Praise for Neil Alexander

'So moving, so transporting and so important.'
Laura Pearson

'Heartbreaking and uplifting at the same time, and so authentic.'
Beth Moran

'Captivating and charming.'
Imogen Clark

'A wonderful storyteller.'
Matt Cain

'Compelling and authentic.'
Julietta Henderson

'Beautifully observed and poignant.'
Alex Brown

Also by Neil Alexander

The Vanishing of Margaret Small

The Lost Past of Billy McQueen

Neil Alexander

embla
books

First published in Great Britain in 2024 by

Bonnier Books UK Limited
4th Floor, Victoria House, Bloomsbury Square, London, WC1B 4DA
Owned by Bonnier Books
Sveavägen 56, Stockholm, Sweden

'Carrick Revisited' from Collected Poems by Louis MacNeice
© Louis MacNeice, 2007, published by Faber & Faber, reproduced by
kind permission by David Higham Associates.

This is a work of fiction. Names, places, events and incidents are either
the products of the author's imagination or used fictitiously. Any
resemblance to actual persons, living or dead, is purely coincidental.

A CIP catalogue record for this book is available from the British Library.

ISBN: 9781471416316

This book is typeset using Atomik ePublisher.

Printed and bound in Great Britain by Clays Ltd, Elcograf S.p.A.

Embla Books is an imprint of Bonnier Books UK.
www.bonnierbooks.co.uk

To my parents, Lorna and Sam.
Thank you for the music, and the stories.

Our past we know
But not its meaning – whether it meant well.

Louis MacNeice, 'Carrick Revisited'

Prologue

Tuesday 11th July 1989

The night Conor Doherty disappears, Northern Ireland is in flames. Across the province, shadowy crowds gather in fields and open spaces to watch the annual Eleventh Night bonfires.

The newspapers are calling this 'The Second Summer of Love'. Soul II Soul are number one in the charts; Steffi Graf has just beaten Martina Navratilova at Wimbledon and Kylie Minogue, my favourite pop star, is about to release her second album, *Enjoy Yourself*. I can't wait!

This is all by the by though, for where I live, all they talk about is Catholics and Protestants fighting. Like most young people round here, I'm sick of it. Who cares what religion you are? Why does it matter? Besides, I've had enough troubles of my own this summer. For a start, there's Mervyn, Mum's new fella. If you think Ian Paisley's method of preaching hellfire and damnation is extreme, you haven't met Mervyn yet. And then there's Conor. Not that Conor's trouble. He's the best thing that's ever happened to me – I just wish everyone else saw it that way.

Conor's the reason I'm here tonight. Alone. Pacing around an abandoned workman's hut on a building site on the outskirts of town. Ever since we started seeing each other in May, the hut has become our secret hideaway. It's a complete dump, with high-vis jackets and hard hats hanging on rusty nails. Photos of topless models torn from dirty magazines and tacked to the walls like hunting trophies. It's *our* dump, though. Apart from us, no one else comes here.

1

Rolling up the sleeve of my denim jacket, I check my watch. It's almost nine. Conor's an hour late, which isn't like him at all. *Where is he? Has something happened?*

Pressing my nose to my wrist, I breathe in the woody smell of his favourite aftershave, Jazz by Yves Saint Laurent. Earlier, he gave me a half-empty bottle as a present. 'Put a wee squirt on your pillow at bedtime,' he assured me. 'That way, I'll always be by your side, even when I'm not here.' I try to focus on his words, his scent, to slow my thumping heart.

Without him, the building site feels eerily quiet. The air is clammy, swarms of midges darting about the bushes. Sitting down on the hut steps, I wrestle my Puma backpack off my shoulders, placing it on my lap. I check my watch again. Five past nine. Something isn't right. My mind races, panic creeping in. *Is he not coming? Has he stood me up?*

Across town, the Orangemen are rehearsing for tomorrow's Twelfth of July parade. The shrill whistle of their flutes echoes in the night air, my heart keeping time with the fast beat of the Lambeg drums. Unzipping my backpack, I take out my Walkman and put on my headphones. I press play, watching the magnetic rollers of the cassette spin slowly round.

The first song is 'Suddenly', the theme to Scott and Charlene's wedding in *Neighbours*. Like all the songs on Conor's cassettes, the lyrics have a special meaning for us. 'Suddenly' is about showing someone your true feelings, showing them the real you. As the drums kick in with the chorus, I nod my head in time to the music, tapping my feet along to the beat, allowing myself to get lost in the emotion of the song until the track fades out and I realise it's ten past nine. Still no sign of him.

Switching the tape off, I stand up, peering across the fields. The sun is low in the sky and the band have stopped playing now, the only sound my new Converse trainers shuffling about on the gravel. My mouth is dry, my palms sweaty. *How much longer do I wait?*

I check my watch one last time and, panicking, perform a counting ritual. Something I've been doing ever since I was a wee boy, to calm my nerves. *If Conor isn't here in the next ten seconds*, I tell myself, *he isn't showing up at all.* I take a deep breath, begin the slow, familiar countdown . . . *ten, nine, eight . . .* praying that before I reach the end, Conor will come running towards me – a rolled-up copy of the latest *Smash Hits* in his hand, his cute anxious face full of apologies. But my hopes fade when I get to zero. He's still not here. *Where are you, Conor? Where?*

As crowds wait for the bonfires to cast their red and orange glow across the fields, I pull my backpack over my shoulders and reluctantly head towards home.

1.

Monday 7th August 2023

'You went to school in Northern Ireland?' The woman in Café Del Margate looks down at my CV, frowning. 'You don't *sound* like you come from that part of the world.'

Behind me, a coffee machine sputters to life. The interview has only just started, but already I feel like I've disappointed her, that maybe I should apologise for not sounding like the happy-go-lucky Irish leprechaun she had me down as on paper. 'I've lived here over thirty years,' I mumble, my voice drowned out by the hiss of frothing milk. 'The accent's pretty much gone now.'

So far, not the best of interviews, but I'm used to things not going my way. I've lost count of the number of jobs I've applied for over the past few months – must be well into double figures. And right now, I'm beginning to wonder if there's something fundamentally wrong with me.

The woman, whose name is Sue, according to the badge pinned to her striped apron, licks her finger, turning a page on her clipboard. 'That's a shame. I love the Irish accent. You should've held onto it, darlin'. Customers like it too. It's friendly.' She pauses. 'Ain't it funny, the way some people lose their accent, and some don't? I have an uncle. Uncle Terry. He moved to Australia in the eighties, but he still speaks like an East End barrow boy.'

I nod, staring up at the digital clock on the wall: 11.53 a.m. *If the minute changes in the next ten seconds, I'm not going to get this job*. I begin my countdown. *Ten, nine, eight . . .*

'So, tell me, Billy. Why do you want to work here?'

I pause, allowing myself a moment for the question to sink in. *Seven, six, five, four . . .*

Sue looks at me, tilting her head. Smiling.

Three, two, one.

I glance at the clock again, breathing a sigh of relief when I see that the minute hasn't changed. It's still 11.53 a.m. *You've got this, Billy McQueen. The job is yours.*

Why do I want to work here? Good question. Does she want the honest answer, or the not-honest answer? Well, the honest answer is I need this job. I'm desperate for it, in fact. Not least because the electric meter in my flat is gobbling pound coins faster than a fruit machine, and if I don't find the money to pay my landlord for the three months' rent I owe him, I'm not going to have a home, let alone a job. So I choose to give her the not-honest answer. 'I guess I want this job because . . . well, Café Del Margate is my favourite coffee place in town. I come here *all* the time. And I love working with people. I'm friendly, you know. A people person. I'm a very people person.'

Oh my God, Billy McQueen, will you listen to yourself? When was the last time you spoke to someone who wasn't actually *paid* to talk to you? Not the doctor, who prescribed you pills this morning for your nerves, or the young girl who hands you a bottle of red wine in the off-licence every night. Or the Royal Mail customer service representative you complained to earlier because the parcel was left on your doorstep *in broad daylight, in the pouring rain*. Admittedly this was more of an online than an in-person 'chat'. And who, apart from a complete eighties music nerd like yourself, would want to nick a second-hand vinyl copy of *Jason Donovan's Greatest Hits*, anyway? Face the facts, Billy. You're fifty, you've no friends or family and you're a big, hopeless loser. Why would anyone want to employ *you*?

I stare at the falling-to-bits Converse trainers I've chosen to pair with a crumpled navy M&S suit I bought in a charity shop especially for this interview. When I put the outfit on this morning, I thought I looked OK. I thought I looked trendy, hipster even, but now all I can see is the bright streak of a yellow sock poking through a hole in the toe of my left trainer. More hobo than hipster, more boho than barista.

'Describe how you deal with an angry customer?' Sue asks, scribbling a few notes down on the piece of paper attached to her clipboard. Like a panic-stricken contestant on one of those daytime quiz shows I've been watching far too many of lately, I search for a buzzer to press. Out of the corner of my eye, through the café window, I spot a solitary magpie landing on the back of a patio chair on the terrace. I wave, muttering, 'Hello, Mr Magpie, how's your wife?' under my breath. Sue looks away, rubbing the back of her neck, as I rack my brain, trying to think of the last time I had to deal with an angry customer. But the truth is, I haven't got any hospitality experience. My last – and only – job, before I got made redundant last year, was working in the communications department of the local council, a solitary role which mostly involved writing press releases about potholes, street lighting and bin collection days. Come to think of it, I liked the fact that it was solitary; most of the time I could hide behind my computer and deal with people via email rather than by phone or face to face.

I glance at Sue, looking for help, desperate for some kind of prompt or cue, but she's busy typing something on her phone. Probably an email to another candidate to tell them they've got the job. I need to think fast. *How do I deal with angry people?* Well, I suppose there was that time last week when my landlord was hammering on the door for his rent money and I pretended I wasn't in. He was very angry, fuming even. I'd hardly class him as a customer, though, and by hiding from him, I avoided the situation entirely, so . . .

Think, Billy, *think*. 'It depends,' I say, playing it vague. 'But if in doubt, I'd smile and apologise. Maybe offer them a complimentary tea or coffee?'

Sue looks up from her phone, placing it face down on the table. 'Good answer, darlin'.' She sighs. 'I mean, most of our customers are very satisfied, but you do get the odd tricky one, you know, the sort who leave one-star reviews on Tripadvisor?' She leans in, putting her hand over her mouth to stifle a yawn. Did she have a late one last night with the girls, or am I boring her to death with my inane responses? 'So, tell me, Billy, how would you handle the stress of being a barista?'

Being a barista is stressful? Jeez. Taking another deep breath, I pinch my thumb and forefinger, plucking another hair from my beard and taking ritualistic comfort in the mild pulling sensation. 'To be honest with you, Sue, I'm dead calm, you know? I don't tend to get stressed easily.'

'Not one to flap.' She nods, scribbling a few more notes. I look away in case she thinks I'm trying to peep at what she's writing. She puts her pen down, clearing her throat. 'So, this last question is slightly quirky, but it's my favourite.' She pauses. 'If you were a hot beverage, what would you be, and why?'

I stare at her, lost for words. There's a moment of excruciating silence. To help me out, or maybe speed up this car crash of an interview, Sue tells me if she was a drink, she would be a cappuccino because she's frothy and fun and very popular with the customers.

Looking out the window, I watch Mr Magpie spread his wings and lift off, launching himself into the wide grey yonder. Desperate for an idea, I snatch a menu from the table, frantically scanning the list of hot beverages. Americano? Vegan iced coffee? Mocha choca latte? None of them sound remotely like me. My brain is fogging over, a real pea souper, but I can't not give her an answer. 'A flat white?' I shrug, blurting out the first thing that comes to mind.

'A flat white? Interesting.' She narrows her eyes. 'Why would you describe yourself as a flat white, Billy?'

'Because I'm . . . um . . . warm, you know, and . . .' *And what, Billy? Milky? White? Say something.* 'And I might look a bit pale, but I'm still full of beans?' *Oh my God.* Squirming in my seat, I fiddle with an open sachet of sugar, accidentally spilling the contents all over the table. I use my palm to wipe up the mess, brushing it discreetly onto the floor.

Sue pouts, tilting her head. 'Fascinating. Well, look, I've got a few more candidates to interview this afternoon. It was nice meeting you though, my darlin'. I'll be in touch.' She stands up and we shake hands, awkwardly. My palm is sticky with sugar, but if she notices, she doesn't say anything, thank God.

Mortified, I close the door of the café behind me, breathing a huge sigh of relief. I step onto the wet pavement, waiting until I'm safely outside the building before putting up my umbrella. Cringing, I recall the utterly banal answers I gave to some of Sue's questions. What must she think of me?

The seafront is miserable today, the normally bright pastel colours of the various shops, bars and arcades dull and muted under a grey sky. A family of day trippers huddle under a single umbrella, staring down at their phones, googling things to do on a wet afternoon in Margate, and debating whether to make a last-minute dash for shelter in the Turner Contemporary, or brave the rain and take a ten-minute walk to the Shell Grotto in Cliftonville. Even though they look glum, I can't help feeling a pinch of envy at their togetherness.

On my wander home, I pass all the usual places: The Old Kent Market with its striking, fire-engine-red brick exterior; the shop selling beach memorabilia – inflatable rubber rings, windbreakers, buckets and spades – a sign outside saying 'Come to Margate and Catch Crabs'; and the Tivoli amusements arcade, which I've lived above, in a flat (a nicer word than bedsit), for the past twenty-five years.

Moving to Margate was never part of the plan. I just sort of ended up here. This was in the nineties, and I'd just finished university with a 2:1 in English. Unlike many of my friends, who went back to London, or the Home Counties, to live with their rich parents, returning to Northern Ireland wasn't an option for me. Forced to fend for myself, I'd taken the first job I could find. My role at the council may have been boring and paid peanuts, but it gave me the financial stability I craved – at least it did until they made me redundant. While I'm not exactly what you'd call adventurous, even I never dreamt I'd still be living in Margate nearly three decades on.

I'm not in the mood to go back to my flat. The fridge is bare and the last place I want to be right now is at home, alone, mentally flagellating myself for today's failures. So, after popping to the off-licence for a cheap bottle of red wine, I pay a visit to the chippy, thinking I deserve a treat after that balls-up of an interview. Once inside, I feel instantly warmed by the bright neon menu display and the cheery chatter of the staff, busy operating the various fryers, shouting instructions to one another. I ask the girl behind the counter for a small sausage and chips and, while she fetches my order, I fumble in my pocket for change.

'Salt and vinegar?' she asks, rapidly assembling my food on the countertop in front of me. I nod, my mouth watering as I watch her tip a generous sprinkling of both over my meal. Wrapping everything in white paper, she slides the steaming parcel into a plastic bag. 'That'll be £4.50, my love.'

Horrified, I realise I'm a pound short. I no longer have a credit card, a consequence of having racked up a ton of debt at university, debt which took me nearly twenty years to pay off, and my Universal Credit payment isn't due for another week. I decide my best option is to fess up and admit I haven't got enough money.

'I was sure I'd four pounds,' I say, going through the motions of sliding a hand in each of my pockets; a last-ditch attempt to convince her I'm not skint, just a little forgetful.

The girl, still clutching my order in her hand, gives me a

sympathetic look. 'You're local, aren't you? If it's easier, you can always drop the money in later. I don't mind.'

My stomach rumbles with relief, and just as I'm about to agree to her trusting offer, a voice pipes up behind me. 'I have a spare pound, if you want it.'

Turning around, I see a boy, no older than eighteen, holding a coin between his thumb and forefinger. His hands are dirty, his nails broken and bitten down to the quick. He's wearing an oversized puffer jacket over grey tracksuit bottoms and Adidas trainers. He reminds me of someone, I can't think who. 'Take it,' he says, looking down at my ripped Converse. 'I know what it's like not having enough money to eat.'

'Thank you,' I say. 'That's really kind of you. I can pay you back, though. I just need . . .'

The boy shakes his head and laughs. 'No worries, fella. We've all been there.'

I accept his offer of help, patting him gently on the shoulder, thanking him again, then quickly pay the girl behind the counter. It's only when I turn to leave, I realise he must think I'm homeless. He smiles and I smile back, embarrassed and a little horrified, but with a heart full of gratitude. He didn't need to give me his money. My stomach growling, I make my way outside. I need food. And, more importantly, I need a drink.

The wind has picked up, sheets of rain battering the esplanade, but rather than go home and eat alone in my bedsit, I continue walking along the seafront. Careful to avoid any cracks in the pavement, I pass Swirly Whirly ice cream parlour and Cinque Ports restaurant where, through the window, I catch a glimpse of couples, groups of friends and families eating and drinking in the warm, brightly lit interior. When I reach Dreamland, I cross the road onto Royal Crescent Promenade. In recent months, the Nayland Rock Shelter has become a favourite hangout of mine. It was here T. S. Eliot wrote Part III of *The Waste Land*, when he was in Margate recovering from a nervous breakdown.

Sitting down on one of the wooden chairs, I reach into my bag and take out my sausage supper, placing it on my lap. I unscrew the wine and put the bottle to my lips, gulping down a generous slug. Eating my chips, I think back to one of the questions Sue asked me in the interview earlier: *Where do you see yourself in ten years' time?* My mind had gone completely blank. I couldn't think of anything to say.

Lately, I don't know why, I've been feeling disconnected, not only from the people around me, but from myself too. Maybe it stems from the fact that I recently turned fifty and have nothing to show for it. No home, at least not one I can call my own. No friends, no family. No job. What led me here, to this point?

After I've finished eating, I take my old Walkman out of my bag. I know no one listens to cassettes these days, but I don't care. In my mind, there's still plenty of charm attached to tapes. Even though the player is scuffed, and the battery compartment needs Sellotape to keep it shut, I've never had the heart to throw it away. Besides, if you look hard enough, you can still see the remains of a Garfield sticker Conor once gave me stuck on the front. The finer features of Garfield's face may no longer be visible, and the top hat and cane he once held have worn off, but he's still recognisable. Still Garfield. Printed on the sticker are the words *I am what I am.*

I swig another mouthful of wine, enjoying the warm feeling spreading over my chest. Slipping on my headphones, I lean my head back against the shelter wall, taking comfort in pressing the play button with its reassuring, plasticky click. Recently I've found myself listening to 'Belfast Child' by Simple Minds on repeat. It's a song that teenage me had written off as a depressing dirge. But now, when Jim Kerr sings the line urging Billy to come on home, the hairs on the back of my neck prickle, for only years later do I get the sentiment behind the lyric. Only now do I understand that feeling of loss, of wanting to return to a place – an Ireland – I had to leave behind. Gently rubbing my finger

11

over the Garfield sticker, I can't help thinking of Conor, the boy I was in love with, the boy who no one would let me love because it wasn't the right place or time. The boy who vanished without a trace. Never to be seen again.

You might wonder why I'm still grieving after all this time. *It's been thirty-four years*, you might say. *You should be over it by now, Billy McQueen, you should've moved on*, and, who knows, you might be right. But remember this: everyone's grief is different. Yes, I've had relationships since; all of them ended badly, though. None of those men were as good to me as Conor Doherty. He was kind, *so* kind, and what happened to him remains the big unsolved mystery of my life. He was my soulmate and, apart from my dad, the only man who ever showed me genuine kindness, the only man I ever loved. Not a day goes by that I don't think of him. Staring up at the vast Margate sky, I ask the clouds for answers. *Where are you, Conor? Where?*

2.

Before

Monday 8th May 1989

Conor opens the door wearing neon-green bicycle shorts and a baggy Acid face T-shirt.

'All right?' I say, lowering my gaze to the floor to avoid staring at his enormous Lycra bulge.

'Come in,' he says, turning round and bounding up the stairs two at a time. Closing the front door, I kick off my DMs in the front porch and follow him inside.

Conor's bedroom, which he calls his 'penthouse', is in the loft. You reach it via a wooden ladder. It's huge and luxurious, like something out of the Freemans catalogue, with its soft cream carpet, modern furniture and private, ensuite bathroom. While I love it here, it makes me slightly ashamed of where I live. Which is one of the reasons why I don't invite Conor over to my house that often.

Conor leaps onto the bed, leaning his back against the wall, his head brushing up against a poster of Belinda Carlisle.

'I take it your da's working tonight then?' I say.

'Aye, he's on lates this week.'

Conor's dad is in the British Army. He started drinking a lot when Conor's mum died a few years ago. Conor and him are always fighting, so I avoid coming over when he's home. I've never actually seen Mr Doherty. He's like the adults in the Charlie Brown cartoons: I've only ever heard his voice, but that alone is enough to make me want to stay well clear of him. I'd never say this to Conor, but I think his dad is a nasty piece of work. A bully.

'Wanna see my new twelve-inch?' Conor quickly changes the subject to our favourite one. Pop music. I nod, avoiding eye contact, and take a seat on the floor. Reaching down the side of the bed, he pulls out a plastic carrier bag from Caroline Music. 'London Boys. "Requiem",' he says, showing me the record sleeve; a photo of two grinning musclemen in tight white vests and high-waisted trousers. 'Bought it today. I can tape it for you, if you want?'

'Go on then,' I say, slipping my denim jacket off. I always feel dead awkward when I'm in Conor's bedroom. At school, when we're hanging around in a big group, we get along fine, bouncing off each other's jokes like we're in a *French and Saunders* sketch, but when it's just the two of us I get so tongue-tied I can barely string a sentence together.

Conor shrugs. 'No bother at all. Sure, have a look through my records. See if there's anything else you want taped.' He points to his hi-fi in the corner. It's one of those big cabinet ones with a glass door, like Mum has. A record player on top, a double cassette deck and a radio. The records are all stacked upright at the bottom. I shuffle across the carpet on my knees and start flicking through them. Every so often I'll take a sneaky glance at Conor, watching him turn the pages of the latest *Smash Hits* magazine.

I've always thought that if Conor was a pop star, he'd be the lead singer in a band, or a hugely successful solo artist like George Michael or Rick Astley. He's got the kind of boy-next-door face – cherubic pout, dinky wee nose and sparkling blue eyes – which makes teenage girls (and boys like me) want to crush themselves behind crowd barriers, waving posters and screaming '*Conor!*' Jostling and shoving each other, swooning with horniness. Don't get me wrong, like, he's not perfect. He's got dark shadows under his eyes, and slightly chapped lips, which he sometimes picks at, slowly peeling off the translucent, blood-specked skin and rolling it into a ball between his fingers. But these imperfections are nothing a good make-up artist with a ChapStick can't fix. Unable to resist, I take another sneaky peek at his face, before choosing a few seven-inch singles I like: Debbie Gibson's 'Electric Youth', 'Miss You Like Crazy' by Natalie Cole and 'Don't It Make You Feel Good' by Stefan Dennis, better known to us as Paul from *Neighbours*.

'Here,' says Conor. 'Did you see that picture of Andy Bell from Erasure in *Smash Hits* this week?'

'No,' I say, lying. But I know *exactly* the one he means. I'm not sure why I can't quite bring myself to admit it.

Conor holds up his magazine. 'So, what do you think of his t-t-tight leotard?'

For the past year or so, Conor's been having speech therapy lessons to help him with his stutter. A lot of the time, it's barely noticeable, but you can hear it when he's nervous. I think it's cute, but some people at school take the piss out of him.

In the photograph, Andy Bell is sitting on top of an upright piano. He's dressed in a black leotard with matching black tights, a sparkling red bowler hat and ruby slippers. One of his legs is dangling provocatively over the side of the piano.

'I dunno. It's a bit weird, isn't it?' I shrug, trying to seem indifferent.

'Aye. I suppose.' Conor looks put out. He flicks to another page in *Smash Hits*, his face brightening. 'Here, do you know what Yazz's favourite sandwich filling is?'

'Cheese and pickle?'

'Nope.'

'Chicken salad?'

'Nah. One more go.'

'Prawn cocktail?'

Conor raises his eyebrows, adopting the serious tone of BBC *Mastermind*'s Magnus Magnusson. 'It's actually t-tofu and mayonnaise.'

'What's tofu?' I say.

'No idea. Here, grab me that dictionary from the shelf, will you. I'm going to look it up.'

I hand Conor a school dictionary. He skims through it, reading the words aloud. 'T-toe. Toenail. Toffee.' He pauses. 'I can't find tofu. It's not there. Maybe it's a London thing.'

Me and Conor think London is the epitome of cool. One day we both want to move there, so he can realise his dream of becoming a performer, or a DJ on Radio 1, and I can find a job as a music journalist. None of these things are possible if you live in Carrickfergus though. Last term, for example, when I told Linda Dunne, our school careers adviser, my big dreams for the future, she replied in her dreary, monotone voice, 'Why don't you write a wee letter to the local paper?' I stared at the faint shadow of a moustache on her upper lip, only half listening as she droned on about the difference between a university and a polytechnic, and government-funded youth training schemes. 'Or, if you like books,' she said, 'you could always become an English teacher?'

I mean, don't get me wrong, I love English – it's my best subject – but the thought of having to teach literature to girls like Janine Curran and Adele Penney scares the crap out of me. They're far too interested in hairspray, smoking and snogging boys in the bushes behind the Science block to give a toss about similes, subjunctive clauses or *Pride and Prejudice*. I hate to admit it, but sometimes I envy them. Their lives seem so much less complicated than mine.

If the thought of Adele and Janine snogging boys has given me a redner, Conor is too engrossed in his magazine to notice. 'Does it say what Kylie's favourite sandwich is?' I ask him, trying to distract myself from my lustful fantasies, which right at this moment are making me feel all hot and bothered.

'Aye,' he says, not looking up. 'Jesus, that's mingin'!' He scrunches his face in disgust.

'What is?' I say, jumping onto the bed next to him for a peep at the photo of Kylie wearing a glossy red bomber

16

jacket with a black collar. As I lean in, my head brushes his shoulder.

'A chocolate sandwich,' he says, aghast. 'Not chocolate spread though. We're talking a *whole* Mars bar shoved between two slices of bread.' He turns to face me, to gauge my reaction, and in my rush to look at the magazine, we knock heads, our noses briefly touching. For a split second, things get awkward. I lean away from him, my ears burning, a weird sort of swirling in my stomach.

There's a pause. He lies back, his blond hair covering one eye. 'Here,' he says. 'Guess what I nicked from my da's bedroom?'

'What?' I say, my face glowing hot.

He lowers his voice to a whisper. 'Durex. He has loads of them.'

He leans over and opens his bedside drawer, pulling out a white sports sock. Holding it by the toe, he shakes its contents onto the carpet. Five or six shiny red square packets come tumbling out. 'Do you want one?'

'Aye, go on,' I say, my stomach now churning away like Mum's tumble dryer on full speed. Is Conor flirting with me?

He hands me one and I run my finger over the glossy foil wrapper, which is exactly the same colour and sheen as Kylie's bomber jacket. I've never touched a condom before and, though I'd never tell Conor, part of me is really turned on. At the same time, I'm frightened, 'cause when I think of condoms, I can't help seeing those AIDS adverts on TV. The tombstone falling forward. The crumbling white cliff face. The deep, Doomsday voice booming, '*Don't die of ignorance.*' Hands shaking, I start to tear the foil open.

Conor stops me. 'I don't mean for you to put it on now, like!' He laughs.

'Obviously not,' I say, coughing. 'That would be *weird.*' I put the condom in my jeans pocket, pressing it down as deep as it will go.

3.

Now

Monday 7th August 2023

If you asked me what it was like growing up in Northern Ireland during the Troubles, I'd tell you my childhood ended when I was six years old; my youth, when I was sixteen. In the space of those ten years, I lost the two most important men in my life: my dad, and my soulmate, Conor Doherty.

My dad was the loveliest man you'd ever meet. On the nights when he came home from working a long shift at the cigarette factory, he'd scoop me in his arms and carry me up to bed, where he'd tuck me in, snug as a wee bug under my *Magic Roundabout* duvet, and say, 'Which Mr Man are we reading tonight then, son?' In the six precious years I shared with him, he read me them all: *Mr Jelly*, *Mr Bounce*, and my favourite, *Mr Impossible*. Mr Impossible had magical powers. He could do anything, from walking up trees to flying. In the book, he makes friends with a boy called William who takes him to school, where Mr Impossible helps him with his maths. I loved Mr Impossible. I could always tell the nights when Dad was tired though, for he would try to skip out sentences, whole pages even, but there was no fooling me. I knew those *Mr Men* stories back to front. So I'd nudge him and say, 'Daddy, you missed a bit,' and he'd smile and yawn and say, 'All right, Mr Clever, why don't you read *me* a story then?' And so I did.

The Troubles started in August 1969, the week of my parents' honeymoon, which isn't to suggest my parents had a turbulent relationship. On the contrary, they were the perfect couple, full of life. Belfast's very own Rock Hudson and Doris Day. Our home in Carrickfergus was always a place of music and laughter. One of my earliest memories is of Dad putting 'their song' on the record player. The opening chords of Don Williams' 'You're My Best Friend' were Mum's cue to kick off her cork wedge shoes and throw herself into Dad's arms, the pair of them swaying around the living room, madly in love, safe in the knowledge that they were each other's bread, shelter and anchor in life's storm. No word of a lie, I never once heard them argue, or bicker even. They were made for each other, my parents; two proverbial peas in a pod.

Every Saturday night, Mum and Dad would invite the neighbours round for a party. Everyone brought carry-outs from the off-licence: the women drank vodka and Babycham, the men Tennent's Lager, with photographs of glamour models – Janis, Shona and Norma – on the sides of the cans. As the room downstairs filled with smoke, Dad played guitar. 'Sylvia's Mother' by Dr Hook, Led Zeppelin's 'Stairway to Heaven', The Eagles' 'Hotel California', as well as old Irish standards 'Mick McGilligan's Ball', 'Carrickfergus' and 'The Mountains of Mourne'. Woken by the noise, I would sneak out of bed and sit at the top of the stairs, listening to the craic coming from below, breathing in the warm camaraderie of their cigarette smoke. I remember on one of these nights, a neighbour – Bev, she was called – came out onto the bottom landing to use the toilet. She spotted me peering through the banisters. 'Auch, what are you doing on your own, son?' she said, taking my hand and leading me down into the living room. 'Sure, come and join us. Sing us a wee song, Billy.'

On those golden, short-lived evenings I became the entertainment at my parents' parties. Every Saturday, I used to twirl in front of the electric fire dressed as Kate Bush in one of Mum's silk slips and a wig, belting out 'Wuthering Heights' for a crowd of half-cut adults, the smoke from their Embassy and Regal cigarettes creating the sort of dry ice effect you used to see on *Top of the Pops*.

'More, Billy, more,' they'd chorus when I finished, so I'd do a few impressions. My three favourites were Sue Ellen from *Dallas*, Madame Medusa from Disney's *The Rescuers* and our then Prime Minister, Margaret Thatcher.

'He's a geg, a wee character,' the women would giggle, sipping from their Babycham coupes as I batted my long eyelashes and whispered, 'I hate you, J. R. Ewing,' in my best drunk Texan drawl.

But not everyone found me amusing. 'You better watch that one,' I overheard Bev's husband, Norman, saying to my dad one night. 'You don't want him turning into a fruit.'

I didn't know what a fruit was, aged six, but Bev was quick to shoot him a dirty look. 'Catch yourself on, Norman,' she said. She turned to my dad then. 'Auch, sure it's a phase. He's a youngster, so he is. He'll grow out of it.' Dad just looked at her, though, his face all serious. 'He's my son, Bev,' he said. 'I'll love him whatever happens.'

Dad lived for me and my mum. When I was a child, he always stressed to me the importance of getting an education. 'You work hard, son, and the world's your oyster,' he'd say. 'No matter what your starting point in life is, if you put the hours into your education, you can achieve anything, be anyone.' I remember telling him I wanted to be Wonder Woman, or a Charlie's Angel, when I grew up, but he just laughed. Ruffling my hair, he said, 'You be who you like, son. You're my special boy. Don't you ever let anyone dim your light, Billy McQueen, do you hear me?' To this day I wonder how different things would have turned out if he'd lived. As I got a bit older, living in a place where men wore their masculinity with pride, I learned to suppress the more feminine side of my nature. But I've never forgotten how he always encouraged me to be true to myself.

Dad was killed in an explosion in July 1979. One night, after work, a colleague in the cigarette factory who'd had too much to drink asked if he'd mind taking his keys and driving his car back to Carrick for him. In those days, everyone drank at work, it was part of the culture, so Dad thought nothing of it. Besides, he'd had to sell his own car a few months previously because the rising interest rates meant he couldn't afford it. He was glad of the free ride.

Earlier that day, Mum had taken me shopping for new shoes in Belfast, a pair of red Mr Men trainers she'd seen in the window of Anderson & McAuley's department store. Dad met us in town on his way home. He was driving his colleague's brown Ford Cortina, which he'd been given specific instructions to park outside a pub in Carrick. All the way back from Belfast, Mum had this strange feeling the car was being followed. She kept turning round, but Dad told her she was imagining things. I was in the back seat, all warm and cosy, snuggling my Humpty from *Play School*. 'Annie's Song' by John Denver was playing on the radio. As always, Dad sang the main verse and chorus and Mum did the harmonies. I lay there, listening to their soothing voices, my eyes half-open, watching the sky whizz past, enjoying the gentle thrum of the car in motion. It always made me feel safe.

Even now, I feel partly responsible for what happened next. Stupid, I know, for I was only a child. After Dad parked the car, the three of us started walking home, but on the way, Mum noticed I was missing one of my new shoes. I started crying, which quickly escalated into a tantrum. Dad said not to worry, he would go back and fetch it. Mum took my hand then, and we carried on walking, but I was raging. The whole time I kept looking down at my shoeless foot, bunching my fists. Digging my heels in. Trying to get her to go back. It wasn't long before I got my way. She stopped walking. Grabbed my pudgy arm. Crouching down on the pavement, she pulled me towards her. 'Shush now, Billy,' she said, brushing her hand over my wet cheeks, wiping the tears away. 'Your daddy won't be long. Listen to Mummy, now. I'm going to do a wee countdown, like your teacher does at school. And when I get to zero, I want you to stop crying, OK?'

'*Five, four, three, two . . .*'

Out of nowhere, a massive bang. Mum stood up, shielding her eyes from the sun, staring ahead into the distance, her face white as a sheet. I turned round to see dark clouds of smoke, orange and black flames billowing from the burnt-out shell of a car, spilling over the Marine Highway like waves. I remember Mum swearing, calling out for help. I remember holding onto her hand for dear life as we started running back the way we'd come. I remember treading on a stone with my bare foot, crying out in pain, 'Mummy, stop! Mummy, Mummy! I hurt my foot!'

But Mum was no longer listening. As she told me, years later, the only thing she could hear then was the sound of her own screaming.

When I get back to the Tivoli amusements arcade after finishing my chips and wine, I spot Kirk, my landlord, pacing around outside, next to a pavement sign which reads *FREE TO USE ATM CASH MACHINE*. He's dressed in his standard sheepskin coat and flat cap combo, puffing furiously on a cigarette, and shouting at someone on his mobile. I can't hear what he's saying, but I know if he sees me, he's only going to start having another go about the overdue rent. I do my usual trick, pulling the hood of my raincoat over my head and ducking into the entranceway of a nearby shop. Plastered all over the walls are torn posters promoting club nights, community groups, local taxi ranks, and so on, but my eye is drawn to one poster in particular: a photograph of a man with his back to the camera. He's looking into the distance as if lost, as if he's got nowhere to turn. I stare at the words next to the image, my focus slightly blurry from the bottle of wine. It reads: '*I'm going to be all right, it's not so bad spending a lot of time alone*'. I laugh, recognising the voice, thinking it's the sort of thing I'm always telling myself. Am I really that desperate, though? Surely not. I place my hand on the poster, letting it rest on the damp wall, feeling a slightly sentimental connection to this stock image of a man at the end of his tether. Pulling my phone out of my pocket, I take a photo of the Samaritans helpline number. I'll never ring it, I reassure myself, but it's always good to have options.

Peering around the corner, I'm pleased to see Kirk is no longer standing outside the arcade. I cast an eye up the street and spot him walking in the other direction, past the Margate Clocktower, heading towards the Marine Gardens. The coast is clear; I can go back to my flat now without him hassling me.

Even during the daytime, my flat is always dark inside. Pushing open the front door, I flick the light switch on. Nothing happens. The electric meter must be out of credit again – a pain because I don't always have the cash handy to top it up. Cursing myself for spending my last ten quid on chips and a bottle of wine, luxuries I really can't afford right now, I ransack the flat for spare change – which over the past few months has become a well-rehearsed routine. First, I push my hand down the back and sides of the sofa and armchair cushions, feeling around for any money that might have dropped out of my trouser pockets. Aside from toast crumbs, a wine-stained cork and half a Polo mint, I find nothing. Next, I go through all my coat pockets, where I manage to cobble together the grand sum of seventy-two pence. Somewhat relieved, I tell myself I only need another twenty-eight pence and I can take it to the newsagent's next door and exchange it for a shiny pound coin. My last resort is always the drawer next to the kitchen sink, or the 'Drawer of Crap'. While my house is generally tidy, this is the black hole where I dump everything: extension leads, Sellotape, balls of string and screwdrivers. Shoving my hand in, I rummage around for some loose change, eventually finding a green-tinged pound coin stuck to the bottom. The coin is covered in gunk, where a battery has leaked all over it, but it will do. When I go to slot it in the meter though, it won't budge; the meter is full of coins that Kirk has failed to empty. Grabbing a knife from the draining board, I wedge it into the slot in a bid to make some room, twisting the blade to the left and right, wiggling it around until something which feels like a miracle happens. The power comes back on. Light floods the room. Kitchen appliances start humming again. Alexa lights up, a blue circle hovering around her head like a halo. Even better, as I wiggle the knife back and forth, I notice the tiny clock hand on the meter moving forward a fraction until it reaches full credit. 'Who needs money for electricity when all it takes is a kitchen knife? You're a genius, Billy McQueen,' I say out loud, chuckling to myself. 'This will save you a fortune!'

I'm still marvelling at this new hack of mine when my mobile rings. The number on the display is unfamiliar, but my first thought is that it's Sue from Café Del Margate calling about the job. Buoyed from my discovery of free electricity, I answer it immediately.

'Yes?' I say, my hands shaking.

'Billy, is that you?'

A woman's voice, unmistakably Northern Irish. My heart flutters. Is this my mum calling? Why would my mum be calling, though? She hasn't made any attempt to contact me in over thirty years.

'Yes,' I say. 'Who is this?'

'It's Bev. Your mum's next-door neighbour? You probably don't remember me. Only I've a spare key for her house. I found your number in her address book.'

The fact that my mum has my number in her address book makes my heart jump, but why is Bev calling me?

'I remember you, Bev.' I swallow. ''Course I do.'

'Listen, son, are you sitting down?'

'Yes, I'm at home. Why?'

24

'Look, there's no easy way of saying this, love. Your mother's in hospital. She's had a bad stroke.'

I drop the phone, staring up at the speckled patch of mildew which has been gradually spreading over the kitchen ceiling. There's that old superstition that bad news comes in threes. First my dad died, then Conor went missing. For years I've been wondering, dreading in fact, what the third thing is going to be and now, finally, I have it. The lights in my flat may be on, but this revelation plunges me into unexpected darkness.

Estrangement, like grief, never goes away; the feelings of hurt and loss remain on your skin like invisible tattoos. Even though Mum cut all ties with me after I left for university, refusing to accept that I was gay, I'm still not prepared for this. I've always sent a card at Christmas, on her birthday and for Mother's Day. Not once has she ever written back, or picked up the phone to say thank you, but for me it was important to maintain contact. I'd like to think she read my cards and letters, but they probably went straight in the bin as soon as she saw my handwriting on the envelope. I suppose in some ways my relationship with Mum was a bit like her relationship with God. It relied on one-way communication, a suspension of disbelief, faith even. The cards I've sent her every year were like prayers. The comfort came from the way they allowed me to express my feelings, even if nothing ever came back.

'Are you there, son? Can you hear me, Billy?' Bev's tone is soothing, full of empathy, the kindest voice I've heard in ages. I pick up the phone again, putting it to my ear.

'Yes,' I say, a lump rising in my throat. 'So . . . what happened?'

'We don't know exactly. The doctors reckon she might've tripped when she was hanging the washing out. Banged her head. They think that's what triggered the stroke.'

After the shock, my next reaction to this news is panic. What if I don't get the chance to make amends, to make up for all our years of not speaking? I pause for a second, letting the gravity of the situation sink in. 'When?' I say. 'When did it happen?'

Bev hesitates. 'Last Friday. I would've got in touch sooner, but I only just got hold of your number. I'm sorry.'

'Don't apologise. It's hardly your fault. Is it serious?'

Bev has a sharp intake of breath before speaking. 'Son, the doctors aren't sure at this stage whether she's going to survive. Your mum . . . she's in a coma.' Her voice falters. 'I mean, it's just as well I found her when I did. Luckily, I'd bumped into her in the Euro Spar a few hours before it happened, and she'd asked me over for a cup of coffee. I thought she was looking well, so I did, which just goes to show you can never tell what's round the corner. I must've been knocking on her front door for a good couple of minutes, and when she didn't answer, I went round the back thinking I'd find her sunbathing or doing a bit of gardening. As soon as I saw her lying there, I called the ambulance. Awful, so it was. I'd hate to think what would've happened if she hadn't invited me over.'

'Where was Mervyn? Was he not at home?'

Bev pauses. 'Did you not hear? Sure, Mervyn died about five or six years ago. He'd been ill for a while. Dementia. Your mum was the sole carer. Poor woman, she was struggling. I used to pop round and help her out up at their big house, cooking and cleaning, and so on.'

I slide down onto the floor, my mind reeling with regrets. If only Mum had let me know she needed support. I would've gone over and stayed with her. If only she hadn't been so upset over what happened with Conor . . .

Stop blaming yourself, Billy McQueen. None of this is your fault.

I swallow, realising my only option right now is to return home. Whatever happens, I need to see Mum. I need to speak to her, to tell her how much she means to me before it's too late. I'll need money, though. How am I going to pay for a flight when my Universal Credit only amounts to £85 a week? I panic.

'The thing is, Bev,' I say, my voice shaking. 'I lost my job not that long ago and I'm skint. It sounds awful, but I don't know how I can afford to get there.'

Bev interrupts. 'Auch, don't be ridiculous. I can give you the money. I'm sure she won't mind me telling you all this, but after Mervyn died, your mum asked me if I would take on the role of her power of attorney. She was worried there'd be no one to deal with her estate if she passed away, and she said I'd always been good to her. When I agreed to it, she left me specific instructions to look after you if anything happened to her, so I can help.'

Bev is being so kind. She doesn't need to do all this for me. My eyes well with tears. 'Are you sure? I can pay you back.'

'Of course. Besides, it's your mum's money, not mine. If you give me your bank details, I'll do a transfer right now so you can book yourself a flight. It's what she would want.'

I have so many questions for Bev – not least why my mum seems to have had such an abrupt turnaround towards me – I feel overwhelmed. For the first time in thirty years, I'm heading home to Northern Ireland.

4.

Friday 12th May 1989

From my bedroom window, I watch Mum stepping out of a white BMW. She's all dolled up in her latest purchases from Dunnes Stores: a jade-green jumpsuit paired with a huge gold belt and matching strappy heels; a magenta scarf draped casually over her massive, *Dynasty*-style shoulder pads. She looks class. I haven't seen her put this much effort into her appearance for donkey's years. A man I've never seen before holds the car door open for her like a chauffeur. He's tall, with tanned skin and Crest-white teeth, and his flashy beige suit is the kind of thing you see J. R. Ewing wearing to the annual Oil Baron's Ball in *Dallas*. Mum flutters her eyelashes at him, pointing to the house with her clutch bag. As she pushes open the front gate, I duck behind the curtain, listening to her heels clip-clopping down the path. A key turns in the front door.

'Do you fancy a coffee, Mervyn? I can pop my new percolator on.' Mum's putting on her 'posh' voice, like the flirty woman in the Gold Blend advert, casually dropping the word 'percolator' into the conversation to show off her knowledge of mod cons. What she doesn't tell him is that the percolator came with her first order from Kays catalogue – one of many free gifts she's sent off for, from different catalogues, over the past year, which include a set of crystal glasses, a 5 Minute Body Shaper and a jazzy-patterned continental quilt.

'If it's no bother, Sadie, aye. I can't stop for long, though.' His voice is broad and deep. He doesn't sound like he comes from round our way.

'I could make you a wee Slim-a-Soup too, if you're hungry?' says Mum. 'I've got Minestrone, or Chicken and Leek with croutons.'

'Just a coffee,' he says.

I start worming my way downstairs, curious to know who this man is. Mum is hanging her scarf and bag over the banister. When she sees me, she turns to the man and says, 'This is my son. Billy?' She looks up at me then. 'Billy, this is my new friend, Mervyn.' Reaching the bottom stair, I pause, almost eye level with him.

The man is standing in the hallway with his back to the front door. His shape casts a tall shadow along the floor. He comes forward, holding out his hand. 'Nice to meet you, Billy.'

'Hi,' I mumble, clenching my teeth as he squeezes my hand with his Superman-strength grip.

'Your mother's been telling me all about you.' He looks me up and down then, shaking his head, tutting at my Kylie T-shirt and blue Primark jeans, ripped at the knees and turned up at the ankles the way Bros wear them. 'Those are a queer pair of shoes you have there,' he says when his eyes reach my feet, his face taking a darker turn.

'DMs,' says Mum. 'Dr. Martens? They might look like dockers' boots, but they're all the rage with youngsters these days.' She laughs, ruffling her hand through my hair, which is so sticky with gel and hairspray it doesn't budge. 'He loves his fashion, don't you, Billy?'

Mervyn rolls his eyes. 'Fashion? You don't need fashion if you have Christ. In the Bible, God tells us to set our minds on heavenly things.' He furrows his brow, his eyes still fixed on my fake Dr. Martens, which I've customised with Grolsch bottle tops I bought off Janine Curran at school, who sells them for 15p each. 'What are those things hanging out of your lace holes?'

29

Mum glances at my shoes and gives a nervous laugh. 'I'll put the percolator on, shall I?' she says, clearly trying to divert Mervyn's focus away from me and my 'queer' sense of style. 'Kitchen's just through there, if you want to make yourself at home.'

'And the bathroom?'

'Upstairs on your left. Next to the hot press.'

In the kitchen, Mum pulls a Tupperware tub of coffee down from the cupboard and bangs it on the work surface, flipping the plastic lid open.

'Who's that man?' I say.

'I'll tell you in a minute,' she hisses, thrusting the percolator jug at me. 'Here, fill this up with cold water, will you?' Taking a filter bag out of one of the drawers, she opens it into a cone shape and places it in the machine, spooning in ground coffee.

'Mum, is that man your boyfriend?' I say, turning on the tap and holding the glass jug underneath. It's been almost ten years since Dad died, and I've never known her to show interest in any man other than Patrick Duffy in *Dallas*. I'm not sure how I feel about her seeing someone else.

'Shush, you,' she snaps. 'He's from the church.'

'Church?' Is she having me on? Mum's never been the religious kind, and she's never pushed me in that direction either, apart from maybe when I was at primary school and she used to send me to The Five-Day Club, a week of Bible study sessions for children, which Old Moira Hopkins ran every summer holiday in her back yard. I always thought that was just so Mum could benefit from the free childcare and sit on her sun lounger drinking vodka all day long. Not that I minded. Old Moira might have scared the bejesus out of us with horrific stories about the Apocalypse and the Second Coming, but the free sweets and lollies she doled out afterwards more than made up for her terrible tales of fire and brimstone.

I hand Mum the water and watch her pour it into the

top of the machine, snapping the lid shut. Setting the jug underneath, she presses the switch. As the percolator gurgles to life, she chucks a few mugs down on the kitchen table and begins rummaging for food in the cupboards, which are mostly filled with the kind of low-calorie stuff Mum eats when she's on a diet: packet soups, SlimFast powder and Ryvita. Still, she manages to throw together a last-minute supper consisting of a multipack of Wotsits, which she opens and pours onto a plate, a bowl of nuts and a few United Biscuits.

'Mervyn and me, we're an item, yes,' she whispers, making it sound like they're on sale at the Spar, but before she has a chance to elaborate, Mervyn reappears. Taking his place at the head of the table, he reaches for a Wotsit. He sniffs at it first, like he's never tasted one before, then pops it cautiously in his mouth. 'That was a lovely service,' he says. 'We must've had about ten new people come to Christ tonight.'

'Aye, it was,' says Mum, nodding. 'It must be rewarding for you, Mervyn, saving all those wee lost souls.'

'It is, yes,' he says. 'Nothing beats that feeling of rescuing a sinner from eternal damnation.' He pauses to lick his orange lips. 'Speaking of sinners, do you know Gilly Gorman?'

'I don't think so,' says Mum, shaking her head.

'Auch, you do. Always sits in the front pew at church. Mousy-blonde perm. Tasselled leather boots.'

'Oh yes,' says Mum. 'I know Gilly. Married to the sheep farmer from Balleybogey?'

'That's her,' says Mervyn, leaning in and stroking his earlobe. 'Well, you wouldn't know to look at her, but Gilly told me that before she was saved, she and her husband went to the Costa del Sol. It was one of those package holidays, which attract heathens like flies. You should hear some of the perverted things they got up to round the pool. Topless sunbathing, cocktails. The way she described it, it was like Sodom and Gomorrah-on-Sea. In broad daylight, too. Disgusting!'

As he says this, a glob of orange Wotsit flies from his mouth, landing on my hand. I pretend not to let on, but I'm conscious of it the whole way through our conversation, which is less of a conversation and more of a monologue because, boy oh boy, this Mervyn seems to love the sound of his own voice.

Mum tells him she often holidays on the Costa del Sol. But is quick to add that she won't be going again after what he's just told her.

'Oh really?' He reaches across the table, grabbing himself another Wotsit. I brace myself for a second round of spit, but he seems to be sucking on the Wotsit this time, rather than chewing it, moving it slowly, rhythmically even, in and out of his mouth. It looks weird, and part of me wants to laugh. I fiddle with the wrapper of my United Biscuit to distract myself.

'To be honest, Torremolinos was never really my sort of place,' says Mum. 'It was a good few years after my husband passed, you know? I just needed a wee break. A bit of time to myself.'

Mervyn nods. Listening intently, he moves closer to Mum, gently placing his hand on her arm. 'If only you'd come to Christ sooner, Sadie,' he says, softly. 'It would have saved you an awful lot of heartache.'

'Don't get me wrong, like. It wasn't bad,' Mum continues. 'In the evenings, the hotel put on entertainment – discos, tapas, bingo – but after a few days of lying on a sun lounger reading *Flowers in the Attic* . . . well, it's not the same when you're on your own.' She pushes a bowl towards Mervyn. 'Help yourself to one of my wee nuts.'

'I better be off, actually,' he says, looking at the kitchen clock, which has just gone half eight. 'Didn't realise it was that late.' He stands up to leave. 'I'll give you a wee ring in the week. Thank you for supper. Good to meet you, Billy.'

'Well,' says Mum, after he's gone. 'What do you think?'

'I'm not sure,' I say, rubbing the dried-up remains of Mervyn's Wotsit spit off my hand. 'He's very serious, so he is.'

She frowns. 'You'd be serious too if you worked for the church. Saving souls is no party, Billy.'

'So – does this mean you're religious now?'

Mum stands up, pushing her chair back. She fiddles with an earring. 'Well, yes, I suppose I am, son.'

'Since when?'

'Not long. A month or so? I didn't want to make a big deal of it until I was sure it was my kind of thing.'

It's all starting to make sense now. A while back, Mum started going to these 'meetings' on Friday and Sunday nights, but she never said where. As she's recently given up the drink, I just assumed she'd gone back to Alcoholics Anonymous and didn't want to talk about it.

'So, this Mervyn,' I say. 'Where did you meet him?'

'In a bar, of all places. I was with a few friends. He approached me with a flyer, asked me if I'd heard of his church. I thought he was good-looking, like Howard Keel with a Belfast accent. Anyway, he invited me to one of their services one night. I really enjoyed it.' She starts clearing away the plates and cups, stacking them in a pile by the kitchen sink. I have my doubts about this Mervyn, but I don't want to hurt Mum's feelings.

And then, out of the blue, she asks me the question I always dread. 'What about you, son? Have you found yourself a wee girlfriend yet? You're getting to that age now.'

I shrug my shoulders. Slipping my hand into my jeans pocket, I touch the condom Conor gave me the other day, still in its foil wrapper. 'I-I don't have time for a girlfriend,' I say, the blood rushing to my cheeks. 'I'm too busy with exams.' Not a lie as such, but I can't tell Mum about these feelings I have for Conor. She'd kill me. Besides, I'm saving that conversation for when I see my best friend, Aine, tomorrow. I've been building up to telling her for weeks and I've no idea how she's going to react. I feel sick just thinking about it. Changing the subject, I tell Mum I'm going to Belfast in the morning.

'You be careful now,' she says. 'I don't like you going into town on your own. It's not safe.'

'I'm not going on my own.'

'Who are you going with?'

'Aine.'

'Aine Kelly?' She gives me a dirty look. 'If I've told you once, I've told you umpteen times, you don't want to be hanging round with her.'

'You're just saying that because she's Catholic,' I say, folding my arms against my chest.

'I couldn't care less what religion she is. It's not about that.' She raises an eyebrow. 'Here – you're not seeing her, are you? You know me, Billy. I'd love you to have a girlfriend. Not Aine Kelly, though. Her family is trouble.' She reaches for the pair of bright pink Marigolds dangling over the side of the draining board.

'She's just a friend,' I say, watching as she pulls on the gloves, snapping them around her wrists.

'Just as well. And what about this Conor fella?'

'What about him?' My stomach tightens. Is she getting suspicious over the amount of time we've been spending together recently?

She turns on the tap, squirting a dash of Fairy Liquid into the basin. 'Well, he's good-looking, isn't he?'

'Like I would know, Mum,' I say, laughing it off, trying to keep my voice as light as possible, despite the fact my cheeks are roasting.

'He's a wee stunner. Bet he has girls queuing round the block. If I was twenty years younger, I'd have a good mind to . . .'

'Mum! Don't be gross. That's disgusting, so it is!'

'Seriously, Billy, boys need plenty of male company, especially at your age. I'm glad you've finally found

34

yourself a friend like Conor. He seems like a nice boy, so he does.'

My palms are sweating now. I wipe them on my jeans. *A nice boy?* Jeez, Mum, I think to myself. If only you knew the half of it.

5.

Now

Saturday 12th August 2023

The key to Mum's house, which Bev gave me on our drive back from the airport, is attached to a fob. A white circle, gold-rimmed, with the words 'Jesus Saves' written in the middle. I push the key into the lock, turning it.

Opening the door for the first time in over thirty years, I feel like Dorothy in *The Wizard of Oz*, the moment her house – swooped up in a tornado – crashes down on Munchkinland, and her world goes from black and white to colour. Only for me, it's the other way round. My world has gone from colour to black and white, which is how Mum viewed everything. She lived her life in binaries: man, woman; good, bad; heaven, hell. She didn't believe in anything in between.

Mum wasn't always like that, though – only in her later years, after she met Mervyn and found God. The big change in her personality happened the day my dad died. It was as if someone had flicked a switch inside her. Overnight, she went from being this carefree, fun-loving young girl to a nervous wreck who preferred staying at home in front of the TV, with a bottle of vodka, to going out.

Before we lost Dad she was always immaculately dressed. A former Miss Belfast beauty queen, she'd taken great pride in her appearance. And while she briefly recovered her love of fashion when she began dating Mervyn in 1989, in the years following Dad's death she was a complete mess. Growing up, I had got used to hearing her tell people the same story. How the day after Dad died was the only time in her life she ever went out of the house in her dressing gown and slippers. How she left me in the care of a neighbour before walking the mile into town, her hair dishevelled, a bottle of bleach in one hand, a bucket and brush in the other. The way I've always pictured it, she was walking slowly that day, her eyes half-closed, as if she was in a trance. As if an invisible thread was pulling her forward.

Our town was a small, friendly place, where everyone knew each other, but Mum said the people who had passed her on the street that morning ignored her, choosing instead to lower their heads, or turn their gazes away. I can't imagine they were being rude. They would have heard about our family tragedy on the news, or through the local grapevine. It was far more likely they didn't know what to say; perhaps they felt it was too soon, too raw, to stop her and say hello, to offer their sympathies. For what words do you give a woman whose husband has just died in a car bomb? What use are words when something like that happens?

Car horns tooted as she crossed roads without looking. On the pavements, women pushing children in buggies swerved out of the way to avoid crashing into her. Not that Mum would have noticed. She was far too numb with grief to care about physical injuries.

The sky was clouding over, she said, when she reached the spot where Dad died, a square of empty car park facing the pub. Hitching up her nightdress, she knelt on the ground and began scrubbing. She scrubbed and she scrubbed, until her knees hurt and her hands spasmed in pain. Then the rain came, sheets of rain, but she continued to scrub, pouring on more and more bleach; scrubbing and sobbing until every trace of his blood, congealed on the tarmac due to the scorching heat that summer, was gone.

My own recollections of what happened the rest of that day are hazy, but I remember Mum returning home drenched from the downpour and putting the electric fire on to dry out. As the bars warmed, I watched her pour herself a large vodka, drink it neat, then roll herself into a ball on the settee. She lay there for the next few hours, her eyes red from crying, her damp hair bedraggled and clinging to her forehead like dulse. 'Where's Dad?' I kept asking, because I still didn't understand what had happened. I kept thinking any minute now the door would open and he would come in, pick me up in his arms and give me a big kiss like he always used to. But she shook her head. 'Your dad is with the angels, son,' she said. 'Don't you worry your wee head now. They'll look after him.' Even though I was hungry, my six-year-old self knew she was upset. I didn't want to make her worse, so I copied what Mum used to do when I wasn't feeling well. I covered her with a blanket and gave her my Humpty to cuddle. She pulled Humpty close, patting the settee, always her signal for me to curl up next to her. Tucking her knees behind my legs, she gripped my chest, spooning into me. I remember lying there, listening to her sobs, wondering why there was nothing I could say or do to make her feel better.

In the years following Dad's death, up until she met Mervyn, really, I'd watched Mum become increasingly insular. Apart from her annual solo holidays to Spain, when she left me in the care of Granny McQueen, she barely travelled anywhere; as far as she was concerned, the rest of the world was a barbarous jungle. This coming from a woman who lived in Northern Ireland throughout the height of the Troubles. She'd been to England a few times in the sixties and seventies, but she didn't like it. She said the people weren't friendly. As soon as they heard your accent, they assumed you were a terrorist. To be fair, this was how many living on the mainland viewed the Irish then and, in the past, both my parents had experienced prejudice because of where they were from.

Looking around the house, it strikes me how spacious it is. As a teenager, I always felt it was small, claustrophobic even, but for a modest 1970s semi-detached it feels positively palatial compared to my flat in Margate. How strange that, even after all this time, it's kept its familiar smell: polished wood, new carpet, vanilla pot pourri. Always vanilla, Mum's favourite. It takes me right back to when I lived here in the eighties. Picking up a messy stack of yellowed newspapers, leaflets and bills piled by the door, I put them on a table in the hallway, telling myself I'll sort through them later.

The living room door is open. I pause at the entrance, take a sharp breath. Inside, everything is the same as I remember it: beige walls, beige carpet; heavy burgundy curtains tied loosely round the middle with sagging bronzed ropes. When she was younger, Mum loved her mod cons, always keeping up with the latest gadgets and home furnishing trends, even if she couldn't afford them – most of her things were purchased on credit, or freebies from the catalogue. After she met Mervyn, though, she became more frugal. She stopped spending money on what she called 'frivolous things'. Broken electrical items could be fixed. Worn clothes could be darned, patched and mended. In fact, the only evidence in the room of what you might call a 'recent' purchase is the television: a small flatscreen, with a copy of the *Radio Times* lying next to it on a pouffe, the slightly yellowing pages still spread open on the date she had her stroke. My eyes are drawn towards the electric organ, with its flashing lights and primary-coloured buttons (*Rumba, Cha-cha, Waltz*); the worn crimson stool where I sat for hours struggling to read the notes to 'Mary Had a Little Lamb' from *John Thompson's Easiest Piano Course*. Above the organ, framed in dark wood, is a religious tract from the Psalms: *Thy word is a lamp unto my feet and a light unto my path*.

It's like I've time-travelled, like the interval between now and when I left for university in the early nineties is a matter of days, not years. I make my way through to the kitchen, which is just as retro as the living room. Dark wood kitchen cabinets filled with Eternal Bow plates, cups and saucers, the floor covered in a swirling orange 1970s lino, a straw mat concealing a large black burn mark where Mum dropped a casserole once. Opening one of the cupboards releases a waft of old Schwartz herbs and spices, long past their sell-by date: paprika, coriander seed, oregano; a jar of cloves marked *Best before October 1982*, the contents stuck together at the bottom like playground jacks. I shake the jar. Unscrewing the lid, I hold it to my nose, inhaling the warm, spicy aroma. A winter memory of making Christmas decorations with Mum, studding mandarin oranges with cloves and pinning red ribbons on them, then hanging them in the hot press to dry.

The doorbell rings, pulling me out of the past. I pause at first, unsure whether to answer. More knocking, and a woman's voice. 'It's only me, Billy, are you in there?'

I open the door to find Bev standing on the front step, holding a Tupperware box in her hands. She's petite and bottle-blonde with huge bosoms and a tiny waist. Ulster's answer to Dolly Parton.

'I brought you some of my home-made stew to help keep your strength up.'

'Aww. Thanks, Bev,' I say, taking the plastic box from her outstretched hands. 'That's very kind of you. Look, why don't you come in? I'll make you a cup of tea.'

Earlier that morning, Bev had been waiting to pick me up from Belfast International Airport. I'd had mixed feelings on the journey back, half of me wondering if I was making a huge mistake coming home, the other half taken by the urgency of the situation. I had to see Mum. I wasn't bothered about leaving my life in Margate behind. Besides, what did I have left there? The day after Bev rang with the news of Mum's stroke, I'd received an email from Sue at the café saying that regrettably she was unable to offer me a job. Panicked, I'd got straight on the phone to my landlord to tell him I was moving out. He wasn't happy, but, given the circumstances, and my reassurance that he'd get his rent money in due course, he let me go without a fight. It had only taken me a day or two to clear out the flat. Packing what few possessions I had into a small suitcase (one benefit of having pawned most of my clutter over the past year or so, I suppose), I dropped my keys off at the letting agency and caught a coach to the airport.

'I've no milk. I didn't think to get any. Will you take it black?'

'Have you nothing stronger, son?' Bev looks at me with a naughty twinkle in her eye.

'Stronger?'

'A wee vodka, maybe. Scotch, or something?'

It's not even gone 11 a.m. I open and close a few of the kitchen cupboard doors, looking for alcohol.

'Mum quit drinking years ago, didn't she?' I say. 'After she turned good living?'

'You're right,' says Bev. 'She keeps a wee stash of bottles for visitors, though. In the cupboard under the sink. I can give you a hand looking, if you want?'

'You're all right,' I say, following her instructions. Sure enough, I find several bottles of red wine, a litre of Bushmills and a couple of miniature Baileys.

'I've got wine, whiskey or Baileys, Bev.'

'I'll have a whiskey.'

I take a couple of glass tumblers from the cupboard, pouring a generous measure into each one. I bring the drinks into the living room, handing one to Bev, who is sitting on one of mum's armchairs, feet up, her fluffy white slippers resting on the pouffe.

'Cheers,' she says, taking a glass. 'Well, this is a blast from the past. I haven't seen you since you were a wee lad. It's a shame it's such a sad occasion.' She smiles at me, an impish glint in her eye. 'Here, I used to wipe your dirty nose, do you remember?'

I shake my head, laughing. 'Not really, Bev. It was a long time ago.'

'Aye, so it was. Doesn't feel like it though. Not to me,

41

anyway. Flip me. Time flies, so it does. What's it like being home then?'

I shrug. 'It feels weird. I've not been back here for donkey's years. There are ghosts everywhere I look.'

Bev gives a thoughtful nod. 'Aye, I'm sure there are. Do you like it here, though?'

'I do, yeah. Nothing beats that feeling of coming home. That smell of cow shit when you come off the plane.'

Bev smiles wistfully, her eyes crinkling at the corners. 'You've been away too long. Welcome back, son.'

We raise our glasses in a solemn toast to Mum and then sit for a moment in silence. Outside on the street, children are playing, kicking a ball about, their voices loud and excitable. I think about when I was one of those kids, those long summer evenings when it didn't get dark until past ten o'clock. When we stayed out late, getting bitten to death by midges, playing Hunts, British Bulldog and Thunder and Lightning, the game where we knocked on random people's doors and ran away. We stopped playing that when a man we called J.R., because of his temper, came out with a gun one night and threatened to shoot us.

Bev takes a sip of her whiskey. 'So, if you don't mind me asking, son, what happened between you and your mother? Why were you not speaking?'

'There's a few things I need to tell you,' I say, stroking my beard for reassurance.

They say the act of coming out is never a single event, but one that you repeat, again and again, throughout your life. Over the course of several more drinks, I tell Bev about what happened between my mum and me all those years ago, her shame over what she termed my 'life choices', her decision to cut all ties with me.

Bev listens in silence, her eyes widening, then she says, 'Maybe it's time for some food, son. We both need sobering up. Otherwise we'll end up plastered.'

She bungs the plastic container she brought over in the

microwave and, once it has heated, divides the contents into two bowls. 'Get that into you,' she says, handing me a bowl wrapped in a tea towel. I rest it on my lap, feeling the warmth on my thighs. I haven't had Irish stew in ages. Comfort food, it calms me. I like Bev. She might have a brash exterior, but she's a good person. I was expecting more judgement from her, but she has proved me wrong.

'I love Gay Pride,' she says, blowing on a mound of mince, potato and onion to cool it before spooning it into her mouth. 'You know they have it in Belfast now? I've been going the past few years. Some quare sights. All that leather. You gay fellas know how to put on a parade. You could teach those Orangemen a thing or two.'

This makes me laugh, and I find myself relaxing in Bev's company. It's nice to hear the accent again and I find my own coming back as we sit there talking.

'Come to think of it, son, your ma's funny about stuff like that. She's got strong views about certain things, you know. Abortion, sex . . . She can be difficult at times. I love her to bits, though. She's always been a good friend to me.'

I look around me, wondering why Mum chose to keep hold of this house, especially since she married Mervyn. Hadn't she moved in with him years ago? I ask Bev the question, as it's been playing on my mind all day.

'She did, aye. I don't know if you remember, but Mervyn owned that lovely big house on the Shore Road. They called it Graceland. It was stunning. It put my own poky wee home to shame. Every time I went round there, I felt like the maidservant. They even had one of those big brass dinner gongs. Honestly, it was out of this world, like something you'd see on *Downton Abbey*. Fair play to your ma, though, she insisted on keeping hold of this place, partly because Mervyn didn't own his house, the church did, and she always said this was her safety net in case anything happened. Between you and me, though, I think she kept it out of respect for your dad. She never got over his death, not really.

Even after she married Mervyn, she still came back here every weekend to do a bit of housekeeping or gardening. Then she'd take a walk up to Victoria Cemetery to visit his grave. She might've remarried, but your father still has a very special place in her heart.'

I tear up at this mention of my dad, and the knowledge that Mum has remained loyal to his memory, even after all these years. She kept the house as a shrine. Like me, my mother finds comfort in the past.

'What happened to Dad, exactly?' I say. 'Mum never really told me who was responsible.'

Bev sighs. 'It was an accident. The bomb wasn't meant to kill him. He'd borrowed the car off this fella he worked with – Tommy something or other – who was involved with one of the paramilitaries. Your da didn't know that at the time, obviously. He just thought he was doing Tommy a favour by driving the car for him.'

'So, who was the bomb meant for, then?'

'Barry Beggs. He owned the pub which Tommy told your da to park the car outside. Barry was refusing to pay protection money, you see. To be honest, I don't think the bomb was meant to kill anyone, it was supposed to be a threat. A warning.' Bev looks down at her hands, fiddling with her wedding ring. 'That sort of thing used to happen all the time back then. Awful, so it was. Your poor ma. She never got over losing him.'

Bev rubs her eyes, before continuing. 'Did I tell you she wants to be buried in the same plot as your father, not Mervyn? I thought you'd want to know.'

This is news to me. Despite it being many years since we lost Dad, I'm finding it hard to hold back the tears. I feel desperately sad for her. She married Mervyn when she was still in love with Dad. For over half her life she's had to hide her love away.

'You know she's gifted you the house?' says Bev, her voice brightening just a little. 'If you want it, that is. And there's a lot of money coming your way, too. Not that it's something you'll want to think about now.'

This revelation sends my mind racing. Why has Mum left me an inheritance? She's made zero effort to contact me in decades. Even after Mervyn's death she stayed silent.

'Seriously?' I say. 'Was she planning on getting in touch with me then? Was she going to tell me about this?'

Bev shrugs. 'I assume so.' She stares down at her lap. 'Sorry, I thought you might've known.'

I shake my head. 'Like I said, we haven't spoken for a long time.'

'Now I think of it, she has been talking about you more recently. Before the stroke, she said to me, "I wonder what my Billy's up to these days?" She even mentioned writing to you at one stage . . . I encouraged her, of course. I get the impression she still feels bad about what happened.'

My throat tightens. Resting my spoon on the side of my bowl, I swallow, turning my head to look at the gold-framed photograph of Mum, which has lived on top of the mantelpiece for as long as I can remember. She wanted to make contact, then. Was she ready to forgive me? Still staring at the photograph, I go to speak again, but my voice comes out croaky. 'Do you think I'll be allowed to see her? At the hospital, I mean?'

Bev widens her eyes. 'Of course. You're her son, aren't you?'

'Will she recognise me, though?'

'She's asleep, so she probably won't even know you're there. When I go up to the hospital, I always hold her hand and talk to her. She doesn't react, but that's not to say she isn't listening. One of the nurses there told me patients take comfort from our voices.'

'Would you come with me?'

'Of course, love. I can drive you up there tomorrow, if you want?'

'I'd really appreciate that, Bev,' I say, mopping up the last of the gravy with my bread. 'It's so kind of you to do all this for us. Mum's lucky to have such a good friend.' I pause, thinking to myself how this is the first time in my life I've been able to be truly myself at home. 'Thank you for listening,' I say. 'And for not judging me over the whole gay thing.'

Bev laughs. 'Auch, wise up, will you. Who am I to judge? Sure, I'm no angel myself. I could tell you stories which would make your hair curl.' She stands up, taking our dirty dishes into the kitchen, where she washes them and lays them on the draining board to dry. 'I better be off, love,' she says. 'But if you need anything, just holler. I'm only next door.' I follow her into the hallway. She pauses by the front door, taking an envelope from her coat pocket. 'Oh, and here's a wee map I drew for you earlier. Directions to your da's grave in Victoria Cemetery, in case you've forgotten. I was thinking you might want to take a walk over there. He won't have had any visitors since your mum went into hospital. It'll save you getting lost.' She presses the map into my hand.

'Thanks, Bev,' I say. 'You're a lifesaver.' I watch her go down the garden path. When she gets to the gate, she turns to me and waves.

'You're a good son, Billy McQueen. You look after yourself now. I'll see you tomorrow.'

Later that afternoon, I go upstairs to my old bedroom. The drinks I had with Bev have made me drowsy, but I'm too restless with the novelty of being home to bother with a nap. Earlier, it dawned on me that my old bedroom is the only room in the house that has been redecorated since the eighties. No more bold, colourful wallpaper plastered with Kylie posters I'd torn from *Smash Hits* and *Number One*. No more shelves overflowing with stuff: Letts revision guides, Penguin Classics, stacks of Commodore 64 computer games. The corkboard pinned with old concert ticket stubs and photographs is gone, too. Now, the walls are painted magnolia, the sparse furnishings equally bland and colourless.

Opening a wardrobe, I spot an old Clarks shoebox lying on the top shelf, with 'Billy' written on the side in Mum's handwriting. I lift it down, before sitting on the bed. Opening the lid, I look inside.

The first thing that catches my eye is a cheque, made out to me, for fifty thousand pounds. With a sharp intake of breath, I examine it more closely. This is a joke, a mistake, surely? I turn it over in my hands, holding it up to the light to make sure my tipsy brain isn't playing tricks on me. But no, the cheque is mine, all right. It's written out in my name and signed by Mum. The date: Thursday 3rd August 2023. The day before she had her stroke. Was she intending on posting this to me? An olive branch, in the form of money? I clutch it to my chest, my eyes wet with tears. Just last week, a young guy gave me a pound so I could afford to eat, and now I'm holding a cheque in my hand for fifty thousand pounds. This can't be real. Did Mum really write this? Folding the cheque neatly in half, I slip it in my jeans pocket. Tomorrow, I'm going to ask Bev what she thinks I should do with it.

I continue rummaging through the contents of the box, which is full of my things: old Polaroid photographs – of me as a child, looking terrified on Santa's lap in Anderson & McAuley's department store; a day trip to Portrush; my first day at school. There's a slip of paper with my GCSE results on it, pages of old song lyrics from *Smash Hits*, and then something which stops me in my tracks. A missing persons notice, ripped from an old copy of the *Carrickfergus Advertiser* and paperclipped to the front of a padded envelope. It reads:

Conor Doherty, aged 16. Last seen 11th July 1989, 3.30 p.m. Blond hair. Blue eyes. Fair complexion. Height 5 feet 10 inches. Wearing a denim jacket with grey corduroy collar, white jeans and Timberland boots.

Even now, I can picture him so clearly. His denim jacket with the giant cartoon Fred Flintstone printed on the back, which used to make me so envious because I wanted one just like it. Lifting the newspaper cutting, I examine the front of the envelope. While it's clearly addressed to me, it's been Sellotaped at the back, like someone has opened it and then resealed it. The postmark is dated 13th July 2013. I tear it open. There's a TDK cassette, in a broken plastic case, and a note. The note is typed. It says, 'This belongs to you, so returning it. Sorry for keeping it so long.' Written on the label in blue biro are the words *For Billy, 11th July 1989*.

I click open the plastic cassette cover, my eyes scanning the track listing: 'Wind Beneath My Wings' – Bette Midler, 'Eternal Flame' – The Bangles, 'I Don't Wanna Get Hurt' – Donna Summer, 'Ain't Nobody' – Rufus and Chaka Khan, 'You'll Never Stop Me From Loving You' – Sonia. I shiver, recognising the handwriting at once. It's Conor's.

That's impossible, though. How can it be? I put on my reading glasses, leaning forward to double-check the date and postmark on the envelope. There's no mistaking it. This cassette was posted to Mum's house from Belfast in July 2013, twenty-five years *after* Conor went missing. Given the date – a date I'll never forget – and the fact that it's clearly Conor's handwriting, this can mean only one thing. Conor was planning on giving me this mixtape on the night he disappeared. Mind racing, I turn the cassette over in my hand to see if there's anything written on the back, contact details for the sender, but there's nothing. No name, no address. Who sent this, and why did they wait twenty-five years? Is there someone out there who knows what happened to him that night?

Later, looking at the map Bev has drawn for me, I decide to take a wander down to Victoria Cemetery. I need to sort my head out, mull things over. Before leaving the house, I slide Conor's mixtape into my Walkman to keep me company on the journey, the opening piano notes of Bette Midler's 'Wind Beneath My Wings' tinkling as I close the front door behind me. I pull the handle down three times to make sure it's fully locked, then before I'm even halfway down the garden path, I go back, touch the handle again, just to make sure it's secure.

It's only a twenty-minute walk to the cemetery, but one that takes me past many of my old haunts. As a child, I remember coming this way with Mum. She always let me carry the flowers she'd cut fresh from the garden that morning for Dad's grave. I loved pressing them into my face, breathing in the sweetness of their wet petals. She used to stop off at the corner shop too, to buy me sweets for the journey: a Cadbury's Fudge, or a bag of Rowntree's Tooty Frooties. She never let me eat them until we were back home, though. My reward for being such a brave wee soldier, she said.

The empty fields Conor and I used to hang around in as teenagers have morphed into new housing developments, new roads. There's very little left I recognise. I try to cast my mind back, to remember what was here before, but it's impossible. Stopping off at the garage to buy flowers, I continue walking until I pass the church. When I reach the new roundabout, I cross over the road, making my way to the cemetery.

It doesn't take me long to find my dad's grave. The plot looks lonely and bare, the only evidence of visitors a single vase of wilted, dried-out flowers placed in front of the headstone, presumably by Mum. I pull them out, replacing them with fresh ones. This grave is my responsibility now, I tell myself. While Mum is in hospital, I am its sole caretaker. I look around to check I'm alone before kneeling on the pebbled pathway. Closing my eyes, I whisper a silent prayer. I don't think I've prayed since I was a teenager, and I'd forgotten how reassuring it can be, chatting to the big fella upstairs. In my prayers, I tell my dad I love him dearly, how I hope one day to be reunited with him in a place where we can be a family again. I tell him the reason why Mum hasn't been to visit him recently, and not to worry because I will be looking after her. I'm not sure I believe half of what I'm saying, but still, there's comfort to be had in prayer, in ritual.

When I get home, I take off my headphones, collapsing on Mum's sofa. Exhausted, I pick up my phone and do my usual mindless scroll through Amazon and eBay looking for bargain eighties cassette tapes, but my mind is too preoccupied by the events of the past few hours to allow me to switch off. There's the question of who sent me Conor's mixtape, and then seeing my dad's lonely grave got me thinking about my own lack of friends. It's been a long time – years – since I've felt part of a community. I haven't had contact with the old Northern Irish crowd since I left for university. To be fair, keeping in touch was difficult back then. We didn't have the technology, the instant access people have to each other's lives nowadays, so if you moved far away it was easy to drift apart. I do miss the friends I had here. Conor obviously, but others too. I wonder if any of them might be able to shine a light on the sender of the mixtape?

I've always avoided friendship apps, finding them a horrible invasion of privacy, but tonight, after pouring myself another large glass of whiskey and putting on my reading glasses, I download Facebook on my phone. Within minutes, I've managed to set up an account and a basic profile. I type the name of mine and Conor's old schoolfriend, Aine Kelly, into the search bar. As it turns out, there are hundreds of Aine Kellys, but I keep scrolling. Eventually, I find a match. The profile blurb gives little information apart from the name @aine_kelly73 and the fact she lives in Carrickfergus. I click the 'Add friend' button and in less time than it takes me to finish my glass of whiskey, a message pops up on my phone screen.

OMG, BILLY MC QUEEN! HOW THE HELL ARE YOU? A XXX

Straight away, I start typing a reply.

6.

Before

Saturday 13th May 1989

It might be blowing a gale when I leave the house, but even
the wind is no match for the rock-solid Rick Astley quiff
I've spent hours hairspraying to perfection for today's trip
to Belfast with Aine. I need to tell her about this Mervyn
fella Mum brought round on Sunday, the fella she's secretly
been seeing for a few months, but more importantly I need
to talk about these weird feelings I've been having for boys.
As I battle my way down the road, my coat hood pulled up
over my head to protect my hair, I listen to the latest cassette
Conor has made for me on my Walkman. The first track is
'More Than You Know' by Martika, which is about fancying
someone but being too scared to tell them. Both Conor
and I are massive Martika fans. Earlier this year, for the
school talent show, he devised an interpretive dance routine
to her debut single 'Toy Soldiers', all about the Troubles. He
performed it solo in his dad's old army khakis and a black
balaclava. It was totally mega. Not only did he look sexy,
but he came first place, which secretly made me dead proud.

When I get to the bus stop, there's no sign of Aine.
Punctuality's not her strong point. Still, I'm early and the
bus isn't due for another ten minutes. Hugging my denim
jacket, I lean over the pebbled coastal wall. To my right is
Carrickfergus Castle, built in 1177. At school, we learned that
the name of our wee town originally comes from two Gaelic
words: *Carraig*, meaning rock – or rocky headland – and

Fergus, which means 'strong man'. Which is a pretty apt description for this place, come to think about it. For round here, there are loads of strong men. It's the weedy boys like me who stick out like a sore thumb.

A sea mist is creeping up the lough, and further along, through the fog, I can just make out the tall yellow figures of Samson and Goliath, the two cranes in the Harland & Wolff shipyard in Belfast. A ferry floats past in the gloom. I watch as it slowly disappears, thinking of the passengers on board, where they're heading. Somewhere better than here, no doubt. I wish I could join them.

If only I lived in London, life would be a lot easier.

I've been meaning to talk to Aine about these strange feelings I've been having for fellas for a while now, as she's the least likely of all my friends to be fazed by it. I've tried to broach the subject with Mum, but I chicken out every time; my last attempt, a few months ago, ended with me working myself into such a state that I was dry-heaving over the kitchen sink. Just when I was on the verge of blurting it out, she said, 'I'm going next door to watch *Coronation Street* with Bev.' I realised it was just a normal day for her. She hadn't a clue what was going on in my head. I couldn't tell her after that.

One reason it's so hard for me to talk about my feelings is that, apart from Gordon and Chris in *Brookside*, and pop stars like Boy George and Holly Johnson, I don't know any gay people. Real-life ones, that is. Ordinary gay folk. And while I've always had my suspicions about Mr Boyle, our French teacher, who all the rugby lads at school call 'Bender Boyle', he's never going to admit it. Teachers aren't supposed to talk about gay stuff, you see, because Mrs Thatcher has introduced this new law, Section 28, banning what she calls the 'promotion of homosexuality' in schools. Which is a shame, 'cause I know for a fact that Miss Wright, my English teacher, would be cool with me liking fellas as she's dead on with people who are a bit eccentric, or different. Like, when we read *A Midsummer Night's Dream* in her class last year, she explained to us how in Shakespeare's times, men performed the women's parts because women weren't allowed to act in the theatre. So, when Miss asked for volunteers to read at the front of the classroom, naturally Conor and me both put our hands up. He chose the male part, Pyramus, and I played his lover, Thisbe, which made me take a redner at first, but I don't think anyone noticed. Miss explained to us that Pyramus and Thisbe are doomed lovers who live in the city of Babylon. Like Romeo and Juliet, their parents are rivals, so they can't have sex, despite the fact they're both completely gagging for it. They live next door to each other and secretly communicate by whispering sweet nothings through a big crack in the wall.

The whole performance was a geg. Davy Dodds, the tallest, thinnest boy in the fourth year, played the wall. As Thisbe, Miss encouraged me to put on this high-pitched voice and when I said the line, 'O wall, full often hast thou heard my moans', Tracey McGookin shouted out, 'Sounds like the noises my ma makes when her fella stays over', and everyone burst out laughing. Even Miss Wright was creasing up at her desk. Things got worse when, at one point, Pyramus says, 'O kiss me through the hole of this vile wall', and Thisbe replies, 'I kiss the wall's hole, not your lips at all'. As the wall, poor Davy Dodds was doing his best to stay as still as possible, but he was shaking with laughter – seriously, his face was redder than the Red Hand of Ulster – and, as soon as I whispered the word 'hole', everyone lost the plot. Tracey McGookin yelled, 'Up your hole with a big jam roll, Billy McQueen', and the class erupted into a riot. Miss stood up and told us all to be quiet, but you could tell she was secretly pissing herself. She could barely keep a straight face. Like I say, out of everyone, I reckon she'd be fine with me being gay. It makes me anxious that I can't talk to her about stuff like that.

Behind me, a car swishes through a large puddle, spraying

a shower of water along the pavement. Aine jumps out, slamming the door behind her. 'I'll see you back here at five,' she says to her ma, Bronagh, who gives me an enthusiastic wave from the driver's seat. Aine puts up her umbrella and runs over to me, squealing. 'Jesus, it's pissing down,' she says.

I press the stop button on my Walkman, taking off my headphones. 'I thought you liked the rain?'

'I do. But not when I'm outside. It's all right when I'm indoors and all cosy, like.' Aine blinks at me with her feline eyes. She's dressed head to toe in black today (black duffel coat, black dress, black tights and black DMs) which is the look she normally goes for, being an 'alternative' indie type who worships Morrissey, avoids meat and lives under the daily threat of a nuclear cloud; Aine is what you might call a rebel with various causes.

While she's my best friend, music is one thing that Aine and I can never agree on. It's the root cause of most of our arguments. Aine's dad, Alan, owns Carrick Rocks, the local record shop, and she sometimes works there on Saturdays for a bit of extra pocket money. Just like her opinions, Aine's tastes in music are very left-field. She listens to bands like Depeche Mode, the Pixies and The Stone Roses; she wouldn't be seen dead reading *Smash Hits* (she buys *NME* and *Melody Maker* every week) and, most days, she carries an LP around school under her arm. It's usually a Morrissey album, but sometimes it's the latest Cure or R.E.M. record. At lunch and break, she makes me stand outside the Sixth Form Study Centre while she badgers the older pupils to play her records on the school hi-fi, which is one of the massive perks of doing A levels. It's usually not that hard, to be honest, as being a record shop owner's daughter, Aine has instant kudos with the cool kids who hang out at Carrick Rocks and know her dad – Carrick's answer to John Peel.

The blue Ulsterbus pulls up at the stop and we clamber on, relieved at last to have some shelter from the rain. We pay our return fare, Aine rolling her eyes at the driver when he tells her to 'take her wee ticket'. Aine loathes the word 'wee'. She especially hates it when people call her 'wee', but everyone does it because she's so petite. At school, they've even nicknamed her 'Wee Aine', which does her head in because, according to her, 'wee' is nothing but a pathetic attempt to infantilise her, and it's even worse if a man does it. Of course, in Northern Ireland everything is 'wee' – a 'wee' bun, a 'wee' cup of tea, a 'wee' chat – so for her, living here must be a nightmare. One time, I tried to reassure her there's nothing wrong with being 'wee' by showing her a feature I'd spotted in *Smash Hits* called 'How Tall Are Pop Stars?' I was ecstatic to learn that, at five feet tall, my favourite actress and singer Kylie Minogue is *exactly* the same height as Aine. Anyone would think being compared to Kylie might make her feel better about her own 'wee' proportions, but she was frigging livid, not least because, according to her, Kylie is a puppet and her music is 'manufactured shite'. For as Aine is forever reminding me, there's a hell of a difference between what she calls 'real' music and 'manufactured' pop. Pop music is evil and capitalist, whereas 'real' artists, like Morrissey, use their music to carry important political messages about issues like corrupt establishments, nuclear weapons and vegetarianism.

As always, we head straight for the middle of the bus, as far back as possible – but not right at the back as that's the smoking area and we don't want to come home stinking of fegs. We take our seats on the hard plastic chairs and, as the bus lurches forward, Aine rubs the steam from the window with the sleeve of her duffel coat, but not before turning around to give the woman behind her, who is smoking, a dirty look. 'If I get lung cancer, I'll know who to blame,' she deadpans. Aine's bolshiness gives me a fit of the giggles, which I eventually manage to get under control by thinking about Mum's new fella Mervyn and what a weirdo he is. I mention all this to Aine.

'Oooh, gossip,' she says. 'Where did she meet him?'

55

'Some pub in Belfast.'

'Your ma still goes to pubs? Seriously, like?'

'Aye. She only started going out again recently, though.'

'She must be in her forties. At least.'

'Thirty-nine.'

'Jesus, she's hardcore. You wouldn't catch Bronagh drinking in pubs these days. She's the same age.'

'Your ma's all right though.'

'Aye, she's sound.'

The bus stops outside a housing estate. From the window, we can see the residents are already busy making preparations for the 12th July parades. Union Jack and Red Hand of Ulster flags hang from poles stuck above porches; flagstones are painted red, white and blue, and the sides of some of the end houses are painted with murals of King Billy and covered in graffiti: slogans such as 'No Surrender', 'Remember 1690' and 'Fuck the Taigs'. Behind the estate, there's a big field, in the middle of which they've already started gathering items for this year's bonfire: old furniture, books, newspapers, crates, cardboard boxes, and so on. A woman gets on the bus with her baby. She's carrying a red-and-white-striped fold-up buggy in one hand, a cigarette hanging from her mouth.

'You're going to have to put that out, love, until you're in the smoking area,' the bus driver says to her, as she hands him the money. The woman scowls. Dropping the cigarette on the ground, she stamps on the butt with the heel of her trainer, kicking it out the door. 'Well, that's a waste, so it is,' she says. She grabs her ticket and heaves the baby and buggy on board, sitting down on one of the seats facing us. The child is wearing a T-shirt which says 'Baby Annie's First 12th July' in orange bubble writing, with Union Jack and Ulster flags either side. Below is the line 'Following in my Daddy's Footsteps'.

'Jesus Christ,' Aine mutters under her breath. 'What kind of parent dresses their child in shit like that? Why do they have to shove their dumb slogans in our faces?'

'Have you looked at your bag lately, Aine?' I laugh.

'What do you mean?' she says.

'Talk about slogans.'

I point to the blue Army & Navy canvas messenger bag on Aine's lap. It's plastered with pin badges – The Cure, Morrissey, Echo & the Bunnymen – and covered in slogans scrawled in black marker pen: *CND, MEAT IS MURDER, BAN THE BOMB.*

Aine tuts. 'Wise up, Billy,' she says. 'I'm promoting peace, not violence. Anyway, that's not the point. I'm not the one putting slogans on my kids.'

Aine is the most political person I know. She's absolutely obsessed. Her heroine is the Independent Republican Bernadette Devlin, who, at twenty-two years old, was the youngest female MP ever to be elected to Westminster. Aine aspires to be just like her, carrying a battered, dog-eared paperback of Devlin's autobiography, *The Price of My Soul*, everywhere she goes. It's her Bible, she says. Her da gave it to her as a present on her twelfth birthday and she read it cover to cover in one sitting. 'Bernadette Devlin changed my life,' she told me once. 'Everything – the whole shitty Northern Irish political situation – suddenly made sense to me.' Aine's parents had met at Queen's University in Belfast in the late sixties and were both very active in the Civil Rights movement, so I suppose she gets her political aspirations from them. Back in the day, they used to go on marches and demonstrations, campaigning for better housing and employment opportunities for Catholics.

The baby starts screaming. It clenches its tiny fist, pushing it into the woman's cheek. 'For crying out loud, Annie,' says the woman. 'Will you give my head peace?' She reaches into a plastic carrier bag and pulls out an orange dummy, which she puts in the baby's mouth. The screaming stops.

'Do you want kids?' I say to Aine.

She sighs. 'I've not really thought about it, to be honest. Probably not, like. I wouldn't want to be responsible for bringing up another child in this shit-hole.' She draws a smiley face in the steamed-up window, staring at it for a few seconds, weighing up its artistic merits, before wiping it off with her sleeve. 'Here. Don't say anything to Bronagh, though. Being Catholic, it's kind of assumed I'll be popping them out once I'm married.' She pauses. 'What about you?'

I shake my head. 'As soon as I get a chance, I'm outta here. No time for kids.'

'Really?' says Aine. 'Where are you going to move to?'

'England.'

Aine pulls a face. 'Englaaand?' she says, putting on a fake British accent and laughing.

'What's wrong with England?'

'Nothing,' she says. 'Doesn't that make you a traitor, though?'

'A traitor? Why?'

'Sure, you may as well get yourself a T-shirt like that wee girl has – with a big Union Jack on the front.'

'Piss off.'

'Well, why would you want to move to England?'

'To get away from here?'

'What about Dublin?'

'I want to live in London.'

Aine howls with laughter. 'How the hell are you going to afford to live in London? Do you know how much it costs to buy a house there? It's like a billion pounds.'

'I'll get a job.'

'Who do you know in London?'

'Loads of people,' I lie.

'Like who?'

'Like . . . I dunno . . . Kylie Minogue, the Pet Shop Boys.'

'I mean *real* people, Billy.'

'Kylie Minogue *is* a real person.'

'Don't be a smartarse. It doesn't suit you. Seriously, tell me the name of one person you know who lives in London. A real person, like, not somebody off the TV.'

The bus is slowing down. We're nearly at our stop.

'I don't know anyone,' I say, quietly. 'I'm planning on getting a job though. It's one way of meeting people, I suppose.'

'Where are you going to work?'

'*Smash Hits*,' I say. 'I want to be a music journalist.'

'Well, good luck with that, mate,' says Aine, starting to gather her things. 'How many Northern Irish journalists working for *Smash Hits* do you know?'

'None,' I say, standing up. 'I'll be the first.'

We turn a corner and I lurch forward, grabbing onto a pole to stop me from falling, as the bus pulls up near the entrance to Royal Avenue.

Any minute now, I think, I'm going to tell Aine my secret.

7.

Now

Sunday 13th August 2023

'Not far to the hospital now.' Bev fiddles with the knob of the car stereo, turning the volume up a notch, but not so loud that we can't hear each other speak. All the way here, we've been listening to *Glen Campbell's Greatest Hits*, an album which always brings back fond memories of my childhood.

'Mum used to play "Rhinestone Cowboy" all the time when I was kid,' I say, wistfully. 'It used to drive me bonkers, but it's growing on me now.'

Bev nods, tapping her fingers on the steering wheel. 'Your ma loves her music. You must take after her then. We used to have some quare parties back in the seventies, with your da on guitar and me and your ma on backing vocals. Those were the days.'

As Glen begins singing the line about all the compromises he's had to make, I decide now is a good time to broach the subject of the money Mum left me.

'Did Mum ever mention anything to you about a cheque?' I ask her.

'A cheque?' Bev shakes her head. 'She talked about you in her will, if that's what you mean.'

'Only I found one last night. Made out to me and signed and dated by Mum, the day before she had her stroke.'

'Really?'

'Yeah. In a shoebox in my old bedroom. No note or anything, just a cheque – for fifty thousand pounds.'

Bev whistles. 'Fifty thousand smackeroos? Seriously, like? To be honest with you, son, that doesn't surprise me. Your ma inherited an absolute fortune when Mervyn died. He'd a lot of assets tied up in that church.'

I pause, listening to the rain pattering on the roof of the car, while Glen croons on about the dollar tucked away inside his shoe and what he plans to do with it. 'Only I've been wondering whether I should cash it or not. It seems wrong given that she's in hospital.'

'Auch, catch yourself on. Sure, she wouldn't have written it if she didn't want you to have the money. Besides, you've come all the way over here to look after her now. She'll want to make sure you're OK financially, so don't you worry your wee head. Your ma's not short of a bob or two.'

'You think I should just go ahead and bank it then?'

'Absolutely!' says Bev. 'That's exactly what I think you should do.'

Bev's practical advice is just what I need to hear right now, not to mention a relief, given I've been stressing over how I'm going to pay my old landlord and afford groceries. I wonder if I should tell her about Conor's mixtape too, but not now. Maybe later.

'This is it – this is the place,' says Bev, turning into the car park of Belfast's Royal Victoria Hospital. I stare out the window, my stomach in knots. Any minute now, I'm going to be reunited with my mum. Am I really ready for this?

'I've not been here in years,' I say, peering up at the large white building, which looks completely changed from the last time I visited. 'This is where I came to have my tonsils out when I was seven or eight. I remember the nurses feeding me ice cream and wheeling the big TV into the ward, so I could watch *Dallas*.'

Bev lets out a throaty chuckle. 'Sure, do you remember I used to come over to your ma's house every Saturday night for *Dallas*? You always got dead excited by the cliff-hangers, running around the living room in your knickers like a wee monkey. Hyper, so you were. Your ma had a job trying to calm you down before bedtime. You loved that show.'

'Mum loved it too,' I say, recalling our many nights spent cuddled on the sofa together, completely engrossed in the latest twists and turns in the Ewing family's fortunes. To be fair, they made our own crazy life look almost normal, which was comforting in a way. All that money, and they were still unhappy. 'Here, do you think my being here will be too much for Mum? I don't want to cause her any stress.'

'She's asleep, son. She won't know. It'll be a comfort for her, hearing your voice.'

I nod, mentally trying to prepare myself for a reunion with my mother. It's a moment I've been dreaming of for as long as I can remember, even if the circumstances aren't quite how I'd imagined them. As we make our way to the entrance, I take comfort from all the signs Mum's given me so far that she wants us to be close again. I'm hoping that, like me, she's been longing for this day. Our reunion.

'Your mum's doing OK,' the young nurse tells me after we sign in. 'Her condition hasn't changed much, but she's stable.'

'What are the odds of her making a recovery?' I ask, as she leads us down a long corridor.

'I can't answer that question. You'd need to speak to the doctor. The stroke was quite severe, though, Mr McQueen. It could take a while. For now, the main thing is that you're here for her.'

I nod and try not to worry as we weave our way through various passages. 'This is her room,' says the nurse as we turn a corner and come face to face with a white door. I hold my breath as she pushes it open, not knowing quite what to expect.

Bev pats me gently on the arm. 'Are you OK, love?'

'I think so,' I murmur, pausing in the doorway for a moment, my eyes closed, bracing myself for what I'm about to see. I listen to the sounds on the other side. Mum's gentle breathing, the steady beep of the heart monitor, the soft shuffle of the nurse's shoes as she moves around the room, checking everything is as it should be. At the sound of the curtain being pulled along its rod, I step into the room.

Mum is lying on the bed, an oxygen mask over her mouth, an IV drip attached to her arm. The last time I saw her, she was in her forties, so it comes as a shock to see how old she is now. Her once-brown hair is grey, her face covered in deep lines. She looks smaller, too, as if the stroke has caused her to shrink in size.

The nurse points towards the armchair next to the bed. 'Take a seat, if you want,' she says.

Lost for words, I turn to Bev. 'What should I say to her?'

'Anything you want, son.' She smiles. 'Maybe start by letting her know you're here.'

Mum looks so pale and fragile, like the Lladró ornaments she used to bring home from her trips to Spain. I'm too scared to touch her in case she breaks, so I let my hands rest on the crisp white bedsheets, stroking the soft fabric, as if it's part of her. 'Mum,' I whisper, my voice shaking. 'It's me, Billy. Your son.'

No answer, no movement, just the sound of her low breathing, in and out, in tandem with the beep of the heart monitor.

'I'm here with Bev,' I say. 'You know Bev? She's been very good to us both, so she has. She's looking after me.'

I can feel my eyes welling up. I've been building up to this moment for days, and now that it's finally here, I can't cope. Swallowing, I try to choke back the sobs, but this is too much. I let it all pour out of me, this pain I've been holding inside for so long.

Bev stands behind me. She wraps her arms around my shoulders, drawing me into her warm bosom. 'There, there, now,' she says, over and over, the way Mum used to do when I was a wee boy and I'd fallen over and grazed my knee. 'It's all right, son. Like the nurse said, you being here, it's all that matters.'

8.

Before

Saturday 13th May 1989

'For flip's sake, as if that oul doll is going to be carrying explosives,' Aine hisses, as we join the short queue at the security gates to enter Belfast city centre. 'She must be at least ninety.' She starts doing a little jig on the spot, fidgety to get to the shops. An armed soldier, leaning casually against a wall, catches her eye. He stares at her as if to say 'wise up'. Aine freezes, her face stuck in an awkward grin. We wait in line while the old lady in front of us takes off one of her gloves. Unclipping the gold clasp of her handbag, she passes it over to the security woman. It's a well-rehearsed routine, one which everyone round here is used to. The security woman is in her forties and dressed head to toe in uniform. Neatly permed hair sticking out the sides of her black military cap. She doesn't smile, or show any hint of friendliness, as she rifles through the handbag. Satisfied the old lady hasn't got a bomb hidden among her things – which, from what I can see, mainly consist of her purse, a few scrunched-up tissues and a bottle of Estée Lauder's Youth Dew – she returns the bag to its owner. The old lady puts her glove back on and wanders through the gates.

'Next,' says the security guard. I'm not carrying anything with me today, so she ushers me straight through. 'Wait there,' she says to Aine, who already has the buckles undone on her canvas bag, ready for inspection. The security woman gives her stuff a customary glance and nods. Flinging the

65

strap of her bag over her shoulder, Aine struts through the gate like she's a model on *The Clothes Show*. Catching my eye, she sniggers; then she looks back at the soldier to check he hasn't seen her taking the piss. He's facing the opposite direction, thank God.

The rain is easing off now, but several storm clouds looming over City Hall suggest it'll be back again before long. Belfast is quiet today. It's lunchtime, so mostly mums doing their shopping, or Saturday workers nipping out for a bite to eat. We mooch around the city centre for an hour or so, down Donegall Place, browsing a few shops in Cornmarket. Aine hasn't stopped talking since we got off the bus. Seeing that woman with the baby earlier has got her on her political soapbox.

'I mean, what is it with people like her?' she says. 'It's like they're always having to prove they're British the whole time.' I'm listening, but I'm finding it hard to concentrate on what she's saying. All I can think about is my secret: how – and at what point this afternoon – I'm going to slip it into the conversation.

Aine is after a single by a new band she's read about in *NME*. They're so new that even her da hasn't heard of them yet. We duck into Caroline Music, the coolest of several record stores in Belfast. As we pass through the bright red and yellow storefront, a huge cardboard cut-out of Simple Minds' *Street Fighting Years* LP on display in the window, the familiar guitar strums to 'People Are Strange' by Echo & the Bunnymen buzz from the shop speakers, the rhythm marked by a series of finger clicks which suddenly explode into a burst of drums and melody. The song's lyrics give me a momentary swagger of confidence, gently reminding me that it's OK to be different.

All the latest chart releases are shelved on racks along the walls. Aine makes a beeline for the alternative section, her fingers flicking rapidly from one record to the next. She pulls out a seven-inch single, 'Love Buzz', by a band called Nirvana. 'You won't like them, Billy,' she says when she sees me glancing, seriously unimpressed, at the blurry black and white cover, which features long-haired men with beards. 'They're way too heavy for your tastes. They're going to be massive, though. I've been looking for a copy of this for ages.'

As we head over to the tills to pay, a voice screams, 'Aine, Aine!' A tall guy, wearing a black bomber jacket, jeans and a baseball cap, waves at us enthusiastically from the queue.

'Do you know him?' I whisper to Aine. I recognise him from around Carrick, but I've never spoken to him myself.

'Big Gay Willy,' she says, waving back. 'William Carson. We used to go to choir together.'

'Is he actually gay though?'

Aine rolls her eyes. 'Jesus, Billy. You don't half ask stupid questions.'

Big Gay Willy runs over, kissing Aine on both cheeks. He is holding the twelve-inch vinyl of Kylie Minogue's 'Hand on Your Heart' under his arm. I can't help noticing he has a small gold stud in his right ear, which everyone knows is code for being gay. 'This is Billy,' Aine says, introducing me.

He smiles, eyeing me up and down in a way that makes me feel a bit weird and uncomfortable. 'Are you two together then?' He turns to Aine, winking.

'Catch yourself on,' she says, with a look of horror. 'Billy's a mate.'

'I see.' Big Gay Willy grins. 'What are yous up to?'

'Nothing much,' says Aine. 'Just a bit of shopping.'

'I'm looking for a new summer job,' he says. 'Not having much luck though, and these new trainers are killing me.' He points at his feet, revealing a bright red pair of Converse All Stars.

'Those are *so* cool,' says Aine. 'Where did you get them?'

'American Madness.'

'Is that the place that does all the vintage clothing?' I say, amazed that anyone our age can afford to shop there.

'Aye – and look.' Big Gay Willy turns round, drawing our attention to his bum. There's a red handkerchief sticking out of the back pocket of his jeans. 'I got a wee bandana to match. They're all the rage, so they are.'

Big Gay Willy tells us that he bought the trainers with the money he's saved from his job at the petrol garage. 'The pay is crap like,' he says. 'But I'm looking for another job, preferably in retail. Not in a supermarket though. They make you put on an embarrassing shite-brown uniform, which personally I wouldn't be seen dead in. At least in the petrol garage they let me wear what I want. I can retain some of my individuality, know what I mean?'

Aine nods in agreement. 'I'm never going to wear a uniform for work,' she says. 'Fuck that. No way am I hiding who I am behind some bullshit corporate dress code.'

'Don't you have to wear a uniform in your da's shop?' I say.

'Only black jeans and a black T-shirt,' she says, frowning. 'I'd hardly call that a uniform, Billy.'

'Only saying like.' I stare down at my Primark trainers, which look cheap and nasty next to Willy's Converse.

'Here. Don't yous be having a domestic now.' He laughs, a very loud, high-pitched laugh. 'Jesus, what have I started?'

He seems nice, Willy. Friendly, but full-on. Not the sort of person who blends easily into the background. Here in staunchly conservative Belfast, he stands out from the crowd, and, in my eyes, he's both terrifying and fascinating. I might not have met anyone like him in my life before, but I'm weirdly curious to find out more; the fact that Aine's OK with him being gay gives me some reassurance that she's going to be cool with me, too.

'Next,' says the man behind the till, a tall, skinny, softly spoken Goth with hair like Robert Smith from The Cure. Big Gay Willy steps forward to pay for his Kylie record.

'Shall we see if Willy wants to join us for lunch?' says Aine.

'I don't know about you two, but I'm starving.' Big Gay

Willy pushes open the door to Wimpy, pressing his back against the glass and holding it for us as we squeeze past. The three of us bomb upstairs, chucking our shopping bags down on the nearest available seats.

Wimpy is Belfast's premier burger joint. It's one of the few big restaurant chains we have. McDonald's haven't made it over here yet, probably because of the Troubles. Why put all that effort into building a fancy new restaurant if it's only going to get blown up by the paramilitaries?

Big Gay Willy watches our stuff while we go downstairs to order the food. He gives Aine a five-pound note and asks her to get him a Bender in a Bun, which makes us all snigger. 'And a *large* Diet Coke,' he says, as if the bigger the Diet Coke, the greater the slimming benefits. Aine and I go back downstairs and take our place in the short queue. We stare up at the menu board above the counter, with photos of perfectly presented burgers, salads and mixed grills. I'm not really that hungry, but I end up going for my usual, a cheeseburger. Aine, being vegetarian, orders a salad and fries.

Once we're back at the table, I unwrap my cheeseburger. I take one look at the salty processed meat, though, and put it straight back down on the tray. My stomach is churning with nerves. I end up just nibbling on a few chips. I watch Aine picking at her salad and fries, wondering how she's going to react when I tell her I'm gay.

Big Gay Willy squirts ketchup and mayonnaise all over his Bender in a Bun and takes a huge bite. 'So, tell me a bit more about you, Billy,' he says, his mouth full. 'Are you seeing anyone?'

Not this question again. I give my usual excuse about being too busy with exams, not having enough time. 'What about you?' I say, turning the spotlight back on him.

'Well, there is someone.' He looks around to check no one is listening in, but apart from the three of us and a couple of oul dolls slurping coffee two tables down, the top floor of the restaurant is empty. As he leans in, I can smell his aftershave.

It's nice and gives me that warm, fluttering sensation in my belly, like the way I feel when Conor's around. I do my best to ignore it.

'Swear to God you won't tell anyone?' Willy whispers. 'Only he's what you might call *in denial*.'

'In denial?' Aine picks a cherry tomato from her plate and pops it in her mouth.

'He's not out, you see,' he says. 'No one knows he's gay.'

Silence. Willy puts a straw in his mouth and takes a noisy suck of his Diet Coke.

'Is he . . . gay?' I say, both intrigued and horrified at the same time.

'Actually, he's bisexual. His name's Nigel.'

'Where did you meet him?' says Aine.

Willy gives a coy grin, running his hand over the back of his freshly trimmed head. 'Castle Cutz. The men's hairdresser's in Carrick.'

'How old is he?' I ask.

'Seventeen. He's got a girlfriend, so he has.'

Aine's jaw drops in shock. 'Jesus, Willy. Are you asking for trouble?'

Willy parts his lips, smiling. 'He's a total ride, though, Aine. You should see him.'

'Ride or not,' says Aine. 'Don't you think what you're doing is a bit wrong?'

'How old do you have to be to have gay sex?' I ask.

'Twenty-one, according to the law.' When he says 'the law', Willy makes a quotes sign with his fingers.

'Do your parents know?' says Aine.

'Do they fuck! My da's a peeler. He'd kill me!'

'What about your ma?' I say.

'She'd kill me too. She hates "fruits". She says fruits give you AIDS, and AIDS is a plague sent by God to get rid of them.'

At the mention of the word AIDS, my stomach does a leap over itself. Feeling queasy, I lean back in my seat and fold my arms against my chest. I'm noticing how sweaty Willy looks. He might smell really good, and he might be dressed in the latest fashions, but his whole face glistens with perspiration. There are large, damp patches under the arms of his Madonna *Like A Prayer* T-shirt. Has he managed to catch AIDS from this Nigel fella? I'm feeling slightly faint, like I'm about to lose consciousness in the middle of Wimpy and slide off my plastic chair, underneath the table.

'So have you, you know . . . done the deed?' asks Aine.

'Technically, no.' He gives her a sly, knowing glance. 'We've done other stuff though . . . if you know what I mean.' He leans over his large Diet Coke and, taking the straw between his fingers, places it slowly between his lips. I think I know what he's hinting at, but I can't quite believe it. I mean, I've heard the nasty rumours that Tracey McGookin from school gives 50p blow jobs in the bushes behind the Home Economics block at breaktime, but I've never actually seen it myself. And as for boys giving other boys blowies, surely that doesn't happen in a town like Carrickfergus?

Big Gay Willy plays with the gold stud in his right ear. 'The sex,' he says, 'wasn't really proper sex. The first time we did it was at my house.'

Aine gasps. 'You had sex at your parents' place? Are you mad? Weren't you worried they'd catch you at it?'

'Not really,' he says. 'My da was on duty that day and my ma was working up in Ballymena. She's a rep for Schwartz herbs and spices, so her job is to go round all the supermarkets, checking their displays. She's rarely home before six o'clock. Handy for me, like. I can do what I want. So, as I'd a free house, I invited Nigel over. He only gets an hour for lunch, so we agreed it would be a quickie. Honestly, he couldn't believe the effort I'd gone to when I took him upstairs to show him my bedroom. I'd made it all romantic for him, pulled the venetian blinds down, lit a scented candle, put a tape on – Sade's *Stronger Than Pride*. I even sprayed my quilt with Lynx Oriental. I wanted our first time to be special, you know?' He pauses to finger the rim of his Diet Coke.

'And . . . was it?' asks Aine. 'Special, I mean?'

Willy grins, licking his lips. 'Totally special. Nigel only stayed about twenty minutes but, swear to God, it was the hottest twenty minutes of my *life*!'

'Do you not feel guilty that this fella has a girlfriend, like?' Aine says.

'Not really. To be honest, it's all happened so fast. I haven't had any time for regrets. It was love at first sight, though. And the feeling's mutual. Naughty Nigel said he has a hard job keeping his hands off me.'

'We need to get going, Billy,' says Aine, standing up. 'I've got stuff to do this afternoon. No offence, Willy, I'm in a bit of a rush. It was nice seeing you, so it was.'

Big Gay Willy gets up and gives Aine a hug. For a moment I'm scared he's going to try and do the same to me, but he just smiles and winks and says, 'See you around, Billy.'

We leave him to finish off his Bender in a Bun and make our way downstairs. Pushing open the glass door on to Donegall Place, I check my watch. It's almost two o'clock and I'm still no nearer to telling Aine my secret. I'm just waiting on the right moment, I tell myself, the right opportunity. It will come. And it does. Sooner than I thought, as it happens.

An hour or so later, after walking off our lunch, Aine and I are sitting on a bench in front of the City Hall. There's a breeze blowing. Aine brushes her hair from her eyes, turning her head towards me. 'So, what did you make of Big Gay Willy?'

I shrug. 'He's pretty full-on, isn't he?'

'Full-on?' Aine grins. 'He's a total headcase. I've never met anyone like him.'

Across the road, a preacher has set up a stall on the corner next to the pedestrian crossing. He's holding a megaphone and shouting, 'Repent! Repent! Repent of your sins and come to our Lord Jesus Christ!' Standing next to him a woman hands out religious tracts to anyone who will take them. A couple of drunks swagger past, raising their cans of Harp at the preacher, jeering at him.

I'm desperately trying to think of what to say next, how to bring up the subject of my feelings for Conor. Just as I'm on the verge of blurting everything out, a fat pigeon swoops down, cooing noisily and flapping its wings. It lands directly in front of us, pecking around the pavement for scraps. Distracted, I try to shoo it away with my foot, watching as it lifts itself off the ground, only to land again a short distance away, continuing its search for food. I decide to steer the conversation back to Willy.

'Has he always known?'

Aine is looking at the pigeon. 'Known what?' she says.

'That he's . . . you know . . . gay, like?'

'I'm not sure.' She shrugs, turning her attention back to me. 'Why are you asking?'

The words I want to say to Aine are buried so deep inside; I can't seem to build up the courage to let them go.

Aine repeats her question, her voice softer this time. 'Billy, what's wrong? Tell me.'

I go to speak, but my throat closes, and then the tears come. I look at her, my watery eyes telling her everything I've been too afraid to say.

9.

Now

Saturday 19th August 2023

The pub where I've arranged to meet Aine for our first catch-up in over thirty years is an old school haunt. A crowd of us used to come here as teenagers, no one seeming to mind that we weren't quite old enough to drink. True to form, Aine has just sent me a message on WhatsApp to say she's running late. New technologies aside, some things never change. I order a pint of Guinness from the barmaid, who looks around the age I was in the late eighties. She's heavily made-up, with a smooth, shiny brow and glossy pout. I can't help wondering what young Aine would've made of her. Aine, who once told me she thought women who got perms, or shaved their legs, were antifeminist. The barmaid fills the pint glass halfway and leaves it to settle. 'Put your wee card there for me,' she says, handing me the machine.

I tap my card, half expecting it to be declined. And then I remember that, for the first time in ages, my bank balance is in credit. I had the exact same feeling last week when I went shopping in Belfast for new clothes. I spent three hundred pounds on some essentials – a new jacket, jeans, a few T-shirts and trainers – and for a horrible moment I panicked, convinced I didn't have enough money to pay for them. The sense of relief when the transaction went through was enormous. I can't remember the last time I felt so relaxed about spending money.

'I've not been in here for years,' I say, looking around the bar. 'Not since I was at school.'

The girl studies my face, her eyes narrowing. 'How long ago was that? The noughties, or something?'

I laugh. 'The eighties.'

'No way! You don't look old enough to be an eighties person.'

'I'm fifty.'

'Fifty, seriously? My da's fifty-seven and you look way younger than him.' She calls out to her colleague, who's downstairs changing a barrel. 'Here, Kelsie, c'mere and tell me how old you think this fella is.'

Kelsie emerges from the cellar, her face hidden behind two boxes of Tayto she's carrying. She groans, dropping the crisps on the floor. Stockier than the girl serving me, she has short-cropped hair and no make-up and wears a pink T-shirt with the slogan *Girls, Gays, Theys*.

'I dunno, Abbie. I'm shite with ages, so I am.'

'Go on. Have a wee guess.'

The stocky girl glances at me, shifting from one foot to the other, avoiding eye contact. 'Fifty-two?'

Abbie laughs. 'No freakin' way does he look fifty-two! Are you blind?'

'I said I was shite with ages, didn't I? How old's he then?'

'I'm fifty,' I interrupt, keen to put a stop to this guess-my-age game before my fragile gay ego completely implodes.

Kelsie looks seriously unimpressed. 'See. I wasn't too far off.' She shrugs. 'How old did you think he was then?'

'Late thirties.'

'LOL!' Kelsie snorts, rolling her eyes. She turns her back on me and retreats downstairs to the cellar.

'Ignore that one, they haven't a clue about fellas.' Abbie slowly pours the rest of the Guinness, handing it to me. I take a large gulp of the thick, treacly liquid, wiping my mouth with my hand, keen to avoid a creamy moustache.

Just at that moment, Aine walks through the door. We clock each other straight away. Time may have added a few extra pounds to our bodies, and wrinkles to our fifty-something skin, but if you squint hard enough, underneath the additional layers you can just about see the youthful faces we once had. Aine's is less angular now, softer; her once short, spiky hair chopped into a neat, shoulder-length bob. Gone are the black clothes. Today she's wearing a floaty summer dress and green Dr. Martens.

'Billy McQueen,' she says, her voice deeper and huskier than I remember. 'C'mere and give me a big hug, you. Auch, I never thought I'd see you again.'

We hold each other and I feel a wave of nostalgia. It's so comforting to be back in the arms of my old friend again, after all this time.

'This is mad,' I say. 'How long's it been? Over thirty years?'

'Jesus, it must be,' says Aine, rummaging in her bag for her purse.

'Let me get you a drink,' I say. 'What are you having?'

'Vodka lime soda, please. May as well. I'm not driving tonight.'

I turn to Abbie, who's staring down at her phone, tapping at it with her long jade fingernails. 'Can I get a vodka lime soda for my old friend here?' Abbie looks up, slipping the phone into the back pocket of her jeans.

'Sure,' she says.

'Less of the old, Billy,' Aine chips in. She gestures at me to Abbie with her thumb. 'Here, you wouldn't think it, but me and him were at school together. I bet you thought I was his daughter, didn't you?'

Abbie, who has her back to us, holds a glass up to the optics, releasing a measure of vodka. 'Yous were at school together? That's so cute! I was just sayin' to him how young he looks. I thought he was only in his thirties.' She turns round, filling the glass halfway with soda, topping it with a dash of lime cordial.

Aine grins, her green eyes twinkling mischievously. 'He looks great, doesn't he? I'm only messing with you, Billy. You look a million dollars.'

Aine and I take a seat at a small round table in the corner. Initially I thought things might be awkward between us, but I needn't have worried. As soon as we start talking, the years melt away and, before long, it feels as if we've never been apart. Aine admits she's been trying to get in touch with me for years, that she couldn't believe it when my friend request popped up on Facebook.

'I was so excited, Billy,' she enthuses. 'I was like, *that's my best friend from school*.'

There's a pause, both of us realising, and appreciating, how much this moment means to us. I try to remember the last time we saw each other. It would've been just before I went to university. A small crowd of us had met up for farewell drinks. It might even have been here, in this very pub. My memory of that time is extremely hazy, though. I do know we drank a lot of cider. We'd a lot on our minds, to be fair.

'To old friends,' says Aine, raising her glass in a toast. 'We've loads to catch up on.'

'To old friends,' I say, leaning over and tapping her glass with mine. I wonder if, like me, she's thinking of Conor right now. If she senses his absence. He should be here with us.

'So, you're in London now?' she says.

'Margate. Kent,' I correct her.

'That's right. I remember you saying. What is it you do for a living again?'

I pause, doing my best to shut out my inner confidence crusher which has chosen this lovely moment to remind me that I'm useless and unemployable.

'I write. Well . . . I sort of write,' I say, as if I'm not quite convinced by the words coming out of my own mouth. 'You know, copy.'

'Auch, that's brilliant, so it is. You always wanted to be a journalist. I remember you telling me you wanted to work for *Smash Hits*.'

I realise I've made the job in Margate sound way more

glamorous than it actually was. 'It wasn't exactly *Smash Hits*,' I say. 'I worked for the local council. It was mostly admin, writing press releases about local fetes, that sort of thing.' I take another sip of Guinness. 'I worked there for about twenty years, doing various roles, then a while back they made me redundant. Not going to lie, it's been tough.'

Aine gives me an understanding nod. 'I bet it has. Poor you. Have you managed to find another job?'

'Not yet. And not for want of trying either. It's hard, isn't it? When you get to our age.' I fidget with my beard, pulling at a hair. 'I'll be staying here for the foreseeable, though, so I'm going to see if I can find something locally.'

'You'll find a job here no problem,' she says brightly. 'It can take a bit of time, that's all.' She reaches over, squeezing my forearm. 'Listen, I was sorry to hear about your mum. How is she?'

'As well as can be expected. Not a lot I can do at the moment, apart from hope for the best.'

She looks at me, her expression full of concern. 'And are you managing OK? If you need any help, I'm more than happy to drive you up to the hospital, or whatever.'

A lump is rising in my throat. I swallow it down. To think that only weeks ago I was in Margate, without a penny to my name and staring at a poster for the Samaritans, thinking how alone I was. Now I have a home, a few quid in my pocket and friends around me; people who care, people who are willing to give me a hand. While it's lovely, it's overwhelming too.

I describe my visit to the hospital with Bev, how emotional it was seeing Mum in that state.

'I just feel so conflicted by the whole thing,' I say. 'Does that make sense?'

Aine looks puzzled, and then it dawns on me. She knows nothing about the estrangement.

I take a deep breath. 'I haven't told you this yet, but Mum and me . . . well, we hadn't spoken to each other in years. We had a sort of falling-out over me being gay.'

'I knew she wasn't exactly over the moon when she found out about you and Conor, but I thought she might have come round, especially after . . .' Her voice falters, dropping to a whisper. 'Especially after everything that happened.'

There's a lull in the conversation, both of us lost in our memories of that eventful summer. After Conor went missing, there was a huge police search, stories in the local newspapers, posters of him all over town; they even held a vigil in school assembly. While not under suspicion, Aine and myself were both interviewed by police officers. We were only sixteen. It was a traumatic experience. We were already under huge amounts of stress with exams that summer. It put a lot of pressure on our friendship. While we didn't exactly fall out, Conor's disappearance caused a sort of unspoken rift between us. Neither of us was the same afterwards. It's me who eventually breaks the silence. 'I think about him every day, you know.'

Aine pauses, biting her lip. 'Me too,' she says, quietly.

I want to mention the mixtape, to see if Aine has any idea who might have sent it, but now's not the right time. I'll save it for later when we've both had a bit more to drink. Right now, I'm feeling the need to lighten the mood. I begin by bringing up the subject of our schooldays, and we have a good laugh swapping stories about our most loved and most hated teachers.

'Here,' says Aine. 'Do you remember Mr Murphy?'

'How could I forget Old Spud? He scared the bejesus out of me in PE. Do you remember when he told me I looked like a pregnant duck? I was only bending over to pick up a shuttlecock.'

Aine laughs. 'The things they used to get away with then. Shocking.'

'Another time he kept kicking a ball against my leg till I burst into tears. I hated that man. He was a sadist, so he was.'

'God love you, you were never the sporty type,' says Aine. 'Didn't some of the boys used to call you Queen Billy?'

I roll my eyes at the recollection. 'Those boys knew I was gay before I did.'

'Bless you,' says Aine. 'So, what about now? Do you have a partner?'

'No. I'm single,' I say. 'I was seeing a guy back in Margate for a bit, but it wasn't to be. Totally my fault, like. He was lovely, but as usual I pushed him away.' I don't mention to Aine how relieved I was that I'd finished with him just before I was made redundant. At least that spared me even more humiliation.

Aine opens her mouth in surprise. 'Auch, that's a shame. Seriously, look at you, Billy. You're a catch.'

I've never thought of myself as a catch, far from it, so it's nice of Aine to say so, even though I reckon she's just being kind. I look down at my new jeans and trainers, grateful to be able to afford new clothes for the first time in ages.

'I don't know. To be honest, I think I'm the problem, you know?' I rub the back of my neck, trying not to smile at Aine's kind comment on my appearance. 'I've had plenty of time on my own to think about it. It probably has something to do with what happened with Dad, and then Conor . . .' Aine nods, as if she gets it. 'So, how about you?' I ask, realising I'm in danger of bringing the mood down again. I don't want our first reunion in years to be sad. 'Are you single? Married? Divorced?'

Aine sighs, fiddling with the straw in her glass. 'I'm a single parent. Their da, Paul, dumped me not long after they were born. I've pretty much brought them up on my own.'

Aine has children. This is news to me. I realise there's a whole side to her life I don't know anything about. It's like I've been living in a dream these past thirty years and just woken up.

'That must've been tough,' I say. 'Lovely to have children, though. I bet you wouldn't change things for the world. What are their names?'

'I've only the one. Eighteen. They just passed their driving test last week. They're picking me up later. You'll get to meet them.'

'Oh, I see. When you said them, I thought . . .'

'Aye, I meant as in *they, them*. Alex is non-binary.'

'And you're cool with that, I take it? I mean, it's nothing to be ashamed of these days, right?' I raise my pint as a show of solidarity.

Aine looks down at her drink. 'I wish everyone thought like you, Billy. Don't get me wrong, I love Alex to bits, but everyone seems so divided on the whole gender issue. I worry for them, for their future.'

'Of course. Of course you do. But at the end of the day, if it makes Alex happy . . . I mean, isn't that what *all* parents want for their children? For them to be happy?'

Aine's voice falters. 'I've not told anyone this, so please don't repeat it, but . . .'

'God, no, Aine, I won't say a word.'

She gulps down her drink. 'I found it hard at first, you know? It was tough for me, as someone who's always prided myself on my identity as a woman, who grew up preaching feminist ideals, reading Adrienne Rich at university, vowing to smash the patriarchy. And then to have a child who . . .' She pauses, looks up at the ceiling. 'Help me out, God. What am I trying to say here?'

I reach across the table and take her hand, squeezing it lightly. 'It's OK, it's OK. You don't have to explain. I understand.'

'The thing is, I spent my whole life standing up for women's rights and then suddenly all my beliefs, everything I'd fought for, was being challenged. Not only that, but by my *own child*, my own flesh and blood.'

'Isn't that what children do, though?' I say. 'Challenge their parents' beliefs?'

An old eighties song lyric floats into my head, about how every generation blames the one that came before it. I withdraw my hand, drain the last of my pint. 'I mean, look

81

at me and Mum. I certainly challenged her views on things. At least you're accepting of your child's difference.'

Aine sighs. 'And that's the thing. I *do* accept them. And it's lovely seeing their confidence grow. I guess, what I mean to say is, I just want all the fighting to stop. Not between me and Alex – we don't fight. It's everyone else. Social media is the worst. It's got so nasty. And when I feel like the attacks are aimed at my child, it becomes personal. That's when the lioness in me comes out.'

As if on cue, the opening bars to Katy Perry's 'Roar' blare out of the pub jukebox. We both laugh.

'This might be why I've never really done social media,' I say. 'I've only just discovered Facebook.'

Aine chuckles. 'You're well behind the times. What's happened to you? I love a good oul argy-bargy on my phone, so I do. Gets my pulse going in the morning.' She pauses to fiddle with the charm bracelet on her wrist. 'Saying that, I have been cutting down on social media a lot, lately.'

'How come?'

She shrugs. 'It's like a drug, isn't it? I was addicted. It took me a long time to realise I was spending so many hours on phone apps, I was missing out on real time with my friends. I lost the need to see them in person. I thought I already knew what they'd been up to because I'd seen their posts about holidays, birthdays, and so on.' She tilts her head to the side, smiling. 'Which is one reason why it's so lovely seeing you, because I haven't a bloody clue what you've been doing since we last saw each other.' She reaches down, giving my knee an affectionate squeeze.

'Cheers to catching up,' I say, raising my glass again. 'Here, can you imagine if we'd had social media when we were young?'

Aine snorts. 'I'd have been arrested. Or killed.'

'Tell me about it. You couldn't keep your bake shut. Your mouth was always getting us into trouble.'

Aine blushes at this reminder of her younger self. 'I was

such a gobby wee madam, wasn't I? I wanted to be Bernadette Devlin, or Sinéad O'Connor. God rest her soul.'

'Meanwhile, I wanted to be Jason Donovan, or Rick Astley.'

She shoots me a mock-withering look. 'You always had shite taste in music.'

'I beg to differ,' I say. 'So, what are you doing for work these days?'

'I teach A level politics. After I finished uni, I carried on working in my dad's record shop to earn a bit of extra money while I was doing my PGCE. I've been teaching ever since.'

'Do you enjoy it?'

'Aye. It's hard work, like, but every day is different, you know? And I love working with young people. It's a rewarding job.' She pauses. 'Listen, I need the loo. How about I get us some more drinks on the way back. Same again?'

I nod, watching her head off in the direction of the ladies', enjoying that slightly woozy feeling of warmth and connection you get when you catch up with an old friend over a few beers. As I wait for her to come back, my mind returns to Conor. Unzipping my backpack, I take out the envelope I found at Mum's house and place it on the table.

Time to find out what Aine has to say about Conor's mixtape.

10.

Before

Monday 15th May 1989

I'm still confused about a lot of things, but talking to Aine about my feelings over the weekend has lifted some of the weight off my shoulders, giving me a little more confidence in myself. Even so, when Conor invites me round to his house, I lie to Mum, telling her I'm going to Aine's to revise for my GCSEs. It's only a white lie, but it trips off my tongue so easily, so convincingly, I almost believe it myself.

Conor's dad is on nights this week, so we have the house to ourselves. Normally, we hang out in his bedroom, but today – after a few hours of studying – we're sitting on opposite sides of the living room sofa, watching our second favourite Australian soap, *Home and Away*.

It's been a tense week on Summer Bay, even tenser than mine, with Kerry Barlow being shot by her crazed husband. I don't know why, but the sad piano music playing during her funeral scene makes me well up.

'Are you crying?' Conor jabs me in the ribs with the toe of his white sports sock.

'Get lost.' I grab a cushion, throwing it at him.

'You wanna fight?' he teases, leaning towards me, his head cocked to one side, a cheeky grin spreading over his face. Without warning, he whips a cushion from behind him and whacks me over the head with it.

We pounce on each other then, our bodies merging in a pretend wrestling match. Both of us are wearing near-identical white T-shirts and grey tracksuit bottoms. Our faces are flushed, our breathing fast and furious. Through the flannel fabric, I feel something hard pressing against my leg, which makes me gasp. Sliding my body down the sofa, I push my groin against his, enjoying the weird swirling sensation in my belly. Conor positions himself on top of me, a strand of his Jason Donovan blond hair brushing my cheek as he leans over. I look up at him, our eyes locked in mock combat, and then he moves in. We kiss, and even though I'm scared, I can't stop.

Afterwards, we lie holding each other on the sofa. 'What just happened?' he says, stroking the back of my head. Even though all we did was kiss, my whole body feels like it's about to explode.

'I don't know,' I say, swallowing back the saliva rising in my throat. 'I liked it, though.'

'Me too,' he says, pausing to pull at a loose thread on his tracksuit bottoms.

'Does this mean we're . . . you know . . . gay?' I say, thinking about the photos of Boy George and Andy Bell in *Smash Hits*. They wear make-up and women's clothes, though. Conor and me aren't like that.

'We're so not gay,' he says.

'What are we then?'

He shrugs, awkwardly shifting his weight around on the sofa. 'Me and you, well, we're just . . . us. Does it matter?'

Not to me, it doesn't, but I can't help wondering how Mum and Mervyn would react if they knew what we've just done. And Conor's dad? He'd go ballistic. I shudder, leaning into him for protection, my eyes twitching at the thought of our parents finding out.

'We can't tell anyone, though,' whispers Conor.

'What, not even Aine?'

'Not even Aine. We have to keep this our secret, OK?'

11.

Saturday 19th August 2023

Aine stares at the TDK tape. 'So, this was sent to your mum's house in 2013? That's ten years ago. I know you weren't on speaking terms, but surely she could've forwarded it on to you?'

I shrug. 'She pretty much severed all ties with me once I went to uni. Looking back, I blame Mervyn. He had a lot of influence over her. He was the one who kept telling her I was a sissy, that my "lifestyle choices" went against God's will. I remember him saying to me once in private that I'd broken my mother's heart. He told me I'd be doing her a favour if I stayed out of her life. Those were his exact words.'

'Jesus, Billy. When was this?'

'Not long after Conor's disappearance.'

'And you believed him?'

'Yes. Yes, I did. I was still a teenager and terrified of the person I was becoming. He blamed me for what happened with Conor. He said it was God's way of punishing me for my sins. He made me believe everything was my fault.'

'Jeez, Billy, that's awful. I'd no idea.'

'Seriously, it was bad. They couldn't bear the idea of us being together. After Conor went missing, they wouldn't even let me grieve, especially Mervyn. If he caught me crying, he'd slap me round the head, tell me to stop acting like a woman. Then he'd make me sit with him for two hours watching some boring western on the TV. As a Protestant evangelist preacher, he didn't watch much television, and believed the cinema was sinful, but he made an exception for John Wayne. "Now there's a real man, Billy," he'd say, pointing at the screen. By then, I couldn't wait to finish my A levels and get out of there. It was like he hated everything Conor stood for. Both he and Mum just wanted me to be "normal", to fit in with their beliefs, their narrow way of seeing the world.' I pause to take another drink, shaking my head in disbelief as more memories from my past come flooding back. 'There was this one John Wayne quote he was particularly fond of spouting: "If everything isn't black and white, I say, why the hell not?" I think Mervyn based his entire moral compass on the Bible and John Wayne.'

'What about your mum, though? Did she not stick up for you or anything? I mean, he sounds like something out of a cult.'

'Not really. I don't think she would've dared, especially the longer they were together. After I left for university, she moved in with him to his big house on the Shore Road and I never heard from her anymore.'

Aine tuts. 'I can't for the life of me imagine disowning my own child because of who they are. He must have had some power over her.'

'He did, but it was the eighties, remember? Everyone hated gay people. I mean, I'm as guilty as anyone for looking back on the past with rose-tinted glasses, but in those days we were either seen as a dirty joke, or something to be scared of.'

Aine tears open a packet of Cheese and Onion Tayto crisps, placing the bag in the middle of the table. I take one, the taste transporting me back to happier times in my childhood, when my dad was still alive.

'Did I mention Mum's friend Bev told me Mum plans to leave me the house in her will? It came as a shock after all those years of not speaking.'

'Seriously? She must still love you, then. She wouldn't do that otherwise.'

'I dunno.' I shrug. 'Maybe she's just feeling guilty. We don't have any other family, so . . .'

'Don't think like that, Billy. Times have changed. Your mum will have different views on things, I know she will.'

She picks up the mixtape again, reading the titles of the songs, neatly handwritten in blue biro on the cardboard insert. Her eyes narrow as she carefully studies the track listing and the typed note that came with it. 'Hold on a minute,' she says. 'Conor went missing on the Eleventh Night, yeah?'

'Yes. The 11th of July, 1989.'

'So, he made this tape the day he disappeared?' She looks up at me, confused.

I nod. 'It doesn't make sense, does it?'

She scratches her head. 'So basically, someone kept this tape for twenty-odd years and then decided they were going to post it back to you? Why would anyone do that, though? Why would they leave it that long?'

'And why did they have it in the first place?'

'Good point.' Aine chews on her fingernail, deep in thought. 'It must be someone we know, or someone who knows you. How would they have your mum's address otherwise?'

I nod, trying to think of all the people we were friends with that summer. 'Maybe Conor gave the tape to someone the day he went missing?'

'It's possible, I guess.' Aine bites her lip. 'Do you think we should contact the police? Or at the very least try and get in touch with Conor's family? I can't imagine what it must be like to lose a child and never know what happened . . .'

'His mum died when he was thirteen. I'm not sure about his dad though.'

'Actually, forget I said that. I think Mr Doherty's dead, you know,' says Aine. 'I'm sure I read his obituary in the paper. It must've been about ten years ago now. I can check.' She takes out her phone and starts googling.

Ten years ago. I do the maths in my head. 'So, if Conor's dad was still alive in 2013, it could've been him who posted this tape to Mum's house, right?'

'Possibly,' says Aine, her eyes still focused on her phone. 'Why would he do that, though?'

'Maybe he found the tape in Conor's bedroom. Maybe he wanted to make up for the way he treated Conor in the past. People change. He might've come round to the fact his son was gay. It might've been his way of apologising.'

Aine looks up from her phone, frowning. 'It says here he died in 2009, so it can't have been him.' Folding up the crisp packet, she wedges it underneath a candle in the centre of the table. She pauses for a moment, then says, 'This is so weird, Billy. I mean, obviously I've never forgotten what happened to Conor, but in a way, I'd made peace with the not knowing. I don't think I ever told you this, but I had some counselling in my late teens. It was my parents' idea. They could see the effect his disappearance was having on me, the stress of it.' She reaches across the table, resting her hand on mine. 'I feel for you, Billy, I really do. It must have been so much harder for you not having the support network at home.'

'What happened to Conor was the tipping point for me leaving Ireland,' I say, nursing my pint of Guinness. 'Don't get me wrong, things at home were bad, but if I'd stayed here, I would never have coped. Too many ghosts, too many triggers.' I pause for a moment, the pain I felt as a teenager resurfacing in the present. I push it away. 'I don't remember anyone offering me any counselling. I remember them praying for me though, of course. Lots of prayers . . .'

Aine nods. 'So how does it feel, being back?'

I rub my eyes before looking up at her. 'It feels strange. It's early days, but everyone I've met so far has been so lovely. You. Bev, my mum's neighbour. I suppose if my life had turned out more "normal" and people had been more accepting of me, I would've stayed.'

Saying this feels like a confession. I fiddle with a hair in my beard, twisting it between my fingers, pulling at it lightly, until I feel a slight resistance. It's not like me to talk so openly about things. I'm used to secrecy, to hiding my feelings, but there's something to be said for those friends who know us from our formative years, who shared our past, growing up, who knew us in the days when we still had hopes and dreams, before life dragged us down.

Aine looks surprised. 'Really? I always thought you couldn't wait to get away from this place?'

'As a youngster, maybe, but that was because I felt I couldn't be myself here. It wasn't the place as such, it wasn't Ireland.'

We sit in silence. The jukebox is playing U2's 'I Still Haven't Found What I'm Looking For'. One of Conor's favourite songs. I have a memory of us, lying on his bedroom floor, holding each other, as we played *The Joshua Tree* LP from beginning to end. It might be the alcohol, but the lyrics hit me hard tonight. Bono is singing about love, about burning desire, about someone who carried his shame, someone he has spent his whole life searching for. Now, more than ever, I want to find out what happened to Conor that night. I need to know the truth. I need to stop blaming myself.

After several more drinks, and a lot more reminiscing and soul baring, Aine mentions a school reunion with our old year group she was invited to on Facebook. She says she wasn't planning on going but suggests it might give us an opportunity to talk to people who remember Conor. At first, I'm not too sure, a school reunion being my idea of hell. I worry that part of me is going to revert to my insecure sixteen-year-old self: the effeminate wee fella in the Kylie Minogue T-shirt, turned-up jeans and fake Dr. Martens. And I'm even more reluctant to go when Aine tells me the reunion, which is next weekend, is being organised by Wendy Johnson. I dated Wendy that summer of 1989, in a short period during which Conor and I had separated – both of us trying to convince ourselves we weren't gay. This was all thirty-five years ago, though. Wendy is married with kids now.

'You two couldn't stand each other, do you remember?' I say, laughing at a memory of Aine and Wendy tearing into each other at my sixteenth birthday party.

Aine drains her glass, spitting out an ice cube. 'She nearly wrecked our friendship. Your ma thought she was the bees' knees, though, which tells you *everything* you need to know about Wendy Johnson.'

'I wonder what she's like now?'

'I dunno, but I'm kinda curious to find out. Shall we go?'

I blow out my cheeks. 'Only if you promise not to get in a catfight with her again. We're not living in the eighties anymore.'

'I'll do my best,' says Aine, grinning mischievously. 'Absolutely no promises, mind.'

12.

Before

Sunday 21st May 1989

Since last Monday, Conor and I have been spending more and more time together. School is officially over and we're on study leave – and the fact that his dad works so many night shifts makes it easier for us to carry on our relationship in secret. Not that we're calling this a relationship as such – we would never refer to ourselves as 'boyfriends' – but we still grab every opportunity we can to meet up. One night, Conor suggests I stay over at his house. 'As long as you're gone by the time my da gets back from work,' he says, 'it'll be safe.' I tell Mum we're having an all-night revision session for our science exam the following week (not a complete lie) and try not to feel too guilty when she tells me she's proud of all the extra studying I've been doing recently.

It's a warm night, the sky as pink as Birds Angel Delight, and on my way to Conor's, the smell of mince dinners wafting from the houses is making my mouth water. When I reach his place, he's already waiting for me by the front door. He pokes his head out to check none of the neighbours are watching, before ushering me inside. 'I hope you're hungry,' he says. 'I've made us some dinner.' Beaming with pride, he takes me through to the dining room, where he's set the table up all posh with a candle and serviettes. 'My speciality,' he says, putting down two plates of Crispy Pancakes, beans and microwave chips and pouring us each a glass of Shloer. Seeing all the effort he's gone to gives me a redner. I'm not used to such romantic gestures, especially coming from a fella. I pinch myself, wondering if this is all a dream.

Over dinner, we talk about what grades we hope to get in our GCSEs, the subjects we're studying in sixth form and where we want to go to university. We both agree we don't want to stay in Northern Ireland.

'I want to get as far away as possible,' says Conor. 'London, or Brighton, ideally.'

'You'll need to earn loads of money. How are you going to afford it?'

'I've been saving up. Plus, I'll get a part-time job, while I'm doing my A levels.'

'Does your da know you're planning on leaving?'

Conor frowns. 'Who cares what he thinks? It's my life, my decisions. I'll do what *I* want.'

'So you haven't told him?'

He puts down his knife and fork. 'Nah. He'll go ballistic. It's not worth the hassle.'

'Maybe we could apply to the same universities?' I suggest. 'That way we won't have to sneak around all the time. We can just be ourselves.'

Conor agrees this is a good plan and we make a pact. Over the next two years, we're going to work really hard, so we can do well in our exams and get away from this place. I remember then what my dad always told me: *You work hard, son, and the world is your oyster. No matter what your starting point in life, if you put the hours into your education, you can achieve anything, be anyone.*

After we've finished eating, we cuddle up on the sofa together, talking about the latest Top 40 on Ceefax before watching one of our favourite videos, *Victoria Wood: As Seen on TV*, both of us laughing hysterically and shouting out the lines to the sketches we've learned by heart.

Later, upstairs, I strip down to my Mickey Mouse boxer shorts and climb into Conor's single bed. 'Budge up,' he says, squeezing in next to me and sliding one arm underneath my shoulders. He pulls me close to him.

'Are you cold?' I say.

'Not really.'

'Take your clothes off then.' I reach down and start lifting the bottom of his T-shirt, but he lays his hand on mine, stopping me.

'Don't,' he says.

'Why not?'

'Just leave it on.'

'Why?'

'Because I said so.'

He leans over to switch off his bedside lamp, tentatively pulling me towards him, our bodies touching. As we kiss in the dark, I feel like I'm falling, like that scene in Walt Disney's *Alice in Wonderland* where she tumbles down the psychedelic rabbit hole and her skirt puffs out and there are strange objects spinning all around her. Is this what love feels like? I wonder. And if so, how come something this wrong feels so good?

13.

Friday 25th August 2023

'Jesus, Alex, will you give my head peace? How can you listen to this shite?' We've only been in the car for five minutes and already Aine is on one. This doesn't bode well for our school reunion.

'It's not shite, Mum. It's Sam Smith and Kim Petras. This song's a bop. You're just old, so you are.'

'Old? Listen, kiddo, I'm totally cool with whatever dirty shenanigans Daddy's getting up to in the body shop, but the tune, if you can call it that, is an unholy mess.'

Alex has agreed to be our chauffeur for the night, driving us to our 'Class of 89' reunion in an old bottle-green Morris Minor. The car was a gift from Aine for passing their A levels with flying colours. They seem shy with me at first (or possibly disinterested, fossil that I am), but once we get on to the subjects of music and drag, they become more animated and engaged in conversation.

'You're not a Sam Smith fan, Aine?' I laugh. 'Why doesn't this surprise me?'

'Don't you start. If we left you in charge of the car stereo, we'd be listening to Kylie and Jason.'

'Kylie Minogue?' says Alex, turning the music down slightly. 'I love her. "Padam Padam"'s a banger, so it is.'

'I was a huge Kylie fan as a teenager,' I say, ignoring the obvious eye roll from Aine. 'Still am, in fact. I've grown up with her music. She's an ally – for *all* of us. Who are your icons, Alex?'

Aine chips in. 'Alex is obsessed with *RuPaul's Drag Race*. We must've watched every season about twenty times. Not just UK *Drag Race*, either: Australia, Canada, Thailand . . .'

'It's my dream to be on the show,' Alex says, wistfully. 'I've got a place at fashion school next year. I want to be able to create my own outfits.'

'Alex has an incredible eye for colour,' says Aine, beaming with parental pride. 'Have you seen those talons? I get them to do mine, too. Look!' She holds up her hands to reveal a set of perfectly manicured, emerald-painted nails. 'Alex, you could do Billy's. What colour would you like, Billy? Orange? Red, white and blue?'

'You're all right.' I laugh, gazing down at my hands and realising what a state my nails are in. They're a mess, where I'm constantly picking at them. Maybe I *should* get Alex to have a go? I'm not so sure about nail polish though.

Alex says, 'I wish they'd bring RuPaul's DragCon to Belfast. I keep asking Mum for tickets to the London shows, but they're dead pricey.'

'Teenagers, huh?' says Aine. 'They think we're made of money.'

'We were the same, though, weren't we?' I say.

'Speak for yourself,' says Aine. 'I was working part-time at my da's record shop when I was fourteen. I never asked him for a penny.'

'Times have changed,' I say. 'Young people are living with their parents longer.'

'Not this one,' says Aine, laughing. 'They can't wait to get out of Carrick.'

Alex drops us off on the corner of Donegall Place, jokily warning us not to get too drunk. It's cloudy for August, the sky spitting with rain. I put up my umbrella and Aine takes my arm. Together, we look every bit the devoted heterosexual couple. In front of us is Belfast's City Hall.

'This is where I came out to you,' I say, pointing towards the building. 'On those benches out the front. Do you remember?'

'Aye, 'course I do.' Aine squeezes my arm. 'You were terrified. You thought I was going to fall out with you because of it.'

I think back to the shy, uncertain teenager I was then. If you'd told me that in thirty years' time, Belfast would have its own Gay Pride event, that Aine would have a non-binary kid and that I would be living openly as a gay man, I wouldn't have believed you. Nothing seemed possible in the late eighties. I feel a sudden surge of love for my old friend.

'Aine, I've never told you this, but I really am grateful for everything you did for me back then. Seriously, I was in such a dark place with my mum, and Mervyn, and everything that was going on with Conor. You got me through some tough times. You helped me cope. I don't know what I would've done without you.'

Aine squeezes my arm, leaning her head against my shoulder. 'You two were so sweet together. It can't have been easy, being yourself. The pair of you must've been so scared.'

'Aye.' I nod. 'I was. It was a different world. It's hard to describe. I felt like there was something wrong with me, that I was abnormal.'

'Jesus, Billy. Who's normal? More to the point, who wants to be normal? We'll leave normal to the Wendy Johnsons of this world. They're welcome to it, as far as I'm concerned.' She tugs on my arm. 'Right, you, this isn't the time for us to be getting all maudlin. I was thinking we should start the night as we mean to go on, with a couple of porn star martinis. What do you reckon?'

'I'm totally up for porn stars. Bring them on.'

The school reunion is at Nora McNasty's, a trendy new venue on Donegall Square. It's the sort of cool, New York-style bar, serving cocktails and American-themed food, that has been popping up all over Belfast for the past twenty or so years, since the peace process began bringing more business and tourists to the city. Inside it's all traditional wood and exposed brick. Rustic, but chic. Before heading in, Aine stops outside for a vape, puffing furiously on a Lost Mary.

'They named these things after me, you know,' she quips. 'I'm the original Lost Mary.'

'You're still Catholic, though, aren't you?'

'*Lapsed* Catholic,' she corrects me. 'Have been for years. How about you? You still a practising Prod?'

'Church of Ireland. I've always thought that put me somewhere in the middle.'

Aine chuckles. 'You're bi-religious then?'

'I'm not really anything. I just don't want to get my head kicked in round here for saying the wrong thing.'

'You're a geg, Billy McQueen.' Aine pops her vape back in her coat pocket. 'Right, shall we go in?'

A young girl, dressed all in black, stops us by the door. 'Are yous here for Mrs Pratt's private party?' she asks.

'Who's Mrs Pratt?' I say.

Aine laughs. 'Are you serious? You used to go out with the girl, Billy. Remember?'

The penny drops. Pratt is Wendy's married name.

'Your names?' says the girl in a bored tone, pointing to a batch of stickers on a table in front of her.

'Aine Kelly and Billy McQueen,' says Aine. The girl roots among the pile, handing us both a sticker. We laugh and pat them on our chests before heading through the doors. Already it feels like we're back in school.

'Wendy's had a bit of work done, hasn't she?' says Aine, pointing to the woman coming towards us in a flowing red evening dress, waving frantically in our direction.

'Well' – beams Wendy, her face barely moving, her lips plumper and glossier than Pete Burns from Dead or Alive – 'if it isn't Aine and Billy. If it wasn't for the name badges, I don't think I would've recognised you two.' She pauses, then lets out a very fake laugh, not that dissimilar to the laugh Elaine Paige does on her BBC Radio 2 show on Sundays. 'Just bein' sarcastic. *Of course* I recognise you both. How could I forget?'

Aine clearly isn't impressed. 'I have to say, I wouldn't have recognised *you* either, Wendy. You're looking, well ... *different.*'

If Wendy is giving Aine a dirty look, it's hard to tell because her face is moving less than the contents of the Iceland freezer section.

Wendy sighs. 'I'll be honest with you, Aine. Good looks cost money. But then I am married to Colin Pratt, one of the top plastic surgeons in Northern Ireland. You might have seen one of his advertisements in the *Ulster Tatler*?' Aine and I look at her blankly. 'When you get to our age, every little helps. These days it's the people who *haven't* had procedures that stick out like a sore thumb, don't you think?'

'I wouldn't know,' says Aine. 'Personally, I prefer the natural look.'

Wendy smirks. 'Really? I would never have guessed.' She pauses, then lets out another fake laugh. 'Just bein' sarcastic,' she whines, turning to me. 'What about you, Billy? Do you prefer the natural look?'

I shift from one foot to the other. 'I don't mind either way. Whatever makes you happy. That's always been my motto in life.'

'Speaking of happiness,' says Wendy. 'Are you still flying your wee rainbow flag? Or don't they call it that anymore since they brought in the additional colours?'

'I'm still gay, yes, if that's what you mean.'

'Well, at least you know who you are. Honestly, I can't keep up with all these new identities. He, she, they. I mean, who *cares*? Things were a lot simpler in our day, right?'

'Actually, my child identifies as non-binary,' says Aine.

There's an awkward pause, then Wendy says, 'I'm sorry to hear that. It must be hard.'

'On the contrary,' says Aine, stiffly. 'I'm incredibly proud of my Alex.'

Sensing my old friend is on the verge of saying something she might regret, I tell Wendy we'll catch up with her later, dragging Aine towards her favourite place, the bar.

'I thought old Barbie doll over there might've mellowed with age, but she's got worse,' she hisses, once we're out of Wendy's earshot. 'I was ready to punch her lights out.' She mimics Wendy's fake sincerity. *'Just bein' saaarcastic. Sarcastic, my hole.'*

'Calm down,' I say. 'We've a long night ahead of us. Don't forget why we came here in the first place. We need to stay on everyone's side.'

The room is beginning to fill up, as the DJ cranks up the eighties tunes. I order two porn star martinis from the barman. 'Good Thing' by Fine Young Cannibals starts playing, and a group of women in virtually identical flowery dresses swarm towards the dance floor, throwing their limbs in all kinds of awkward shapes. Aine pulls me towards her, shouting in my ear. 'This is freaking me out, Billy. Everyone looks so middle-aged. I feel like I've time-travelled forward thirty years. It's like *Back to the Future*, or *Cocoon*!'

I laugh. 'Have you looked at yourself in the mirror recently? We're middle-aged too.'

'You know what I mean. I don't see us like that, though.'

'Time to embrace the ageing process, otherwise you're going to end up miserable.'

'Like Wendy, you mean? She's clearly not happy with getting older.'

'Exactly. But why judge? If a bit of cosmetic surgery makes her feel better about herself . . .'

Aine shrugs. 'So, how's the job hunting going?'

'Slowly,' I say. 'I've signed up with a couple of recruitment agencies and sent my CV to a few places, but I haven't heard back yet.'

'What sort of work are you looking for?'

'Anything, really. I've got a bit of money to tide me over in the meantime, so I'm in no rush.'

Aine grabs my arm. 'Here. Is that Davy Nugent over there?' She points at a stocky, bald guy in a white shirt which is open at the collar, exposing his hairy chest and thick neck. He's standing in a corner on his own, by a red velvet curtain, gripping a pint of lager with his hairy tattooed fist. While the name rings a bell, I don't recognise him.

'I'm sure it's him,' says Aine. 'He was in our year, remember? His big brother Marty was that bouncer at Club Babylon, that place we went to with Conor, the week before he disappeared. Marty let us in that night, even though we were underage. Let's go and say hello.'

Aine takes my hand, dragging me in Davy's direction. Davy looks up from his pint when he sees us coming. He squints at our name badges, a look of recognition slowly forming on his ruddy face. Grinning, he reveals an incomplete set of teeth in various shades of brown, grey and gold.

'All right, Davy,' says Aine. 'Long time no see.'

He scans her body from head to toe, his red eyes lighting up. 'Bloody hell, Aine. You're lookin' well.'

'Do you remember Billy?' She points at me.

'Auch, aye. Billy McQueen. Here, didn't we used to call you Queen Billy at school?' He lets out a raspy laugh, reaching out and giving me a bone crusher of a handshake.

'You did, yes,' I say.

He gives me a friendly thump on the back. 'Sure, there was no harm in it. Everyone had a nickname at school. It was our sense of humour. Besides, I always thought it suited you.'

'Good turnout, isn't it?' says Aine, sensing my awkwardness. She takes a sip of her martini, surveying the room. 'Have you spoken to anybody else, Davy?'

101

He shakes his head slowly. 'Only just got here, myself. Still tryin' to put names to faces, if you know what I mean.'

'You here on your own?' says Aine.

'Aye. The wife and I split up a couple of years ago.'

'Sorry to hear that.'

'Don't be, love,' he says. 'It was my fault. You might remember, I was a bit of a ladies' man at school.'

Aine does her best little girl smile. 'Speaking of ladies' men, how's that hunky big brother of yours?'

'Marty?'

'Aye, that's him. He was awful fond of the women too, if I remember rightly.'

'Still is. He's slowing down a bit in his old age, though. Ever since the heart attack a few years ago. You'd hardly recognise him now. He's lost a stone, so he has.'

'Really? God, I haven't seen Marty in years, not since he used to work the door on Club Babylon.'

Davy laughs. 'The good old days. We were all youngsters then.'

'Tell me about it,' says Aine. 'Where has the time gone?' She pauses. 'You know, I've just thought of something. The last time I went to that club was just before Conor Doherty went missing. Do you remember him?'

Davy looks down at his pint, nodding. 'Aye, that was awful, so it was. They never found out what happened to him, did they?'

'No,' says Aine, shaking her head, 'and I never went back to the club after he disappeared. My ma grounded me for weeks. She was terrified the same thing was going to happen to me, so – yeah – that would've been the last time I saw Conor.'

Davy rubs his eyes and sighs. 'Loads of people went missing during the Troubles, sure. Years later, and they're still uncovering bodies.'

'Terrible . . . but then I've never thought Conor's disappearance had anything to with the Troubles.'

'No?'

'He was only sixteen. A good kid. I don't think he would've got himself mixed up in any of that paramilitary crap.'

Davy's face takes a sudden dark turn. 'Crap? Is that what you call it?' He's slurring his words. Only now do I realise how drunk he is.

Aine takes a step back. 'Sorry, that came out wrong. I didn't mean . . .'

Davy holds up his empty pint. Pausing for a beat, he loosens his grip, letting it drop to the floor, where it smashes into pieces. The floorboards glisten with shards of broken glass. Davy leans towards Aine, like he's about to kiss her, then pulls away.

'A word of warning,' he says. 'Watch what you're saying, love, especially round here.'

'Let's go and catch up with some of the others,' I tell Aine, trying to disguise the shakiness in my voice. As we go to leave, Davy steps on the pile of broken glass, crushing it under the heel of his boot.

14.

Before

Monday 22nd May 1989

I wake up to the sound of running water. Next to me, the bed is empty. Conor must be in the shower. I glance at the alarm clock: ten o'clock. His dad won't be back for a few hours. From the wall, Belinda Carlisle is smiling down on me, like she's giving me her sign of approval. Busting for a wee, I jump out of bed, making a dash for the bathroom.

When I open the door, Conor is already out of the shower. He's naked in front of the mirror, towel-drying his hair. He jumps when he sees my reflection behind him.

'Whoa, you nearly gave me a heart attack, Billy! You should've knocked.'

He goes to cover himself with the towel, but not before I've spotted the massive purple bruise on his torso.

'What happened to your ribs?'

He pulls the towel tighter around his body. 'Nothing. It's nothing. I t-t-tripped and fell against something the other day.'

I want to believe him, but I know he's lying. If it was an accident, why would he feel the need to hide it from me? As I pee, there's the sound of a key turning in the lock downstairs.

'Shit!' hisses Conor. 'It's my da. He's home early.'

'Conor!' his dad yells from downstairs. 'Are you still in bed, you lazy wee shite? It's gone ten. Get your arse down here and make your da a cup of tea. It's about time you started earning your keep.' There's a crashing sound, of something being knocked over.

Conor pushes me out of the bathroom. 'You need to go. Quick!'

'How am I going to get out without him seeing me?' I stare at him, unsure what to do.

'Just get dressed, Billy. Now. Hurry up, for God's sake!'

I run back into the bedroom and scramble around, gathering my clothes together. 'My watch,' I say. 'I can't find it. I think I left it downstairs on the sofa!'

Conor slaps himself on the forehead. 'Jesus. Well, you'll just have to leave it. I'll say it's mine, or something.'

'My shoes are down there too. By the front door.'

Conor's dad is calling his name again. 'I'm dying of thirst here. Will you hurry up and make me a frigging tea.'

Conor yells back. 'I'll be down in a minute!'

'Is he always like this?'

'Yes,' whispers Conor. He picks up my backpack from the floor and thrusts it into my arms. 'I'll go down the ladder first and keep him talking, while you sneak out the front door, OK?'

I nod, strapping the bag to my shoulders and watching as Conor descends the ladder from his bedroom. I follow him down, then wait for a minute at the bottom of the stairs while he goes to distract his dad in the kitchen. Almost as soon as he walks in, I hear shouting, and then a horrible thud. Conor cries out in pain. I feel sick, and my palms are so slippery I can barely open the latch. I can't believe I didn't know this was happening to Conor. I don't want to leave him, but my gut tells me if I stay I'll only make things much worse.

Sliding my feet into my DMs, I slip out the front door, closing it quietly behind me.

15.

Friday 25th August 2023

Shaken by what just happened with Davy Nugent, Aine and I grab a stool at the bar and order another round of porn star martinis.

'I'll get these,' I say, taking my wallet from my pocket and placing it on the bar.

'Wow, that was horrible,' says Aine, shuddering. 'And weird . . . did you see the reaction on his face when I mentioned Conor's name? I think he knows something.'

The barman places our drinks down in front of us, and we raise our glasses.

'Maybe he's protecting his brother,' Aine muses, grabbing a handful of peanuts from a bowl. 'I think we should try and get hold of Marty Nugent.'

I shake my head. 'I think we need to stay well clear of Marty Nugent, friend. That was a definite warning from Davy to back off.'

She pauses for a second before picking up her phone. 'I've just had a thought. Don't judge, but a few months ago, I signed up to Tinder.'

'Remind me what Tinder is again?'

'It's a dating app, you dinosaur.'

'Oh yeah. Don't forget you're talking to the guy who only just discovered Facebook.'

Aine laughs. 'I love how you're so clueless when it comes to technology. Let me explain,' she says, putting on her best teacher voice. 'Tinder allows you to flick through guys' profiles. If you like what you see, you swipe right. If you don't, it's left.'

'That's brutal,' I say, grimacing at the thought of my smiling face being swiped to the left.

'Also efficient,' she counters. 'So anyway, I was swiping through Tinder a while back, and . . .' She stops, puts her hand on my knee. 'By the way, don't say anything to Alex about this. I don't want them knowing I'm on dating apps.'

'I swear I won't mention anything to Alex.'

'Brownie's honour?'

'Brownie's honour.'

'OK, so as I was saying, I was swiping away and who should pop up on my phone screen but Marty Nugent?'

'Aine, I'm slightly disturbed by the direction this conversation is heading.'

'He's actually looking quite hot these days,' she says, ignoring my comment. 'His brother's right, he has lost weight.'

'That'll be the heart attack,' I say, raising an eyebrow.

'Oh, shut up, you. Seriously, he was looking all buff and muscly, like he'd been working out. Bit of a ride, in fact.'

'So which way did you swipe? Left – or right?'

'I didn't swipe either way. I just shut down the app and went back to watching *The One Show*. Honest to God, it completely slipped my mind that I'd seen him on there until our conversation just now with his thug of a brother.'

Aine leans forward on her stool, crossing her legs. She lifts her drink, putting the straw between her lips. 'So,' she says. 'How about I go on a date with Marty Nugent?'

'Are you serious?'

'Look, I'll play it safe, obviously. Arrange it somewhere public. A bar, or something. You can come with me. Maybe sit somewhere close by, keep an eye on things. Nothing's going to happen if we're surrounded by other people.'

'I'm not sure about this. At least don't make it so obvious

that you're wanting information about Conor this time, yeah?'

'Give me some credit, Billy. I'll have you know I got a grade A in GCSE Drama. Marty Nugent will be like putty in my hands.'

'You've got me thinking of that scene in *Ghost* now, with Patrick Swayze and Demi Moore.'

Aine covers her mouth with her hand. 'Eww, can you imagine? Me and Marty Nugent getting messy with a pottery wheel. To be honest, I was thinking more Sharon Stone in *Basic Instinct*.'

'Don't you dare do a Sharon Stone!'

Aine screams with laughter. 'You crack me up, Billy. As *if* I'd flash my lady bits at Marty Nugent.'

Now it's my turn to laugh. 'OK, fine, you're on. Let's do it. I'll be nearby the whole time though, mind, looking out for you. So nothing can go wrong.'

16.

Before

Wednesday 24th May 1989

'We can't meet at my house anymore,' Conor says. 'It's not safe.'

It's the first time I've spoken to Conor since the incident on Monday. He's calling from a phone box, as we can only ring each other at home at certain times of the day: usually around seven thirty on weekday mornings, when his dad is still on night shift.

'Are you OK?' I say, my voice full of concern. 'I was worried about you.'

There's a moment of silence, then he speaks. 'I'm fine, yeah. My da gets like that now and again if he's had a rough night at work. It's nothing I can't handle.'

'Are you sure, though? If there's anything I can do to help . . .' I want to ask him about the bruises on his ribs, but now is not the time. Not over the phone.

'Honestly, I'm fine. Don't worry about me, Billy.'

'When can I see you again?'

'Whenever you want. Just not at my da's house.'

'Where, though?'

'I've been thinking. How about the old hut on the building site? No one goes there.'

The hut is this place we discovered last summer. It's basically an abandoned shed. The door is hanging off its hinges and it's full of cobwebs, but we used to like chilling out there: me, Aine and Conor. It was somewhere we could talk in private, a parent-free zone. One of us would bring a cassette deck and we'd sit around just chatting and playing our music.

'Meet me there tonight,' says Conor.

I smile. 'What time?'

'After *Neighbours*.'

And then he hangs up.

17.

Tuesday 5th September 2023

Bev and I are sitting outside The Clock Tower Café in the Marine Gardens. This morning, she drove me over to the hospital to see Mum again. Depressingly, nothing much has changed. She's still unresponsive, but the nurses continue to assure me she's stable and there's every chance she will begin to make a recovery soon. I spent a good half hour by Mum's bedside, talking to her about what I've been doing since I've been home; how I've been looking after the house, and started working on my CV, that I'm hoping I'll find a job here. I tell her how much I've enjoyed catching up with old friends over these past few weeks, but I don't mention names. Mum was never Aine's biggest fan, and if she is listening to me, the last thing I want to do is upset her, even though I would hope any grudges she once held against my best mate are in the past.

It's warm for September. The neighbouring park is empty apart from a lone mum pushing her toddler on a swing. Bev and I watch in silence, listening to the squeak of the chains as the chair sways back and forth.

'Do you remember coming here as a youngster?' Bev takes off her cardigan, resting it over the back of the chair. 'Me and your ma used to always bring you down to the park in the afternoons when your da was at work. You loved the slide. Your ma used to get on it with you and I'd wait at the bottom, pretending to catch you both.' She chuckles.

'Then your ma and I used to sit together gossiping on that wee bench over there, drinking Blue Nun while you mucked around in the sandpit. You were always so happy. Until it was time to go home, of course. All hell broke loose then. You'd throw a tantrum. God love you, you were mustard.' She looks at me and laughs, her eyes crinkling at the corners.

'Was I?' I say, feeling grateful to have someone like Bev still around who can fill in the gaps in my childhood memories. The good and the bad.

A young waitress arrives with our order. 'Here's your wee large pot of tea,' she says, nervously placing it down on the table. 'I'll bring your wee cakes and sandwiches over in a minute.'

'Cakes and sandwiches?' cries Bev, her face beaming.

'My shout,' I say. 'You've been so good to me since I came home. To be honest, I don't know how I would've coped without you.'

I mean every word of this. I'm so thankful for Bev's friendship. She has been so welcoming, so kind – helping me deal with everything life has thrown at me recently. If someone had told me last month, when I was standing in the chippy in Margate, hungry and groping in my pockets for loose change, that I'd soon be splashing out on a cream tea, let alone a cream tea for two, I would've told them to wise up.

The food arrives and Bev and I start tucking into a delicious spread of finger sandwiches, fruit scones and cakes.

'Well, this is a treat.' Bev grins, licking a blob of cream from her lips. 'I can't remember the last time a fella took me out for lunch. It was probably Norman, my husband, and he's been dead twenty-five years, God rest his soul.'

'Twenty-five years? What happened?'

'Heart attack. Dropped dead during an episode of *Countdown*. I blame yer woman, Carol Vorderman. He couldn't take his eyes off her. He always used to say he watched it for the conundrums, but I knew better.' She smiles.

'I mean, I can laugh about it now, but it was an awful shock at the time. He was only in his late forties.' She leans over and picks up a macaroon. 'What about you, are you seeing anyone?'

'No. I've been single most of my life. I've had the odd fling, you know, but nothing serious.'

'Why's that then? I thought living in England you'd have loads of fellas to choose from?'

I take a sip of my tea. 'I don't know, really. It's hard to explain. I was never that open about my sexuality in England. You'd think that being away from home, I would've explored that side of myself a bit more. Don't get me wrong, like, I had a few affairs, but I never told anyone about them.'

'Why? What did you have to be ashamed of?'

'Nothing, really. I guess, after everything that happened with Conor . . .'

I pause, realising it's the first time I've spoken to Bev about him.

'Conor Doherty?' Bev puts her macaroon back down on the plate, untouched. 'You mean the wee fella who went missing years ago? I remember you and him were good friends.'

I nod. 'We were more than friends, Bev. We were seeing each other.'

Bev lifts her hands to her face, her mouth open in surprise. 'Yous were courting? You're kidding me. Fair play to you, son, you kept that one quiet.' She pauses for a beat. 'Although, come to think of it, me and Norman did have our suspicions. I always remember the pair of yous messing around with your ma's garden hose one summer. I had to tell you both off, 'cause I'd just pegged my washing out and all this water was pouring over the top of my hedge, like frigging Niagara Falls. Wee bastards, so you were. Me and Norman used to call you the Wham boys.'

'Really?' This makes me laugh. Conor would have found it hilarious too, I think to myself. He absolutely worshipped George Michael. 'Mum knew about us,' I say.

113

'Did she now?'

'And Mervyn. They found out.'

'I never knew that. She never mentioned it.'

I tell Bev what happened after Conor disappeared. How it caused the falling-out between Mum and me. How Mervyn told me it was God's way of punishing me for my 'perverse' nature.

Bev frowns. 'Did he really say that?' she whispers, her eyes full of sympathy. 'That's terrible, son. I mean, I believe in God and call myself a Christian, but it makes me cross the way some of them carry on, preaching hate about people who are different. That's not Christianity, in my book. Whatever happened to "love thy neighbour"?'

I tell Bev I've always blamed myself for Conor going missing because Mervyn drummed it into me that it was my fault. Bev shakes her head.

'You know, I always respected that man. I knew he had some funny ideas about things, but I've gone right off him now.'

I begin telling her about the mixtape and the investigation. Bev listens intently, every so often stopping to ask questions and offer me her sympathy. 'I need to find out what happened to Conor,' I say. 'If I don't, I think part of me will always feel guilty, that maybe there was some truth in what Mervyn said.'

'Nonsense,' snaps Bev. 'Don't you believe a word of it. The man had extreme views.'

'Extreme or not, he had a huge impact on the way I viewed my sexuality. I need to know what happened, not least so I can prove to myself that Conor's disappearance wasn't my fault.'

Just at that moment, my phone pings. It's a message from Aine. Hey, good news! I've managed to land a date with Marty Nugent. Mark my words, kiddo, I'm going to find out what happened to Conor, if it kills me.

18.

Wednesday 24th May 1989

I get to the builder's hut fifteen minutes early for my meet-up with Conor. I haven't been here in ages. Inside is like a bizarre shrine to last summer, when Conor, Aine and me gave the space a makeover, covering the walls with pages we'd torn from *Smash Hits*: Madonna, Tiffany, T'Pau and Wet Wet Wet, along with a few token pictures of Aine's favourite indie bands from *NME* and *Melody Maker*. The posters have yellowed a little, their corners peeling away from the wall. I push them back in place, pressing the Blu Tack down with my thumb.

There's a crunch on the rubble outside, then a voice. 'Billy?'

'In here,' I say, perching myself against an old desk the workmen have left cluttered with paperwork and mouldy mugs of tea.

Conor steps into the hut. He looks handsome with his freshly cropped blond hair slicked back with gel. He's wearing a plain white T-shirt, tight bleached denim jeans ripped at the knees, a black belt with an enormous silver buckle, DMs and a black bomber jacket.

'I was just having a look around,' I say. 'To see if anything's changed.'

'Looks exactly the same to me,' says Conor, taking off his sunglasses and resting them on the V-neck of his T-shirt. He reaches into his pocket and pulls out the watch I left at his house on Monday. 'Lucky I found it before my da did,' he says, handing it to me, producing a cassette from his other pocket. 'I taped you those songs you asked for, by the way.' I thank him, taking the cassette case and turning it over. On the back, in black biro, Conor has written the words 'May 1989' and drawn a smiley Acid face. He watches my face closely as I read through the list of songs.

'Side One is more dance, like,' he says, smiling. 'Side Two is mostly slow numbers.'

'It's class,' I say. 'I absolutely love it. Thanks, Conor.'

'Let me play it for you,' he says, lifting his sports bag off the floor and unzipping it. He pulls out a bright red ghetto blaster, placing it next to me on the desk. 'Give me the tape,' he says, pressing the eject button.

I hand him the cassette, the cassette that he has lovingly curated for me. It's rewound at Side Two. He puts it in the tape compartment, pushing it shut, and presses play. He sits down next to me on the desk, our thighs touching.

From the speakers, the opening chords to Jason Donovan's 'Sealed With A Kiss'.

I reach for the back of Conor's head, feeling the soft fuzz of his buzz cut against my fingers. Placing my hand softly on the back of his neck, I pull his face towards mine. We kiss, slowly at first, our tongues touching. Sliding my hand under his bomber jacket, I lift his T-shirt, gently stroking the curve of his lower back. As I go to move my hand higher, he flinches.

'Ow,' he says, pulling away. 'Be careful.'

I back off. 'What's the matter? Did I hurt you?'

He twists his torso in pain, squeezing his eyes. 'It's nothing,' he says. 'Really.'

I stare at him. His face is pale, his breathing fast and shallow. 'Conor,' I whisper to him. 'What happened to your ribs? Was it your dad?'

He looks at me with an expression of absolute terror. 'Don't you say anything about my da. It's none of your business!'

He pushes me away, putting his head in his hands, taking a series of deep breaths.

116

'We've got to stop doing this, OK?'

'Stop what?' I say, panicked.

'This,' he cries, throwing his hands up in the air. 'Us! This isn't going to work, Billy. I'm not a fucking *gaylord*.'

I watch in a stupor as he switches off the cassette. Ejecting the tape, he pulls it out of the deck and throws it on the floor, kicking it away with his foot.

'Fuck's sake!' he yells, wiping his mouth with the sleeve of his jacket. 'You and me, we're done, Billy. Never call me again, OK?'

Picking up his ghetto blaster, he storms out of the hut.

19.

Now

Tuesday 12th September 2023

Aine and I are sitting at the table she's chosen for her 'date' with Marty Nugent. Fiddling nervously with the cuff of her denim jacket, she asks the waitress for a gin and tonic. I order a glass of white wine and we wait a moment for the waitress to move away before continuing with our conversation.

'Why did I think this was a good idea,' hisses Aine. 'What on earth possessed me? I'm bricking it.'

'You were tipsy.'

'Tipsy? I was shitfaced! I'm surprised I didn't throw my drink in Wendy Pratt's face at the end of the night. She was asking for it, so she was. Just bein' sarcastic, my frigging arse.'

It turns out Aine hadn't wasted any time getting in contact with Marty Nugent. The morning after the school reunion, hungover from far too many porn star martinis, she'd gone straight onto Tinder to track down his profile. Having had no luck, she'd then trawled through Facebook. Finding they had a couple of acquaintances in common, she sent him a friend request, which he accepted instantly, quickly following it with a photo of himself working out at the gym, along with a wink. Aine responded with a 'Hi, handsome' and after a series of brief chats, and a string of flirtatious emojis, which included an aubergine, a taco and, rather bizarrely, a fireman's helmet, they had arranged to meet here, in Dobbins Inn, Carrickfergus' oldest pub.

'What time is old lover boy getting here?' I say, toying with a beer mat.

Aine rolls her eyes. 'Half seven. Please don't call him that, though. You'll make me boke.'

'What else did he say in his chats?'

She shrugs. 'Not a lot. It was mostly banter. Obviously, I was fully prepared for the inevitable dick pic, especially after all the muscle photos he sent, but it never materialised, thank God.'

I laugh. 'Muscle pics?'

Aine screws up her face. 'He sent me all these really gross photos of him standing in front of the mirror . . .'

'Naked?'

'With clothes on the bottom half, thankfully. But he was bare-chested, pulling all these bizarre poses. I mean, fair play to him, he's got a good body for a man in his mid- to late fifties, but I couldn't get past the fact his bathroom mirror was covered in smears. All I could think was, that mirror is in far greater need of a rubdown with Mr Muscle than I am.'

This makes me laugh. 'Did you chat about anything else, other than his Adonis body?'

Aine looks around the room cautiously, then whispers, 'He did ask me at one point if I was into broccoli.'

'Broccoli? Does he know you're vegetarian, then?'

Aine shakes her head. 'No. Wait till you hear this. He sent me a wee emoji of a broccoli and an OK symbol.'

'Why did he want to know if you're OK with broccoli?'

'I had to ask Alex because they're more clued up about emoji language – if that's what you call it.'

'You didn't tell them who you were messaging?'

'God, no! I just said I was asking for a friend. They probably thought I meant you.' Aine laughs.

'What did Alex say?'

'They told me broccoli was emoji for drugs.'

'What kind of drugs?'

'Weed. Marty Nugent smokes weed. He's a stoner.'

'How did you respond to that one then?'

Aine picks up her drink and shrugs. 'I just sent him a wee winking emoji, so I did. Didn't want to put him off meeting me.'

'Fair do's. Look, where do you want me to sit? Obviously, I'll be discreet. I've brought a copy of the *Belfast Telegraph* to keep me occupied.'

Aine gestures towards a small table in the corner, next to the fireplace and facing a stained-glass window. 'Over there. And don't look at me when I'm talking to him. You'll put me off.'

'How are you going to broach the subject of Conor without it sounding like you're up to something?'

'Gin and tonic and a white wine?' The waitress arrives, holding a small round tray with both hands. Aine pauses as the girl sets the tray on the table and carefully offloads the drinks before leaving us alone.

'I haven't quite figured that out yet,' she continues, pouring half a can of Fever Tree tonic into her glass and giving it a taste. 'I was just going to start talking about our schooldays and then slide it into the conversation somehow.'

'We need a safe word,' I say.

'A safe word? Jesus, Billy. You're making me even more nervous.'

I take a sip of my tepid wine. 'Just in case he gets a bit difficult, or nasty. I can be on hand to give you an excuse to leave.'

'I dunno,' says Aine, quickly scanning the room for ideas. 'How about "Harp", as in the lager? Will that do?'

'Perfect. So, if things get too much, just say Harp.'

Aine inhales loudly, puffing out her cheeks. 'Deep breaths, Aine, deep breaths. I better keep a crisp bag handy, in case I have a panic attack.'

'Why do you need emergency crisps?'

'It's not the crisps I need,' she hisses. 'It's the bag! Have you never had a panic attack?'

I shrug. 'Not really, no.'

'Seriously, like? You blow into the bag when you can't breathe. It helps calm you down.'

'I'll go and get you some crisps then,' I say, standing up, pushing my chair back. 'Any particular flavour?'

'Something plain. Ready Salted or Salt and Vinegar. Not Scampi Fries, mind. The bag's too small to breathe into and I don't want to scare Marty off with my fishy breath.'

The bar is in the next room. I take my drink with me, just in case Marty arrives while I'm away. As I approach, I hear a man having a row with one of the waitresses.

'I gave you a twenty, so I did. You've only given me change for ten. You owe me another tenner.'

The waitress, who is young, not much older than Alex, says, 'I'm sorry, mister. I could've sworn you only gave me a tenner. I'll need to check with my manager, 'cause I'm not allowed to give refunds without her permission.'

'Who's your manager? Tell her I want a fuckin' word.'

'OK, OK. What's your name? I'll let her know you're waiting?'

'Marty Nugent. You tell her I've been coming here for thirty-five years, and I've never had service as shockin' as this.'

The waitress whimpers and runs off. So, this is Aine's 'date' for the evening. I'm half tempted to dash back in and tell her to get the hell out of here. I watch Marty take his phone out of his back pocket and write a text. Seconds later, his phone pings in response. And then mine pings too. It's Aine. She's messaging to say Marty's here. I text back saying, 'I know. He's standing next to me at the bar.' She replies with, 'I've moved your newspaper to the table by the fireplace.'

'Sorry for the wait. Are you being served?' I look up from my phone to see the young waitress standing in front of me. She's visibly shaken by the verbal abuse Marty's just hurled at her. I ask for a packet of plain crisps, for Aine, and order another white wine for myself. While she's sorting out the order, a suited woman in her thirties, immaculately presented, appears behind her. She introduces herself to Marty Nugent as the manager.

'Listen, love,' he says. 'I'm meant to be on a date the night, so I don't have time for this sort of carry-on. Long story short, you owe me a tenner. Thon wee doll over there gave me the wrong change, so she did.'

'Auch, I'm terribly sorry about that, Mr Nugent. While I'm not doubting your honesty, I won't know if you've been overcharged until I do the takings at the end of the night. Do you want to leave me your wee number and I'll ring you when I've checked the till?'

Marty Nugent's face looks like it's about to reach boiling point. 'Are you calling me a liar?' he yells.

'No one's calling you a liar, Mr Nugent. It's just that we have procedures . . .'

Marty slams his fist on the bar. 'Don't give me all that procedures shite, love. I'm not interested. I just want my money back. Fact is, I gave that wee girl twenty pounds and she gave me change for ten.'

Shaking, the waitress places my glass of white wine and packet of crisps on the bar, and I hand her a ten-pound note. She takes it, then hovers by the cash register, as if unsure what to do with it. Marty glares at her, then at me. He says, 'Make sure she checks that before she puts it in the till, mate. Maths isn't her strong point.'

The girl looks like she's about to burst into tears. 'Go and have a wee break, Aimee. I'll sort this,' says the bar manager. Taking the money from the girl, she rings my order into the till, handing me a few coins in change. She then turns her attention back to Marty Nugent, who is messaging on his phone again.

'Mr Nugent?' she says. He looks up from his text, his brow furrowed. 'While I can't offer you any refund until I've counted the money later, as an apology for our mistake I can give you a couple of drinks on the house. Is that OK?'

Marty deliberates for a moment or two, then says, 'Aye,

well, if that's the best you can do. I'll have another pint of Harp, and a gin and tonic for my date.'

'Sure,' says the manager. 'If you take a wee seat, I'll bring it over to you.'

Marty nods, wandering off into the other room. Grabbing the crisps and drink, I follow close behind him, slipping discreetly into my vantage point next to the fireplace, where I'll be able to earwig on their conversation.

Aine gets up from her chair when she sees Marty coming. If she's still nervous, it doesn't show. Watching her, I'm not surprised she got that A for Drama. Now that I'm not standing right next to him, I'm able to study the man, who has no idea he's about to be interrogated even more closely by Aine. Like his brother, Davy, he's short and stocky, but – unlike Davy – he still has a full head of hair, which is slicked back in a sort of 1950s quiff. He's wearing a black polo shirt and very tight jeans, the kind so tight you need an extra pair of hands to get them off at the end of an evening. His hands and wrists are heavily tattooed.

When he clocks Aine, he puts both drinks down on the table and, taking a step back, looks her up and down, in the same way a hungry drunk might eye a slab of kebab meat on a rotating vertical skewer; then he holds out his arms and pulls her towards him, leaning his head into her neck and giving her what looks like a crushing embrace. Aine winks at me over his shoulder, making a face, before pulling away and sitting down at the table again.

'You smell gorgeous, Marty,' she says, turning the charm up to max. 'What aftershave's that you're wearing?'

'Burberry Brit.'

'Burrr-berry,' she purrs, dreamily. 'Get you and your designer smellies.'

'Actually, houl' on a minute.' He lifts one armpit up to his nose and gives it a sniff. 'I tell a lie. It's Lynx Africa. My deodorant. I've just come from the gym, you see.'

'Lynx Africa,' enthuses Aine. 'How exotic.'

Marty's face turns serious. 'Are you takin' the piss?'

Aine, who is *clearly* taking the piss, throws him a look of complete innocence.

'Oh, no, Marty. What makes you think that? I'm being deadly serious. I love Lynx, so I do. It's a very *manly* fragrance. Reminds me of being at school, standing next to the boys on the bus, breathing in their Lynx Oriental. All that raging testosterone.'

Marty laughs. 'You're a headcase. I like you, though.' He lifts his pint. 'Cheers. It's good to finally catch up in person. I'm a bit embarrassed to admit this, you know, but I've fancied you for years, since you were sixteen.'

Aine blushes. 'You remember me from our younger days then?'

'I do, aye.'

'Oh God, now I'm embarrassed.'

'Don't be. You were hot . . . for a Fenian.' For a split second, Aine looks horrified. Marty clearly senses he's put his foot in it. 'I'm only messing,' he says. 'I couldn't care less what religion you are. A bit of skirt's a bit of skirt. Know what I mean?'

If Aine feels repulsed, which I know for a fact she does, she's doing a very good job of hiding it. She smiles and says, 'I remember there was a rumour at school that you used to let schoolgirls into Club Babylon without ID, if they gave you a French kiss on the door.'

Marty looks down at his pint, shaking his head at the memory. 'Jesus. Don't go spreading that around. You'll make me sound like a right paedo.'

'Are you still doing bouncer work then?'

'Am I fuck.' Marty wipes his mouth with his sleeve. 'I'm way too old now for that sort of carry-on.'

'What do you do for a living?'

'Burger vans. I've got two. One in the car park by the castle and one in Larne.'

'I love a big dirty burger,' says Aine. 'As long as it's veggie, mind. Will you give me a discount, Marty? Mate's rates.'

He squeezes his eyes shut, grinning. 'You're a geg, so you are. To tell you the truth, I'd happily give you one for free.'

Aine smiles, batting her lashes. 'I'd love that, Marty.' She takes a sip of her drink as he watches her. 'Here, was I at school with your wee brother?'

'Maybe,' he says. 'What school did you go to?'

'Carrick High.'

Marty nods. 'Aye, our Davy went there too. What age are you now, if you don't mind me asking?'

'Fifty.'

'So's he.'

'We were in the same year, then. Doesn't seem like that long ago, does it?'

Marty shakes his head. 'Time flies, so it does.'

'At least we made it to our fifties,' says Aine, clearly sensing an opportunity. 'Not all our friends did . . . I still think about that poor wee Conor Doherty fella. You remember him? He was just sixteen when he went missing.'

At the mention of Conor's name, I shake my head at her, warning her not to go straight for it, but she doesn't see me. There's a pause. Marty takes another slug of his pint.

'Everything OK, Marty? Did you know Conor?' she asks, putting on her best concerned face.

He taps his fingers on the table's smooth surface. 'He was a friend of yours, was he?' Aine nods. 'I should be careful what I say then.'

Aine leans in. 'What do you mean?'

'This is only gossip. Feel free to take it with a pinch of salt.' He looks shiftily around. I bury my head in the pages of my *Belfast Telegraph*. 'After he disappeared, there was a rumour going round he was involved with drugs.'

'Really?' Aine looks at him.

Marty shrugs. 'I dunno. You know what people round here are like, though. Chinese whispers. Anyway, he was your mate, so he was. You'd know him better than me.'

'What was the rumour?' Aine asks.

'I don't know if you remember, you were probably too young, but Club Babylon used to have a bit of a reputation. This was during the "Second Summer of Love", in the late eighties. Illegal raves were happening all over the place.'

Aine nods. 'I only went to Club Babylon once. It wasn't long after we'd finished our GCSEs. I remember going to a few raves in Donegal though, when I was studying at Queen's in the nineties.'

'Happy days,' says Marty. 'They were good times. The drugs were good, too. Pure, like. They weren't cut with the kind of crap you get now. Acid trips, pills, weed, everyone was off their faces. And you know the best thing about it? No one cared if you were Catholic or Protestant. Everyone was in it for the craic.'

'How was Conor involved, though?'

'Like I say, I didn't really know the guy, only to see, but he must've been on the premises once or twice, for I recognised him from the posters they put up around town. If you ask me, I reckon he'd been coaxed into dealing for the club. They used to recruit young lads – sometimes girls – to sell drugs for them. It meant the owners could turn a blind eye to any dealing, when really, they were the ones supplying. They got raided a few times in the late eighties – peelers smashed the place up with sledgehammers, strip-searched the punters. Then, later, in the early nineties, Andy Stone, the owner, got arrested and convicted for supplying drugs. That's when the club was shut down.'

'So, what do you think happened to Conor then?'

'I'm not sure. I mean, I'm no angel, but you wouldn't want to go messing with some of those guys. Seriously, they were nasty pieces of work.'

'Where are they all now?'

'Most of them are dead, or in jail,' he says, swigging from his pint glass.

'What about Andy Stone? Is he still alive?'

126

Marty scratches his head. 'He may well be. Andy was around forty at the time, so he'd be in his seventies now.'

'How long was he in prison for?'

'Not that long – a few years, probably.' Marty gives a grim snigger. 'I'm beginning to feel like I'm on *The Bill*. All these questions.'

Aine laughs, nervously. 'Sorry, Marty. You got me thinking about what happened to my friend, that's all. I'm getting sentimental in my old age.'

'They never found a body, did they?'

Aine shakes her head.

'Aye, it's sad,' says Marty. 'I remember it being all over the papers at one point, and then nothing. Too much else going on in this place for them to bother searching for one missing wee lad.'

He pauses before lifting his pint to his mouth, giving Aine a cheeky wink. 'Anyway, that's all in the past. When am I treating you to one of my big dirty veggie burgers?'

Aine plays with the rim of her glass. 'You know the way to a woman's heart, Marty Nugent.'

He eyes her, seedily. 'It's not your heart I'm after, love.'

'Right,' says Aine, checking her watch. 'Will you look at the time? My Alex said they'd pick me up at nine.'

Marty looks at her, disappointed. 'I didn't know you had a curfew. So – would you like to go on another date then? Some other time, maybe?'

Aine drains the contents of her glass and stands up. 'It's been lovely talking to you, Marty. I'll be in touch.' She leans over and pecks him on the cheek, leaving him to drink the rest of his pint. On her way out, she gives me a wink. A minute or so later, my phone pings.

Good job from DI Kelly tonight! We've got a lead. Meet me outside in 5. A xxx

127

20.

Sunday 28th May 1989

I haven't heard from Conor since our row last Wednesday, and I've been wallowing in misery ever since, playing his cassette tapes over and over, wishing I could pick up the phone and call him. With everything that's been going on, it's been hard concentrating on my exams. I miss our regular meet-ups, the daily phone chats, the secret sleepovers. Lying in bed, I listen to the low, steady hum of the hoover coming from downstairs, and Mum belting out the chorus to Jennifer Rush's 'The Power of Love'. She always plays music when she's doing housework, blasting whatever chart song she's obsessed with at the time. She has this annoying habit of putting on a seven-inch single and playing it on repeat. It's not just my mum; loads of my friends' mums do it too. I'm surprised one of the big record labels like Telstar haven't cottoned on and released a compilation album aimed at housewives: *80s Carpet Busters. Hits to Hoover To*. If they did, Mum would be the first to buy it.

Lying in bed, I stare at the posters and magazine cuttings from *Smash Hits* and *Number One* magazine covering my bedroom wall. Three of my walls are dedicated to the absolute goddess and lyrical genius that is Kylie Minogue, which lately Mum has taken as a sign I fancy girls. The other day I overheard her boasting to Bev next door that I had a 'wee thing for Kylie'. Bev laughed and said, 'God love him. When I was his age, I wanted to marry Adam Faith. Sure, it's normal to have crushes as a teenager. His wee hormones must be all over the shop.'

Hidden away on the back of my bedroom door, though, is something Mum hasn't spotted yet: a huge poster of my favourite boy band, Bros. On the poster, the three boys are sitting on the bonnet of a black Sahara Jeep. Luke is in the middle, his arms around Matt and Craig. They're dressed in sexy leather jackets, black DM shoes and ripped jeans with turn-ups, and staring directly into the camera. Matt's jeans have a small rip in the crotch region, and if you look closely enough, which I have, many times, you can even see the smooth baby-soft pink of his inner thigh. Gazing at it now, I get a sudden urge to visit the bathroom. I grab the Kays catalogue from under the bed, slipping it up my pyjama top.

Once inside, I close the door behind me and pull the bolt across. Downstairs, Mum is still busy with the hoover while Jennifer Rush warbles on and on about being a lady in love. I try to block out her banshee wailing so I can focus on the job at hand.

I turn the shower on and strip off my pyjamas, sitting down on the fluffy avocado-green toilet seat cover. As I wait for the water to heat up, watching the mirror on the bathroom cabinet slowly misting over, I spread the catalogue open on my thighs. My whole body is shaking.

Over the past year, I've been spending a lot of time in the bathroom, the only room in our house with a lock. I've become addicted to perusing the men's underwear section in Mum's catalogue. There are two pages in particular which are well-thumbed and slightly crinkled where I've accidentally dripped bathwater on them. The pages feature several musclemen modelling tanga briefs in a range of colours – jade, orange and topaz – with bold, black zigzags emblazoned on their bulging crotches. The men are standing on a sandy beach. All of them are tanned, their hair slicked back with gel, their bodies glistening with sweat. They smile knowingly at each other, as the frothy white surf crashes in the background.

Once the room is a glorious oasis of steam, I lay the catalogue down and clamber into the bath. Resting my back against the cold bathroom tiles, I slide down into my regular position, so I'm facing upwards with the shower water cascading down on me like a waterfall. As I lie there, I visualise the male models in the catalogue, letting my fantasies play out in my head. Every so often, their faces become Conor's. I try to keep the focus on them, but it's no use. Conor keeps reappearing. So I let my thoughts go where they want to. This is just a fantasy, I tell myself. No point in fighting it.

When I come out of the bathroom, I hear Mum and Mervyn talking downstairs. At the mention of my name, I pause in the hallway to listen, my hair dripping, a towel wrapped around my waist like an untidy skirt.

'You're mollycoddling the wee lad, Sadie. If you're not careful, you'll turn him into a Ginny Ann.'

His harsh words cause me to catch my breath. Shuffling back a step or two, my towel drops to the floor. I scramble to pick it up again, my heart racing.

'Don't say things like that,' says Mum. 'It's not his fault. He lost his dad when he was a child.' It's nice to hear Mum defending me, but I can't help feeling bad for her, guilty almost. It's like she's having to apologise for the way I am.

'Exactly!' says Mervyn. 'I'm not blaming anyone, but it's obvious to me the boy's in desperate need of a father figure. Look at the clothes he wears. It's not natural for a fella to dress like that. He's too . . . *flamboyant*.'

'He's a teenager! He's into fashion. It's perfectly normal at his age.'

Mervyn scoffs. 'Normal? Who buys his clothes, if you don't mind me asking?'

'I do, why?'

'Auch, Sadie, you're as soft as Flora. Too soft. He should be paying his own way at his age.'

'I have said to him about getting a job, but he always tells me he's got too much revision to do.'

'Nonsense. Sure, he'll be finished his exams in a few weeks. I tell you what, let me talk with him. Man to man.'

When I finally pluck up the courage to head downstairs, Mum is hovering outside the living room, nervously clutching a coffee jug.

'Mervyn would like a wee *word* with you,' she whispers, pushing me in the direction of the living room.

Mervyn is on the sofa, reading a copy of the *Evangelical Times*. When he sees me, he puts the paper down and stands up, holding out his hand. I shake it, with the same hand I've just been using to satisfy my lust for the Kays catalogue men. This thought gives me a redner. I hope he doesn't notice.

'Would you like a wee coffee, Mervyn?' asks Mum, but he shakes his head. 'No stimulants for me today, please. A glass of water will do me rightly.'

Mum heads back into the kitchen to fetch his drink.

'What age are you, young man?' says Mervyn, glaring down at me.

'Fifteen,' I say, turning my head away. 'I'll be sixteen in July.'

'Sixteen?' He puffs his cheeks. 'Dangerous age,' he says. 'A very dangerous age.'

My whole body tenses. Given their conversation in the hallway just now, I'm dreading what he's about to say. Mervyn edges towards me, placing his hand firmly in the centre of my chest.

'Do you know what this is?' he says, giving his hand a slight push, which forces me to take a step back, almost losing my balance.

I nod, a heavy, sinking feeling in my stomach. I can feel my pulse pounding.

'Well then?'

'My heart?'

'Correct. Now, let me tell you something, son. The heart is one of the most complex organs in the human body, and sometimes it can rule the head. And when that happens, we become vulnerable to all kinds of temptations. Do you know what I'm getting at here?'

'I-I think so,' I say, my ears and cheeks burning, images of Conor and the Speedo-clad men in the Kays catalogue flashing through my mind.

'You think so?' He nods. 'Well, take my advice. As tempting as it might seem, don't light that fire, Billy, because that fire will start a blaze inside of you and you won't be able to control it. Do you understand?' He pulls his hand away.

'Yes,' I lie, my head in a muddle.

He pauses for a moment, then says, 'Tell me, son, are you saved?'

'Saved?'

'Yes, son. Are you saved?'

Mum returns from the kitchen with his drink. 'Here you go, Mervyn. It's only tap, nothing fancy. I should've got some Perrier in for you.'

He takes the glass of water from her. 'No need to fuss, Sadie. My needs are basic.' Sitting back down on the sofa, he places his glass of water on one of Mum's Costa del Sol coasters. 'I was just asking Billy if he'd come to Christ yet.'

Mum looks slightly embarrassed. 'To be honest, I haven't had a chance to talk to him about it.'

'No time like the present,' he says. 'As my foster mother always told me, "There's no point waiting for the morrow, for the morrow might never come."' He turns to me again. 'Billy, at fifteen you might think you have your whole life ahead of you, but let me tell you something. You could go outside later and get run over by a bus, doomed to face an eternity without the Lord. Is that what you want?'

'No,' I whisper.

Ma puts her arm around me, giving a nervous laugh. 'Go easy on him,' she says. 'He's only a youngster.'

Mervyn ignores her. He leans forward on the sofa, putting his hand on my knee. 'Let me tell you a wee story, Billy. Like you, I lost a parent as a child. Both parents, in fact. My entire family was killed in the Belfast Blitz when I was just two years old. Can you imagine what that felt like, to be orphaned at such a young age?'

'Mervyn was adopted,' says Mum. 'He didn't have it easy.'

'I certainly didn't. But look where I am now. I may come from humble beginnings, but these days I'm one of the biggest evangelists this country's ever seen. The Holywood Church is worth *millions*. As your mother will tell you, our church is something else. State-of-the-art. People come from all over the province. I even had a lady come to Christ, and she was from Rathcoole, an area rife with sin. People queue round the block to see me. Yes, *me*.' He points at himself and grins. 'Of course, it helps that I'm good-looking. Back in the day, people used to say I was a dead ringer for Elvis Presley.' He pauses for a beat and then laughs. 'I'm only joking with you, Billy, only joking. Just my sense of humour.'

'I think you're better-looking than Elvis,' says Mum.

Mervyn gives her a playful slap on the leg, turning to me. 'She's a good woman, your mother. One of the best. I'm a lucky man.'

Mum looks at Mervyn, her face beaming with pride. 'He earns a fortune, so he does. It's a good job, being a preacher. It pays well.'

'Not that I do it for the money, mind,' Mervyn says gravely. 'It's a vocation. A calling, if you like, but the Lord looks after his own.' He puts his hand over his mouth, clearing his throat. 'Saying that, my needs are very simple. No mod cons.'

'No mod cons,' says Mum, and I can't help thinking she sounds a little disappointed. After all, Mum loves a mod con. I look out the window at the white BMW parked in our driveway. Clearly flashy cars don't fall into the 'mod con' category.

'Mervyn's had to work hard for his success,' says Mum,

glancing at him for approval. 'Which is why I'm always telling you you need to concentrate on your schoolwork.'

'Absolutely,' he says. 'I had to bust a gut to get where I am now. If you'd seen the first church I worked for. Boys a dear, it was this old hut that had been bombed to bits during the Second World War. It had a tin roof, which rattled like gunfire when it rained, and a broken washing mangle for a pulpit. And the congregation used to sit squashed up on old potato sacks on the cold stone floor, for we never even had pews!'

Mum is laughing her head off at this story she's no doubt heard a million times. 'Imagine that, Billy!' She pokes Mervyn in the ribs. 'Here, Billy wouldn't even be seen dead working in a shop. There's no *way* you'd catch him sitting on a sack of old spuds.'

I cringe at this comment. Mum obviously reckons I think I'm above shop work, but the truth is I'm too shy to look for a job. I've thought about it, especially as I could do with the extra cash, but I'm too scared to do an interview.

Mervyn glares at me. 'You don't have a part-time job yet? How do you earn your keep?'

'He doesn't,' says Mum, raising an eyebrow at me. 'He relies on the Bank of Mum.'

'Dear oh dear,' says Mervyn, shaking his head. 'That's terrible. You're the *man* in the family, Billy. You should be supporting your mother. When I was your age, I was already getting ready to preach my first sermon.'

Mum looks at me, nodding in agreement. My cheeks are burning up. Maybe they're both right and I'm nothing but a flamboyant, jobless Ginny Ann? Worst of all, I'm a disappointment to Mum, which hurts me badly. Growing up, I've watched her suffer. I know it hasn't been easy for her, being a single mum and missing my dad. The last thing I want to do is let her down, to disappoint her. How would she feel if she found out I was gay? I think about what Mervyn said. *Don't light that fire, Billy . . . that fire will start a blaze inside of you . . . you won't be able to control it.* Maybe I've already lit that fire, though. Maybe it's still blazing. And the boy I lit that fire for has dumped me, leaving me in flames. I realise I've made some bad choices lately. If I do what Mum wants, will it make her happy? Will it make things better for us?

I start to cry, overwhelmed with feelings of guilt and shame over the way I've behaved. Mum leans in, putting her arm around me. 'Listen, son. All we're trying to say is that life would be a lot easier with God on your side.'

'Your mum's right,' says Mervyn. 'If you let the Lord into your heart, he will provide. Whatever problems you have, Jesus will help you overcome them. Whatever you desire, the Lord hears you, but only if you open your heart to him. Let him inside.'

21.

Tuesday 12th September 2023

After Aine's investigative Tinder 'date', we head down to Castello Italia, Carrick's newest Italian restaurant.

'I'm absolutely starving,' says Aine, her eyes roving hungrily over the menu.

'You didn't fancy one of Marty's big dirty burgers then?'

'Oh my God, how gross was he? Such a lech. It took all my strength and willpower not to chuck my gin and tonic in his face.'

I laugh. 'You were brilliant. You deserve an Oscar for that performance.'

We order a few antipasti dishes from the waiter and, Aperol Spritzes in hand, start mulling over the events of the evening in more detail.

'Do you think Conor was into drugs?' says Aine.

'I dunno. Now that I think about it, he could've been on something the night we all went out at Club Babylon. He was all huggy with me in public, which he never would've been if he was sober. Mind you, that was probably just the drink.'

'Maybe Marty was right then. At least we got something out of him. Some guy, the club owner. What was his name?'

'Andy Stone,' I reply.

Aine picks up her phone and opens Google. 'Sounds like a soul singer, doesn't he?'

'What does Google say about him?'

Aine pauses, scanning the article that's just this minute

flashed on her screen. 'He gets a mention here in this piece about rave culture in Northern Ireland and how it allowed for Generation X, now in their mid-forties to late fifties – that's us, then – to mix, irrespective of their religious backgrounds. Hold on a minute.' She picks up her handbag and starts rummaging through it. 'I need my reading glasses to see this properly.' She puts them on. 'Andy Stone . . . blah, blah, blah. OK, so Marty was right. He was jailed for three years for selling drugs on the club premises.' She reads on. 'Oh, now this is interesting, so it is.'

'What?'

'It says here, on leaving prison, Andy Stone found solace in evangelism, joining the Holywood Church in Belfast, where he eventually took on the position of treasurer, taking care of the organisation's funds.' Aine puts down her phone. 'Repenting for his sins, so he was.'

At the mention of the Holywood Church, a shiver runs down my spine.

'You know what this means,' I say to Aine. 'The Holywood Church is Mervyn's church, the one Mum went to. That means they must have known Andy Stone. It would've been Mervyn who employed him.'

22.

Before

Saturday 10th June 1989

The Holywood Church youth group have organised a day trip to Tollymore Forest and, as a treat for finishing my GCSEs, Mervyn has kindly agreed to pay for me to go. 'The wee lad needs a break,' I heard him telling Mum. 'He's had a lot on his plate recently, with exams and so on.'

At first, I thought Mervyn was a bit of a weirdo, but over the past few weeks I've seen how happy he makes Mum. She's given up alcohol, does loads more housework and has even taken up proper cooking. This is all down to Mervyn, who bought her a copy of *Delia Smith's Complete Cookery Course* as a gift, telling her that, next to the Bible, it was the only other book a modern woman of the twentieth century needed.

As such, she's ditched the SlimFast shakes and the packet soups for home-made spaghetti bolognese, beef bourguignon and coq au vin. After years of dishing up burnt chips and microwave dinners for tea, Mum has transformed herself into a culinary goddess. Last night, for example, we ate baked marrow with tomatoes and coriander followed by a traditional apple charlotte. We dined by candlelight – candlelight! – and drank red Shloer from her finest wine glasses (free with her first order from the Great Universal catalogue).

Life has got so much better in the short time since Mervyn joined our family. Sometimes I feel like pinching myself, because it's like living on Southfork Ranch with the Ewings in *Dallas* – if they had been saved. Mervyn was right. Jesus really does provide!

I owe Mervyn my life right now. Through Christ's teachings, he's shown me another path, another way of living. As soon as I accepted the Lord Jesus into my heart it was like a door opened. All the worries of the past year vanished. I saw a way forward. Mervyn made me realise my soul was in danger. Teenagers are especially vulnerable, he said, explaining how the devil takes many forms. 'Satan will try and trick you into going against nature, Billy. He will put all kinds of queer temptations in your path, but you must resist.' I thought of Conor, and Bros, and the male models in Mum's catalogue; I can't say I'm completely out of the woods yet, but for Mum's sake I'm trying my best to be a good son.

I'm feeling nervous about today's trip though. It's my first outing with the church and I don't know anyone else who's going. I'm sure it'll be fine, but I keep thinking of Aine because she laughed when I told her about it on the phone the other day. 'Don't tell me you've joined the Jesus Brigade, Billy?' she said.

It was a typical Aine comment, but it really hurt my feelings. I remembered Mervyn warning me about false friends who would mock me because of my new faith, and I cringed at the memory of my 'coming out' to her a few weeks back. Why had I felt the need to tell her all that stuff? I know in my heart that I'm not like the Big Gay Willies and Boy Georges of this world. Coming to Christ has made me realise it's just a phase. I can turn things around. I can make things right. I know I can. As one of my favourite singers, George Michael, says, I just gotta have faith!

When I get to the church, a group of young people are already waiting to board the coach to Tollymore Forest – a mix of boys and girls. They're standing a good distance apart from each other, the boys at one end, the girls at the other. At the front of the coach, a group of lads are kicking a football around. Now and again their ball hits the side of the coach, just missing the three screaming girls huddling underneath a soggy copy of *Just Seventeen* to protect their perms from the rain. A long-haired guy in skinny, whitewashed jeans, white Converse boots and a denim jacket covered in Jesus patches and pin badges comes over to greet me. He looks a bit like the lead singer in Bon Jovi. He has an acoustic guitar with a rainbow strap hanging over one shoulder. He introduces himself as Aaron. Aaron, it turns out, is one of the youth leaders on the trip.

'Nice to meet you, Billy,' he says. He extends his hand and gives me a floppy but friendly handshake. 'Have you been on a trip with us before?'

'No,' I say. 'This is my first time.'

'Cool. Do you want me to introduce you to some of the others?'

'Aye, all right.' I nod, shyly.

Aaron blows on the whistle hanging round his neck. 'Listen up, everyone,' he says. He waits for the boys to stop kicking the football around and for the girls to stop their chatter. 'I've someone here who I want you to meet,' he says. 'This is Billy. He's new to our church, so please make him feel very welcome.'

There's a brief, slightly awkward silence. 'All right, mate,' says one of the boys. Like Aaron, he has long hair and is dressed head to toe in denim. I learn later that his name is Mike and he plays the drums in Forever Faith, the church's Christian rock band. A girl in a white ski jacket, who has been standing on her own since I arrived, comes over and joins me. Her blonde hair is styled in a sort of Princess Diana bouffant and she's carrying an enormous pink sports bag. 'Wendy Johnson,' she says confidently. 'This is my first trip too. Are you excited? I'm *really* excited, so I am.'

Wendy starts telling me all about herself. She can't half talk; I barely get a word in edgeways. She's a pupil at Belfast Royal

Academy (BRA for short) and has been competing in the semi-finals of the Northern Irish Under Sixteens Gymnastics. 'It's been a tough competition,' she says, 'but I'm determined to win. God blessed me with supple joints and a *very* flexible spine.' Wendy tells me she's so obsessed with gymnastics that everyone at BRA calls her 'Bendy Wendy'. Even her ma, who teaches Sports Science at the University of Ulster, reckons she was born wearing a leotard.

'Mum told me I tumbled out of her fanny like an Olympic gymnast, forward-rolling my way into existence.' She laughs, revealing a set of perfectly straight teeth, the result of two years of wearing braces. 'They were a nightmare,' she goes on. 'A complete nightmare. I had train tracks and elastic bands, the works. If you'd seen me a year ago, you wouldn't have recognised me. You know Plain Jane Superbrain from *Neighbours*? That's me. None of my friends can believe the transformation. Talk about the ugly duckling turning into a swan. Of course, Jesus had a lot to do with my makeover. If it wasn't for him, I wouldn't be here today, on a coach travelling to Newcastle with a whole bunch of new friends. I can tell we're going to be best buddies, Billy. Isn't this *exciting*?'

Already exhausted by Wendy's non-stop chatter, I clamber onto the coach with her. She insists we find seats next to each other but requests not to sit by the window because she gets travel-sick. There's no toilet on the coach as far as I'm aware, so I'm not sure where she plans to boke in an emergency, but I guess we'll deal with that when it happens. A group of boys push past us, like a rugby scrum, grabbing the back row of seats. Not wanting to look like complete geeks, we sit down in the middle of the coach: me by the window and Wendy on the outside.

We haven't even set off yet, but already the coach feels muggy and airless. As the others pile on board, Wendy tells me about her morbid fear of coach crashes. She saw a documentary once on BBC2 about a group of schoolchildren who were involved in a coach crash on a trip to Paris. 'It was awful,' she says. 'These poor weans, with their whole future ahead of them, wiped out in an instant. What a waste!' Wendy tells me she gets regular premonitions when travelling; usually they come just before a vomiting episode, but she's quick to point out they're not always a hundred per cent accurate. Like now, if she closes her eyes, she says she can see a big headline on the front of the *Belfast Telegraph*: CHRISTIAN COACH CRASH! And underneath it says *Top Under-16 Ulster Gymnast 'Bendy Wendy' in a coma and fighting for her life*. Next to the story, there's a photograph of a young Wendy, posing in her leotard in front of a G Plan side cabinet plastered in rosettes and gymnastics trophies. She tells me it only happens when she closes her eyes, though.

I take my Walkman and headphones out of a Spar carrier bag, which contains my packed lunch, lovingly prepared by Sadie this morning (two rounds of jam sandwiches, a United Biscuit, a packet of Tayto Cheese and Onion crisps and a carton of Five Alive) and place them on my lap.

Wendy leans in, her ski jacket rustling like sweet wrappers. She smells like a Strawberry Shortcake doll. 'What are you listening to?' she says. I take a complete redner when I realise it's the latest cassette Conor made for me. 'It's just a compilation tape,' I say.

'Have you got *Now That's What I Call Music 14*?' she says. 'I bought it in Woolworths the other day. I've got it here, so I have. Do you think they'd let us play it in the coach?'

'Why don't you ask the driver?'

'I'm going to.' She reaches into her pink sports bag and lifts out a double cassette. I watch her as she sashays to the front of the coach and hands it to the driver, cocking her head to one side and giving him a cheeky smile. He winks at her (boke, he must be at least fifty, like) and takes the cassette. Wendy gives him a wave and, twirling round, struts back up the coach like she's Miss World. She slides back into the seat next to me. 'Sorted,' she says.

Aaron, the youth leader, blows his whistle. Everyone on the coach, now packed with teenagers, stops talking. 'Right, guys,' he says. 'I need your attention a wee minute. We're just waiting on someone coming back from the toilet and then we'll be on our way.'

A guy gets on the coach. It's Aine's friend, Big Gay Willy.

'Oh my God,' I say out loud, not meaning to.

'What is it?' says Wendy.

'I know him.'

Big Gay Willy takes a seat a few rows in front of us. He's wearing sunglasses, a New Kids on the Block T-shirt and ripped jeans. He has a red bandana tied around his head.

'How do you know *him*?' Wendy whispers.

'I don't, really,' I say, trying to distance myself from the very obviously gay fella. 'Friend of a friend.'

'What friend?'

'My friend Aine. You wouldn't know her.'

Part of me was hoping that joining the church youth group would mean a fresh start, a chance to make new mates and reinvent myself, but it's looking like it might be harder to escape my past than I thought.

The driver starts the engine, and the coach starts moving. The cassette Wendy gave him whirs into action, the grand, sweeping orchestral intro to Marc Almond and Gene Pitney's duet 'Something's Gotten Hold of My Heart' filling the coach with sound.

'God, I love this song,' says Wendy, as the coach turns out of the car park and onto the main road. 'Don't you?'

I nod in agreement, thinking to myself what a small world we live in.

'Here,' says Wendy. 'Did you know Marc Almond's gay?'

'Only six miles to go,' I say, pointing out a road sign flashing past.

'Don't,' says Wendy, who has spent most of the journey with her head in a sick bag. She clenches her stomach,

143

retching. 'I can't look at anything moving. It makes me worse, so it does.'

She's a far cry from the chirpy championship gymnast of earlier. Her Princess Diana bouffant is squashed against the back of the coach seat, her clammy cheeks turning a hot shade of pink.

I dig out the *Smash Hits* magazine I've brought to read on the journey – not that I've had a chance to do much reading yet. On the cover, Jason Donovan is wearing a floral shirt, pink shorts and a cool pair of turquoise Converse All Stars. I'd love to be able to afford designer shoes like those, but I only get five pounds a week pocket money, so it would take me ages to save up. I did think about asking Mum to get me a pair for my birthday, but it's not worth the hassle. She'd only get me spoof ones from Primark, telling me they're just as good, and to stop being such a label snob. Inside the magazine, there's a free gigantic poster of Bros, which I remind myself I shouldn't be looking at. The last thing I want to do is light that flipping fire again.

As I'm flicking through my *Smash Hits*, Neneh Cherry's 'Buffalo Stance' starts playing on the coach stereo. Two rows in front of us Big Gay Willy, who's been dead quiet up till now, lets out a loud whoop and raises his fist in the air. 'This song's an absolute belter, so it is! Who's up for a party?' He turns round to face the back of the coach. When he sees me, his face is a picture. For a split second, it's obvious he's trying to work out where he knows me from, and then it dawns on him. 'Here,' he says. 'You're Aine Kelly's friend, aren't you? We met in Belfast the other day?'

'Aye, so we did.' I'm trying to sound surprised, like I've only just figured out who he is.

He leans over the back of his seat. 'Aine's a geg, isn't she? She doesn't half take herself seriously though. Sixteen going on sixty.'

'I haven't really seen much of her these past few weeks.'

'Really?' Big Gay Willy is clearly sniffing the opportunity

for some gossip. He gets up and moves to the row directly in front of us, squeezing his face in between the two coach seats. He gives Wendy a quick glance and mouths, 'What's up with her?'

'She's not feeling too great. Travel sickness.'

'Oh dear. Has she tried sucking on a sweet? I've got a wee tin in my bag that I use on the plane to stop my ears popping.'

'Are we nearly there yet?' Wendy rolls her head from side to side, the fringe on her Princess Diana bouffant looking a bit messed up.

'Three miles,' I say. 'Not long now.'

'Right, lads, who's up for partying like it's 1999?' Big Gay Willy unzips his sports bag and pulls out a two-litre bottle of Lilt and a multipack of cheesy Quavers. Handing me a plastic cup, he screws open the Lilt, which fizzes everywhere. He pours some into my cup and I take a sip. It tastes like pineapple piss.

'I'm not really meant to have sugary drinks,' says Wendy.

'Why not?' Big Gay Willy says. 'You got diabetes or something?'

'No, it's just my ma won't allow them in the house. She says they'll make me hyper.'

'Sure, that's the whole fuckin' point!' he says, ignoring her protests and pouring her a drink. 'Here, get that down you. What your ma doesn't know won't kill you.'

'Well, maybe a wee one,' says Wendy, reluctantly taking a plastic cup.

'Cheers, girlies,' says Big Gay Willy. 'We're gonna have the time of our *lives* on this trip.' And with that, he pours himself a Lilt and launches into the theme from *Dirty Dancing*.

We're about a quarter of the way into our five-and-a-half mile, wet and windy trek through Tollymore Forest when our group, led by Aaron, arrives at the foot of Parnell's Bridge. Reading from his foldaway map, Aaron explains that the bridge, built in 1842, crosses the Shimna River. None of us could care less about any of this boring historical stuff, but we stop for a moment, watching the clear water rippling over moss-covered stones. Wendy gets her Kodak out of her bag and asks me to take a photo. Grinning at the camera, she shrieks as the wind blows her hair in all directions.

Later on, Big Gay Willy points at Wendy, as she runs ahead of us over the bridge. 'She fancies you, so she does.'

'Do you think so?' I say, taking a redner.

'Aye, I can smell it a mile off.'

'Really?'

'It's obvious. I'll bet you any money yous are seeing each other by the end of the day.'

We carry on walking, tramping through a winding maze of pathways, past follies and grottoes surrounded by conifer trees. Before long we come to a boundary wall. Up ahead is Luke's Mountain, its steep craggy peaks peering at us through the misty drizzle.

'Can you take a photo of us?' says Wendy, handing her camera to Aaron. We stand with our backs against the boundary wall, Luke's Mountain behind us. I'm in the middle, with Wendy on my left. She leans in, resting her cheek on my shoulder. Big Gay Willy, on my right, pulls a stupid face, yelling at us to give a thumbs up.

'Smile,' says Aaron. Winding the film forward, he hands the camera back to Wendy.

We continue our trek in a zigzagging fashion for another half hour or so until we reach another bridge, which Aaron tells us is called 'Hore's Bridge'.

'Whore's Bridge?' Big Gay Willy laughs, running on ahead of us. He freezes dead in the middle of it, posing with his hands on his hips and pouting. 'Here, Wendy,' he says. 'Take another one for the scrapbook, will you?'

On the way home, Wendy and I sit next to each other again. Her *Now That's What I Call Music 14* tape is still playing on the coach stereo and, as we turn a corner, 'First Time', by Robin Beck, comes on. Everyone knows this song from the Coca-Cola advert last year and three of the girls – Sharon, Debbie and Louise – who have joined Mike and the other lads, rowdily sing along from the back seat.

'I love this song,' says Wendy, leaning in, her breath smelling of strawberry Hubba Bubba. 'It's sexy, don't you think?' She stares into my eyes, holding my gaze, before resting her hand on my leg. She starts caressing my thigh with her long nails. 'Do you like that?' she whispers.

I nod and she leans forward. Taking off her ski jacket, she covers both our heads with it, then in the very intimate surroundings of our home-made tent, she brushes her nose softly against mine. We kiss and I'm relieved to discover it's not unpleasant. The coach goes over a few bumps in the road, and we knock teeth, but I do my best to convince myself that this is *exactly* how God intended it to be. Man and woman. *Adam and Eve. Not Adam and Steve*, as Mervyn is forever preaching. You never know, if I keep practising being straight, I might even grow to enjoy it.

23.

Tuesday 13th June 1989

Wendy has suggested we meet in Shaftesbury Park for our first official date. It's a warm day in June and, when I get there, I find her lounging on a blanket by the pond in her bikini, reading the latest *Jackie* magazine, a massive pair of white sunglasses perched on her forehead. She waves when she sees me.

'All right,' I say, shuffling up next to her on the blanket.

'Aye,' she says, pointing at the plastic carrier bag by her feet. 'I've made us a wee picnic, so I have.'

'Mega! I'm starving.' I lean over, taking a peep in the bag. Inside are a few rounds of ham sandwiches cut into triangles and wrapped in clingfilm, along with a bag of beef Monster Munch and a couple of Petits Filous.

'Petits Filous!' I gasp. '*Very* posh.' Mum always buys Yellow Pack yoghurt, the local supermarket no-frills budget label, so this is a real treat.

'I forgot to bring spoons, though, so you'll have to lick it straight out of the wee pot. Is that OK?'

'Aye, no bother.'

'Only the best for my Billy boy,' she gushes, rolling over onto her front on the blanket and placing her magazine in front of her. 'Here, I wanted to read you something from my *Jackie*. Listen to this and tell me what you think.'

Dear Ellie,

    I'm 16. Me and my boyfriend have been going out for two months now. We're head over heels in love and have already talked about getting married in the future and having children together. The problem is, he wants to have sex now and I'm not sure I'm ready. He has reassured me he would use a condom, but I'm still scared I might get pregnant or catch AIDS. Are condoms safe?

'Well?' Wendy says, running her thumb under her bikini top. 'What do you think?'

I ponder this reader's dilemma for a second, then say, 'I think she should go for it.'

Wendy rolls her eyes. 'I don't mean *her*, I mean *us*, Billy. Do you want to have sex with me?' Her directness takes me by surprise. I freeze, trying to work out what to say.

'What about the church?' I stammer, at the same time wondering if sex with Wendy might be God's way of helping me fix this unholy fire, which – if I'm being honest with myself – is still blazing inside of me like a disco inferno.

'Just because we're Christians doesn't mean we can't have sex.'

'But doesn't the Bible say you should only have sex with someone when you're married?'

'The Bible says a lot of things. Loads of it is out of date. I know tons of people our age who are having sex.'

'Like who?'

Wendy looks slightly put out. 'I'm not naming names. I'm only saying, like. It's not a sin though, if that's what you're thinking.'

'What do they say the girl in your magazine should do?' I'm learning that girls' magazines offer so much more advice on sex than boys' magazines, which tell you nothing.

Wendy reads it to me.

Dear Anon,
*   While it's great to hear you are in a loving,*
committed relationship, sex is not something you
should ever feel pressured into doing. If it doesn't feel
right, don't do it. In answer to your question about
condoms, they are an effective way of preventing
sexually transmitted diseases and pregnancy, but
obviously there are still some risks attached. In most
cases, however, they are very effective.

'I've got a condom at home,' I blurt out, reassured by the matter-of-fact advice dished out by *Jackie* magazine's in-house agony aunt.

'Really?' Wendy shoots me a suspicious look. 'Wait, are you telling me you're not a virgin?'

I laugh. 'No. Of course I'm still a virgin. I've not used it, or anything.'

'Why have you got a condom then? Men don't carry condoms unless they're intending to use them, right?'

'It was a present.'

'A present?'

'Aye, a present,' I say. 'From my friend Conor.'

'You've never mentioned a friend called Conor before.'

'We've only just started seeing each other. You can't expect to know everything about me.'

'So, this Conor fella, how do you know him?'

'He's a mate – from school.'

'Why did he give you a condom as a present?'

'It's the sort of thing boys do. I've not opened it. It's still in the packet.'

'I should hope so! Where is it? Have you got it on you?'

'No. It's in the sock drawer next to my bed.'

'So do you want to have sex with me then?'

A mother swan emerges from the pond, her four ducklings in tow. She ruffles her feathers, before curling up on the grass, her babies huddled together next to her.

'When?' I ask her.

'I dunno.' She pauses for a moment, then says, 'How about your birthday, next week?'

I nod and say yes. Even though I'm feeling under pressure, this might be my chance to prove to myself once and for all that I'm normal.

24.

Tuesday 19th September 2023

For the past week or two, I've been setting the alarm two hours earlier than usual so I can devote my mornings to job hunting. Without a routine, it's all too easy to slip into bad habits – moping around the house, watching too much daytime TV. Having spent a lot of time polishing my CV to perfection, I signed up to a few recruitment agencies, and this morning I'm delighted to find an email in my inbox from the editor of one of the Belfast newspapers keen to arrange an informal chat with me over the phone about possibly doing some freelance work on their entertainment pages. I type a quick reply saying I'd be delighted, and to let me know a suitable date.

Later, I decide to take a walk over to the cemetery to visit Dad's grave. On my way, I think about how much calmer I've felt since coming home to Northern Ireland. I've rekindled an old friendship, I have a neighbour I can talk to, and things are even starting to look up on the job front. Maybe being here isn't so bad after all. Is there any point in going back to Margate, I wonder? What would I be going back to?

My phone rings, interrupting my thoughts. It's Aine. She says she's been doing some digging on the internet and has found an address for Andy Stone.

'He runs his own company. E-Zee Records. He's listed as director – since 2014. According to the website, he's still active.'

'Is there an address?'

'Yeah. He's local. Lives in one of those massive houses on the Belfast Road, opposite the primary school. I looked it up on Google Maps.'

'What about his phone number?'

'No number, but there's an email address and a link to his website. He sells second-hand records.'

'What else does it say on there?'

'Jesus, mister. Twenty questions, houl your horses. I'm looking now. OK, so there's another appointment listed here for him. It says here he was treasurer at the Holywood Church from 1999 to 2010. He resigned from there on 31st August 2010. It also gives his date of birth as 1950.'

There's a brief pause while I do the maths. 'He's seventy-three, then.'

'Definitely still alive.'

'So how do you want to play this? Should we drop him an email?'

'Might get his guard up. I reckon we need to be a bit more subtle than that.'

'I have an idea,' I say. 'Better to talk about it in person, though. Do you want to come round mine?'

'What time?'

'About seven thirty?'

'I'll need to run it past Alex first. They've got the car this evening. Give me a second.'

I hear Aine yelling 'Alex!' several times, then the sound of her tramping upstairs. The phone goes quiet. A minute or so later, she's back on the line.

'It's a date. What are you cooking me?'

'Something retro from *Delia Smith's Complete Cookery Course*.'

Aine laughs. 'Hilarious. Looking forward to it already.'

25.

Saturday 17th June 1989

On the morning of my sixteenth birthday, I give Aine a call. She answers the phone after two rings. 'Hey, stranger. I was beginning to think you'd dumped me for Jesus.'

'Hey,' I say, ignoring the sarcastic comment. 'Are you coming to my party later?'

'What party?' She pauses. 'Joke! Of course I'm coming. Happy Birthday, Billy! I wouldn't miss it for the world.'

Since I joined the church a few weeks ago, Aine and I haven't spoken much, so we've got some catching up to do.

'So, what's the gossip then?'

'I met someone.'

'Oooh, how exciting. What's his name?'

'It's a girl.'

'A girl? Seriously?'

I twist the telephone cord around my finger. 'Look, forget what I told you the other day. I don't know what came over me.'

'Really? But I thought . . .'

'I was confused.'

'Okaaay, I see. So, what's her name? Do I know her?'

'Wendy.'

'Wendy who?'

'Johnson. Wendy Johnson.'

'Sounds like a good solid Protestant name to me. At least your ma will be pleased.'

'Mum doesn't care about stuff like that.'

'Are you having me on? She's not exactly one of my biggest fans.'

'What gives you that idea?'

'I rang you while you were away. She was rude to me down the phone.'

'You're joking. Really? What did she say?'

'She said – and I quote – *my son is spending the day with his new Christian friends.*'

'What's wrong with that?'

'It was the way she said "new", like I was an old friend. She was being sly.'

'Mum's not like that,' I say, knowing it's exactly the sort of comment Mum would make. 'She likes you, Aine,' I lie.

'Aye, right. Whatever.' An awkward pause. 'So tell me about this new girlfriend of yours then?'

'She's nice. You'll like her, I think.'

This is such a lie. I'm dreading them meeting. Aine's going to hate Wendy's guts and the feeling will be mutual. It'll be like those *Dynasty* scenes, where Alexis and Crystal hurl each other around a penthouse in a massive catfight, pillow feathers billowing everywhere.

'Is she hot?'

'Jesus, Aine. Let's not get carried away.'

'Hmm.'

'*What?*' I can't help sounding defensive.

'Nothing,' says Aine primly. 'What time do I need to be there?'

'Seven.'

'Cool. I'm meeting up with Conor in the park beforehand.' My stomach flutters. 'Conor's coming?'

'Yeah, why?'

'Oh, nothing, but have you spoken to him recently?'

'Yeah, this morning. He seemed fine.'

'Fine? Really?' So, he's obviously not too upset about the fact we haven't seen each other for a few weeks. Not that it matters, I remind myself. I'm with Wendy now.

'Is everything OK, Billy?' says Aine.

I want to talk about Conor, about the fact we haven't spoken since that night at the hut, but I promised him I wouldn't tell anyone about us, and it would only mean dragging up the whole gay thing again. I've been trying my best to put all that stuff behind me.

'Yeah,' I say lightly. 'I'm good. I'll see you later then.' I hang up the phone, ever so slightly annoyed with myself that Conor still has this hold on me.

26.

Tuesday 19th September 2023

Aine arrives at Mum's house half an hour late. 'Before you say anything, Billy, it wasn't my fault,' she says, handing me a bottle of Tesco's Finest Pinot Grigio. 'Alex was having a meltdown over what to wear. They're on a date tonight, so they are.'

'Oooh, who with?'

'Some fella from school. They showed me a photo of him. He's quite handsome. Looks a bit like a young Kiefer Sutherland.'

Aine tells me they're meeting in Libertines, one of Belfast's newer gay bars, which warms my heart. When I was a teenager, Belfast had only one gay bar, The Crow's Nest, which was on the fringe of Cathedral Quarter, but I was too young to go there myself. It's lovely to hear how the city has changed, to think that young LGBT people now have the freedom to be themselves in a way we didn't.

We go through to the living room. Aine gazes around in disbelief. 'Wow, it's like a time warp. I don't think this house has changed since the last time I was here. How long since your ma decorated the place – 1987?'

I laugh. 'Did I tell you I found a jar of mixed herbs in the cupboard the other day with a best-before date of the early eighties?'

Aine pulls a disgusted face. 'Boke. I hope you haven't used them in tonight's dinner?'

'God, no. I've made a Delia lentil and vegetable moussaka, so I had to go up to the big Tesco earlier and buy fresh parsley and a jar of nutmeg. Although, Mum's old herbs and spices got me thinking. Maybe I could keep hold of them and open the house up as a museum. Charge people entry. The eighties are going through a bit of a renaissance, aren't they?'

She laughs. 'Too right. Alex is constantly raiding my wardrobe. The other day they went out in an old denim jumpsuit and denim jacket of mine. Double denim, like. I always thought that was a fashion no-no.'

Aine points at the gold-framed photo of Mum on the mantelpiece, looking the epitome of 1980s glamour with her permed hair and Elizabeth Duke jewellery. 'Speaking of fashion, look at your mum. She was cool. I know we never really saw eye to eye, but I always thought she was dead stylish. She's probably younger than me in that photo. God, it makes you think, doesn't it? Where does the time go, eh?'

I nod, remembering Aine's turbulent relationship with my mother, in particular a massive argument they had with each other on the night of my sixteenth birthday party. Fetching us a couple of wine glasses from the kitchen, I pour us both a generous glass of Pinot Grigio.

Aine asks me how Mum is doing, and I fill her in on what's been happening on my visits to the hospital with Bev. Later, we move on to the subject of my job search. I tell her about the email I received this morning from the editor of *Belfast Life*. 'They don't pay a huge amount of money, but you never know, it could lead to something more permanent.'

'Sounds right up your street,' says Aine. 'I'll keep everything crossed for you.' She grins, curling her feet up on the sofa and tucking them under a cushion embroidered with the words *God is Love*. 'So, what's this plan you've come up with to do with Andy Stone then?'

'Well, I figured that if Andy knew Mum and Mervyn well, I could approach him for a chat.'

Aine wrinkles her nose. 'Won't that be a bit weird? Especially if he knows you two weren't speaking.'

'Oh, Mum won't have said anything to him about our falling-out. I doubt she would've told him I'm gay. She would've been too embarrassed.'

'Even so, what reason would you have to contact him?'

'I was thinking I could spin him some yarn that I'm researching an article on the rave scene in Northern Ireland in the late eighties and early nineties. And how clubbing helped bring together the two sides of our community, Catholic and Protestant. That, as someone who was heavily involved in music at the time, he'd be the ideal person to interview. What do you think?'

'Sounds plausible. I like it.'

'And at some point, obviously, I can steer the conversation towards Conor and his disappearance.'

'Makes sense,' says Aine, cupping her glass of wine in both hands. 'So, are you going to call him first? Send an email?'

'I thought I'd start with an email. If he doesn't reply, I'll give the number on his website a ring.'

Aine raises her glass. 'Cheers to us, Northern Ireland's very own Cybill Shepherd and Bruce Willis.'

'Cagney and Lacey, more like,' I say with a giggle. 'How about I get the laptop out and we can work on the email together?'

27.

Saturday 17th June 1989

It's the day of my sixteenth birthday and the kitchen table is overflowing with party food. Cocktail sausages and sausage rolls, family-sized bags of crisps, frozen mini pizzas, burgers, crusty baps, huge tubs of coleslaw and potato salad.

While Mum is upstairs getting changed, Mervyn and me have been busy putting up decorations. We've covered the entire downstairs of the house with bunting, balloons and streamers, pinning a giant 'Happy Birthday' banner on the wall behind the sofa.

I'm bursting with excitement but am also a bag of nerves. Not only is this the first big party I've ever had, but I'm introducing my family and friends to my first ever girlfriend. Speaking of Wendy, Mum was absolutely over the moon when I told her we'd started seeing each other. She gave me a massive hug and told me I'd made her the happiest mother in the whole of Northern Ireland. Seeing her so chuffed has made me realise I'm doing the right thing. I can't remember the last time she was so proud of me.

At bang on 5.30 p.m., Wendy is the first to arrive, dolled up to the nines in a denim jacket, denim shorts turned up at the knees, black tights, red ankle socks and a pair of green Converse All Stars. She's even had her hair done especially for my party.

'Loving the new perm!' I say, kissing her on both cheeks.

'Thank you! I based my look on The Reynolds Girls.

They were on *Top of the Pops* the other day. Dead trendy, so they are.'

'You look mega!'

As if on cue, Mum appears at the top of the landing. She and Mervyn decided they were going full-on fancy dress tonight, so she's wearing a tight-fitting lime-green Lycra dress, neon-pink stilettos and a massive Carmen Miranda-style hat, weighed down with plastic fruit, which looks like it might topple over at any moment. Bounding down the stairs like a cash-hungry contestant on *The Price is Right* (no mean feat in six-inch heels), she beams from ear to ear. I've not seen her this happy since before we lost Dad, and it's all down to me – the choices I've made. If anything, this makes me even more determined to please her.

'I'm Sadie, Billy's mother,' she gushes, throwing herself at Wendy, the bracelet on her wrist jangling with novelty fruit trinkets. 'Look at you, aren't you *gorgeous*?'

Wendy blushes, taking a step back. 'I love your outfit, Mrs McQueen. It's fantastic, so it is!'

'Auch, none of this Mrs McQueen nonsense. Call me Sadie.' Mum pats the sides of her hair with both hands, drawing attention to the pair of tiny red cherries dangling from each ear. 'Sure, you're practically family now, so you are.'

Ushering Wendy into the hallway, she offers to take her denim jacket, hanging it over the end of the banister. Just at that moment, Mervyn emerges from the kitchen looking every bit the alpha male. He's dressed in a glittering all-in-one white and silver Wild West costume, a tray of raw sausages in one hand and a pair of barbecue tongs in the other.

'Here, Wendy, check out this big hunk of a Rhinestone Cowboy,' squeals Mum. 'This is my fella, Mervyn.'

Mervyn grabs Mum by the waist, bending her over his knee and smacking her on the backside. 'Yee-hah! Giddy up, love!' he hollers, like he's John Wayne and she's Dollar, his faithful, long-suffering movie horse. What's got into her?

I mean, it's not even as if she's had anything to drink apart from half a SodaStream and lime. Wendy, who must be feeling a bit overwhelmed by all the madness, just waves and smiles as Mervyn introduces himself.

'Howdy-doody, Wendy,' he says, looking her up and down in a way which makes me cringe. 'With a pair of legs like that you'll make a man out of this wee fella yet.'

If I've taken a massive redner, Wendy doesn't seem to have noticed. She smiles politely, before turning her attention back to me.

'Here, I got you something.' She hands me a parcel wrapped in Jesus Saves paper. 'It's only wee, but I thought you'd like it.'

'Thank you,' I say, taking the parcel and tearing it open. A Lynx Oriental gift set with matching deodorant and shower gel.

Mum lets out a cry of delight. 'Auch, Wendy. You know him well. What a lovely present. Billy loves his smellies, don't you, son?'

'I got you this too.' She hands me an envelope. Inside is a Forever Friends card. I open it and read the message:

I love you, Billy McQueen.
Your forever girlfriend,
Wendy xxx

A cloud of cigarette smoke billows from the living room like a bomb just went off. Wendy coughs, which to be fair is how most people tend to react when they encounter Granny McQueen for the first time; she chain-smokes, an alternating mix of full-strength Lambert & Butler and Honeyrose herbal cigarettes (which are even smellier than the real ones). God help anyone who tries to tell her smoking is bad for her health – she's as staunchly loyal to her beloved 'fegs' as she is to her great Protestant hero, King William of Orange.

'Is that the wee girl?' Granny croaks from her place on the settee. 'Bring her in here. I want to meet her.'

A sixty-a-day smoker from the age of fifteen, Granny McQueen has inhaled so many cigarettes over the course of her lifetime, she's started to resemble one. Thin as a match, with a tuft of orange nicotine-stained hair, she puts down her copy of *People's Friend* and takes off the reading glasses hanging on a chain round her neck, to get a better look at my girlfriend.

'Jesus, you know who she's the spitting image of?' she cries, pointing a gnarled finger at Wendy before even bothering to introduce herself. 'Her off the TV. Yer ginger woman. Fuck's sake, what do you call her?' She snaps her fingers.

'What ginger woman do you mean, Granny?' I say, wondering what on earth Wendy must be thinking of my family right now.

Wendy leans into me, whispering. 'She must mean Pam in *Dallas*. Victoria Principal. People are always saying I look like her.'

'Do you mean Pam in *Dallas*, Granny?' I say.

'God no, not her. Who am I thinking of?' She raps her forehead with her knuckles.

Mortified, Wendy folds her arms across her chest. Mum, interrupting, offers Granny a drink, but she waves her away, telling her to stop fussing.

'Ginger!' She shouts like she's giving clues on a TV game show. 'Singer. Big teeth.'

Mum and I look at each other in total embarrassment.

'Cilla Black, that's it!' Granny McQueen points a finger at Wendy. 'Spitting image, so she is.'

'She looks nothing *like* Cilla Black!' Mum says, turning to Wendy. 'Ignore her. She's blind as a bat without her glasses.'

'I might be blind but I'm not deaf, Sadie.'

'All right, well, why don't I get you that wee Guinness you asked for, Gloria?' says Mum, flapping her hands and disappearing back into the kitchen.

Granny McQueen pats the sofa cushions either side of where she's sitting. 'Come and join your oul gran, the pair of you.'

Reluctantly we both take a seat, Granny McQueen perched between us both. 'Reach us my bag from down the side there, Billy, love,' she says.

Snatching her handbag from me, she snaps open the clasp. Rummaging around inside, she pulls out a half-eaten tube of Halls Mentho-Lyptus and shoves it under Wendy's nose. 'Would you like one?'

'What are they?' says Wendy, with a look of horror, and clearly still raging about being told she looks like a woman more than twice her age.

'Cough sweets,' says Granny McQueen.

Wendy wrinkles her nose. 'I haven't got a cough.'

You will after you've been sat here for ten minutes, I think, but I keep my mouth shut.

Wendy takes a sweet and unwraps it, cautiously. There's some loose tobacco stuck around it. Too polite to say anything, Wendy scrapes it off with her nail before popping it in her mouth. I take one too, wishing I had a normal granny like everyone else. One who offers me Rolos, or Fruit Pastilles, instead of bloody cough sweets.

'So how long have yous two been courting then?'

'Only a couple of weeks,' I say. I'm trying to save Wendy from the embarrassment of having to answer any more of Granny McQueen's random questions.

'Early days then.' She sighs and reaches into her bag for a herbal cigarette.

'I tell you something, Wendy, you've done us all a favour by putting us out of our misery. I've always thought our Billy was a fruit.'

Oh my God. What is my granny like? Right now, I want to disappear down the gap between the sofa cushions and never come back.

Granny laughs, poking me in the ribs with her free

(non-smoking) hand. 'Here, do you remember the impressions you used to do when you were a wee lad, Billy? Auch, you were a geg, so you were.'

'Stop it, Granny. You're embarrassing me.'

Granny McQueen has no intention of stopping, though. 'He's a great mimic. Aren't you, son? Who was that singer you used to do?'

There's a pause. Wendy hazards a guess. 'George Michael?'

Granny McQueen almost chokes. 'Good God, not him,' she says. 'Now there's a fruit if ever I saw one. You know the one I'm on about, Billy. Her with the hair.'

'Her?' says Wendy.

I realise there's no point even attempting to get out of this one. 'Kate Bush, Granny. I used to do an impression of Kate Bush.'

'That's the one.' Granny laughs, her phlegmy chest rattling. 'It was hilarious, Wendy. You should've seen him, prancing around in front of the electric fire in his ma's flameproof nightie.'

Wendy stands up. 'Where's the toilet? I need to go to the toilet.'

'Upstairs on your right, the door next to the hot press.'

She rushes out of the room and bounds up the stairs. I hear the bathroom door slamming, the sound of the bolt being pulled across.

Granny McQueen flicks her ash into a pot plant on the table in front of her. 'She seems like a nice girl.' She takes another quick puff. 'What's her surname?'

'Johnson.'

'You did well there, son. You've made your oul gran awful proud.'

Personally, I'm feeling anything but proud right now. In fact, I'm totally scundered. What is it about Northern Irish people and their complete lack of tact? You need skin as thick as a rhino's if you're going to survive around here.

'I'm just going to check she's OK,' I tell Granny McQueen,

running upstairs after Wendy and wondering what sort of state she's going to be in. I'm also wondering what sort of state the bathroom is in after all of us getting ready in there earlier. It's probably an absolute tip. What will Wendy think of us?

I knock on the door. 'Wendy, it's me. Can I come in?' At first there's no answer, and then the latch clicks. I push open the door to find Wendy slumped on the floor with her back to the towel rail. Her eyes are puffy, and she has mascara running down both cheeks.

'Please tell me I don't look like a forty-year-old woman,' she says, between breaths. 'I mean, don't get me wrong, my family loves Cilla, but . . .' Her voice breaks and she lets out a sob.

I pick up the crochet bride doll toilet roll cover from its place on the window ledge and sit down next to Wendy. Pulling the toilet roll out from underneath, I tear off some tissue, handing it to her. As she wipes her eyes and blows her nose, I fiddle with the multiple folds of the doll's lacy gown. My family are a major embarrassment. I'm actually lost for words.

'Why can't you answer me, Billy? Do I or do I not look like Cilla Black?'

'You look nothing like her.'

'But surely I must look a bit like her for your granny to say that? Is it my teeth? Is that what it is?' Wendy covers her mouth with her hand, choking back more tears.

'You have lovely teeth. Ignore her, seriously.'

'Only I can't believe I went through two whole years of braces – *two years* – for someone to say I look like that.'

'You don't, though.'

'But I *do*!' Wendy grabs the crochet doll off me and flings it at the wall, where it slams against the tiles and drops into the bath.

It sounds really mean of me, but I'm not sure I can put up with any more of this tonight. I know Wendy's upset, but it's my sixteenth birthday. I want to be celebrating downstairs, not stuck in the toilet with my drama queen girlfriend.

The doorbell buzzes downstairs. I stand up. Reaching down, I offer Wendy my hand. 'C'mon, you. My friends are here. We need to get back to the party.'

Wendy refuses to budge. 'You go. I can't face it.'

'Are you joking me? You can't stay in here all night.'

'Just *go*, will you?'

I sigh and leave. Wendy kicks the door shut behind me, sliding the bolt across. At least things can't get any worse. I'll check on her again in a bit.

'Happy Birthday, matey.' Aine grins at me from the bottom of the stairs, giving me a little wave. I rush down and throw my arms around her, feeling instantly better.

'You smell nice,' I say.

'Patchouli oil. My ma reckons I smell like an old hippy.'

'I love it. Just like Madonna.' Everyone knows that Madonna sprayed patchouli oil on the inside sleeve of her recent *Like A Prayer* LP.

'Exactly. Don't tell anyone I listen to Madonna, though. You'll ruin my street cred. Actually, forget I said that. She's cool. I don't mind her latest record.'

Aine gives a twirl. 'What do you think of my outfit?' To be honest, she isn't dressed that much differently than normal: black DMs, black tights, black T-shirt. 'What about the skirt? Is it too short?'

She runs her hands over the stretchy black-and-white fabric. I've seen Carol Decker from T'Pau wearing something similar in one of their videos, but I don't mention this to Aine, as – unlike me – she thinks T'Pau are naff.

'You look amazing.'

'Cheers, kiddo. By the way, I got you something.' She hands me a shoebox. It's unwrapped, but there's a huge pink bow on top. 'I hope they're the right size.'

I don't need to open the box. The massive logo gives the game away. My hands trembling, I lift open the lid. I let out

167

a little cry of happiness when I see what's inside. Wrapped in tissue paper is a brand-new pair of turquoise Converse All Stars, the exact same ones Jason Donovan was wearing on the cover of my *Smash Hits* magazine.

I'm practically jumping up and down on the spot with excitement. 'Wow! Aine, these must've cost you an absolute bomb.'

'You're worth it.' Aine tells me she's been saving the money she earns part-time from Carrick Rocks for weeks now. 'I wanted to get you something special,' she says. 'It's not every day you turn sixteen.'

Taking a seat on the bottom stairs, I kick off my old Primark trainers and slide my feet into my new Converse. They look amazing. I feel just like a pop star.

'Billy, can you give us a hand getting these mushroom vol-au-vents out of the oven?' Mum hollers from the kitchen, bringing me right back down to earth.

'I better go,' I say, quickly tying my trainers. 'Is Conor not with you?'

'He's on his way. I left him drinking in the park with Willy, his new best mate.'

'They know each other?'

'I introduced them the other day. They get on like a house on fire.'

I feel a pang of emotion. Not jealousy, it can't be jealousy. Whatever it is, I shake it off.

'Where's Wendy?' asks Aine.

'Upstairs, getting ready.'

'Ace,' says Aine, waltzing off to the back garden. 'Really looking forward to meeting her.'

'This is a nightmare, Billy. These are burnt to a crisp!'

Mum is bent over the oven, which has more smoke pouring from it than Granny McQueen's mouth. She pulls out a tray of parched, blackened pastry and flings it, clattering, onto the work surface. The smoke alarm starts wailing.

'My goodness,' she says, flapping her hands. 'Do me a favour, love, and switch that thing off.'

I grab a tea towel and wave it underneath the alarm until it stops. I'm just about to go upstairs and check on Wendy when the doorbell buzzes again.

Conor's here. My stomach lurches. He looks great in a long-sleeved hooded top, bleached jeans and Timberland boots. Big Gay Willy is standing behind him in the porch. 'S'cuse me, fellas,' he says, pushing past us. 'I'm gagging for a drink, so I am. I'll leave you two to talk. Happy Birthday, Billy boy!'

Conor blushes. He hands me a cassette tape. 'Sorry it's nothing t-too exciting. I'm a bit skint, so I am.' Without thinking, I breathe in his Jazz aftershave, the familiar scent making my heart race. 'I'd look at it later if I was you,' he adds. 'Somewhere private, maybe?'

I nod, slipping his gift into the pocket of my neon-pink Hawaiian shorts.

'How you been?'

'Not too bad. Yourself?' He stares down at his feet, avoiding eye contact.

'Good, actually. I don't know if Aine told you, but I've started seeing someone.'

'Aye, she said.'

'Her name's Wendy.'

'That's nice.'

There's an uncomfortable silence.

'Aine's already here,' I say. 'She's in the back garden if you want to go through.'

I nip upstairs to check if Wendy has finished having her tantrum. The bathroom door is ajar. She's no longer in there. I pop in to rescue Mum's crochet bride doll from the bath, shoving the toilet roll back up her skirt and returning her, pride of place, to the window ledge.

Coming out, I hear Debbie Gibson's 'Lost in Your Eyes' playing from the stereo in my bedroom. I open the door to find Wendy sprawled on my duvet, the turn-ups of her denim shorts raised slightly to reveal that the black tights she's wearing are stockings.

'Do you like my sexy lingerie?' she says, stroking her legs. 'I hope you haven't forgotten your promise.' She pats the bed, willing me to join her.

'Not now, Wendy,' I stammer. 'We need to go back downstairs. Everyone's waiting.'

Wendy creases her forehead, pouting like a particularly peed-off cherub. 'What's the matter, Billy? Do you not fancy me, then? Might this have anything to do with what your granny said?'

'What my granny said?'

'About you being a fruit.' She stares at me, biting her lower lip. 'Because I know *for a fact* you're not.' She slides her finger into her mouth, letting out a gentle moan.

'Ignore Granny, she loves winding people up. She always says things that aren't true.'

'Fair enough, but do you remember your stepdad's comment?'

'Mervyn's not my stepdad,' I correct her. 'He's my mum's partner. There's a difference.'

'Whatever.'

I shrug. 'Well, what did he say then?'

'He said I could make a man of you.'

'What's that supposed to mean?'

'Don't act all innocent with me. I mean, just look at my lovely legs, Billy,' she whispers, stroking her thighs and giggling. 'What sorta man wouldn't be turned on by these lovely legs?'

On the cassette player, Debbie Gibson is singing about how good she feels being lost in her lover's eyes, but I'm not feeling anything at all. To be honest, all I want to do is get myself away from this embarrassing situation as fast as possible.

'Not now, Wendy,' I say, edging back towards the bedroom

door. As I run downstairs to join the others, I hear her shouting after me, 'Call yourself a man, Billy McQueen! You better start acting like one, or I swear to God, I'm dumping you!'

28.

Now

Friday 29th September 2023

After ringing the doorbell to Andy Stone's rather grand-looking Edwardian house, I take a step back to get a better view of the property. The front of the building boasts four large rooms; directly above the front door is a balcony, presumably leading out of the master bedroom. The house has been modernised, with new windows and trendy black gloss wooden shutters, which are closed, so I can't see inside.

It was a week or so before Andy replied to my email, and Aine and I agreed it would be better if I met with him on my own, to keep any suspicions he might have to a minimum. As I stand in the porch, my phone vibrates in my pocket. It's a text from her: Good luck, kiddo. With you in spirit x

I'm just about to double-tap her message with a thumbs up when the door opens. A young man, in his mid- to late twenties, stands in the hallway. He's wearing a white ribbed vest, thigh-length frayed denim shorts, white sports socks and trainers. Toned, tanned and smooth, he's sporting the faintest hint of a moustache on his upper lip.

'Hey, what's up?' He grins, revealing a set of immaculate Hollywood-white veneers. 'You must be Billy.' He extends a muscular arm, giving me a firm handshake. 'I'm Zach, Andy's PA.'

He has one of those voices that goes up at the end of each sentence, like it's a question. I try to place his accent. Canadian, maybe?

'Nice to meet you, Zach,' I say, stepping inside.

Ahead of me, in the middle of the hallway, is a wide set of stairs, which leads to a landing, where two narrower sets of stairs split in opposite directions. It's the sort of staircase I've only ever seen in films or historic houses. Zach ushers me into a room immediately on my right. Aside from a wall of records and CDs, the room is sparsely furnished with two massive black leather couches and a large, round, glass coffee table, a selection of music magazines – *Rolling Stone*, *Record Collector*, *The Wire* – neatly spread out on it. There's a Bang & Olufsen CD player mounted on one wall, a massive print of the cover of Grace Jones' *Warm Leatherette* album next to it. A large white egg chair faces the window, offering a view of the sea. A few pot plants are dotted around the edges of the room.

Zach points at a black Smeg fridge tucked away in the corner. 'Help yourself to a drink. I'll go and let Andy know you're here.'

I take a seat on one of the sofas, picking up a magazine and flicking through it. My phone buzzes again in my pocket, but I ignore it this time. Eventually, Zach comes back. There's a man behind him, tall, with long grey hair tied in a ponytail at the back. He's dressed in a suede waistcoat, denim jeans and cowboy boots.

'Billy McQueen,' he says, reaching out to shake my hand. 'You don't know me, son, but your mother and I go back a long way. You said she'd had a stroke. How's she getting on?'

'Not great, to be honest. She's still in hospital,' I say. 'They're hoping she'll make a recovery though, so fingers crossed.'

'I'm praying for her,' he says. 'I'll tell you something, though, your oul ma's a tough cookie. Trust me, she'll be OK.' He smiles. 'Sure, budge up there, son. Zach will get us a drink.'

I shift along the sofa to make room for him.

'What can I get you?' asks the young man. 'Beer? Soda?'

'I'll have a beer,' says Andy. He turns to me. 'What about you, Billy? Would you like a beer?'

'Just a Coke, please, if you've got one. Diet, preferably.'

While Zach goes to fetch our drinks, Andy gets comfortable on the sofa, easing his back into one of several massive white cushions and manspreading his legs.

'This is an impressive place you've got here,' I say, looking around me and marvelling at the room's minimalist grandeur.

Andy smiles. 'I bought this house when I was working for the church. Managed to pay off the mortgage very quickly. Just as well. There's no way I'd be able to afford it now.'

'So, you're self-employed then?'

He nods. 'I trade in second-hand vinyl. A lot of what I sell is hard to find: white labels, rarities, promos. It's mostly high-energy dance music, you know. People will pay a fair bit of money for records these days. I do pretty much all my business online. And then this one here helps me out with the social media.'

Zach grins, setting our drinks down on the coffee table in front of us.

'How long have you worked here?' I ask him.

He glances at Andy, then at me. 'I've known Andy for a few years now.'

'You're not from round here,' I say. 'Where's the accent from?'

'Canada.'

'How did you end up in Carrick, then?'

He points a finger at Andy. 'He got in touch with me through my Instagram. I used to promote sportswear for an independent fashion brand. Andy liked my work, so he offered me a job as his social media manager. Plus, I've always loved Ireland. My ancestors were from Cork, so I jumped at the opportunity.'

'And you like it here?'

'Oh, yeah. I love my job. Every day is different.' He laughs. 'Anyway, enough about me! It's Andy you're here to talk to.'

He takes a step back. Standing behind his boss, he rests his hand lightly on the man's shoulder, which strikes me as an oddly intimate gesture. Andy shrugs it off, cracking open his Budweiser. 'So, tell me about this article you're writing? Your ma always said you were the creative type.'

Andy nods as I spin him the yarn I previously rehearsed with Aine, that I'm researching an article on rave culture in late eighties Northern Ireland and the impact it had on the peace process.

Andy laughs. 'Well, if it's clubbing stories you want, you've come to the right guy. Those were crazy days, all right, but I'm an open book. Ask me anything. I've nothing to hide, son.'

'Andy's had the most amazing life,' gushes Zach. 'He's . . .' The man clears his throat, which is all it takes to stop his PA mid-sentence. Zach takes a further step back, biting his lip and fiddling with a small gold cross on his neck. There's an awkward pause.

'You got to know Mum through the church, right?' I ask Andy, keen to break the silence.

'That's correct. I started working there in the late nineties.'

'And before that, you were a DJ?'

'I did a bit of DJ'ing, aye, but I was a promoter, essentially. I used to run a very successful club here in Carrick, back in the late eighties and early nineties. It was packed every weekend with young people, ravers.'

'This is Club Babylon, right?'

'You know it? I didn't think you'd be old enough to remember.'

'I only went once. I shouldn't have been there. I was underage at the time.'

He laughs. 'You weren't the only one. It's a rite of passage, isn't it? Sneaking your way into a club. Everyone does it.'

He looks down at his hands, then at me. 'Look, I may as well tell you now. You might know this already, it's no secret, but before I joined the church, I spent a few years in prison. I wasn't guilty, mind you. It was a miscarriage of justice.'

'What happened?'

'Well, to cut a long story short, a few kids got caught dealing drugs on my premises and the peelers accused me of allowing it to happen. They banged me up for a few years. Not long after I was released, I applied for a job with the Holywood Church.'

'And the church didn't have any issues with the fact you'd been in jail?'

Andy shrugs, taking a sip of beer. 'I was very open with Mervyn when he interviewed me for the position of treasurer. He'd seen the story in the newspapers, and he believed in my innocence. You see, about a year or so before I started working for him, I'd been regularly attending services at the church. Mervyn was a fantastic preacher, so he was. I've never seen anything like him. He was better than Billy Graham, honest to God. The effect he had on people, especially the women. When he stood on that pulpit, preaching the gospel, they used to faint, like he was Tom Jones, or something. There'd be hundreds of people in that congregation every weekend – packed to the gills, it was – and yet he made every single person in the room feel like he was speaking to them personally. He'd a special gift, that man. As his wife, your ma was the envy of many a woman in that congregation. What they wouldn't have given to be in her shoes – or her bedroom.' He chuckles.

I nod, remembering my own relationship with Mervyn. Sure, there were times when we got on OK, but that was before I came out. After learning that I was gay, he no longer wanted anything to do with me.

Picking up on what Andy's just told me, I decide to cut to the chase. 'Those kids you mentioned, the ones who got caught dealing. Do you know who they were?'

Andy narrows his eyes. He peels the label off his bottle of Bud, leaving a white trail of sticky paper residue. 'Why do you ask?' he says, his tone shifting to a less friendly one.

I realise I may have overstepped the mark, but a little voice inside urges me to keep pushing him for answers. 'I – I – just thought I might've known them from school or something. I was thinking of my friend Conor Doherty. He went missing around that time?'

At the mention of Conor's name, Andy sets his empty beer bottle on the table. He closes his eyes and starts massaging his temples with his fingers. 'I'm sorry, Billy,' he says. 'I can feel a headache coming on. I get them every now and again.' He calls out to his assistant. 'Zach, would you mind seeing Billy out? I need a lie-down.'

Without so much as a goodbye, he stands up and leaves the room.

Embarrassed, Zach turns to me. 'Sorry, he gets like this sometimes. It's stress. He works too hard. Maybe you can carry on the conversation another day?'

'It's fine,' I say. 'I understand.'

'Anyway,' he says, sounding apologetic. 'It was lovely to meet you.'

'Likewise,' I say. 'I must check out your Instagram. I've got a bit of a record collection myself.'

'Sure thing.' He tears a piece of scrap paper from a notebook on the coffee table and, picking up a pen, he scribbles down his details, handing them to me.

'@Ezeerecordboy.' I nod. 'Thanks, Zach. I'll look you up.'

As soon as I've left the house, I take my phone from my pocket. I quickly download Instagram and set up a basic profile. I find Zach's page easy enough and, after a quick glance at some of the photographs on his feed, I click the follow button, then dial Aine's number.

'So that was all very strange,' I say, as soon as she answers the phone. I explain how Andy cut the meeting short as soon as I mentioned Conor.

'A headache?' says Aine. 'Sounds convenient.'

'Exactly what I thought.'

'Did you manage to find anything out?'

I spend a few minutes filling her in on all the details. Andy's admission that he spent time in prison for suspected drug offences but managed to clear his name. His role at the Holywood Church. I mention he had his PA with him the whole time I was there.

'He has a PA?'

'Yeah. Zach. Cute, twenty-something Canadian. Definite gay vibes. I wasn't quite sure what the arrangement was between the two of them. They were, um, pretty close.'

'What do you mean, close? You don't think they're in a relationship, do you? Andy Stone is in his seventies. Boke.'

'Why would that rule out him being in a relationship with a younger guy? Look at Rod Stewart.'

'I'm just saying, that's quite the age gap, so it is.'

'Yeah. Anyway, Zach gave me his Instagram details.'

'Oh, God, don't tell me *you're* flirting with him too. How old did you say he was again?'

'Mid- to late twenties.'

'You do realise you are old enough to be his dad, Billy?'

I laugh. 'I'm not flirting with him! It's his professional Instagram. He runs the account for Andy, to help promote his record business. Wait, let me find him.' I put Aine on speakerphone and open the Instagram app, typing @Ezeerecordboy into the search bar again. 'Oh, that's weird.'

'What's weird?'

I stare at the screen. 'I was able to see his profile just a minute ago, but I can't now.'

'Maybe he blocked you.'

'Why would he block me?'

'I dunno. Maybe Andy told him to? Tell you what, why don't I look him up? Houl on a minute.' There's a pause as Aine fiddles around with her phone. 'OK. What's the name again? Easy record boy?' I spell it out to her, waiting as she types in the characters. 'Found him,' she says. 'I can see his full profile.' She pauses. 'Sorry, mate, looks like he has blocked you.'

Why would he have blocked me? He seemed quite pleasant. I didn't say anything to upset him, did I?

I listen as Aine scrolls through Zach's feed. There are literally hundreds of photos of him, she tells me. In most of them, he's sitting on a black leather couch, posing with a record, flirting at the camera. From what I can make out, his outfits consist of little more than a vest, shorts and socks, each piece of clothing carefully chosen to complement the colours on the record sleeves. She reads out a list of hashtags, which include things like #vinylcollection #vinyllover #vinyljunkie #dance.

'He's cute, I'll give him that,' she says. 'Surely he's not banging a seventy-year-old, though?'

'I don't know for sure if they're together,' I say. 'It was just a feeling. I might have been reading too much into it. Anyway, Andy was part of the church for many years, so surely being gay is against his religion.'

'Maybe his beliefs have changed. To be fair, most churches are relaxed about different sexualities now, too.'

'I didn't get the chance to ask him about his sexuality. He clearly wanted me out of the house pronto. Put it this way, I don't think he'll be inviting me over for beers anytime soon.'

I hear Aine taking a puff on her vape. 'We can't give up, Billy, not now. I've got a feeling we're on to something too. I'm not sure what, though.'

'Who else can we talk to?'

She exhales. 'Well, there was one person I really wanted to catch up with at the school reunion who didn't make it.'

'Who?'

'William Carson.'

'Big Gay Willy?'

'Aye,' says Aine. 'I've always wanted to know what happened to him. He's not on Facebook, though. Or, if he is, I've never been able to find him. He and Conor became good friends that summer he went missing. We lost touch after everything that happened, but the other day I managed to find his profile on LinkedIn.'

'Really? What's he up to these days?'

'He works for a missing persons charity. He's based in London, I think. I sent him a message. He hasn't replied yet, though. I figured he might know something.' She sighs. 'I guess we'll have to wait and see.'

Walking home, I spot a missed call notification on my phone. A voice message from the hospital. Immediately, I press play, holding the phone to my ear, already imagining the worst-case scenario, my hands shaking in anticipation of what I'm about to hear. Is Mum okay?

29.

Saturday 17th June 1989

It's six o'clock, and more and more guests keep arriving. Before I know it, the back garden is heaving with school friends, relatives and people from church. Technotronic's 'Pump Up the Jam' blares out of Mum's ghetto blaster, encouraging everyone to get their booties on the floor.

'Crikey,' says Aine. 'Who's the Reynolds Girl over there in the denim shorts?'

'That's Wendy,' I say, noticing she's flirting with a bloke from my school. Laughing and joking with him and refusing to look me in the eye.

Aine covers her mouth with her hand, stifling a giggle. 'Oh, Billy, I'm sorry. Trust me to put my foot in it.'

'It's OK,' I say. 'Listen, can I get you a drink? Some punch?'

'Punch? Very posh! Don't mind if I do.'

When I say punch, it's just a large plastic bowl filled with six cartons of Um Bongo juice and a tin of Del Monte fruit cocktail. I grab a ladle and scoop some from the bowl, pouring it into two plastic cups. I hand one to Aine. She sniffs it. 'I take it there's no alcohol in here?'

'What do *you* think? Mum hasn't had any alcohol since she started seeing Mervyn.'

'Just as well I brought my own then.' Aine lifts a silver hip flask from her bag. She unscrews the lid, discreetly pouring some clear brownish liquid into her cup. 'I stole this from the drinks cabinet at home.'

'What is it?' I look around to check no one is watching us.

'Bushmills. It's Dad's, but he never touches it. Do you want some?'

I want to say no, but I'm feeling pretty shaken by what just happened in the bedroom. Maybe a drink will calm me down.

Aine pours a generous slug of whiskey into my punch. I take a sip, choking at the taste. I can't say it's improved things, but it gives me a warm feeling inside.

'Do you know where Conor is?' asks Aine.

'No idea,' I say, giving the garden a glance for signs of him. 'I haven't really had a chance to speak to him yet.'

'He's in a bit of a funny mood tonight,' says Aine.

'What do you mean?'

Aine shrugs. 'Distant, you know? Anyway, I'm sure he's fine. Besides, isn't it about time you introduced me to this new girlfriend of yours?'

Before I can object, Aine grabs my arm and drags me across the garden towards Wendy, who is now sulking alone under a gazebo, holding a paper plate filled with cucumber slices and lettuce.

'Wendy, this is Aine, my best friend,' I say. 'Aine, meet Wendy.'

Wendy scowls down at her limp salad.

'Do you like my trainers?' I say, sheepishly pointing out my new Converse. 'They're a birthday present from Aine.'

Still avoiding eye contact with either of us, Wendy gives my feet a dismissive glance. 'They're all right, I suppose. I mean, if you want *my* opinion, I wouldn't have chosen that colour. It's a bit gay-looking, if you know what I mean.'

I cringe when she mentions the 'G' word. Aine folds her arms. 'Billy chose them,' she snaps. 'They're the ones *he* wanted.'

Before Wendy has a chance to come back with another snarky comment, the music stops. We turn around to see Mum standing by the ghetto blaster. She's holding a saucepan, banging on the side of it with a wooden spoon. Everyone falls silent. 'Where's Billy?' she says, looking around the garden. 'Where's my lovely son?'

I raise my hand and she calls me to come and join her, leading the guests in a rowdy rendition of 'Happy Birthday'. I'm totally cringing, and slightly overwhelmed seeing so many of my friends and family gathered in one place at the same time. There's Granny McQueen, sitting right at the front on a deck chair, fag in hand. Behind her are loads of people from church. I laugh at the sight of Mum's next-door neighbour, Bev, pulling on a party popper, the streamers landing on her husband Norman's bald head like a bad wig. I spy Big Gay Willy, who I've yet to speak to properly. He winks at me, giving me a thumbs up. Mervyn emerges from the kitchen carrying an enormous cake, as big as his John Wayne cowboy hat. The candles flicker as he makes his way through the garden. He sets it down on the small patio table in front of me.

Mum leans over, whispering in my ear. 'Your daddy would be proud of you, son. Make a wish. Make it a good one.'

My eyes well up at the mention of my dad. I close them and wish that I could be with Conor instead of Wendy and somehow please Mum at the same time. It'll never happen, but it's worth a try. I know I shouldn't wish this, but after seeing Conor again at the front door, I can't help it. Wishes are private anyway; it's like a secret that makes me feel better about all the recent drama with Wendy.

Mum starts singing 'For he's a jolly good fellow', and everyone joins in. There are a few cries at the back: 'Speech! Speech!' followed by more clapping and whooping. I'm not used to being the centre of attention, so this is mortifying to say the least.

Once the cheers have died down, I step forward, nervously, to say a few words.

'Um, I'll keep this short because I'm shaking, so I am. Thank you, everyone, for coming tonight, but I especially wanted to thank my mum for organising the party. She spent an absolute fortune in Crazy Prices earlier, so, anyway, yeah . . .'

'Any more of them wee sausages?' shouts Big Gay Willy. Everyone laughs. I glance at Mervyn, who seems less amused.

'Who invited the wee poofter fella?' I hear him mutter under his breath.

'Um, anyhow,' I say, ignoring him. 'I'd also like to thank Mervyn here for helping me put up all the decorations, and for being there for Mum, because I know how happy he's made her.' I turn to look at Mum, and she's crying. Squeezing me close to her, she kisses me on the cheek. Mervyn raises his cowboy hat and takes a bow. Everyone starts clapping like mad.

'Oh, and one more thing,' I say, taking a deep breath and trying to raise my voice over all the cheering. 'There's someone I'd like to introduce to you. I only met this person a few weeks ago, but yeah, so . . .'

'Where are you, Wendy?' shouts Mervyn, addressing the crowd. He spots her, beckoning her over with his hand. 'C'mere, love, and let everyone get a good look at you. Without doubt, the best thing to happen to Billy since sliced bread and, I'm sure she won't mind me saying, an absolute stunner. A lovely-looking girl, gentlemen. Just check out those legs!'

Blushing, Wendy shimmies her way through the garden, waving at everyone like she's royalty. She's very much enjoying this, her moment in the spotlight. When she gets to the front, the crowd start chanting again: 'Speech, speech!'

'Oh, my goodness,' she says. 'You're all too kind. So, firstly I wanted to say Happy Birthday to Billy, and a big thank you to Sadie and Mervyn for putting on this amazing party and, yeah, anyway, I actually have a wee surprise lined up for you all. As some of you might know, I was a finalist in this year's Ulster Under Sixteens Gymnastics competition, so Mervyn asked if I wouldn't mind doing a wee routine for Billy's birthday.' She turns to Mervyn and whispers, 'Do you want to start the music?'

Mervyn presses a button on the ghetto blaster and the hymn 'Lord of the Dance' starts playing. The crowd watches, respectfully quiet, as Wendy stands on her tiptoes, holding her arms out either side in the shape of a cross. Slowly, she begins moving her hands around in tiny circles; circles which gradually increase in size until she's windmilling her arms in great enormous swoops. When it gets to the chorus, she gives us a full gymnastics routine: cartwheels, forward rolls, headstands and high kicks. The crowd clap along, encouraging Wendy into even greater feats of bodily elasticity, and we watch as she twists and flips and bends her body into a range of bold and slightly risqué positions. It's impressive, but slightly mortifying too. Mesmerised, Mervyn can't take his eyes off her, and neither can the other guests. Not Conor though. He's standing next to Aine now and they're whispering to each other. Aine looks like she's about to piss herself laughing.

Things take a turn for the worse when the music suddenly switches to the opening bass line to Sabrina's 'Boys (Summertime Love)'. As soon as the word 'boys' booms from the speakers, Wendy whips off her T-shirt to reveal a neon green boob tube and proceeds to perform what can only be described as an erotic dance, writhing around on the grass in her denim shorts and black tights. Madonna's 'Like A Prayer' video, which recently caused a stir on MTV, pales in comparison, and I catch a massive redner. I don't know where to look, unlike Granny McQueen, who is grinning away and clapping along. Wendy's routine lasts for the song's entire three minutes and fifty-eight seconds and, while technically accomplished, it's excruciatingly painful. Not for the first time today, I wish the ground would open and swallow me whole.

As the finale to her act, Wendy drops down to the ground, performing the splits. Everyone erupts into applause and cheers, apart from Aine, who is doubled over with laughter now. As soon as this is over, we need to have *words*.

As the party gets back into full swing, with everyone dancing to Los Lobos' 'La Bamba', I heave my way through the crowd to look for Aine. I eventually find her upstairs, on her way into the bathroom. She grabs hold of my T-shirt, dragging me in after her, closing and locking the door. She gets straight to the point. 'What the hell, Billy? You can't seriously tell me you like that girl? She's a complete dick!'

Aine's honesty leaves me floundering. The problem is, she knows me too well. I try to think of something to say, but before I get the chance, there's a knock on the bathroom door.

'Billy? Are you in there?' Wendy hammers on the door with her fist. 'Billy! Are you in there? Open up!'

Aine undoes the latch and the door falls open. The look on Wendy's face is priceless.

'What are you two doing in here together?' she snaps, glaring at us. 'Come here *now*, Billy! We need to talk.'

I look at Aine and shrug apologetically. Wendy grabs my arm, pulling me out of the bathroom. She drags me downstairs, through the kitchen and out into the garden.

The music is at full volume now, but thankfully the guests are too busy dancing and having a good time to notice Wendy and me having a row. Wendy barges her way to the punch table, grabs the ladle and pours herself a plastic cup of Um Bongo, taking an angry sip. 'So, what's going on between you and *her*?'

'Nothing,' I stammer. 'She's a friend, that's all.'

'I see. Explain to me why you were locked in the bathroom together then?'

'We were . . . she was upset about something.'

Wendy scowls. 'What's *she* got to be upset about?' There's a pause. 'Oh, I get it. Poor wee Aine's jealous. Is that it?' she says, smirking.

'It's nothing to do with that.'

'Well, why were you on your own in the bathroom with her then?'

Aine arrives with Conor beside her. I do my best to shut out any feelings I have for him, but it's hard. I swallow, my stomach leaping over itself. 'Sorry, have I interrupted something?' Aine says, turning to him. 'Would you like a drink, Conor?'

He nods. Wendy glares at me as Aine picks up two plastic cups and pours punch into them, handing one to Conor.

'Cheers, everyone,' she says, raising her cup. 'Happy Birthday, Billy.'

There's an awkward silence, then a screech of guitars and a clattering of drums as the ghetto blaster plays Transvision Vamp. Aine moves her body in time to the music, a little unsteady on her feet, her words slurring, like she's had way more Bushmills whiskey than she can handle. 'I love this song,' she says. 'Do you know it, Wendy?'

'No,' Wendy snaps. 'Should I?'

Aine turns to me and says, *'Tell That Girl to Shut Up.'*

'Who are you telling to shut up?'

'Calm down, Barbie doll,' laughs Aine. 'It's the name of the song.'

'Don't call me Barbie, you weirdo.'

Aine taps her foot, shooting daggers at her new nemesis. 'So, you're a Christian, are you?'

'What's that got to do with anything?' snarls Wendy.

Aine shrugs. 'I thought Christians were meant to be nice, that's all.'

There's a beat. And then, her face raging, Wendy hurls the contents of her cup in Aine's face. Aine gapes at her, momentarily stunned, before throwing *her* punch over Wendy.

'You're mad!' screams Aine. 'Who do you think you are?'

Grabbing Wendy by the collar of her denim jacket, Aine shoves her face-first into the bowl of punch. Gasping for breath, Wendy emerges, the fringe of her blonde bouffant dripping with Um Bongo and chunks of Del Monte fruit cocktail. Aine takes a step back. She covers her mouth with her hands, as if shocked by what she's just done.

The music stops. People quit dancing and the garden falls deadly silent as Mum barges across the grass towards us. 'What on earth's going on here?' she bellows.

Playing her best little girl act, Wendy bursts into tears. 'It's her, Mrs McQueen,' she cries, pointing at Aine. 'She started it. She's jealous of me and Billy. She wants to split us up.'

Mum gawps at Aine. 'Is that the truth?'

'It's *sher* version of . . . the true . . . the truth,' Aine tries to protest, but her words are coming out jumbled. She shifts her weight from one foot to the other, losing her balance, and almost falls backwards onto a table full of condiments.

Mum turns to me. 'I warned you she was trouble, didn't I? And now she's only gone and ruined your birthday.'

'She hasn't ruined it, Mum,' I say. 'She's . . .'

'What do you mean, she hasn't ruined it?' Mum snaps. She nods her head at Wendy. 'Yon wee girl is in tears there. She's soaking, so she is.' She turns to Aine and says, 'It's time you left now. You're not welcome here. And you can take those two fellas with you.' She nods her head in Conor and Willy's direction. 'Nothing but trouble, you are. Away and leave my family in peace.'

Aine, Conor and Willy look stunned. Conor just stands there, saying nothing. He's taken a complete redner.

Mervyn appears behind Mum. 'What's the matter, Sadie? Have these weans been upsetting you?'

'She has,' says Mum, pointing at Aine. 'The Kelly girl. She's totally ruined Billy's birthday. She physically attacked poor Wendy here.'

Aine sways from side to side, her words slurring. 'You know what? I don't have time to stand here listening to all this shite. Call yourselves Christians?'

'Mind your language,' says Mervyn, tutting. 'I think it's time you went home, wee lady.' He puts a firm hand on Aine's shoulder.

Aine pushes him away. 'Don't call me wee lady, you sexist pig!'

Mervyn turns to me, his face aghast. 'Has she been drinking alcohol?'

'I-I don't think so.'

'The wee girl reeks of it. You can smell it on her a mile off.'

As if on cue, Aine grabs her stomach. Doubled over, retching, she bokes a rusty river of Um Bongo punch all over my new Converse.

30.

Friday 29th September 2023

'She's asleep now,' says the nurse. 'But earlier, when I came to check on her, she had her eyes open for the first time. She was staring out the window, blinking. It's hopefully a sign things are improving.'

Relieved by this tiny piece of good news, I listen to Mum's slow, steady breathing, watching the gentle rise and fall of her chest. I think back to when I was a baby, how she must've done the same with me. Now the roles are reversed.

'Give it time,' says the nurse. 'Stroke recovery can be a slow process.'

'Can I hold her hand?'

'As long as your mum would be comfortable with you doing that if she was awake, then by all means go ahead.'

Would Mum be comfortable? I'm not sure. What if she's still angry with me? It might freak her out, upset her unnecessarily. I turn to Bev, who once again has driven me to the hospital and will be happy to wait patiently, for another hour or so, while I spend time with my mum. 'What do you think, Bev?'

Bev looks up from her *Take A Break* crossword, smiling. 'I can't imagine anything your mother would like more.'

Trusting Bev's advice, I lean over, reaching across the bed, and before I know it, for the first time in over thirty years I find myself holding my mother's hand.

* * *

Later that evening, after pouring myself a glass of wine, I venture upstairs to Mum's bedroom. It's not long before I'm looking through the contents of her wardrobe, sifting through old clothes. A fur coat, which she used to wear in the eighties, feels homely and familiar. I brush it against my cheek, like obsessive old Mrs Danvers in *Rebecca*, enjoying the nostalgia evoked by its soft touch. As a child, I loved being held, like a bear cub, in this mass of fur. Rummaging further, I find an old silk nightie, which reminds me of the many nights when, scared of the dark, imagining all kinds of bogeymen lurking in the shadows, I'd climb into bed with her. She'd hold me close, whisper to me not to worry, that everything was going to be OK.

It's gone 9 p.m., but outside it's still light. I head back downstairs, the evening sun casting a warm glow over the living room. The envelope containing Conor's mixtape is on the arm of the sofa. I pick it up, taking the cassette from its case. Most people got rid of their cassette players years ago, when CDs became all the rage, but Mum still has her old stand-alone hi-fi system with its turntable, analogue radio and double cassette player. Pressing the eject button to open the compartment, I slide the tape into place, pushing the door shut. After pouring myself another glass of wine, I press play.

The first song is Danny Wilson's 'The Second Summer of Love'. Turning up the volume, I settle back into one of Mum's armchairs, smiling and nodding to myself at how relevant some of the lyrics – which reference everything from Jesus to Acid – are to that memorable summer of 1989. Halfway through the song, there's a harmonica solo, which hits me with such familiarity, such a wave of nostalgia, my eyes fill with warm tears. I sway back and forth in my chair, the hairs on the back of my neck raised, my spine tingling in recognition. Next is a song I'd completely forgotten about. 'You On My Mind', a minor hit for Swing Out Sister in

191

1989. A big, sweeping, mid-tempo number, all glossy 1960s production, it's about getting back with someone after a break-up. I picture teenage Conor, alone in his bedroom, curating this mixtape with the closest attention to detail, his brow furrowed with concentration, choosing each song with care. The third track, 'Pink Sunshine' by Fuzzbox, is a joyous burst of pop. I find myself up on my feet, dancing around Mum's living room, spinning giddily, wine glass in hand, laughing out loud, not caring if I'm spilling drink on the carpet. This is followed by another upbeat Stock, Aitken and Waterman classic: Donna Summer's 'This Time I Know It's for Real'. I carry on dancing, singing along to the words this time, crying happy tears, remembering how much we both loved this song; in hindsight, a classic gay anthem. The final track on Side A is 'Days' by Kirsty MacColl. As I listen to the words, I can't help thinking about Conor and the days he gave me.

A memory floats to the surface. This song was playing on the kitchen radio the day after Conor disappeared. I was sitting at the dining room table, eating cornflakes, when a local police officer knocked on the door. Mum let him in, switching the radio off as the policeman sat down opposite me at the kitchen table and began asking me question after question, an interrogation which felt like it lasted for hours. *When did I last see Conor? What was my relationship to him?* I was terrified he'd come to arrest me for being gay.

As I recall the policeman's questions, an idea strikes. If I could remember who he was and track him down, he might be able to tell us something about the case.

'What was his name?' I say out loud, before picking up my phone and calling Aine.

31.

Sunday 18th June 1989

The morning after my birthday party, Mum seems caught up with something, distracted. On my way to the bathroom, I find her standing outside the hot press, her hand on the lid of the laundry basket. She's staring into space, her face frozen as if she's trying to work something out, some problem in her head. When she sees me, she looks startled. She mumbles a quiet good morning and gathers a load of dirty washing in her arms, taking it downstairs. I'd been expecting a difficult conversation today, but now I feel even more worried. What have I done?

The rest of last night's party had passed in a blur. After boking over my shoes, Aine left, taking Conor and Willy with her. Mum spent the next hour or so trying to console a hysterical Wendy and prevent Granny McQueen from plying her with cigarettes in a bid to calm her nerves. Luckily Wendy's mum arrived just in time to save us having to talk to each other. The rest of the guests left in dribs and drabs, and Mervyn went back to his big house on the Shore Road after dropping off Granny McQueen. It was gone midnight when Mum and I had finished tidying up. On the landing, she gave me a cold peck goodnight and said we'd talk about it in the morning, when we'd both had time to cool off a little.

It's only after my shower, when I'm getting dressed, that I remember Conor's gift to me. What did I do with it, though? With all the drama, I haven't even had a chance to look at it yet. I rack my brains, trying to retrace my steps from last night, but the last time I remember seeing it was when I put it in my shorts pocket. And that's when it dawns on me.

Conor's tape is in my shorts.

The shorts that are in the wash.

Fuck.

My stomach twisting in fear, I scramble, half-dressed, to the washing basket, rummaging frantically through it to see if, by some miracle, Mum has left my shorts behind. I check and check again. The basket is completely empty. What was on that tape?

Calm down, Billy, calm down. You're probably making a big deal out of nothing. It'll just be a few dance tracks, or something: a party mix. And then I remember Conor's words to me. You might want to look at it later, he'd said – in private. This was clearly more than just a party mix. I panic. My whole body starts shaking; I feel like I'm about to be sick.

Pulling on the rest of my clothes, a T-shirt – inside out, with the label hanging out the back – I race downstairs, freezing on the spot when I reach the kitchen door. It's shut, but I can hear Mum's voice. She's talking in a low whisper, and every so often I hear my name mentioned. It's then I see the telephone cord, trailing from its plug in the hallway underneath the gap in the door.

Taking a few deep breaths, I hover outside for a moment before pushing the door open. Mum is sitting on a chair at the kitchen table. She has her back to me. She swings round. 'I've got to go, Mervyn. Billy's here,' she says. 'I'll ring you later.' She hangs up the receiver, glaring at me.

Horrified, I catch sight of Conor's cassette on the kitchen table, propped up next to Mum's Tupperware salt and pepper shakers.

'Are you looking for something?' she says, her voice cold.

Without replying, I reach out to rescue the cassette from the table, but she slams her hand on my wrist. 'Don't you dare,' she hisses. 'You've got some explaining to do, Billy McQueen.'

My mind is in a scramble; I can't think straight. As a last resort, I decide to plead total ignorance. 'What do you mean – explain?'

Mum rolls her eyes. 'Do you think I was born yesterday? Tell me, what does it say on this tape here?' She grabs the cassette, waving it in my face.

'I haven't had a chance to look at it yet,' I tell her, which is the truth.

She tuts, shaking her head. 'I don't believe you.'

'I swear to God,' I insist.

'Probably just as well. You don't want to read it.'

I look at her, confused, and she shoves the cassette towards me.

Frightened, I stare at the writing on the cover, forcing myself to read what it says.

Happy 16th Birthday, Billy!

Sorry for being a dick in the hut the other day when we kissed. I freaked out. You were only trying to help. It's just I've never felt like this before, and it's totally messing with my head. I'd do anything to make it up to you, but in the meantime, I wanted to make you a wee tape for your birthday. I hope that one day you'll be willing to give me 'one more try'.

Your friend, always,

Conor x

Side 1
One More Try – George Michael
Miss You Like Crazy – Natalie Cole
Don't Wanna Lose You – Gloria Estefan
Especially For You – Kylie Minogue and Jason Donovan
Cherish – Madonna

Side 2
Stand Up For Your Love Rights – Yazz

Stop! – Erasure
Nothing Can Divide Us – Jason Donovan
There's More to Love – The Communards
Always On My Mind – Pet Shop Boys

Conor's words swim in front of my eyes. He still has feelings for me then. My heart beats madly in my chest.

'Well?' Mum badgers. 'What have you got to say for yourself?'

I swallow, my mind racing, trying to think up a convincing lie. Mum has pushed me into a corner. I can't see a way out.

'Conor's crazy, so he is,' I lie. 'Absolutely crazy.'

For the first time in weeks, Mum reaches for the spare packet of Benson & Hedges she keeps in the drawer and lights herself a cigarette. This is my fault, I think, watching her inhale. She wouldn't be smoking if it wasn't for me.

'I don't get why Conor's doing this,' I say.

'Doing what?'

'Making up lies.'

'Lies?'

'I mean, he reckons I kissed him,' I say, pulling the most horrified facial expression I can manage.

She takes another drag of her cigarette and looks at me, like she really wants to believe me. 'You didn't kiss him then?' Exhaling, she blows smoke all over Conor's cassette.

I shake my head. 'I have a girlfriend, don't I?'

Mum narrows her eyes. 'Why would he lie and say all that rubbish, though?' She tears the cellophane wrapper off her cigarette packet, seeming to come to some decision as she scrunches it into a ball and crushes it with her fist. 'I'm sorry, son,' she says, squeezing her eyes shut, her voice softening. 'I shouldn't have doubted you.'

My shoulders relax, but only because Mum believes me. Or at least, is choosing to believe what *she* wants to believe. Taking another puff of her cigarette, she taps it on the side of the ashtray. 'I'm still fuming about what that Kelly girl did to poor Wendy, though. Seriously, I've warned you about her before.'

'Don't worry, Mum. I can handle her. Besides, I've got my own mind.'

'I'm sure you have, son, but as your mother I'm not about to stand back and let that girl ruin your life, because – trust me – she's the sort to drag everyone down with her. I don't want you seeing her again, or that Conor fella for that matter. Bad influences, the pair of them.'

'But, Mum . . .'

'No buts, Billy. Listen to me. I know a lot more about the world than you do. I might not have O levels, or whatever you call them nowadays, but I do have common sense – and common sense gets you further in life than intelligence. Aine's away with the fairies. She'll be lucky to get a job when she leaves school with an attitude like that, and what man's going to want a cheeky wee gobshite like her for a wife?'

Mum's words come as a shock. I knew she wasn't Aine's biggest fan, but I didn't realise she hated her this much.

'Stay away from them,' she says. 'Otherwise, you're grounded. End of story.'

She stubs out her cigarette in the ashtray, squishing the end of it with her fingers until it stops smouldering. 'I'm going to have a bath,' she says. 'If anyone rings, can you take a message and say I'll call them back.' She grabs her cigarettes and heads upstairs.

As soon as she's gone, I lift Conor's tape from the kitchen table, slipping it into my jeans pocket.

32.

Friday 29th September 2023

While I wait for Aine to answer the phone, I perform another of my counting rituals. *If she doesn't pick up within the next five seconds, we're never going to find out what happened to Conor.*

Five, four, three, two . . .

'Hey,' says Aine.

'What was the policeman's name?' I blurt out, without so much as a hello. 'The one who interviewed us about Conor's disappearance.'

'Oh God, I can't remember. Was it McClean, or McKean? Something like that? Sorry, I'm in the middle of doing a load of marking, Billy. My head's somewhere else entirely.'

'I've got it!' I say, his name suddenly flashing into my mind. 'Constable McKee.'

'He'll be long retired now,' says Aine. 'If he's still alive, that is.'

I pick up my laptop and type his name into the Google search bar, resulting in several hits. 'I think I've found him.'

On the screen in front of me there's a black-and-white photo of Constable McKee, standing in front of a brick wall. To his right is a sign with the words *CARRICKFERGUS POLICE STATION.* He's looking at the camera, his arms folded. A serious expression on his face.

I scroll further down the page until my eye is drawn to a story from yesterday's Belfast Telegraph. The headline reads:

Cinderfella! Former local constable to play pantomime dame.
Sure enough, underneath the headline is a photograph of
Constable George McKee, but not as we know him. I read
the story aloud to Aine.

> Retired police officer and former detective George McKee
> (67) is sure to be an arresting presence on stage this
> Christmas when he joins the bill as one of the wicked
> stepsisters in The DeCourcy Players' latest production,
> Cinderella, at Carrickfergus Town Hall. The play, co-written
> and co-produced with his wife, Barbara McKee, promises
> plenty of laughs, with the occasional 'blue' joke thrown in
> for good measure.

'So let me get this straight,' says Aine. 'The policeman
who undertook the original investigation into Conor's
disappearance back in the eighties is now performing as a
local drag queen.'

'Pantomime dame,' I correct her. 'There's a difference.'

'Dame . . . drag queen . . . whatever,' says Aine. 'We *need*
to talk to this guy. He's going to be able to give us loads
of information about the case. Does it say where they're
rehearsing? Maybe we could pop along?'

I scan the article for more details. Written at the bottom
in italics it says *Auditions take place at Hopehill Presbyterian
Church Hall on Saturday 7th October. Everyone welcome.*

Aine laughs when I tell her this. I know what she's thinking.

'Before you say it,' I warn her. 'There's no way I'm
auditioning for a pantomime.'

'Oh yes you are!' quips Aine. 'So, I'll see you then.'

And with that, she hangs up.

33.

Sunday 25th June 1989

Church is packed. Wendy and I squeeze along the pew, taking our seats. A few rows in front, I spy Big Gay Willy. He turns round and waves at me, mouthing 'I need a word'. What could he need to talk to me about that's so urgent? I wonder.

Earlier this week, after my disastrous birthday party, I made a promise to myself to be good; to think only of Wendy and our relationship, not to get sidetracked by what Mervyn would call 'inappropriate' thoughts. It's been tough though. Even though I know it's wrong, I've been playing the cassette Conor made me in bed. It's the only thing that helps me sleep. I listen to it every night, apart from Sunday, when I tune into Downtown Radio instead. They have this request show, where you can phone in and play a song for someone you fancy. It can be anonymous if you want; you don't have to say your name. Most of the songs they play are cheesy, soft rock ballads by bands like Chicago and Foreigner, but I love it. Often, I lie there in the dark fantasising that 'Lonely Guy' from Carrickfergus, who's requested REO Speedwagon's 'Can't Fight This Feeling', is Conor, and he's sending me a secret message over the airwaves.

The way things are going, though, I'm not sure I'll ever get the chance to speak to either Conor or Aine again. Mum has put a total ban on me seeing them and keeps reminding me of her threat to ground me for a whole month if I make any attempt to defy her. The other day, when she asked me

200

what I'd done with Conor's cassette tape, I lied and said I'd thrown it in the bin.

'Billy, are you OK?' Wendy's hand is on my arm, pulling me out of my thoughts.

'Aye, I'm fine,' I say. 'I was just daydreaming, that's all.'

The church organ starts playing and the entire congregation get up on their feet. The first hymn is 'Give Me Oil in My Lamp', an incredibly uplifting song with a rousing chorus that builds and builds after each verse. Everyone is singing their hearts out. Some play along to the music with maracas, bells and tambourines; others raise their hands in the air, their eyes closed, as if praying. As the hymn ends, the room falls silent, the only sounds the occasional cough, or whispers of 'Praise Jesus' and 'Amen'.

Mervyn strides into the centre of the stage, positioning himself behind the pulpit, his silver fox hair slicked back with Brylcreem. Aside from a pair of tan shoes, he's dressed entirely in white: white jacket and trousers and a white shirt, open at the neck, revealing a silver cross. His arms are open wide, as if he's preparing to embrace every one of us. His eyes scan the room. It's amazing how, even in a space this size, he can make every member of the congregation feel as if they're being welcomed, personally, by him. I guess I should be proud that he's my mum's fella and I get to see him outside of church – but this version of Mervyn is different. It's hard to explain; it's not exactly like he's putting on a performance in church, but the man standing in front of me now doesn't feel like the same man who's round my house a lot. Like the rest of the congregation, I can't help feeling a bit in awe of him.

'Good evening, ladies and gentlemen,' he says. 'Welcome to the Holywood Church. Whether you're a regular, or this is your first time with us, I do hope you enjoy tonight's service.' He closes his eyes, pausing a moment before continuing. 'God came to me with a message last night, which He asked me to deliver to you all today. It's not a comfortable message, but it's one He told me was important. Something that needed to be said.'

He pauses again to look around the congregation. Smiling gravely, his eyes occasionally fix on certain individuals.

'You may have noticed that more and more young people are starting to attend the church. A few weeks ago, we ran our second day trip for secondary school children to Tollymore Forest, and I'm pleased to say that once again, it was very successful, very successful indeed. Many young people came to Christ after that day – many were saved.'

There's a round of applause from the audience, a series of claps, whoops and cheers. A woman with a thick Ballymena accent shouts 'Hallelujah!'

Mervyn raises his hand. 'Thank you,' he says. 'For, as you know, our young people these days face an even greater number of evils and temptations than we did at their age. As such, it's vital that we, as a church, remain relevant to them, and running trips and excursions is one way in which we can increase the numbers of our young – and vulnerable – flock each year, bringing them to Christ.'

He clears his throat. 'What are these new evils and temptations? I can see some of you raising your hands, but it's a rhetorical question. You may have heard that the government introduced a new law last year, a law designed to protect our young people in schools. I for one applaud that decision. This new law is called Section 28, and it forbids, and I quote, "the promotion of homosexuality in schools".'

There is an audible gasp of horror from the congregation.

'As our esteemed Prime Minister, Margaret Thatcher, has said, "Young people are being taught that they have the inalienable right to be gay." Yes,' he says, nodding and pointing at a member of the congregation. 'You did hear that correctly, madam. I said young people are being *taught*.' He pauses for a moment, strokes his chin. 'Now let me ask you something. What kind of education system, whose primary purpose is to morally instruct young people, teaches them that they have a right to be gay? A *right*, I tell you.' He bangs his fist on the pulpit. 'It is a fact that our children are being taught by disciples of the devil. Satanic perverts who tell *our* children there's nothing wrong with two men, or two women, living together, playing happy families and sharing a bed. Yes. Sharing a bed. This is not *natural*. This is not holy. These so-called couples are nothing but filthy degenerates. For doesn't the Bible tell us that homosexuality is against His laws? That homosexuality is a sin. An abomination. Why else did God destroy Sodom and Gomorrah?'

Choking on his words, he pauses to take a sip of water. When he speaks again his voice is much softer, quieter. 'Here's an interesting wee linguistic fact for you all: the Greek word for effeminate is "pervert".'

The can of Heinz soup I had for lunch starts repeating on me and I swallow, the tang of regurgitated tomato sauce stinging the back of my throat.

'I never knew that,' Wendy whispers in my ear.

'Neither did I,' I say, thinking back to my Kate Bush impressions and the time I built a big doll's house out of an old cardboard box for the ladies on the side of my dad's Tennent's Lager cans to live in. By Mervyn's logic, I've always been a pervert.

'That's right,' he says. 'Pervert.' He spits out the word like it's poison. 'Ladies and gentlemen, I am warning you. Look out for your sons and daughters, for they may be possessed. Be vigilant. Beware of the boy who prefers playing with dolls to kicking a football, the girl who cuts her hair short and refuses to wear dresses. These are all signs of perversion.'

Mortified, I realise Mum, who is sitting near the front of the stage, is listening to all this. What must she be thinking?

After delivering his sermon, Mervyn leads the congregation in prayer. This is followed by another hymn, a ballad, which we all sing together. Once the hymn has ended, the piano continues to tinkle in the background as the pastor takes centre stage for the final, climactic part of the evening, when new members of the congregation are asked to come to Christ. He tells us, softly, how he's been saving souls in this church every week since 1978; how over the years he's brought thousands into the church. Collection boxes are dutifully passed down each row, people dropping in coins or slipping in notes. 'Give generously to the work of the Lord,' he says. 'Is there anyone here tonight who wants to come to Jesus?'

Slowly, one by one, people in the congregation start putting their hands up. The pastor acknowledges each of them individually, saying the same kinds of phrases over and over.

'Is there a woman?'

'I see a hand.'

'Where are you, friend?'

'Don't go out of here today without Christ.'

The gentle piano music continues, a queue of people forming at the front, waiting to be saved by the pastor. We watch him perform a brief ritual on each of them, placing his hand on their foreheads and muttering a few words of prayer to yet more cries of 'Hallelujah' and 'Praise Jesus'.

Two rows in front, Big Gay Willy turns round. He catches my eye. 'Toilet,' he mouths. I glance at Wendy to see if she's noticed this little exchange between the pair of us, but she's too enraptured by what's happening on stage. I watch as Big Gay Willy shuffles to the end of the row, making his way up the stairs. I wait for a few minutes before whispering to Wendy that I need the loo. My heart is racing. What does he need to talk to me about?

34.

Now

Saturday 7th October 2023

Hopehill Presbyterian Church is tucked away in a side street just off the Marine Highway. Aine and I stand in front of a poster pinned to the noticeboard outside. It reads: *Local theatrical impresarios George and Barbara McKee invite you to audition for their hilarious and top-notch new production of Cinderella, which runs from 10th to 22nd December in Carrickfergus Town Hall. There is a plethora of roles available (oh yes there is!!!): from singing, acting and dancing, to costume making, set building, stage management and so much more!!! If you have a talent, we can use it!!! Email georgieandbabstheatre@btinternet.com for details!!!*

'They seem like an enthusiastic couple,' I say. 'Judging by the exclamation marks.'

Earlier in the week Aine had emailed them to enquire about auditions. Several hours later, she received a gushing reply from 'Babs' herself saying we were more than welcome, the more the merrier. This was, of course, followed by not three, but *four* exclamation marks. Babs advised bringing a flask, or a water bottle, and a packed lunch, as it would be a long day and their 'pauper's budget' didn't stretch to refreshments.

'How many times do I have to tell you?' I say. 'I'm not auditioning.'

'Chill out, Billy.' Aine grins as we make our way inside. 'Trust me, kiddo. You got this.'

A twinkly-eyed pensioner, sitting behind a trestle table, ticks our names off a list and points us in the direction of a corridor, at the end of which is a large room with high windows and polished wood floors. Around the room, piles of plastic chairs are stacked on top of each other. At one end, a mass of auditionees of all different ages and backgrounds are warming up by stretching their hamstrings, performing lunges and windmilling their arms. At the other end, a group of super-keen hopefuls are chanting tongue twisters, led by a tall gentleman with a waxed grey moustache: *Nine nimble noblemen nibbled nuts* and *I saw Susie sitting in a shoeshine shop. Where she sits, she shines, and where she shines, she sits.* In a corner, perched in front of an upright piano with her back to us, a large woman, wearing a humongous maroon turban, plays 'Memory' from *Cats* while a reedy-looking girl in her late teens screeches along in a nervous, pitchy fashion.

I lean in, whispering in Aine's ear. 'Please tell me I don't have to perform in front of this lot.'

Just at that moment, the pianist stops playing. Turning her head, she stands up to face the room.

'It's her,' I say, nudging Aine. 'Barbara "Babs" McKee.'

Babs claps her hands twice and everyone falls silent, immediately stopping what they're doing. Pulling up the sleeves of her long navy cardigan, she taps on her watch, casting a sweeping glance over the room. 'We're going to take a half hour break now for lunch, but can I just say, both George and I are thrilled by the talent already on display here today, and we wish you all the best with your auditions this afternoon.'

'Good timing,' I say to Aine. 'Shall we make a beeline for George before we have to stand up and perform a duet of "Dead Ringer for Love"?'

Aine nods, stifling a giggle, and we head over to where he's standing. He has his back to us and is rifling through what looks like a stack of scripts.

'Sorry to bother you, Mr McKee,' I say. 'I'm sure you're

very busy today. My name's Billy McQueen and this is my friend, Aine Kelly.'

He stops what he is doing and turns to face us. 'Are you here for the auditions?'

'No, actually,' I say. 'We wanted to have a chat with you about one of your old cases.'

The man raises an eyebrow. 'I'm retired. The only cases I investigate nowadays are fictional ones, when I'm treading the boards as Holmes or Poirot. I'm not sure how much use I can be to you.'

'It's regarding a missing person you investigated over thirty years ago. Conor Doherty?'

George sighs, his eyes clouding over at the mention of Conor's name. He puts the pile of scripts down on a chair and rubs his hand across his mouth. 'One of the biggest disappointments of my career. I can't tell you how much I regret not cracking that case. That poor wee fella. Even today, it still haunts me, what happened to him.' He pauses for a moment. 'Are you police, then?'

Aine shakes her head. 'No. Conor and Billy were . . . *we* were friends of his. You spoke to us both, shortly after his disappearance. You probably don't remember.'

'Did I really?' he says, as if trying to recall the memory. 'I interviewed a lot of people back then. Forgive me if I can't put names to faces.'

'I think you know my mother from church, though? Sadie Ballantine,' I say.

'You're Sadie's son? Boys a dear. I hope she's doing OK? We heard she wasn't well.'

'She had a bad stroke, but she's still with us, thankfully. I've been spending a lot of time by her bedside. She's making progress.'

'Well, I'm glad to hear it,' he says. 'Be sure to give her our love when you see her.' He pauses. 'So – why the sudden interest in Conor Doherty? Have you found out some new information?'

Aine and I look at each other. She nods, as if to say *Go on, then. Tell him.*

'I'm not sure it's new information, as such,' I say. 'But . . .' I pause, looking around me. The room is full of people getting ready to eat their lunch. 'Is there anywhere we can go that's a bit more private?'

He nods. 'There's a kitchen next door,' he says. 'It's open. If you wait in there for me, I'll go let Barbara know where we are.'

Barbara McKee fills the kettle with water and puts it back on its stand, switching it on. She opens the cupboards in search of tea bags. 'I'm sure I saw a box in here the other day,' she says. 'If not, I can always pop out and grab us some coffees.'

'They do a good cappuccino in that new café round the corner,' says George.

'Actually, don't worry,' I say. 'I'm fine with water. Besides, we don't want to keep you too long. By the sound of it, you've got a packed schedule ahead of you today.'

'Same,' says Aine. 'A glass of water will do me rightly.'

'If you're sure,' says Barbara. She fills a couple of beakers under the tap and sets them down on the table in front of us.

'Sorry for gatecrashing the auditions,' I say. 'We probably should've arranged to meet you at a less busy time.'

George sits forward in his chair, twirling one end of his moustache between his finger and thumb. 'Not at all. But it was all a very long time ago now, I'm not sure how much help I can be. I've been retired from the police force for eight years. I would've been in my thirties when it happened.'

'What do you remember about the investigation?' I say, taking a sip of water.

'Well, we certainly had our suspects at the time. The main one being Andy Stone, who ran the nightclub in Carrick for several years. We arrested him for allowing Class A drugs to be sold on his premises, but the courts let him off a few years later, due to lack of any concrete evidence. He was dodgy in other ways, though.'

'What do you mean?' I say, biting my lip.

'Maybe dodgy isn't quite the right word, but . . .' George stops mid-sentence. He drums his fingers on the table. 'How can I put this without sounding offensive?'

Aine and I both look at each other, puzzled, then at George.

He takes a deep breath. 'Andy was gay,' he says. 'Nowadays, of course, being gay is no big deal, but back then there was still a lot of prejudice, you know?'

Babs interrupts. 'Naturally, George and I are very au fait with the gays. We mix in theatrical circles, for goodness' sake. Many of our closest friends are homosexuals.'

George nods. 'Obviously, *we're* not homophobic, but many people back then were. Don't forget, homosexuality in Northern Ireland had only been decriminalised in 1982. Everyone was living in fear of AIDS. Anyway, I'm rather ashamed to admit this now, but . . .'

'Go on,' I say. 'We're not here to judge the way you viewed things in the past. Times have changed.'

He clears his throat before continuing. 'One of my jobs as a police officer involved observing the goings-on, shall we say, in the public toilets in the castle car park. Andy Stone, as it turns out, was a frequent visitor.'

'I take it you don't mean he had bladder issues,' says Aine.

George smiles politely at her facetiousness. 'Let's just say Andy Stone had a bit of a thing for younger men.'

'And you were able to arrest him for that?'

George shakes his head. 'We never arrested him, no. We couldn't just arrest people for being gay, but he – and a few others in the community – were under police surveillance. Obviously if we'd caught him getting up to something in the public toilets, we could have done him for public indecency, but that was never the case.'

'How young were these guys he had a thing for?' I ask. I

think back to my visit to Andy Stone's house. It looks like my gaydar was on point. Zach must be his young lover.

'I was about to say they were of legal age, but I'm forgetting that the age of consent then was twenty-one for gay men. I knew of a few cases of blackmail going on at the time. Younger men soliciting high-profile older men, then threatening to expose them as gay to their families, and so on.'

A horrible thought crosses my mind. Was Conor blackmailing someone? Was he killed because he was threatening to out someone as gay? Andy Stone, for instance? I shudder. Conor wasn't like that, though. Was he?

'Who else do you think might have been responsible for Conor's disappearance?' says Aine. 'Aside from Andy Stone.'

George ponders for a moment. 'Well, we knew for a fact that a lot of the guys working in that nightclub were up to no good. Many were doing a bit of dealing on the side. I remember we spoke to a few people around then who suggested Conor may have been dealing too, but we never had firm proof.'

He pauses for a drink, then says, 'So why are you both suddenly interested in this case again? It's been nearly thirty-five years now.'

'When I moved back here, a few months ago,' I say, 'I found a cassette at my mum's house which Conor had made for me the day he disappeared . . .' I pause for a second, unsure how much information to divulge at this point.

George strokes his chin. 'A cassette?'

I nod. 'A mixtape. You know, of songs.'

Aine chips in. 'I'm sure Billy won't mind me saying, but he and Conor were kind of involved with each other, in a romantic way.'

'I see,' says George. 'That must've been difficult for you both.'

I cradle my glass of water in my hands. 'Yes,' I say. 'Yes, it was.'

'So, this mixtape,' says Babs, leaning in. 'Why do you think it's significant to the case?'

Without going into detail about my estrangement from Mum, I explain how the cassette was posted to our house years after Conor's disappearance with an anonymous note.

There's a moment of silence before George speaks. 'Who do you think sent it then?'

'I've no idea,' I say. 'I've been racking my brains, and I can't think of anyone else who would've had the tape in their possession. It was a present for me.'

Babs says, 'Bit of a wild card, but don't you think there's a small chance Conor might still be alive? He could've run away somewhere. He could've changed his identity. He could be hiding in another country, living under a new name.'

George rolls his eyes. 'Please excuse my wife. She's an eternal optimist. I blame Dame Barbara Cartland. She's read all of her books.'

Babs shoots him a sniffy look. 'I have *not*, George. You're making me sound very lowbrow.' She turns to me then. 'As a matter of fact, you're far more likely to find me reading a Jane Austen or a Barbara Pym.'

He laughs. 'Austen or Pym? What's the difference? They both write far-fetched romantic rubbish. Anyway, it's not that easy to change your identity, and how would Conor have managed to hide himself away for thirty-odd years?'

Babs looks up at the kitchen clock. 'I don't mean to be rude, George, but we've only got five minutes before we need to be back in the hall.'

George, who seems deep in thought, says, 'Like I said, I regard this case as one of my biggest failures as a police officer. We should've caught the person responsible years ago, but the truth is there was so much going on during the Troubles that, as time went on, the case just got pushed to the side. It was as simple as that.' He scratches his head. 'I'm sorry I can't be of more help.'

'It's fine,' I say. 'I understand. It's been really useful hearing things from a policeman's point of view.'

'*Ex*-policeman,' he reminds me, gently.

'Of course,' I say, nodding.

He rises to his feet. 'Anyway, folks. It's been lovely talking to you both. Best of luck with the investigation. Do let us know how you're getting on. You *must* come and watch the show in December. Barbara and I would be delighted to sort you out with a few comps.'

'We'd love that,' I say. 'Wouldn't we, Aine?'

'Absolutely!' Aine grins. 'Count me in.'

George turns to go. 'And don't forget to pass on our good wishes to your mother,' he says. 'She's in our prayers. I hope she gets well soon.'

After they've both left the room, Aine presses her hands to her chest and says, 'I feel like we've hit a brick wall. If George couldn't solve it, what hope do we have?' She sounds exasperated.

I fix her with a look of determination. I can't let this go, and I need her help. I can't do it alone. I need to know that I'm not to blame for Conor's disappearance. 'Aine, we've come so far. Let's not give up now. We need to find out the truth about what happened that night.'

Just then Aine's phone pings. She stares down at it, casually, then her eyes widen in surprise. 'Shit. You'll never guess who's just replied to my message.'

'Who?'

'Only Big Gay flipping Willy!'

35.

Sunday 25th June 1989

When I get to the men's toilet in the church, it's locked. I knock lightly and hear the bolt clicking from behind. I slip inside.

Big Gay Willy is leaning against the sink. He tells me to lock the door. 'What if someone needs the toilet?' I ask.

'Just do it,' he says. 'We need to talk.'

Nervously, I slide the bolt across and turn to face him.

'It's Conor,' he says.

My stomach twists. I knew this had something to do with Conor. Has he told Big Gay Willy about what happened between us?

'What about Conor? Is he OK?'

Big Gay Willy touches the gold stud on his right ear. 'You know fine rightly he's not OK.'

'Do I?' I look up at him. It's obvious from his expression that he can see through my pathetic attempt at playing dumb.

'Conor was drunk the night of your party. We had a chat in the garden. He wasn't making a lot of sense, but he told me his da has been hitting him and then he said that you and he . . .'

A wave of panic hits me. 'What? What did he say?'

Big Gay Willy bites his lip. 'Are you really going to make me spell it out?'

'Spell what out?'

213

He rolls his eyes. 'Don't act all innocent with me, Billy, I knew you were gay the moment I met you in Belfast with Aine that day.'

I want to deny it. I want to call him a liar. I want to tell him he's got it all wrong, but the truth is, I'm struggling to keep up this pretence. It's been exhausting, and hearing him say these words is almost a relief.

I lower my gaze, my eyes watery. 'I'm not gay, though.'

'Two words,' says Big Gay Willy. 'In. Denial. Tell me, what supposedly "straight" man do you know who owns every single one of Kylie Minogue's records on seven-inch, twelve-inch and cassette single? Yes, I'm talking about you, Billy! You must think I came up the frigging Lagan in a bubble.'

I burst out crying then, and start pleading with him. 'Please, Willy, please don't tell anyone. Wendy, my mum . . . she'll kill me if she finds out.'

His voice softens. 'I'm not about to out you, Billy. Do you really think I'd do that to you?'

I look up at him. His expression is full of concern. It's obvious to me he cares. He means well.

'I'm sorry,' I say, choking back the tears, 'it's just—'

I can barely get the words out, but it doesn't matter. He puts his arms around me and gives me a massive hug; his voice is warm and calm and reassuring. 'I know, fella, I know. It's hard, so it is, especially with everyone around you telling you you're a pervert and you're going to hell no matter what, but you need to realise the way people think round here isn't normal. I mean, let's be honest here, Pastor Ballantine's view of normal is fucked.'

This makes me laugh, in spite of my tears.

He lets go of me. Taking a step back, he leans his head to one side and smiles sympathetically.

'There's no point hiding who you are, Billy. You need to start being honest with yourself. If you're not, everything will just eat away inside of you, like it has with Conor. Poor Conor. I haven't told you the half of it yet.'

'What do you mean?' I say, wiping my eyes.

'He's been burning himself.'

'What?'

'With a cigarette. He was doing it when I found him at your party, holding it against his bare arms. They're covered in red marks. Haven't you noticed?'

Oh, Conor. This is all my fault. If only I'd been more open about my feelings. If only I'd tried to talk with him after he ran off on me that night at the hut. I could've done more. I could've helped him.

'It's OK, Billy. He'll be fine in time, I know he will. I've been helping him look for part-time work. He wants to go to university. He's planning on saving up money so he can afford to study in England.'

'I know,' I say. 'We've talked about it. It's what we both want.'

He nods. 'Look, Conor said he really wants to make things up with you, so I've arranged a night out for us all after church next Sunday. It'll give you both a chance to talk.'

'Where?' I say.

'It's a new venue called Club Babylon. You're going to love it.'

36.

Now

Saturday 7th October 2023

'What does he say?'

'Hold on. I'll read it to you.' Aine gets her glasses out of her bag and peers at the message on her phone.

Oh my God, Aine. It's so lovely to hear from you! Your message has really brightened my day. So sorry it's taken me ages to reply, but I don't check this app that much.

On my side, I'm living in London now. I moved over here after my A levels to do a Media Studies degree. I couldn't wait to get out of the shit-hole that was Northern Ireland, at least when we were young . . . I've been back many times since to visit family and had some great nights out in Belfast.

I'm single again, just recently. I was in a civil partnership for ten years with the love of my life, a gorgeous man called Robert, but sadly he passed away last year. I really miss him. It's made me want to come home more often.

I'll be over later in the month, actually, to see my parents. They've just downsized to a wee bungalow in Whitehead, so I'm staying with them for a few days. It would be lovely to catch up with you properly and have a natter about the old days. I still think of you fondly and remember our wild nights out, drinking and clubbing in Carrick! Hope to catch up in person very soon.

Lots of love, William xxx

'So, he's coming to visit?' I say. 'Do you want to meet up with him on your own, or shall we do it together? I don't mind, either way. You knew him much better than I did.'

'Even so, I reckon we should arrange to meet him together.'

'We could always try out one of the new LGBT venues in Belfast?'

'Good idea. I'll send him an email tonight and try and get a date in the diary. I wonder what he looks like these days?'

'Doesn't he have a photo on his LinkedIn?'

'No, it's blank. I did some googling as well, but I couldn't find anything. He was always so trendy. I wonder if he's still the same.'

'I wouldn't bet on it. People change.'

'Not us, though, Billy McQueen. Sure, look at me,' she says, pointing at her feet. 'I'm still wearing DMs. We're rocking fifty, don't you think?'

'Totally rocking fifty,' I say. 'You know, I'm so glad we're hanging out together again. Here's to many more years of friendship – and to Conor.'

'To friendship.' Aine grins, throwing her arms around me and giving me the biggest hug. 'And to Conor. Here's hoping Willy might be able to help shed some light on what happened to him.'

37.

Sunday 2nd July 1989

Club Babylon is Carrick's tackiest nightclub, a complete dive on the outskirts of town. Despite the nasty rumour going round school that it's run by paramilitaries, loads of sixth formers go there because it's free to get in and the drink's cheap: you can buy a pint of cider for a pound. I'm heading there with Willy after church, having lied to Wendy earlier, saying I didn't feel well. Conor and Aine are going to be there tonight and while I'm nervous about seeing them, I'm even more nervous about being caught trying to sneak into a club for over-eighteens.

'How are we going to get in without ID?' I say.

'You don't need ID when you're with Tall Trudy,' says Willy.

'Tall Trudy?'

Willy tells me that Trudy McAllister, aka Tall Trudy, is his best mate in school. A whole year older than us, she's six foot two and built like the proverbial brick shithouse. She wears loads of make-up, like she's seventeen going on forty-seven. All the Club Babylon bouncers know her.

'They're never going to believe us,' I say. 'I mean, look at me. I look about ten years old.'

'Trust me,' says Big Gay Willy. 'That girl can work miracles at the door. Just you wait and see.'

The bus only takes ten minutes. It drops us off round the corner from the club. When I say 'club', I'm stretching the truth a fair bit; it's a complete dump – an old linen factory that's been kitted out with a bar, a dance floor and a dodgy sound system. A banner hangs above the door which says 'Club Babylon – Where the Craic's At!' in bold red lettering. There's a bouncer guarding the entrance: a young, stocky guy in his early twenties, who, despite his munchkin proportions, doesn't look like the sort of fella you'd want to mess with in a hurry. He has tattoos on his knuckles and a red, angry face.

I'm absolutely shitting my pants. There's no way we're getting past him.

Big Gay Willy checks his watch. 'I told Tall Trudy we'd meet her here at half seven.' He nudges me in the side with his elbow and laughs. 'You look petrified, kiddo. Honestly, you're going to be fine.'

Dead on half seven, a tall brunette with a massive perm comes staggering through the entrance to the car park. She totters towards us in six-inch heels with all the grace of a Roly Poly on stilts.

'Fuck, these shoes are killing me!' she says, giving us both a huge grin, revealing a full set of train-track braces.

'You look amazing, Trudy,' gushes Big Gay Willy. 'I love the dress.'

'Primark's finest,' she says, giving us a twirl. 'Sure, you look gorgeous too, Willy. C'mere and give me a kiss, you total ride of a man.'

She grabs Big Gay Willy by the hips, smacking his backside and planting a snog on his left cheek. 'Who's the cute friend?' she says.

'This is Billy.'

'Billy and Willy,' she laughs. 'It's like a kid's TV show. Here, I hope yous are ready to party the night. I'm half-cut already, so I am.'

'You're a geg,' says Big Gay Willy. 'What have you been drinkin'?'

'Peach Schnapps. I brought it back for my ma when I went on that school trip to Austria last year, but she won't touch it. Her loss is my gain, so it is.'

Tall Trudy points out the bouncer. 'Auch, it's only wee Marty Nugent on the door. He's a soft touch. We won't have any bother getting in the night.'

I'd hardly describe the bulldog guarding the door as 'a soft touch', but Tall Trudy doesn't seem fazed.

'Yous two wait here,' she says. 'I'll give you a wave when the coast is clear.'

We both watch in awe as Tall Trudy swaggers towards the entrance like she's Tina Turner taking to the stage at Wembley Arena.

''Bout ye, Marty,' she hollers, raising her hand to high-five him.

The bouncer's face lights up as soon as he sees her; it's like a dial has switched from ferocious lion to playful puppy. 'All right, love,' he says. 'I see you're lookin' as gorgeous as ever.'

'You're a charmer, Marty Nugent. What would my ma say if she saw you checking out my legs?'

I whisper to Big Gay Willy, 'Does he know she's only seventeen?'

''Course he does,' hisses Big Gay Willy. 'They're all a bunch of paedos, these doormen.'

'Ugh,' I say. 'He must be like, twenty-two, or something.'

'I know, but watch what she does next. Tall Trudy's a legend, so she is.'

Tall Trudy leans over and says something in the bouncer's ear. He gives a dirty laugh. 'Is that right?' he says. 'Tryin' to get me horny, are you?'

She carries on flirting with him for a while. I shudder to think what she's saying, but there seems to be a lot of snorting and giggling from both parties. Once she has him under her spell though, she waves one hand behind her back, the signal for us to make a move.

'Let's go,' says Big Gay Willy. 'Follow me.'

We walk past them both and straight into the club. No one bats an eyelid.

Inside, the club is heaving, and I'm relieved to see that most of the people in here are around my age. 'Numero Uno' by Starlight pounds from the speakers, the sound of drums and house piano filling the room. I look around for Conor and Aine, but it's too dark, and crowded, to see clearly: every so often there's a blast from the smoke machine, which covers the dance floor in an opaque mist. I didn't think I'd say it, but there's something really exciting about being here. The club is absolutely buzzing. It's a totally different vibe to what you get at church. People are smoking and drinking and there's a real sense of fun. And instead of hymns, they're playing dance music: the same songs that I tape, without fail, every Sunday afternoon, when I listen to the chart countdown on Radio 1.

We weave our way to the bar. 'My round,' says Big Gay Willy. 'What are you having?'

I gaze at the bottles on display behind the bar. Apart from the sip of whiskey I had at my birthday party, I've never really drunk alcohol before. I think about what Mum usually drinks at home, or used to drink – before she got saved – and toy with the idea of a Bacardi and Diet Coke, but that doesn't really feel like a man's drink. 'I'll have whatever you're having,' I say.

Big Gay Willy orders two K Ciders and hands one to me. 'Bottoms up,' he says. We chink bottles. I take a sip of cider. It tastes sweet, like fizzy apple juice; it's much more drinkable than Aine's whiskey.

We sit down on the stools in front of the bar. The music is so loud we have to shout over it to hear what the other person is saying.

'Any sign of Conor yet?' says Big Gay Willy. We both scan the dance floor for our friends. 'Aine said they'd be getting here around eight.'

'Do they know I'm coming then?'

Big Gay Willy gulps down his cider and nods. 'Don't you worry, kiddo. Your Fairy Godfather here has got it all sorted.'

'What about what happened the night of my party? Is Aine cross with me?'

'You know Aine. She can be a nightmare when she's got a bee in her bonnet about something. She was fuming over the whole Wendy business, but when I said I'd had a chat with you, and told her about you and Conor . . .'

'You told her about me and Conor? Was he OK with that?'

'Of course he was. We had a chat about it before I spoke to her.'

'And what about Aine? What did she say?'

'She was a bit annoyed at first, mainly because you hadn't told her, but she soon came round and, honestly, she was dead chuffed. She just wants you two to be happy.'

Already the cider is going to my head and I'm starting to feel slightly dizzy. It's not a bad feeling, and it's definitely taking the edge off my nerves over seeing Conor.

'I see you two have already got the drinks in,' says Tall Trudy, tapping Big Gay Willy on the shoulder. 'It's all right for some.'

She pulls up a stool and sits down next to us, crossing her legs, her short skirt showing off her thighs. 'I said, it's all right for some.' She clears her throat and points a finger at the optics behind the bar. 'Vodka and Coke, please, Willy. Chatting up Marty Nugent is thirsty work. I wanted to boke at some of the creepy things he was saying to me the night.'

'Creepy?' I say. 'What sort of things?'

'Trust me, sweet cheeks. You don't want to know. You're way too innocent for that sort of carry-on, so you are.'

'Go on, tell me,' I say.

She takes the drink from Big Gay Willy, knocking it back in one go. 'If you really must know, he said he could give me multiple orgasms.'

'Multiple orgasms!' Big Gay Willy roars with laughter. 'As if! Look at the height of him. He's three foot nothing, for God's sake.'

'It's not about size,' she says, as the DJ starts playing 'Hey Music Lover'. Tall Trudy puts her empty glass down on the bar, dragging us both up onto the smoke-filled dance floor. As we start moving our bodies to the rhythm, I feel self-conscious, but soon I'm dancing as freely as the other two, enjoying hearing some of my favourite songs played in a space which isn't my bedroom. The music is mostly excellent, but when 'We Call it Acieeed' by D Mob comes on, I use it as an opportunity to visit the toilet.

The toilets are as grotty as you would expect in a dive like Club Babylon. I stand by the urinal, leaning one hand against the wall, trying to pish in a straight line. The guy next to me in a football top is whistling along to D Mob. His pish seems to last forever. Sometimes it stops and I think he's finished, but then it starts up again, a slow but steady stream. Eventually he does up his flies and staggers towards the condom machine. He shoves some coins into it, slipping a pack of Durex into the back pocket of his jeans. As he goes to leave, he turns to me and winks. 'Missus is in for a treat the night,' he says, his words slurring.

I'm washing my hands at the sink when all of a sudden, I see Conor's face reflected behind me in the mirror. My whole body freezes. For a moment I think I'm going to boke.

'Billy,' he says. 'Are you all right?'

I quickly turn off the tap, pulling on the wall-mounted towel to dry my hands.

'Not bad. Yourself?'

'Same,' he says. 'Not bad, not bad.' He looks around to check we're alone, but apart from the two of us, the toilets are empty. 'Listen,' he says, awkwardly. 'About the fight we had the other day. I didn't really get a chance to speak to you – to say sorry – at your party.'

'It's OK,' I say. 'Really, I understand.'

He shuts his eyes, squeezing them with his fingers. I can't help thinking how cute he looks tonight in his black jacket, jeans and stripy blue and white top. 'Look, I'm sorry I freaked out like that. I shouldn't have stormed out on you.'

'And I shouldn't have jumped on you,' I say, embarrassed.

223

'Did you like the t-tape?'

'I did, yeah, thanks. My mum found it, though. She read your note.'

'Shit! I'm so sorry, Billy.'

'It's not your fault. I should be more careful with my stuff.'

'What did she say, like? Was it all right? Did she go mental?'

'I managed to talk my way out of it,' I say, cringing when I remember that I pretty much put the blame on Conor for everything.

'How did you do that?'

'I just made up some excuse. I said it was a joke.'

'Did she believe you?'

'I think so.'

'You think so?' Conor raises his eyebrows.

I shrug. 'It's easier for her to trust me when I say I'm straight than have to deal with the alternative.'

'What's the alternative?'

He waits for me to answer, his eyes locked on mine. No matter how hard I try though, I can't bring myself to look at him. I want to tell him the truth about how I feel, but I can't. Something is stopping me. The words won't come. I stare down at my feet.

And then he touches my arm and my whole body begins shaking. When pop stars sing about electricity, they're not wrong: it's exactly how this feels. He leans in to kiss me. Part of me wants it so badly, but I can't help hearing Mum and Mervyn's voices in my head, telling me what I'm doing is a sin.

Conor's lips are almost touching mine. I put my hands around his waist, and he pulls me closer to him. For a moment, I forget all about everyone else and what they want. All *I* want is Conor.

The door bangs open and a drunk man stumbles in, pulling at his belt, his zip already open, ready to pish. Conor immediately steps back, but not before the man has given us both a dirty look. *Is there nowhere in this town where we can enjoy a bit of privacy?*

224

The man swaggers over to the urinal. He has his back to us, but every so often he turns around to glare. He mutters the word 'fruit' under his breath and clears his throat, gobbing into the urinal. If I don't act now, we could be in big trouble. Time to employ some of those acting skills Miss Wright taught us in class when we were studying Shakespeare.

'Yeah, Tall Trudy's fit as anything, so she is,' I say, raising myself to my full height, pushing my shoulders back and mustering as much laddish bravado as I can. 'I'd definitely give her one.'

Conor looks at me, horrified, as if to say *what the hell are you talking about?*

'Have you seen her tits?' I say, really getting into character now, but hating myself for being a sexist wanker. 'They're massive.'

This crap 'lad' act of mine seems to be working, as the drunk man doing a pish suddenly starts laughing and jeering. 'Nothing beats a pair of big tits,' he slurs, turning round and tucking his visibly shrivelled willy back in his pants. 'I wish I was your age again, son. If I had your looks and stamina, I'd be riding half the women in Carrick.' He pulls up his trousers and makes a drunken attempt to do up his flies.

The thought of this man having sex with anyone makes me feel sick, but I play along, laughing at his comment. 'Don't you worry, mate,' I say. 'I intend to.'

'Good lad,' he says, slapping me hard on the back. 'May as well make the most of it while you're young. Sure there'll be days when you're dead.'

He turns around and staggers out the bathroom door.

'Billy, what the hell was *that* about?' says Conor, as soon as the man is out of earshot.

'I was only putting on an act, Conor. That guy would have killed us both if he knew what we were doing. Look, we can talk about everything later,' I say. 'This isn't the time or the place, it's way too dangerous. Where's Aine, by the way?'

'She went to get a drink.'

'Let's go find her,' I say, pushing open the toilet door and stepping back into the club.

Aine is sitting on a bar stool waiting to be served. She's looking glum, waving a five-pound note impatiently in her hand. Her mood changes immediately, however, when she sees me standing with Conor.

'Billy!' she squeals, leaping off the stool and throwing her arms around me. 'You came! I'm so glad you came! Honestly, I thought I'd never see you again.'

'Don't be stupid,' I say. 'Like we've ever fallen out for long.'

'I'll get the drinks in,' says Conor, putting on a brave face. 'What are yous all having?'

'I'll have another one of these, please,' I say, holding up my nearly empty bottle of K Cider.

'Whiskey and lemonade, please,' says Aine.

Conor moves further down the bar to get the drinks. Aine leans back against her stool. It wobbles slightly as she heaves herself back onto it and turns to me.

'Is that girlfriend of yours here?' she says, sounding annoyed all of a sudden.

'Wendy, you mean?'

'Aye, that's her,' she scowls. 'The blonde bitch with the attitude.'

'I've come on my own,' I say. 'I left her at church.'

'Good!' Aine pulls me towards her and whispers in my ear. 'We need to have a chat. So Willy told me about you and Conor?'

'Yeah, he said.'

'So?' Aine gives me a big dopey grin, her eyes half-shut.

'I was seeing him for a bit, yeah. But I'm going out with Wendy now,' I say, wondering why I'm still feeling the need to deny things to my best friend, who knows *exactly* what's been going on.

Aine flicks her hand dismissively. 'When are you going to be you, Billy? You can't keep on pretending.'

As terrified as I am of admitting it, I know Aine's right. I need to call it off with Wendy before things get more complicated. It's time I was honest. In the meantime, I fill her in on everything that happened between Conor and me, and the fallout. She listens, upset that I felt the need to keep our relationship a secret from her, but glad things are out in the open now.

'To be honest with you, this is why I came here tonight,' I say. 'To sort things out with Conor. And you, of course.'

Aine pulls me into a warm hug, apologising for getting on my case. 'I just want you to be happy, Billy, to be yourself.'

Conor comes back with our drinks, and soon Big Gay Willy and Tall Trudy join us. Aine leans in and whispers to me that we can talk more later.

'Here, you'll never guess who I've just been talking to,' says Big Gay Willy, lifting his nose in the air as if he's a VIP. 'Only the club manager. Andy's his name. I've seen him around town. He gets his hair cut in the same place I do.'

'Does he know you're underage?' says Aine.

'Shush, you!' says Willy.

Tall Trudy laughs. 'Seriously, I leave him alone for ten minutes while I join the women's queue for a pish and he's already picked himself up a sugar daddy.'

'Andy's offered me a job in the club,' says Willy. 'Something to do with promotions. Cash in hand.'

'Drinks on you then,' says Aine, grinning.

I check my watch, remembering I need to be back home by ten o'clock. It's only half eight, which means I've got at least an hour before I have to leave. I'm on my second drink now and the alcohol is definitely beginning to kick in. I can feel myself starting to loosen up a bit and the music seems to be getting louder. It isn't long before we're back on the dance floor. We form a small circle and Tall Trudy puts her handbag in the middle of it, the five of us laughing and joking and dancing around it. I've never been clubbing before, and I love it. I feel like I'm in the audience for *Top of the Pops* or something. Big Gay Willy asks the DJ to play 'French Kiss' by Lil' Louis and, when it comes on, he grabs Tall Trudy and they perform a super-raunchy dance routine in the middle of the dance floor, which has the rest of us creasing up.

We're having such a good night that none of us pay much attention to the hostile looks we're starting to get from some of the other punters in the club. The booze has made us oblivious to our surroundings. We order a few more rounds of drinks, each time saying, 'Just one more.' I'm so wrapped up in the dancing that I've completely lost track of time. I'm past caring, in fact. Right now, I'm living for the moment, loving this chance to express myself through the music.

After a while, we decide to take a rest and the five of us pile onto a huge circular sofa next to the dance floor. I end up sitting next to Conor, who is every bit as drunk as I am. Every so often his leg touches mine and I feel that little spark of electricity again. This time, I don't move away from him. I'm happy to linger, enjoy the warmth from his body. My head is spinning; it feels like I'm in motion. I let it drop on Conor's shoulder, inhaling the scent of his Jazz aftershave. I look across at Big Gay Willy, who is sitting opposite me. He smiles, and it's obvious that he approves of Conor and me. I watch him lean in and whisper something into Aine's ear, and now she's looking at us and smiling too.

My friends are cool with this, I think to myself. Maybe this is OK.

It's nearing the end of the night, and the DJ has started to slow down his set. 'That's The Way Love Is' by Ten City is playing and Big Gay Willy grabs Tall Trudy for one last dance. I brush Conor's hand with mine and mumble a drunken apology.

'Sorry for being a dick,' I say.

'It's OK,' he says. 'I was being a dick too.'

'We're both dicks then,' I say, and we laugh.

228

His hand brushes mine, and our fingers touch. In the darkness of the club, we take each other's hands. And it's then that he whispers the words I've secretly been longing to hear. 'I think I love you, Billy McQueen.'

38.

Thursday 26th October 2023

'We should've arranged to meet Willy somewhere quieter. I can hardly hear myself think.'

Aine stirs her Aperol Spritz with a straw. We're in The Maverick, a new gay club in Belfast. It's early evening and the venue is already packed. A drag queen wearing a short blonde wig and ripped fishnet tights lip-syncs on stage, while the entire room vibrates to the booming bass of Kim Petras' 'Coconuts'. Aine picks up her phone to check her WhatsApp messages. 'Willy's five minutes away.' She glances towards the main doors. 'I'm nervous. Are you nervous?'

'What's there to be nervous about?'

'We haven't seen him for donkey's years. What if it's awkward?'

'We hadn't seen each other for years either. We managed to hit it off again straight away, though. Right?'

Aine nods. 'Yeah, but that's different. I wasn't as close to Willy as I was to you.'

'Relax, it'll be fine,' I say, nodding in the direction of the drag queen. 'This is the kind of thing your Alex could be doing in a few years.'

Aine folds her arms and says, 'Over my dead body.'

'Who wants a wee sip of my Snake Charmer?' We turn around to find Big Gay Willy standing behind us with a huge jug of yellow-green liquid. He lets out a massive cackle, slamming the jug down on the table, along with three tumblers. Sitting down on the empty chair between us, he gives both of us a hug and a kiss on the cheek.

'This place is fab, isn't it?' he says, gazing around the venue. 'I never thought I'd see the day when Belfast would have bars like this.' He pours us all a drink. 'You two haven't changed a bit. You're both looking well. What's your secret? Botox? Fillers? Anyway, cheers, queers! It's good to see you again.' He raises a toast, and we chink glasses.

Looks aside, he hasn't changed much but, like Aine and me, he's at least a stone or two heavier than he was in his youth. He's wearing a chequered shirt, blue jeans and black trainers. His lips look visibly plumper, his forehead suspiciously shiny and motionless, and he's every bit as loud and flamboyant as he was in the eighties. My mind flashes back to how intimidated I was by him. In part, I think this was to do with my own internalised homophobia, but equally, I was in awe of how he always appeared so confident and sure of himself. While in some ways he terrified me, I also wished I was as brave as him. He never seemed to care what anyone thought.

'What happened to your accent?' Aine says to him. 'You're sounding very English these days.'

'Fuck knows.' He sighs, taking a sip of the green cocktail and grimacing at its tangy sweetness. 'I have what they call "Wandering Accent Syndrome". I can't help it. One minute I'm talking with a Northern Irish twang and the next I sound like I'm from the Home Counties.'

'Me too,' I say. 'It's hard keeping up the accent, isn't it? Mine's only come back since I moved home.'

Aine leans in. 'Sorry to hear about what happened with your partner.'

He nods. 'Thank you. Yeah, things haven't been so great recently. To tell you the truth, I'd rather not talk about it. Not tonight, anyway.'

'Of course,' says Aine. 'So, spill the beans. What have you been up to? What's it like being home?'

'Honestly, Aine, I love being home. I've been thinking about moving back here permanently, actually.'

'Really?' says Aine.

'Aye,' he continues. 'My parents are both in their late seventies. They've no other children, so I'm the only person able to care for them. Looking back, I would never have imagined them being comfortable with me being gay. They were so homophobic, but they've mellowed with age. It took them a while, but we get on great now.'

I think of my own mum. I'm so glad I now have a chance to make peace with her, to make up for the years we've lost.

'What about work?' says Aine. 'Are you going to look for a new job?'

'I'm only in the office two days a week. My employer's happy for me to work remotely, so it's no big deal.'

'What's your job?' I say. The music has got louder. Another drag queen, who introduces herself as Sandy Craic, has taken to the stage in a leopard-print bra and thong combo. She is belting out a Miley Cyrus number. The crowd, which includes Tia's Hen Party, wave their arms in the air, drunkenly singing along.

'I work for a missing persons charity,' he says, practically shouting to be heard. 'In the public relations team.'

'Do you help find people who've gone missing, then?' says Aine.

'Not quite. We mainly support the families of missing people and people who are thinking of running away or leaving home.'

'That must be very rewarding,' she yells.

'Recording? Recording what?'

Aine leans towards him, repeating what she just said.

He nods. 'It is, yes. Very rewarding.'

If it wasn't for Miley Cyrus and her deafening wrecking ball, this would have been the perfect moment to bring up Conor, but our fifty-something ears are struggling to hear each other over the speakers. Browned off with the noise,

I suggest going somewhere else and grabbing a bite to eat. 'We can always come back here later,' I shout. 'What do you think?'

Big Gay Willy grins. 'You know me. I'm always up for food. There's a decent Chinese round the corner. Shall we try there?'

'You can't beat sweet and sour chicken balls,' says Big Gay Willy, spinning the Lazy Susan round and spooning a dollop of gloopy orange sauce onto his plate.

We've spent the last few hours catching up on our shared past, exchanging funny memories and anecdotes about things we got up to in our youth. So far, however, neither Aine nor I have broached the subject we really want to talk about tonight: Conor's disappearance. In the end, it's Aine who bites the bullet.

'So, I'm really fascinated by this missing persons job of yours, Willy,' she says, playing with a forkful of veggie chow mein. 'Billy and me have been reminiscing about Conor a lot lately. Do you ever wonder what happened to him?'

Willy raises a pint of lager to his mouth, taking a few gulps. 'I do, yes. That was sad. He was a lovely guy. Gorgeous-looking, too.'

Aine takes a moment to top up our glasses with water. 'You might know more about these things than us, given your line of work, but they never found a body or anything, so technically, he's still missing. Do you think there's a chance he could show up again?'

Willy swallows, then shakes his head. 'No. I mean, don't get me wrong, some people go missing for a long time, but in Conor's case, it's been thirty-odd years. The more time that's passed, the less likely it is . . .' He looks down at his plate, then at me. 'You two were made for each other, so you were. It's such a shame . . .'

Aine interrupts. 'You were seeing someone back then too, weren't you? A guy?'

He dabs at his mouth with a napkin. 'I was seeing a few guys. LOL! It was so long ago, though, Aine. I can't even picture their faces now.'

She looks at him. 'I remember you telling us once that you had a boyfriend. If not a boyfriend, some guy you were dating. An older guy, maybe?'

He pauses for a moment. 'Like I say, I had a couple of guys on the go, but it was all very discreet in those days. Besides, I've a terrible memory for names.'

'What did this older guy look like?' says Aine. 'Did we know him?'

He gives a nervous laugh. 'I – I've no idea. They all roll into one after a while. Men, that is. God, I'm making myself sound like a right slag.' He picks up a spring roll and pops it on his plate. He's lying, I think to myself. Nobody forgets their first time, surely?

I glance at Aine, who raises an eyebrow. She stands up. 'I'm just popping out for a vape. Do you smoke, Willy?'

'No. I gave up years ago.'

'Do you mind if Billy comes with me?'

'Not at all. You two knock yourselves out. I'll stay here and mind the table.'

I follow Aine outside, wondering what she's up to. Leaning her back against the wall, she takes a Lost Mary from her pocket and inhales. 'Why's he lying to us? Did you see his face when I mentioned Conor?'

I nod. 'He looked really awkward.'

Aine breathes out a cloud of fruit-infused vapour. 'He's being cagey about something.'

'Maybe it's to do with drugs,' I say. 'Maybe he was dealing.'

Aine pauses. 'You know, I've just remembered something. That night we all went to Club Babylon together, didn't Willy mention something about working for Andy Stone? Hold on a minute: what if he was *seeing* Andy Stone? Andy has a thing for younger guys and, from what George McKee told us, he's a bit of a shady character. Maybe Willy and Conor were both dealing for *him*? I mean, we all went to Club Babylon together once. It's possible they knew him.'

The thought of Willy and Conor working for Andy Stone makes me flinch. How well did I know Conor? He'd never struck me as the type of guy to be mixed up with the drugs scene.

Aine clenches her vape tightly in her hand. 'Maybe he'll loosen up a bit after a few more drinks.'

'He's already had half a jug of Snake Charmer and three pints,' I say. 'How much more booze is it going to take? Besides, I can't keep up. I'm half-cut already.'

'I know. I'm feeling a bit better now I've had some food, though. Let's stick to soda water from here on. If he's pissed, he's not going to notice we're not drinking.'

'OK,' I say. 'In that case, let's get ourselves back to The Maverick.'

If the music at The Maverick was playing at maximum volume when we left, it feels like it's been pumped up to infinity on our return. As we reach the venue, two of Tia's Hen Party are standing outside: one girl is throwing up into a gutter, while her friend stands behind her, holding her hair back. Making our way inside, a young woman in her twenties with shaved pink hair and a nose piercing deliberately brushes shoulders with Aine on her way past. The girl winks at her, before heading into the toilets.

'She might be fifty, but she's still freaking fabulous!' yells Willy. 'You must be giving off BDE tonight, Aine.'

Aine glares at him. 'What's BDE?'

'Big Dyke Energy.'

She shoots him her stern teacher look. 'Put a lid on it, you, or I'll use some of my BDE to knock your melt in.'

'Promises, promises,' says Willy, making a beeline for the bar, where he orders three shots of flaming sambuca.

Oh God, we're doing shots. I haven't done shots for years.

I give Aine a look as if to say *we need to be careful here or we're going to end up off our faces*. 'One more drink,' she mouths back at me.

We down the shots, grimacing as the aniseed-flavoured alcohol scorches our throats. Aine offers to buy the next round, ordering a pint of lager for Willy and two fizzy waters for us. Willy announces that he needs 'a slash', so Aine and I take our drinks and head to a booth in a quieter corner of the club, away from the dance floor.

Willy comes back from the toilet with a huge wet patch on his shirt. He's carrying another jug of cocktail. 'Shove up, Billy,' he says, putting the jug down on the table and squeezing himself into the space next to me. His face is looking flushed, his skin even shinier than it was earlier and his pupils are dilated. Around one nostril, I spot the telltale traces of white powder.

'Jesus, those toilets stink of pine disinfectant,' he says. 'I can't stand that smell.' He strokes his adam's apple. 'So, you're both single?'

'Separated,' says Aine.

'What about you, Billy?' When I tell him I'm single too, he looks at me wide-eyed, a massive grin forming on his face. Grabbing a tumbler, he pours himself a porn star martini. 'If you don't mind me saying so, Billy, I think you're an attractive guy.' He leans in, close enough that I can feel his warm breath on my neck. I thank him for the compliment, shifting along a little in my seat.

The drink is clearly going to Aine's head, despite her best efforts to stay sober. She leans towards Willy, slurring her words loudly over the thumping bass. 'Conor Doherty was his one true love,' she says, her eyes glazing over. 'We've been trying to find out what happened to him.'

Willy's face freezes. He's about to raise his glass to his lips, but he sets it down on the table again. 'What do you mean, *find out*?'

Aine puts her elbow on the table. She tries to rest her head on her hand and misses, her head flopping forward slightly. She straightens herself up. 'Me and Billy have been doing a bit of investigating,' she says.

'Investigating? Are the police involved, like?'

'No police,' I say, taking over the conversation before Aine manages to balls everything up. 'They gave up on the case *years* ago.'

He looks at us both, his eyes narrowing. 'So why are you two looking into it again?'

I tell him about the mixtape that was posted to my mum's house ten years ago and how we're trying to work out who sent it.

Willy is swaying in his seat, his face a ghostly shade of pale. Clutching his stomach, he says, 'You'll have to excuse me a minute, I think I'm going to be sick.'

He stands up, knocking his glass to the floor, where it shatters into little pieces. We watch him half run, half stagger to the exit.

39.

Monday 3rd July 1989

It's a quarter to one by the time I get back from Club Babylon. The lights at the front of the house are off. I turn the key in the lock and step into the gloom of the hallway. Immediately I'm hit by the smell of cigarette smoke coming from the kitchen. Mum's still awake. Shit. I'm about to creep upstairs when she swings open the door.

'A word,' she says. 'Now!'

Reluctantly I join her in the kitchen. The first thing I notice is the bottle of vodka on the table. She's been drinking. As far as I know it's her first drink since she got together with Mervyn and joined the church. The second thing I notice is the cassette tape Conor made for me, lying next to the bottle of vodka, its plastic case open – the track listing and letter he wrote for me in plain sight. She picks up the cassette's inner sleeve and waves it in my face.

'You told me you were going to throw this away,' she says.

I panic. My drunk brain is scrambling for an excuse, but I can't think of anything. 'I thought I did.'

She looks at me sceptically. 'You *thought* you did? Why was it still in your cassette player then?'

'I dunno. I must've put it there by mistake.'

As excuses go, I'm really scraping the bottom of the barrel here, but Mum wants to believe me, so, at this point, anything is worth a go.

'You must think I was born yesterday,' she says. 'What is

it, son? Do you think your oul Ma's stupid or something? Do you think I can't see what's been going on under my own roof?'

'Nothing's been going on, I swear to God.'

'Don't you swear to God in front of me. You're a wee liar, Billy McQueen. And are you *drunk* as well? What's got into you?'

'I'm not a liar, Mum. I'm telling the truth.'

'You're a liar, do ye hear me? Why are you so late getting home?'

'Dunno.'

'You don't know? Catch yourself on, Billy. It's gone midnight. Where were you?'

'I went to church.'

'I know you went to church, smart Alec. I mean after that.'

'I went to Wendy's.'

Ma slams her hand on the kitchen table. 'No, you didn't! I know for a *fact* you didn't, because Wendy rang here at half ten looking for you.'

'Did she?' I say, trying to look confused. 'What did she say?'

'She said you left church early because you said you weren't feeling well. She saw you leaving with that Willy Carson fella.'

'Oh yeah, that's right,' I say, trying to sound vague.

Mum sits down at the table and sparks up another cigarette. 'Tell me something,' she says, inhaling. 'Are you on drugs or something, son? Only you seem to be having some quare memory problems the night.'

I take a deep breath, lowering my voice. 'I'm not on drugs, no.'

'Are you sure?'

I nod.

'Because if you are, I've a right to know. I'm not having any of that carry-on in my house. Under my roof.'

'I'm not on drugs, Mum,' I say, slowly and deliberately.

The two of us sit in silence, Mum smoking her cigarette,

me with my head down, tracing imaginary circles on the kitchen table with my finger. Hesitantly, she leans across and places her hand on mine.

'I know you're lying, Billy,' she says, her voice low and husky.

'I'm not lying,' I say, defensively.

'This Willy Carson's gay, isn't he?' There's a slight pause as she takes a long puff of her cigarette.

'I think so, yeah.'

'What do you mean, you think so?' she says, choking on her own smoke. 'It's flipping obvious he's gay, even your Granny McQueen said so.' She pauses, her voice softening a little. 'So, are *you* gay?' she says. She rests her cigarette on the side of the ashtray and leans in. 'Look at me when I'm talking to you, Billy.'

I stare at the rip in the knee of my jeans, pulling at the loose threads. 'Just because I've a friend who's gay doesn't mean I am.'

'Do you want a sex change? Is that what it is? I read a story in the *News of the World* the other week . . .'

'A sex change? No! No, Mum, I do not want a sex change.'

'What is it then?'

My throat feels tight. Part of me wants to stay silent, but I can feel the words rising inside me like vomit. 'It's Conor.'

When I say his name, my voice comes out croaky. Mum stubs her cigarette out in the ashtray.

'I knew it,' she says, abruptly. She leans back in her chair and folds her arms. 'Is that who you were out with the night then?'

'We went to a club.'

'A club?' Mum sits up with a jolt. 'Jesus, Billy. You're sixteen. You're too young to be going to clubs. What club?'

'Club Babylon.'

'My God, you do realise that place is run by one of the paramilitaries?'

I shrug.

We argue some more. She tells me I'm grounded for a whole week. She asks if anything has happened between Conor and myself and I say we've kissed, that's all. I can tell she's uncomfortable with me talking about it though, because every time I so much as mention his name, she can't look me in the eye. She has to look away. And, to be honest, I'm not too comfortable talking to her about my love life either.

'So what's this Conor got that Wendy hasn't?' she asks me, her tone accusatory, like it's my fault I like him more than her.

'I don't know. It's hard to explain. He's—'

'Does Wendy know about the pair of you?'

'No, of course not.'

'Have you thought about what this might do to her?'

'Yeah, yeah, I have. It doesn't make it any better.'

'I know it doesn't. You do have a choice here though, you know?'

'What choice?'

'Stay with Wendy, or—'

'It's not a choice, Mum. It's who I am.'

She raises her voice. 'This is *not* who you are, Billy. Don't talk nonsense. Were you even listening to what Mervyn was saying in church the other week? People these days would have you believe being gay is normal, but it's not. Why do you think the government have banned teachers from talking about it in school? Why are so many gay people dying of AIDS? There's *nothing* normal about being gay, son. It's not normal at all. Do you want to be lonely and unhappy for the rest of your life? Because that's what will happen.'

Her words feel like an attack. I feel a sudden surge of anger. 'What do you know about *anything*?' I scream.

There's a pause. She glares at me, then, raising her hand, she slaps me hard in the face.

I lean back in the chair, shocked by the sudden sting in my cheek. I can't remember the last time she lashed out. Apart from the odd smack on the backside with the wooden spoon, or the dreaded slipper, when I was a kid, Mum has never laid a finger on me. My eyes fill with tears.

Hands trembling, she reaches for her trusty cigarettes, lighting up another.

'I'm sorry, love,' she says, turning her head away from me and pulling a clump of her fringe over her face. 'I didn't mean to hit you.'

40.

Friday 27th October 2023

The next morning, I wake up to my phone ringing. Reaching out, I grab it from the bedside table, swiping to take the call. It's Aine.

'Here's me thinking we were pretty sensible last night,' she rasps. 'I'm actually feeling quite rough.'

'*Quite rough?* I'm basically dead. We're getting old, Aine,' I say, 'we can't handle our drink anymore.'

'Tell me about it. And what the hell happened to Willy?'

'Have you heard from him this morning?'

Aine has a sharp intake of breath. 'Not a dickie bird. I messaged him earlier asking if he was all right. No reply.'

'Weird.'

'He literally walked out on us. I mean, I know he was drunk, but still.'

'Drunk? He was coked up to the eyeballs.'

'So you said last night. Do you think I should call him?'

'You can try. I'm not sure he'll want to speak to you, though.'

'He went funny on us, didn't he? As soon as we mentioned Conor and the investigation.'

'I'm still convinced he knows something,' I say.

'Oh, I agree, one hundred per cent. What, though?'

'I reckon we were right, you know, about him being involved with Andy Stone.'

'Listen, how about I give him a call? If he doesn't pick up, I'll leave a voicemail.'

243

'OK. Let me know how you get on.'

'Will do, kiddo. I'm not sure what to do, though, if he won't speak to us again . . .' There's a pause.

'I'll have a think,' I say.

After my chat with Aine, I take some painkillers for my pounding head, then I lie in bed scrolling through my phone. I open Instagram and spot a red dot next to the heart at the top of the screen. Social media virgin that I am, I press it, surprised to discover I have a notification. It says, @Ezeerecordboy started following you. So, Zach has unblocked me? Why the change of heart? Clicking on the blue button, I follow him back, then realise, for the first time, Instagram also has a messaging feature. I find a message from Zach, sent three days ago.

> Hey, good to meet you! Andy asked me to contact you to apologise for having to cut your meeting short the other day. Would you like to rearrange to talk another time? He said he has more to tell you.

I reply, saying I'd love to have another chat and, within seconds, a pink circle appears around Zach's profile photo. I stare at the flashing *typing*, waiting for his message to come through.

> Great! How about this afternoon? 4pm?

I reply with a 'yes' straight away, then send Aine a WhatsApp message to let her know what I'm up to. I watch the three dots shuffle along the screen as she types. 'Do you want me to come with you?'

'It's fine. Probably best if I go alone.'

Her reply when it comes through is a thumbs up. OK. You're on your own, kiddo! Shout if you need me. A x

41.

Before

Tuesday 11th July 1989

'Hello, Mr Magpie, how's your wife?' Conor waves at the black and white bird perched on top of the tombstone.

It's the first time we've seen each other since Mum grounded me over the whole Club Babylon incident last week. The sky is overcast, and we're huddled next to the old Victorian crypt in St Nicholas' churchyard, leaning our backs against the cold grey stones. 'Aren't you going to wave too?' Conor says, turning to me. 'It's an old superstition, so it is. My ma told me once. If you see a magpie on its own, you should always wave. It's bad luck otherwise.'

'I'm not sure I believe in all that stuff.' I shrug, noticing the purple bruise on his left eye. Gently, I touch his cheek, turn his face towards mine. 'What happened to your face?'

'Do we have to t-talk about it now?' He pulls away, digging the toe of his trainer into a tuft of moss. I can tell he's on the verge of crying, and all I want to do is reach out and comfort him, to try and make him feel better, but not here, not now. It's too risky. What if someone sees us? Conor blinks back tears and sniffs, reaching for his Fila sports bag. 'I brought you a couple of wee things. They're nothing much,' he says, his voice faltering. Unzipping the bag, he takes out a bottle of Jazz. 'It's half-empty, like.' He hands it to me, avoiding eye contact, as if he's embarrassed by his own kind gesture.

'I thought you could put a wee squirt on your pillow at night. That way, I'll always be by your side, even when I'm not here.'

'Thanks,' I say, taking the black and white plastic bottle from him. I spray a bit on my T-shirt, inhaling the fresh, woody fragrance. It fills my senses, giving me a warm and swirling sensation in my stomach.

'I got you this too,' he says, opening his wallet and pulling out a sticker. He hands it to me; it's a picture of Garfield wearing a top hat and holding a cane. Underneath are the words 'I am what I am.'

'I love it,' I say, looking around the graveyard before leaning in and giving him a discreet peck on the cheek. 'Where are you going to put it?'

I think for a moment. An idea comes to me. Taking my Walkman from my bag, I peel off the sticker's adhesive backing, pressing it down onto the cassette door. 'Looks all right, doesn't it?'

'It looks cool, so it does.' Conor nods, a small grin forming on his face. It's the first time I've seen him smile in ages. 'So, are you still seeing that Wendy?'

At the mention of her name, I feel myself taking a redner. 'No,' I say. 'She dumped me.'

'There's a surprise,' says Conor, laughing to himself. 'Does she know about us?'

'She has her suspicions, but I think I managed to persuade her otherwise.'

'Good.' Conor takes a deep breath. 'And how are things at home – with your ma?'

I shrug, putting my Walkman back in my bag. 'Come to think of it, she's been acting funny all week. One minute she's as nice as pie and the next she's giving me the silent treatment. What about you? How's your da?'

Conor scoffs. 'Don't even go there. The sooner I can leave home, the better.' He scratches his head. 'You know, I've been thinking a lot about that chat we had a while

246

ago – about applying to the same university. Are you still up for that?'

'Totally. I've been worrying about it, though. What if only one of us gets the grades?' I panic, for I can't imagine life without him. 'What will we do then?'

He shakes his head. 'It won't happen. Not if we both work our arses off next year.'

'Easy for you to say. You're smarter than me.'

'Wise up, Billy.'

'You are, though. I can't do maths to save my life.'

'I'm the same with French, aren't I? We're good at different things, that's all. Besides, at A level you can choose what *you* want to do. So just do what you're good at and you'll be fine.'

'It's expensive, though, isn't it? University. How will we afford it?'

'They give you a grant.'

'Will that be enough money, though? To live on, I mean.'

'Probably not, like, but we can both get wee part-time jobs, or something. We'll support each other.' I feel a rush of excitement thinking about this strange new life of ours, where we can do all these things together, be together. He reaches across and squeezes my hand. 'Besides, I'm planning on saving loads of money before we go.'

'How?'

'I've got a few things lined up. Trust me. We'll be all right, you and me. It'll all work out for the best.'

I close my eyes and, for a brief moment, allow myself to imagine what life would be like if only we were free to be ourselves. We could rent a place together, see each other whenever we wanted. We could go on holiday, share a bed, talk on the phone whenever we liked. All the things normal couples do, without having to hide their feelings from the world. Seriously, how amazing would that be? I look at him and he's smiling at me, and I realise we can make it happen, we really can. We just need to sit tight, keep our heads down and work hard. My face breaks into an enormous grin, the chorus of my favourite Jason Donovan song playing in my head. *Yes*, I think. *Jason's right. Me and Conor, we're going to be OK. It's true what he says. We're in love – and nothing can divide us!*

42.

Friday 27th October 2023

When the door opens, tentatively at first, I'm surprised to see Andy Stone waiting on the other side, not his assistant. He undoes the latch and, in a gruff voice, ushers me into the hallway.

Once I'm inside, he closes the door. Immediately, I sense that something isn't right. For a start, Andy looks different from the last time I saw him. His hair is dishevelled, his eyes yellow and bloodshot. Is that whiskey I can smell on his breath?

'Is Zach not working today?' I ask.

He shrugs. 'He's gone.'

'Gone?'

'Back to Canada.'

'When?'

'A few days ago.'

He's slurring his words slightly. Is he drunk? I feel a tingling sensation in the back of my neck. If Zach has left, who was messaging me on Instagram this morning?

'Take a seat,' he says, pointing in the direction of the front room. 'I'll be with you in a second.'

When I visited the house a few weeks ago, Andy Stone's front room was a masterclass in minimalism. Sleek black furniture, artfully placed magazines, exotic house plants. Now it looks as though a bomb's hit it: there's a huge crack down the centre of the glass coffee table; magazines with pages torn out are strewn all over the floor; there are knocked-over plant pots everywhere, and the framed photograph of Grace Jones is smashed and hanging lopsided on the wall. What on earth happened in here? Was he broken into?

Cautiously, I take a seat on one of the black leather sofas, being careful not to sit on what looks like an explosion of white powder. It's then I hear the front door locking, the sound of the latch being drawn across. My heart thuds in my chest.

Andy Stone staggers into the room, clutching his stomach as if he's in pain. He's drunk.

I wipe my clammy hands on my trouser leg, wondering if I should make a run for it.

'The room,' I say, nervously. 'What happened?'

He glares at me, shifting his weight from side to side. There's an uncomfortable silence. I look away from him, towards the window. The shutters are closed, blocking any natural light.

'We had a fight,' he says.

'Who did?'

'Who do you think? Me and Zach.'

'Is that why he left?'

'I threw him out. He wasn't to be trusted.'

'I'm sorry to hear that, Andy.'

'Don't be. Good riddance, I say.' He blunders forward, almost falling over as he throws himself down on the sofa opposite me, grabbing a cushion and holding it over his stomach.

He stares at me, his eyes dead with drink. 'It was me who sent you the message. I didn't invite you here to talk about your article, though,' he slurs.

'Oh?' I say, my leg shaking uncontrollably. 'Why did you want me to come over then?'

He slumps back on the sofa, his eyes rolling.

'Andy,' I say. 'Are you OK? What is it you wanted to tell me?'

Silence. He leans forward, his neck stiff, his voice hard. 'He shouldn't have burst in the way he did. He should've knocked first. Was the wee lad born in a field, for fuck's sake?'

'Who are you talking about, Andy? Is this about Zach?'

'Zach? Zach!' He throws his head back, gives a snort of dismissive laughter. 'I'm not talking about Zach. Who cares about him?'

'Who then?' I lower my voice. 'Who are you talking about?'

He sucks his cheeks in, staring at me the whole time, his body swaying back and forth. 'You really don't know?'

I shake my head. 'Tell me,' I say. 'Who?'

He becomes unnaturally still.

'Andy,' I whisper, leaning forward. 'What is it?'

He takes a deep breath, then buries his head in his hands, sobbing. 'It wasn't my fault. None of it was my fault.'

It's then that I notice the gun lying on the floor by the table. The sight of it makes me freeze. I need to message Aine. I need to get out of here. But I also need to know what Andy is trying to tell me.

'I don't know who you're talking about, Andy,' I say, my voice faltering.

He looks up, his wet eyes shooting darting glances at me. His face is pale, haunted. 'You *do* know,' he says. 'It was you who asked me about him. Conor. Conor Doherty. Like I say, though, it wasn't my fault. It wasn't me who killed him.'

At the mention of Conor's name, my thoughts turn fuzzy. I can't think straight. Touching my throat, I ask him, 'Who was it? *Who* killed him?'

43.

Before

Tuesday 11th July 1989

When I get home from seeing Conor that afternoon, I spot Mervyn's white BMW parked outside our house. Pushing open the front door, I throw my sports bag down in the hallway. Just as I'm about to sneak upstairs, Mum emerges from the kitchen, a plate of Fig Rolls in her hands.

'You're back,' she says. 'Just in time.'

'In time for what?' I say, unaware she was planning a surprise party.

'I need you in here,' she says, pointing her plate in the direction of the living room.

When I enter, Mervyn is sitting on the sofa drinking tea out of Mum's best china. He looks up at me before resting his cup on its saucer and setting it down on the coffee table. He doesn't say anything. He simply stares at me, his expression serious. I get a horrible feeling that I'm about to be told off for something. Does he know I've spent the afternoon with Conor?

Gingerly, Mum sets the plate of biscuits down in front of us and takes a step back. She wipes her hands on her apron, nervously perching herself on the arm of the settee, next to Mervyn. I watch him place his hand on her knee.

Silence, apart from the ticking of the gold carriage clock on the mantelpiece.

Eventually Mervyn speaks. 'Son,' he says. 'You were at the sermon I gave a few weeks ago, where I told the story of Sodom and Gomorrah, the two cities destroyed by God because their people pursued unnatural passions. Do you remember?'

'I think so,' I say, my voice a half-whisper, thinking of my secret nights with Conor, my heartbeat pounding in my ears.

Mervyn fixes his eyes on me. 'You think so?'

'Aye. I mean, yeah . . . I remember it,' I say, wiping my sweaty palms awkwardly on the pockets of my jeans.

'Sit down,' he says, pointing to the space next to him on the sofa.

I do as I'm told, my thigh briefly touching his. I move it away.

Mervyn turns to look at me, his gaze penetrating. He places both hands on the crown of my head, pressing down, his fingers digging into my scalp. He closes his eyes and then the strangest thing happens. He starts to pray. 'Oh, heavenly Father,' he says. 'This boy has fallen for the devil's lies. And who can blame him? For as it says in the Bible, Satan will disguise himself as an angel of light.'

Is he trying to tell me that Conor is the devil? My stomach tightens.

'Conor's no devil!' I shout, trying to escape, but he has me locked firmly in his grip. Mum looks away, covering her mouth in shock, as he pushes down harder, my skull trapped under the weight of his heavy hands. In a flash of frustration, a memory comes to me. I hear a voice. A man's voice, rising above Mervyn's. It's my dad, saying, *You be who you like, son. You're my special boy. Don't you ever let anyone dim your light, Billy McQueen, do you hear me?* His words echo in my mind. They give me strength, for it dawns on me that these people are powerless, ridiculous even. Mervyn can't stop me being myself. He can't stop me being gay.

'*You're* the devil,' I yell, grabbing at his hands and pushing them away from me. Leaning forward, I duck my way out from under his grasp, sliding onto the carpet.

'Leave me alone,' I scream, scrambling to my feet and

lurching towards the door. 'There's nothing wrong with me. You lot are the crazy ones.'

'It's Lucifer talking,' he booms. 'Trying to convince the boy that we're nothing but heretics.'

Mum screams after me, 'Come back here, Billy! I know this isn't really you, son. It's just a phase you're going through.'

I pause in the doorway, my cheeks burning with rage.

'It's not a phase, Mum. Jesus was a phase, OK? I'm gay. You know it's true. You're my mother.'

Mum lets out a cry, falling to her knees, her hands raised in prayer. Mervyn looks like he's about to kill me. I dash into the hallway, make a bolt for the front door. Pushing it open, I take a deep breath, my lungs desperate for air. Slamming the door behind me, I leg it down the driveway. On my way past Mervyn's white BMW, I'm unable to resist scraping my house key down one side, then, turning a corner, I run.

I keep on running until I reach the phone box at the end of our road. Although I'm only meant to call Conor at certain times, I have to talk to him. 'Pick up, Conor! Pick up!' I yell, waiting for what feels like an eternity before he finally answers, whispering that his dad's asleep upstairs. I tell him what happened with Mervyn, how he tried to 'cure' me. Conor's livid. 'Listen,' he says. 'I'm just about to head out the door, but let's meet up again later. I'll see you in the builder's hut. Eight o'clock.'

'Don't be late.'

'I'll be bang on time, I swear.' He pauses. 'Don't worry, Billy. Like I said, this will all work out for the best, OK?'

44.

Now

Friday 27th October 2023

Andy Stone leans over the edge of the sofa, grabbing the gun from the floor. My heart hammers in my chest. What the hell is happening? This is madness.

He sits up, his body straight, raising the gun in his right hand. 'This is what killed him,' he slurs, gesturing to the gun. 'But it wasn't me. It was an accident.'

'An accident?' I say, my mouth so dry I can barely get the words out.

He nods, his chin and lips trembling. His voice is a whisper now. He stands up, knocking the sofa cushion to the floor. He's swaying from side to side, his movements muddled with drink. 'You want to know the truth?' he slurs.

'Yes,' I say, trying to avoid looking at the gun in his hand. My pulse is racing to the point where I think I might have a heart attack. All it will take is for me to say the wrong thing and he's going to pull that trigger. He's not in his right mind; he's not thinking straight. My legs feel weak, black spots float in front of my eyes. My whole body is shaking. If I die now, I tell myself, at least I'll die knowing the truth about what happened to Conor.

Andy opens his mouth to speak, but no words come. He drops the gun, his body doubling over. Sinking to the floor on his knees, he squeezes his eyes shut, covering his face with his hands, and lets out a primal scream. The whole room feels like it's closing in on me. Every sound feels magnified a million times. I think about running, but something makes me stay. I look at my watch. *If the minute changes in five seconds*, I tell myself, *then I'm going to die. Right here, right now. Five, four, three, two . . .*

I hear a loud crashing sound. When I open my eyes, Andy Stone is lying on the floor. Is he dead?

Pulling up his sleeve, I check his pulse. His heart's still beating. He's still alive, still breathing. 'Andy?' I whisper. 'Andy? Are you OK?' He mumbles something incomprehensible.

The gun is lying by his feet. I shiver, realising how close he came to using it just now. I'm desperate to find out what he knows about Conor, but I'm not going to get the answers I want tonight. Rolling Andy onto his side, I place a cushion under his head and dial 999 for an ambulance.

After I've ended the call, I notice I have two WhatsApp messages from Aine:

Hey, how did it go with Andy? Just had a voicemail from Willy. He wants to meet us in The Crown tomorrow night.

And then:

I get the feeling he knows what happened to Conor.

I try to call her back, but it goes straight to voicemail, so I leave a rambling message telling her everything that's just happened. My hands are shaking so much I can hardly hold the phone. Part of me has always known Conor is dead but, hearing Andy say those words has sent my brain and body into a strange kind of free fall. I need to get home, and more than anything I need to know the whole story. Until then, I will just have to keep the grief at bay. As I wait for the ambulance, my mind is fixated on one question only.

What was Andy about to tell me?

45.

Saturday 28th October 2023

The Crown is one of Belfast's most historic pubs, famous for its distinctive gin-parlour-style decor: gas lamps, etched glass and carved mahogany snugs. Lined up in a row like confession boxes, the snugs cater for pub visitors who want to meet and drink in private, and Willy has reserved a spot for us in one of them. When Aine and I arrive, he's already sitting inside, nursing a pint of Guinness. He looks a far cry from when we last saw him in Belfast, his face pale and drawn.

'Sorry I disappeared without saying goodbye the other night,' he says, as we take our seats in the booth. 'I was drunk and, to be honest, a bit triggered by being back home and seeing you guys after all that time.' He pauses. 'You might want to get yourselves a drink,' he says soberly. 'I've got a lot to tell you.'

I head to the bar and order a round. Three pints of Guinness. When I get back, I find Aine and Willy both sitting there, silent, as if they've been waiting for me to return before resuming the conversation.

'Look,' says Willy, his hands shaking. 'Seeing the pair of you again the other night, I realised I can't keep this to myself any longer. I know the truth about what happened to Conor. I've kept it a secret for over thirty years. Please don't judge me, just hear what I have to say.'

My heart is racing, my mind working overtime. What does Willy know of Conor's murder? And how could he have kept it to himself for so long? Taking a sip of his Guinness, he begins to tell us his story.

46.

Now – Willy

Back then, in 1987, I used to get my hair done at Castle Cutz in Carrick. At fourteen, I already knew I fancied men, but it wasn't something I was ready to admit to myself. One afternoon, waiting for my usual short back and sides, I was flicking through a magazine of men's hairstyles. This fella I'd never seen before came into the shop. He looked very respectable in his white suit. And he smelt great. Whatever aftershave he was wearing, I could tell it was expensive. This strong, musky smell, very masculine. He sat down on the chair next to me and glanced at the magazine. 'Do you enjoy looking at that?' he said to me.

'Aye,' I said, and he nodded like he understood. He told me then he belonged to the church. 'You should come to one of our services,' he said, sliding his business card onto my knee, letting his hand rest there a split second longer than necessary. 'It's free,' he said. And then he stood up and left.

In those days, I had a secret crush on Nigel, the guy who worked in the barber's. A youngish fella. Seventeen. He wore Fred Perry polo shirts and tight stonewashed jeans. Blond highlights. Crew cut. A gold stud in his right ear. I thought he was the spitting image of George Michael, but looking back he was more like a budget Glenn Medeiros. I fancied him like rotten, though. And sometimes, when I was in the barber's chair with my hands on the armrest, he'd lean over and press his crotch against my knuckles. I'm sure he did it on purpose, but I didn't mind. It turned me on, so I never made any attempt to move my hand away. In my teenage fantasies, he was enjoying it as much as I was.

After the man from the church left, Nigel said, 'Do you know that fella you were talking to just now?'

'No,' I says, easing myself into the big leather chair. 'He was telling me about his church.'

He picked up his hair clippers and started running them over the back of my head. I always loved that feeling.

Nigel told me the man's name then. 'He's a pastor,' he said. I shrugged, for I'd never heard of Mervyn Ballantine.

'Are you religious?' says Nigel.

'Not really. I used to go to church when I was younger, but not anymore.'

'He's a powerful guy, Mervyn. He gives me the willies, though. They say he earns an absolute fortune, preaching the word of God. Drives a big white BMW, so he does.'

'What about you?' I asked him, impressed that a guy who works in a church has so much money. 'Are you religious?'

'Not really.' He laughed. 'Mervyn's always popping in here, trying to save me, but I just tell him my family are Catholic. Usually shuts him up.'

'Do you believe in God, though?'

He switched off the clippers, pausing to gaze at his reflection in the mirror. 'Aye, I suppose I do. Yeah.'

A few weeks later, I was on the bus and who should get on but Mervyn Ballantine. He was holding this bunch of leaflets. I thought he must be doing his missionary work, for why else would a man in his forties who owns a BMW take the bus? He obviously recognised my face from the barber's, for he sat down next to me and said hello. We started talking and throughout the journey, he told me all about Jesus Christ and the importance of being saved. He was leaning in quite close to me, too close, and at one point, I thought I felt him brushing his fingers against my thigh, but I wasn't sure. When the bus reached my stop, and I got up to leave, he handed me a leaflet. Grabbing my arm tightly, he said, 'God asked me to give you this message today. He told me you're in danger. He said the devil has been trying to tempt you with forbidden desires.'

I was scared. It was as if he could see into my soul. I thought of the magazines I liked to look at in the barber shop, the strange fantasies I'd been having. Maybe this Mervyn was right. Maybe it *was* the devil trying to tempt me. I was confused and upset, for you remember what that time was like? And I was lonely, too. I didn't have many friends then, and he told me the church was full of young people like me. 'Teenagers,' he said.

So, a week later, I joined the Holywood Church. I was fourteen. The first time I went, I sat on my own in the congregation listening to Pastor Ballantine preach his usual spiel about homosexuality being a sin. It might sound like I'm exaggerating here, but throughout the sermon, I had this weird sense he was staring right at me. I remember sitting there on my own, tears streaming down my face, thinking I was evil. As soon as he began calling people up to the stage to be saved, I stood up and joined the queue. When it was my turn, he placed his hands on my head and leaned in, whispering in my ear that he saw an angel of the Lord standing behind me, watching over me. If I wanted to be saved, he said, I had to accept the Lord Jesus into my heart.

That wasn't the only time Pastor Ballantine put his hands on me, though. The second time was a chance meeting in the public toilets by the harbour car park, and even though we knew each other, we never said a word. I think I knew, after the bus ride, that it would happen eventually. There was no acknowledgement on either side. Whatever we did then, we did in silence.

From then on, our liaisons always took place late at night, sometimes in his car. A white BMW, which he parked near the toilets. I knew it was wrong, and I hated myself for it, but I couldn't stop. Afterwards, when he saw me in church, he ignored me, except when he was preaching about perversion, the sins of the flesh. Then, I swear to God, he'd fix his eyes on me, as if *I* was the target of all his rage. All his pent-up frustration.

It carried on for a few months and then one day, it just stopped. I never saw his car parked in the harbour again. I kept on going to church, though. By then I no longer believed half the things he was saying about gay people, for I knew what a hypocrite he was. In a strange way, I suppose, this knowledge gave me strength. And I'd made lots of friends in the church, it had become my social life. There was no gay scene then, nowhere I could meet people like me, so my friends there were like family.

By the time I was sixteen, I was gaining a bit more confidence. Don't get me wrong, I was still full of insecurities, but I hid them with bravado. I'd started messing around more with guys, including Nigel from Castle Cutz, and – even though it was all still fairly secretive – I was no longer feeling so guilty about it. In the summer of '89, I met another guy in the barber shop. Like the pastor, he was sitting in line next to me while I waited for a haircut, staring at my cherry-red bomber jacket and Levi's 501s.

'Are you one of them Bros boys?' he said. I was scundered, my cheeks turning as red as my jacket. 'It's a compliment,' he laughed. 'Only you look like them, so you do.'

'Cheers,' I says, flattered by the comparison.

'Those clothes must cost you a bomb. Do you have a job?'

'I've just started working on the tills at the petrol garage three days a week.'

'How much do they pay you?'

'Ten pound a day.'

He shook his head, laughing again. 'Ten pounds? You'd make ten times that amount working one night a week for me.'

Intrigued, I asked him what he did for a living. He told me he was an entrepreneur. 'What's that?' I said, for French was never my strong point at school.

'I own a nightclub in town. Have you heard of Club Babylon?'

Club Babylon? I couldn't believe it. This guy who owns a nightclub was offering me a job. Dollar signs floated in front of my eyes. I thought I'd made it.

'What's your name?' he said.

'Willy.'

He leaned in, whispering in my ear. 'You look like you know how to have a good time, Willy. Do you know what I'm saying?' His breath smelt of Wrigley's Juicy Fruit.

'Life and soul of the p-party,' I stammered, thinking about all the clothes I could buy with a hundred pounds.

When I bumped into him a few weeks later at the club – the same night we all went out together after church – he offered me a job. My first shift went brilliantly. I was in my element. I felt like I was working in Carrick's answer to Club Tropicana. Afterwards, Andy called me into his office. It was this poky wee room next to where they used to hang the coats. A desk with a small window behind it. A filing cabinet, and a massive yellow Acid face painted on the wall. Andy was sitting in a hooded top and baseball cap, feet up on the desk, smoking a cigarette. 'Take a seat,' he said, throwing me a pack of twenty Benson & Hedges. 'Got those in duty-free when I was in Ibiza last month,' he says. 'A wee present from me.'

'Cheers, Andy,' I said, catching the shiny gold box in my hands, even though I didn't smoke. He asked me if I fancied earning more money. At the time, I had my eye on this designer leather jacket I'd seen Luke Goss wearing on the cover of *Smash Hits*. It was ridiculously expensive, but I was desperate for it, so I nodded. 'I would, aye.'

He took a puff on his cigarette. 'I was wondering how you'd feel about doing me a wee favour. Paid, of course.' Stubbing out his cigarette in the ashtray, he put his hand in his pocket and pulled out this small plastic bag. It was full of tiny white pills. He set the bag on the desk in front of him.

'People come to Club Babylon to have a good time,' he

263

says. 'It's our job – yours and mine – to make sure they have the best night possible.'

I nodded, wondering where this was heading.

He held up the bag of pills. 'Ecstasy's illegal,' he says. 'You can be put in prison for dealing these. The way I see it, though, loads of things are illegal. It doesn't mean people don't do them. I mean, think of all those Acid House tracks we play in the club: Frankie Knuckles, Lil Louis, Orbital, The Beloved. All mainstream, right? All getting airplay on the radio. Do you know what I'm getting at?'

'Aye, I think so.'

'Drugs and music go together. Everyone knows it. I'm running a nightclub here. I want my punters to keep coming back. If they have a good time, we make money. Simple as that.'

'So, what do you want me to do, Andy?' I said, curious and petrified at the same time.

'I want you to sell these pills to our customers,' he said, matter-of-factly.

Not going to lie, I was bricking it. I asked him what would happen if I got caught.

'You deny it,' he said. 'Say you found them on the floor, you were just passing them on. But at no point do you say you got them from the club. Understood?'

'Yes, Andy,' I said, gripping the sides of my chair, my hands slippery with sweat.

'I mean it, son. You can't involve the club in any of this.'

I swore I'd be careful.

'Good lad,' he said. 'Now – do you know anyone else who might be looking for a job? I could do with a few more good-looking young fellas like you working for me.'

I remembered a conversation I'd had with Conor earlier that week. He'd told me he was looking to save some cash. 'I do, yeah. My friend, Conor Doherty.'

To begin with, Conor wasn't keen on the idea. He said it wasn't worth the risk. He said his dad would go mental if he found out. Like me, though, he was desperate for money. He'd told me he wanted to save up so he could go to university in England. The way he saw it, education was his ticket to freedom. His dad was a total git, though. He didn't want Conor to leave. He was insisting he study in Northern Ireland, so he could stay at home and look after him. Conor knew his dad would never financially support him if he went to England, and his worst-case scenario was that he'd end up with a place at Queen's in Belfast, living at home. He was determined it would never happen. 'Over my dead body,' he said.

So, on the afternoon of 11th July, 1989, I arranged for Conor to meet with Andy at the club. We went together. Conor was in a right state, fuming over something Mervyn had done. 'I'm meeting Billy later tonight,' I remember he told me. 'He's really upset. I'm worried about him, you know?'

Conor's head wasn't in the right place for a job interview, and when we got to the club he was still angry about everything that had happened earlier that day. I kept telling him to calm down, to forget about things until after the meeting, but he was too upset to focus. All he cared about was being able to see you, Billy. As such, Andy's first impressions of him weren't great. He was looking for someone friendly and enthusiastic and Conor sulked his way through most of the interview. Andy ended things by saying he was going to have to think about it, and so we left. That is when things went wrong. So badly wrong.

We were on our way home when Conor suddenly started swearing to himself. 'Shit. Shit. Shit,' he said, stopping dead in his tracks and searching through the pockets of his denim jacket. We were halfway down the Belfast Road by this point.

'What's the matter?' I said. 'What have you lost?'

'The cassette.'

'What cassette?'

'The one I made for Billy. I think I left it in the club.'

'It's OK. We can go back for it.'

'I promised Billy I'd meet him at eight o'clock, though. I can't be late.'

I checked my watch. It had just gone half past four. 'Relax,' I said. 'You've got loads of time.'

So, we headed back in the direction of Club Babylon. They were shut that night, for the 11th, and I remember hoping Andy hadn't left. When we got there his car was still outside. There was another car I recognised, too. A white BMW. It had a huge scratch all the way down one side, like someone had keyed it. I remember thinking it was strange, that it couldn't be Mervyn's car. It must belong to someone else. There were always all sorts coming and going at the club.

The door to the club was ajar. I said I'd wait outside while Conor went in to get the mixtape. Not long after, though, I heard shouting. It was Conor. He was yelling, 'You bastard! You slimy, hypocritical bastard!'

Panicking, I ran inside, but the door to Andy's office was shut. There was a mighty commotion going on. Conor was still yelling, and Andy kept telling him to calm down. There was another voice, too. A voice I recognised. The voice that had once told me he saw an angel standing behind me.

'Listen, son,' Mervyn said. 'It's not what you think. I – I was just trying to comfort Andy. He's had some bad news today. He . . .'

'I'm not st-stupid!' I heard Conor yelling. 'I saw what you were doing.'

'Nonsense!' Mervyn snapped. 'This is the devil talking. Whatever you think you saw, you're wrong. Your eyes are playing tricks on you.'

'Piss off!' Conor screamed at him. 'You're full of shit. I can't believe you've the balls to stand in church in front of loads of people, calling us perverts, saying we're going to die of AIDS and you . . . here *you* are, with your tongue down another man's throat.'

'You're twisting things. You're a liar.'

'*I'm* a liar?'

'You're a fantasist. A homosexual fantasist.'

Andy started shouting then. 'Right, young man, you've said your piece, now piss off!'

'Nice,' says Conor. 'You got yourself a charmer of a boyfriend here, Mervyn.'

'Didn't you hear me?' yelled Andy. 'I said piss off, or I'll call the police.'

'The police?' Conor laughed. 'Are you having me on? Like you'd want the police coming anywhere *near* this dump. If they find out what you've got stashed away in your wee filing cabinet, you're going to jail for a very long time.'

'Is that a threat?' says Andy. 'Because if it is . . .'

My hand was hovering over the office door handle. Part of me wanted to barge into the room and drag Conor out of there, but part of me was terrified. I backed away from the door, hiding myself under the clothes rail with all the coats people had left behind.

Conor was even more livid now. 'Aww, poor wee Andy. How are you going to cope in prison without your boyfriend? Never mind. I'm sure Merv the Perv here will come and visit you.'

I heard Andy yelling, 'You better shut your mouth, or I swear, I'll . . .'

At that moment a terrifying sound split the air, silencing everything. A gunshot. The clothes rail I was hiding under shook, the metal hangers clinking like broken glass. I put my hand over my mouth, hugging my knees to my chest, trying to make myself as small as possible.

Silence, for what seemed like forever. I hardly dared breathe. I kept praying it wasn't what I'd feared. I kept hoping, any minute now, I'd hear Conor's voice, reassuring me he was OK. Andy was the first to speak.

'W-what have you done, Merv? You've shot the wee lad. You bloody shot him!'

'I – I didn't mean it,' Mervyn cried. 'It was an accident.'

'What are we going to do? My mates are coming here soon, for a few drinks before the bonfires.'

The office door swung open then, casting a rectangle of light across the floor in front of where I was hiding. I heard footsteps, the hasty muttering of prayers. 'Dear God, forgive us our trespasses . . .' I tried not to make a sound, my heart beating madly in my chest, my breath quick, as tears streamed down my face. I wanted to run, but they had a gun. I had no doubt they'd shoot me if they knew I was there.

'I've checked the car park. The coast is clear,' I heard Andy whisper.

'Let's get him in the boot,' Mervyn said.

'Should we wrap the body in something? Jesus, there's blood all over the wall.'

'Stop panicking!'

'You just shot the wee lad!'

'We can clean that up in a minute. I'll drive the car to the door, then we can lift him straight into the boot.'

Not long after, I heard a car pulling up, the heavy breathing of the two men as they carried Conor's body outside. As they left, something dropped on the floor, landing not far from my feet. Conor's cassette. It must have fallen out of his coat pocket. As soon as they were gone, I picked it up.

When they came back, I heard Mervyn telling Andy to clean up and he would take care of the body. He kept telling him to stay calm, act normal. If anyone came in asking questions, Andy was to say he had been busy going through the takings. He was to tell the police he'd been alone all afternoon.

'I guess I'll see you when I see you, then,' said Andy.

'I guess so,' said Mervyn. And then he was gone.

I stayed where I was, hardly breathing, listening as Andy filled a bucket with water and went back into his office, closing the door behind him. The smell of pine disinfectant was everywhere. I waited until I could hear him scrubbing the walls, and then I ran.

I ran, and I ran, and I never looked back.

47.

Now

Saturday 28th October 2023

Willy is staring down at his empty pint glass, his eyes red and swollen. Speechless, I get up from the table and stagger towards the toilets, my head pounding. Aine calls after me. 'Billy. Wait, Billy!' I ignore her. All around me, people are talking and laughing. A group of American tourists, in matching shamrock T-shirts and Guinness hats, gush about how quaint everything is. I barge past them, knocking over a chair in the process. I don't stop to pick it up. I stumble on, lurching into a cubicle, slamming it shut. Pulling the bolt across, I squeeze my eyes tightly shut, pressing my head against the door.

Whatever theories I had about what happened to Conor, nothing could have prepared me for this. I curse Mervyn under my breath, raging at the man's hypocrisy. Not only did he tear our family apart, but he also killed my boyfriend, the only man I ever loved. I then do something I've never done in my life before. Like an angry teenager, I punch the wall. There's a shooting pain in my fingers, but it's nothing compared to what I'm feeling inside. I want to scream. I want the whole world to know my sorrows. I think of Conor, his young life cut cruelly short before it could even really begin – by an evil man, who had the gall to call himself my stepfather. A pastor. I think of my poor mother, lying in hospital. The years she sacrificed. The years she wasted. And for who? For what? This monster of a man. Because that's what he was.

I don't know how long I'm in the cubicle for, but eventually I hear Aine knocking on the door. 'Are you in there, Billy?' she whispers. 'Will you come out now. Please. I'm worried about you.'

I hesitate, my hand resting on the bolt, and then I open the door, falling forward into the arms of my best friend.

When I get back to the booth, Willy looks up at me, his eyes full of sadness. Aine has gone to get us all another drink. I sit down opposite him, and then I reach out my hand, gently squeezing his.

'I'm sorry for storming off,' I say. 'I just didn't . . . I didn't know how to . . .'

'It's OK,' he says. 'I don't blame you.' He pauses. 'Are you angry with me?'

'Why would I be angry with you?'

'I dunno. I've just, always blamed myself, you know? I'm so sorry, Billy. If I hadn't taken him to that job interview, if I hadn't introduced him to Andy, none of this would've happened.' He shakes his head. 'I should've gone to the police. I should've told someone, but I was young. I was scared.'

'It's not your fault. I used to blame myself too. But that was because of Mervyn. He used to say what happened to Conor was God's way of punishing me.'

'Fuck's sake,' Willy mutters under his breath, biting his lip. 'God forgive me, but I hope that man is rotting in hell. He deserves nothing less.'

I pause. 'So I take it it was you who sent me the mixtape?'

'Aye. I'd held on to it so long. It wasn't helping with the guilt. I was going to throw it away, but then I figured it belonged to you. And I know Conor would've wanted you to have it. I'm sorry I didn't send it sooner.'

My eyes well up as I remember Conor's kindness. Willy is on the verge of tears, too. I realise this is the first time we've had a proper chat. A genuine conversation. And it's because, for the first time since we've known each other, we're both able to be honest about who we really are.

The three of us continue talking until closing time. There is so much still to process, so much grief and anger. In the end, we're the last ones left in the pub. The staff are putting chairs on tables, sweeping up. Willy orders taxis for us all and we hug each other, saying our goodbyes.

Aine and I take a cab back to my house, where we sit up late talking, in Mum's conservatory, wrapped in blankets under an old patio heater. It's already gone 2 a.m. As soon as we got home we'd ordered pizza, but while we've managed to get through a bottle of red wine between us, we haven't touched any food yet. Aine lifts the lid off the box, peering at the cold, cheesy mess inside. 'I'm not hungry anymore,' she says, pushing it towards me. 'You should try and get something down you though.'

'I need a glass of water,' I say, heading to the kitchen. 'Do you want one?' She nods.

When I come back, I find her sitting with the blanket over her head like a shawl, staring up at the stars, her eyes red and puffy. I put the glasses down on the table and we sit in silence for a while, both utterly exhausted from everything we've learned today.

'How are you feeling?' says Aine eventually. She reaches over and rests her hand on my shoulder.

'Still numb.' I shrug. 'It's all so hard to process, you know?' I take another glug of water, which doesn't seem to be doing anything right now to quench my insane thirst. 'I mean, I wasn't expecting the truth to be pleasant, but this – this is so much worse than I ever imagined.'

'It's awful,' says Aine. 'Conor had so much to live for. It's just so unfair.'

I rub the heel of my palm against my chest, thinking about all the plans we'd made, all the hard work we'd put into our exams that year. More than anything, we wanted to succeed so we could escape to England, be ourselves. All those dreams, wasted.

'Do you think the pain will ever go away?' I say, taking a deep breath.

Aine covers her face with her hands. 'Who knows? I hope so, Billy. I really do.' She wipes her eyes, reaching for the box of tissues which both of us have all but emptied in the space of a few hours.

'I'm worried about Willy,' I say. 'He was in a bad way when we put him in the taxi home. I hope he doesn't do anything stupid.'

'I'll message him in the morning to make sure he's all right. He said he was going to go to the police. I can't imagine what it must've been like carrying that for so long.'

'Is it any wonder he moved away?'

Aine shivers, pulling the blanket around her chest. 'I'm cold sitting here, Billy. Shall we go into the living room?'

Beside the upright piano is a crate of my old LPs. I found them in the loft the other day when I was having a clear-out. A glass of wine in one hand, Aine kneels next to the crate, quietly flicking through the records.

'Aww, look, it's one of your favourites.' She sniffs, holding up a copy of Kylie Minogue's 1989 record, *Enjoy Yourself*.

'A classic,' I say, my words slurring; '1989 was a good year for . . .' I trail off, remembering Conor never made it that far. He was really looking forward to that album coming out, but he died a few months before it was released. He missed out on so many incredible pop songs. He never got to hear 'Better the Devil You Know', or 'Ray of Light', or Cher's 'Believe'. He never got to see Abba re-form, forty years after they split. He would've loved the fact that Kylie Minogue is still absolutely smashing it with 'Padam Padam'.

'1989 feels like such a long time ago,' I say, my voice wistful with wine. 'A lifetime, really.'

Aine nods, pulling another record from the crate. This time it's one she approves of. The Cure's *Disintegration*.

'One of my all-time favourites,' she gushes. 'Here, let's put this on.'

She opens the glass lid of Mum's hi-fi and slides the album from its paper sleeve. Laying it carefully on the player, she presses the button to release the record arm. A click. The faint crackle of the needle, then the sound of a xylophone; a kaleidoscopic burst of drums and guitar, and Robert Smith's melancholy voice singing 'Plain Song'.

We lie on the carpet, letting the music wash over us, crying throughout 'Pictures of You' and 'Lovesong'. Both songs had been on mixtapes Conor made for me. When it gets to 'Lullaby', Aine gets up and does this weird, swaying little dance, before staggering to the kitchen to get more wine. She comes back with another bottle, filling both our glasses.

'To Conor,' she says, raising her glass, her eyes full of sadness. 'May he finally rest in peace.'

'To Conor,' I repeat, tears sliding down my face.

As I drink, I can't stop my mind working through all the revelations of the past twenty-four hours, the implications . . . Did Mum know about Mervyn? Did she suspect he was having affairs? That he was gay? I really hope not, but if she had she might've turned a blind eye to it all. She'd already lost one husband. I don't think she could've stood to lose another.

Out of nowhere comes a burst of anger. Mervyn drove a wedge between us. He turned Mum against me, then he killed my boyfriend. Part of me, I think, wishes he hadn't died. Part of me wishes he'd stuck around to face the consequences. I would've loved the chance to tell him exactly what I thought of him. Like loads of those other high-profile men who abuse, who lie and cheat and kill, Mervyn went to the grave with his reputation still intact, while my poor mum is in hospital, quite possibly unaware that the man she loved, the man she gave up her son for, was a liar, a hypocrite and an abuser. A murderer. If there is a God, I hope he slams those pearly gates in Mervyn's face. That man has no right being in heaven.

'He's no right to be in heaven,' I say, wiping the tears from my eyes.

'Who are you talking about?' Aine turns to look at me, her expression glazed. We've both had way too much to drink. We should call it a night.

'Mervyn,' I say, my voice full of bitterness. 'I hope he goes to hell.'

A lump is forming in my throat. I try to swallow it back down, to stop the tears from coming, but I can't. I'm angry – not only for Conor, but for Mum, too. Aine puts her arm around me, pulling me close to her. 'It's OK, Billy,' she says, holding my head against hers. 'It's OK to be upset, but don't beat yourself up. None of what happened is your fault.'

'I know,' I say. 'It's just . . . it sounds stupid, but there was a tiny part of me that hoped he was still alive.'

Aine smiles sadly at me. 'But he *is* still alive, Billy. He's here, do you understand?' She puts her hand on my heart. 'You'll always have those memories, I promise. No one can take them away from you.'

48.

Nine months later

Wednesday 3rd July 2024

Castleview Court is a private nursing home for the elderly, with beautiful sea views and leafy surroundings. Mum has been living here ever since she left the hospital earlier in the year. While she's regained some movement, her recovery has been slow: she still can't speak, and requires round-the-clock care. After giving it some thought, I made the difficult decision to put Mum's house up for sale. Considering everything that's happened, it's unlikely she would ever return there, and I realised I needed a fresh start. The old house holds too many memories; it was time to say goodbye, to put the ghosts of the past to rest. I wanted to remain close to Mum, though, and early next week, I'm due to complete on the purchase of a one-bedroom apartment I've bought here in Carrick, overlooking the Marina. The new place is only a short walk from Mum's care home, which is handy for me; I can pop in and see her whenever I like, which I do most days.

At reception, Cathy, one of the support managers, gives me her customary cheery greeting, telling me Mum has just had breakfast and is back in her room, resting.

The staff and facilities are wonderful here, but I'm glad Mum has me to look after her, too. I'd hate to think of her being without family, and I dread to think what would have happened if Bev hadn't reached out and persuaded me to move over here from Margate last year.

When I open the door to Mum's room, she is sitting up

in bed. As soon as she sees me, she leans her head against her shoulder, her eyes lighting up.

'All right, Mum,' I say, leaning over to give her a peck on the cheek. 'How are we today?' I lift the small gift I bought for her from its carrier bag. 'Look, I've got you a wee present. Do you want me to open it for you?' Mum makes a *humph* sound, which I now understand means yes, her eyes keenly tracking my movements as I tear open the cardboard Amazon packaging to reveal a *Dallas* DVD box set, Seasons 1 and 2.

'I thought this might keep you entertained when I'm not here,' I say. 'Do you remember we used to watch *Dallas* together? Der-der, der-der, der der der-der der.' I hum the theme tune while Mum gazes at me, deep in thought, like she's lost something important: her purse, or a set of house keys. Like she's retracing each step in her mind, trying to remember where she was, and what she was doing, the last time she had them. And then something clicks and she starts tapping her hand excitedly on her lap.

Taking the DVD from its case and sliding it into the player underneath the television, I sit down next to her on the bed. Wrapping my arms around her, I pull her close, the way she used to hold me as a child and, as the opening credits to *Dallas* start, I take her hand in mine, squeezing it gently. Mum stretches her neck to look round at me, her eyes wide and twinkling. My heart swells with love as I watch her mouth open, ever so slowly, to form the beginnings of a smile.

49.

Monday 8th July 2024

It's only when I've finished most of the packing that I find Mum's letter. It's on the floor behind the telephone table in the hallway, the last piece of furniture to be shifted. The letter must have slipped down the back. A white envelope with a first-class stamp. My name and address in Margate written on the front in her handwriting. The envelope hasn't been sealed yet. I take out the several pages of blue lined paper inside and I begin to read.

3rd August 2023

My dear son,

I know this letter will come as a surprise, but you've been on my mind a lot lately. I wanted to get in touch to apologise for the way I treated you all those years ago. All the time I've wasted since. You are probably very angry with me, and I don't blame you. But the truth is I love you, son. I always have.

I realise words are not enough. They will never be enough to make up for the pain I caused you by refusing to accept who you are. Or to excuse my decision to cut you – my only son – out of my life for over thirty years. For all these things, Billy, I am so, so sorry. If I could turn back the clock, I'd do things very differently.

After your daddy died, Billy, I fell apart. You were so young then, and I hope I protected you from the worst of it. But the truth is my whole world had collapsed, and until I met Mervyn, my life was a mess. Mervyn saved me. I'm not trying to excuse the things I did, but if it hadn't been for him and the church, I don't know how I would've carried on living. Mervyn gave me the love and the stability I craved – but because of him I had to make a terrible sacrifice.

I've never told anyone this, but just before you left home for university he said to me, 'It's me or Billy, Sadie. You must choose. I can't marry a woman who has a homosexual for a son. My reputation is at stake. We've done all we can for Billy, but it's his decision to walk the path he has chosen for himself.'

It may be hard for you to understand, but I was frightened. I didn't have the financial stability to go it alone, and I suppose I loved him, in a way. Not like I loved your daddy, but Mervyn pulled me out of my dark days. He looked after me, and I respected him. Needed him. And he was a powerful man, Billy, you will remember. I wasn't the only one he had a hold over.

Mervyn died a few years ago. He had dementia for almost a decade, and in his final months he barely recognised me. It was difficult, but I was lucky to have the support of my church friends and Bev, my neighbour. You remember Bev? She always thought you were a geg. If only I had been able to see you through her eyes, but I was so blinded by Mervyn. He changed me. He changed the way I saw the world. It's only now that he's gone that I can see this wasn't always for the best.

During his illness, I saw a different side to him. Some days he would sit in his armchair, rambling about the past. He often talked about 'the wee lad'. At first, I thought he meant you, but then he would mention the name Conor. He'd shake his head and cry, and I would take his hand and say, 'Who do you

mean, Mervyn? Who are you talking about, love?'
He'd just look at me, his eyes wild, and repeat, 'Conor,
the wee lad', as if I should know who he was on about.
The only Conor I knew was your friend. But what did
he have to do with Mervyn? I wondered maybe if he
remembered praying for him in church after he went
missing. Whatever it was, it clearly had a profound
effect on him.

Anyway, it reminded me that, ages ago, there was
a letter sent to you here, no name or address for the
sender, with a tape inside, from your friend Conor.
I remember thinking it was strange at the time, but
I never went to the police, or forwarded it on to you,
because Mervyn told me not to. He said what had
happened to Conor was God's punishment for you
being the way you are, and that if I passed the tape on
to you it would only ignite God's wrath. I'm ashamed
to say I believed him. He frightened me sometimes,
Billy. But I've kept the tape and the letter safe in a box
for you. I don't want to make you sad, but would you
like me to return it?

I hope you have managed to read this far and not
torn up my words in anger or frustration. I wish I
could see you now, give you a hug. I know what I'm
about to tell you could never make up for the dreadful
mistakes I made as a parent, but I hope it will make
life easier for you. I've left you my house in the will,
and all my savings. My way of saying sorry for all the
hurt I've caused you, all the time we've lost. I have
missed you every day, Billy. My beautiful boy.

I love you, son. If you can find it in your heart to
forgive me, I'd love to come over one day and visit
you in England. Maybe you have a partner now, or
children of your own? In which case, I'd love to meet
them.

You'll see that, for now, I've enclosed a cheque.

*Please don't feel you need to accept it, but Mervyn left
me a lot of money, and it feels only right that I should
share some of it with you.*

    God bless,
    Your loving mum x

*PS I read all the cards and letters you sent me over
the years. Every single one. Thank you. I am so sorry I
never replied.*

Blinking back tears, I look again at the date on the letter.
The 3rd of August 2023. So, Mum wrote this the day before
her stroke. She'd obviously planned on putting the cheque
I found upstairs in this envelope, but never got round to it.
It all makes sense now. Holding on to the pages, I lean my
back against the wall, pressing Mum's words to my heart,
letting the sadness pour out of me like rain. *I love you, Billy*,
I whisper, repeating her words over and over, hearing her
old voice in my head. *I always loved you.*

50.

The key to Mum's house is still attached to its 'Jesus Saves' key ring. With my fingernail, I prise the metal loop open, sliding the key off the spiral. I put the key ring in my pocket and drop the house key, which I need to hand over to the estate agent later this morning, in an envelope.

It feels bittersweet saying goodbye to my childhood home. This is the last time I will ever stand inside these four walls. This house, which has been in the family since before I was born. This house, where I spoke my first words, took my first steps.

Stripped of its 1980s furnishings, the living room feels cold. Only the fixtures remain. Gone is the bookcase with its complete collection of the *Encyclopaedia Britannica*. Gone is the glass cabinet filled with Murano clowns and Lladró ornaments. Gone is the G Plan dining room table and chairs, which I managed to sell on eBay for several hundred pounds, and Mum's old hi-fi. I've given it to Alex, who's slowly started building their own vinyl collection and wanted something to play it on.

There's a knock on the front door. Recognising Bev Duff's petite silhouette through the frosted panel, I open it to find her holding a Tupperware box in her outstretched hands.

'I've brought you a wee leaving present,' she says. 'Soda farls and potato bread. Made them fresh this morning for you.'

'Aww, thanks, Bev, you didn't have to go to any bother,' I say, taking the box and peering inside. 'Besides, I'm only moving down to the Marina. You'll be sick of the sight of me before long.'

She chuckles. 'No chance. You're like a son to me now. I'm going to miss having you next door. I've enjoyed our wee chats, putting the world to rights.' She takes a hanky from her pocket, wiping her eyes.

'Oh, Bev, don't be sad. You can visit me anytime. Why don't you come over later? I'm having a wee housewarming. Nothing big, just a few friends. Everything's still in boxes, but I thought it would still be nice to celebrate with a glass of fizz.'

Bev sniffs, then her eyes light up at the mention of bubbles. 'I'd love to.' She pauses. 'Is it OK if I bring the dog?'

'Of course.'

She smiles, her eyes turning wistful. 'It'll be strange having different people living next door after all these years. What are the new neighbours like, do you know?'

'A young couple in their early thirties. First-time buyers. Apparently they like a project, so this place is perfect for them. It beats me how Mum put up with that dreadful honey oak kitchen and avocado bathroom suite for so long.'

Bev shrugs. 'Sure, Mervyn wouldn't let her spend tuppence. All that money, and he was tight as a frog's arse. Besides, he never liked this house. He hated the fact your mum insisted on keeping it.' She pauses. 'By the way, I saw the headline in the *Belfast Telegraph* last week. It's good to hear that Andy Stone finally got his comeuppance. Shocking, isn't it?'

Following his recent appearance in court, Andy Stone was sentenced to fifteen years in prison for accessory to murder and intent to supply drugs. When questioned, he claimed not to know what Mervyn did with Conor's body, so I guess we'll never know.

I nod. 'Awful, but at least the truth is out now. We can try and rebuild our lives.'

'God love you, son.' Bev sighs. 'You haven't had it easy. But here's to new beginnings.'

Glancing at my watch, I realise Aine's due here any minute. 'Sorry to rush you, Bev, but I better go and get ready. I've got a friend picking me up shortly to drop the keys off.'

'Right you are, love,' says Bev. 'I'll see you later then.'

'It's only a little thing.' Alex hands me a small rectangular package. Peeling off the Sellotape at both ends, I undo the pastel-pink, white and blue-coloured gift wrapping. 'To say thank you for giving me your old hi-fi.'

'Oh, no bother at all,' I say. 'I'm glad somebody's getting the use out of it. This place isn't big enough and, besides, I've got myself a new stereo. It's a little more compact.'

Alex's gift to me is a TDK cassette, just like the ones Conor used to make for me. I turn it over in my hands. On the label on the spine, written in pink biro, are the words: *A Mixtape for Billy – Luv, Alex x*.

A tear forms in my eye. 'Aww. This is lovely, Alex. I'm feeling a bit choked up.'

'Mum told me all about Conor. It sounds like he was a lovely guy. You two must've had something really special together.'

'We did. It was really special.'

Before I have time to get all sentimental again, Aine reaches her arm out, tugging at the cassette in my hand. 'What songs have you put on there, Alex? Let me guess. Sam frigging Smith?'

'Yes!' I laugh, rubbing my eyes and peering at the track listing. 'We've got Sam. And Kim Petras with her "Coconuts". Who else? Dua Lipa, Anne-Marie, Olivia Rodrigo, Charlie XCX, Lizzo, Billie Eilish, Maisie Peters and Taylor Swift. You have *such* good taste, Alex.'

Aine sighs, looking at us both in despair. 'Jesus, I must be getting old. I hardly know who any of them are. Here was me thinking I was cool listening to Ed Sheeran.'

'Ed Sheeran's in his thirties now, Mum,' says Alex. 'You're showing your age.'

Aine shrugs. 'I don't care. I'll take Robert Smith over Sam Smith any day.'

I chuckle. 'In that case, we might have to start calling you *Granny* Smith.'

Aine nudges me with her elbow. 'Shut up, Billy. Just because you've always had the music taste of a teenager. Steps, Kylie Minogue . . .'

'Maybe I'm making up for my lost youth.'

'*Lost* youth? What do you mean? You never gave it up in the first place. By the way . . .' She leans in and sniffs my neck. 'Is that Jazz aftershave you're wearing?'

'It is indeed,' I say. 'Yves St Laurent, 1988. A vintage year for pop music – and fragrance.'

Aine laughs. 'You really are stuck in the past, Billy McQueen. Isn't it about time you moved on from the eighties?'

'No chance! They were the best, and the worst of times, as the saying goes.'

'*Hard times*?' Aine grins, appreciating my nod to Charles Dickens. 'Weren't they just! But from *Hard Times* come *Great Expectations*, and look at you now, Billy McQueen. You made it through. I'm so proud of you.' She squeezes my arm affectionately. 'So, tell us all about this new job of yours then.'

Only last week, the editor of *Belfast Life* offered me a full-time contract off the back of some freelance work I did for them earlier in the year: a series of music reviews, along with an investigative piece about Conor's disappearance, and our efforts to find out what happened to him.

'I'm going to be writing for the entertainment pages. My own column.'

'Wow!' gasps Aine. 'I'm dead chuffed for you. Amazing! Things are really looking up.'

'I've just finished a music review for them last night, actually,' I say, my face beaming. 'A retrospective thirty-fifth anniversary review in celebration of Kylie's *Enjoy Yourself* album.'

'Congratulations,' says Aine. 'I can't think of anyone better qualified than you to write a Kylie tribute. Seriously, my friend, dream commission.'

The doorbell rings. 'That'll be Willy,' I say, sliding the cassette tape into my pocket and making my way to the front door.

While we've kept in touch online, I haven't seen Willy for several months. To say he looks different would be an understatement. He's completely transformed himself.

'Willy,' I say. 'You look amazing!'

He steps into my new hallway dressed in a leather jacket, crisp white T-shirt, jeans and black leather boots. 'These are for you,' he says, handing me a bunch of fresh flowers. 'Congratulations on your new place. It looks fab.'

'So do you,' I say. 'What's your secret?'

To tell you the truth, I've never really thought of Willy as handsome, but today he looks great. No longer red and puffy-faced, the dark circles under his eyes have completely disappeared, and his skin is glowing.

He slips his boots off. 'Slimming World. I've lost two stone.'

'In that case, sign me up now,' I say. 'I could definitely do with shifting a few pounds.'

'Honestly, it's brilliant. I'm the only fella in the group, but everyone's so friendly and supportive. You should come with me one night.' He pauses. 'If you want to, that is?'

'I'd like that,' I say. 'It's a date.'

Smiling, I lead Willy into the kitchen where Aine is waiting, ready to throw her arms around him. They squeeze each other in a tight embrace.

'Here,' he says, putting a carrier bag down on the kitchen table and lifting out several bottles. 'I brought you some fizz. The Nosecco's for me, but you're all welcome to try it.'

'Nosecco?' says Aine, sounding surprised.

'Another reason I've lost weight,' he says. 'I've given up the booze.'

'Good for you,' I say, taking the bottles and putting them in the fridge. 'You're looking well on it.' I turn to Aine. 'Maybe we should think about quitting?'

She doesn't respond, but I know she is thinking the same thing as me. For far too long we've both been drinking to forget a past which, until recently, made no sense to us.

Last to arrive is Bev. She's holding Sindy, her Yorkshire Terrier, under her arm like a shaggy handbag.

'You're just in time, Bev,' I tell her. 'We're about to open the fizz.'

'You know me.' She laughs. 'Sure, my Norman used to say I could hear a cork popping from Timbuktu. Welcome to your new home, son,' she says, putting the dog down on the floor and kissing me on both cheeks.

As we gather in the kitchen, I look around, my heart warm and utterly overwhelmed with love. For the others, my housewarming party might feel like an everyday occasion, but to me it's beyond special. Not only is this my first proper home, it's also the first time in many years that I've felt part of something, part of a community. I think back to my old life in Margate, the grey days spent wandering alone in the rain, peering in at lit restaurant windows, wishing I had friends like the people gathered round tables, eating and drinking together, enjoying each other's company.

Pouring my friends a glass of fizz, I raise a toast to our futures, chatting excitedly about what they might bring. Later, I take a moment to myself, stepping out into the garden. I watch the sun sinking lower in the pink and orange sky, and I think of Mum, wishing she was here with us all, celebrating. Choking back tears, I look at my watch, beginning another of my counting rituals, telling myself that if the sun disappears behind the fence within the next ten seconds, all will be well. Mum is going to make a full recovery. I close my eyes and begin my countdown. *Ten, nine, eight* . . . But then I hear the warm laughter and conversation coming from inside, and I stop counting, because what's the point in trying to predict the future? The future is here.

I open my eyes and smile, allowing myself to breathe in the beauty of this moment. And as I stare at the sunset, I swear I can hear my mother's voice whispering in the evening breeze. She's saying, '*It may have taken you over thirty years, Billy McQueen, but don't worry. You're here now, son. You've come home.*'

Playlist

The Lost Past of Billy McQueen

Enjoy Yourself
Kylie Minogue
3:44

Wuthering Heights
Kate Bush
4:29

Back to Life
Soul II Soul, Caron Wheeler
3:48

Especially for You
Jason Donovan ft. Kylie Minogue
4:00

Requiem
London Boys
4:19

Electric Youth
Debbie Gibson
4:58

Miss You Like Crazy
Natalie Cole
3:54

Don't It Make You Feel Good
Stefan Dennis
3:50

Wind Beneath My Wings
Bette Midler
4:53

Eternal Flame
The Bangles
3:58

I Don't Wanna Get Hurt
Donna Summer
3:28

Ain't Nobody
Chaka Khan
4:40

You'll Never Stop Me Loving You
Sonia
3:23

More Than You Know
Martika
4:06

A Note from the Author

I grew up in Northern Ireland during the Troubles and, while this is a work of fiction, some of the events and characters described in this book are loosely drawn from real-life experiences.

In terms of additional research, the following sources were extremely useful: *Say Nothing: A True Story of Murder and Memory in Northern Ireland* by Patrick Radden Keefe; *Making Sense of The Troubles: A History of the Northern Ireland Conflict* by David McKittrick and David McVea; *The Price of My Soul* by Bernadette Devlin; *Fault lines: Fractured Families and How to Mend Them* by Karl Pillemer and *Lost, Found, Remembered* by Lyra McKee. The Radio 5 podcast *Blood on the Dance Floor*, the untold story of the murder of Darren Bradshaw, a gay police officer in Northern Ireland, was also invaluable, as well as various news articles about the late eighties rave culture in Northern Ireland (in particular "90s bangers, friendly faces & gardai raids: remembering the Point Inn 30 years on" by Laura Grainger, on the Belfast Live website), online church sermons and old copies of *Smash Hits* and *Jackie*.

I am also indebted to *Stories from Silence*, an incredibly moving online oral history project featuring the voices of around a hundred individuals who lost a loved one during the conflict in Northern Ireland. The project was undertaken by WAVE (Widows Against Violence Empower), an organisation originally formed in 1991 to empower women whose partners or husbands were murdered during the Troubles in Northern Ireland, now expanded to include those who were injured and/or traumatised in the Troubles (www.wavetraumacentre.org.uk).

Acknowledgements

A huge thank you to my editor, Jane Snelgrove, for your patience and guidance in helping me shape my rough first draft into the book you are now holding in your hands. Thank you also to the wonderful team at Embla for your endless passion and enthusiasm, and for everything you do to help my books succeed.

Thank you to my superstar agent, Rowan Lawton, and everyone at The Soho Agency, for all that you do behind the scenes. It is hugely appreciated.

Thank you to my parents, for the stories you've told me over the years. Some of these have made it into the book, albeit as very fictionalised versions of the truth!

Special thanks to Dan, my partner, for putting up with my many silences and lapses in conversation because I'm busy mulling over some plot issue, or a tricky line of dialogue, in my head, and for your excellent fact-checking abilities. And to Prudence, our rescue cat, who has rarely left my side in the four years it has taken me to write this book.

Finally, to all my readers, who have been sharing the love for my characters and stories on socials. You lot are the ones who keep me going when the going gets tough, as we used to say back in the eighties! A massive thank you to everyone who has read and reviewed one of my books or taken the time to send me a lovely wee message over the past few years. It really means a lot. Readers who wish to get in touch can find me on X @neilalexander_ and Instagram @neilalexanderwriter.

Acknowledgments

THE
Vanishing
OF
Margaret
Small

Can the secrets in Margaret's past
explain the mystery in her present?

NEIL ALEXANDER

Meet Margaret Small: 75, plain spoken, Whitstable native and a Cilla Black super fan. Shortly after the death of her idol, Margaret begins receiving sums of money in the post, signed simply 'C'.

She is convinced it must be Cilla, but how can it be? To solve the mystery of her benefactor Margaret must go back in her memories almost 70 years, to the time when she was 'vanished' to a long-stay institution for children with learning disabilities.

An absorbing and page-turning mystery with a dual timeline, *The Vanishing of Margaret Small* takes readers into a fascinating past, and introduces an unforgettable literary heroine.

Perfect for fans of Libby Page and Gail Honeyman.

About the Author

Neil Alexander is an author, teacher and journalist whose writing has featured in the *Independent*, *Daily Telegraph* and the *Daily Mail*. His debut novel, *The Vanishing of Margaret Small*, an Amazon Top 5 bestseller, was inspired by the voices of people with a learning disability, and the incredibly moving first-person accounts of living in long-stay institutions, which he heard while working for the UK charity Mencap. Neil, who has an MA in English Literature from the University of Kent at Canterbury, began his career working in health journalism. Originally from Northern Ireland, he now lives in the seaside town of Whitstable in Kent.

About Embla Books

Embla Books is a digital-first publisher of standout commercial adult fiction. Passionate about storytelling, the team at Embla publish books that will make you 'laugh, love, look over your shoulder and lose sleep'. Launched by Bonnier Books UK in 2021, the imprint is named after the first woman from the creation myth in Norse mythology, who was carved by the gods from a tree trunk found on the seashore – an image of the kind of creative work and crafting that writers do, and a symbol of how stories shape our lives.

Find out about some of our other books and stay in touch:

X, Facebook, Instagram: @emblabooks
Newsletter: https://bit.ly/emblanewsletter